My pulse did a little soft-shoe in my chest.
I stuck the ampoule in my pocket and swallowed to
cleanse the tarnish of guilt from my tongue.

I grabbed O'Lachlan's arm and pulled up and toward the curb. "C'mon."

Since his hands were bound I had to hoist him up into the SUV. He wriggled across the seat, and I followed him. Morales glanced back over the seat. "Everything okay?" He was frowning like his instincts were telling him otherwise.

I wiped my damp palm on my jeans. "Yep. Why?"

"You're all flushed."

I tilted my head and prepared to verbally punt. "Morales, I just spent the last fifteen minutes chasing down a leprechaun. Sorry I'm not looking spring fresh."

I worried I'd overplayed my sarcasm. But he blew out a breath. "All right then." He turned back toward the steering wheel. "Settle in, Mr. O'Lachlan, we'll have you at the Hoosegow Hilton in no time."

The perp spat on the floor. "May the devil cut the head off ye and make a day's work of your neck."

"First of all, don't spit in the car. It's disgusting," I said. "And second, the devil can do his worst so long as he buys me dinner first."

O'Lachlan looked me directly in my eyes. His own had lost the fevered glow from the potion he'd taken earlier, but, even sober, his irises retained the icy-blue hue of a dirty magic addict. "Once the Blue Moon gets here, you'll all be praying for the devil, bitch."

BY JAYE WELLS

Prospero's War

Dirty Magic

Cursed Moon

Deadly Spells

Sabina Kane

Red-Headed Stepchild

The Mage in Black

Green-Eyed Demon

Silver-Tongued Devil

Blue-Blooded Vamp

Sabina Kane Short Fiction

Violet Tendencies

Rusted Veins

CURSED MOON

PROSPERO'S WAR: BOOK 2

JAYE WELLS

www.orbitbooks.net

Orbit
Hachette Book Group
237 Park Avenue, New York, NY 10017
HachetteBookGroup.com

First Edition: August 2014

Orbit is an imprint of Hachette Book Group, Inc. The Orbit name and logo are trademarks of Little, Brown Book Group Limited.

The Hachette Speakers Bureau provides a wide range of authors for speaking events. To find out more, go to www.hachettespeakersbureau.com or call (866) 376-6591.

The publisher is not responsible for websites (or their content) that are not owned by the publisher.

Library of Congress Cataloging-in-Publication Data
Wells, Jaye.
    Cursed moon / Jaye Wells. — First edition.
        pages cm
    ISBN 978-0-316-22846-6 (trade pbk.) — ISBN 978-0-316-22845-9 (ebook)
    I. Title.
    PS3623.E46898C86 2014
    813'.6—dc23
                                2013043009

10 9 8 7 6 5 4 3 2 1

RRD-C

Printed in the United States of America

For Margie Lawson: Thank you for helping me take it to the next level.

"Everyone is like a moon, and has a dark side
which he never shows to anybody."
—*Mark Twain*

"You're only as sick as your secrets."
—*Recovery program saying*

Chapter One

October 17
New Moon

If you want to know your future, the last person to ask is a fortune-teller. Most of them don't have an Adept bone in their body, much less a sixth sense or whatever bullshit Mundanes called the ability to know the unknowable.

"Come closer, lady," said a three-pack-a-day voice. "For ten bucks I'll tell you your fate."

I paused by the carnival stall and glared at the gypsy who had the misfortune to choose me as her mark. She sat behind a card table covered with a cheap crushed-velvet scarf. A red kerchief covered her gray hair, and dozens of gold bangles clinked together on her weathered arms. Her eyebrows were drawn in too thick and black, and her teeth too crooked and yellow, like a sepia image of a rickety fence. I couldn't tell if she was 50 or 150, but the twinkle in her eyes told me she was a natural-born bullshitter.

"No need," I said, my smile like a pink worm on a hook. "I already know my future." In my five years as a cop, I'd seen too many desperate people hand their last nickels to charlatans like this not to fuck with her a little.

Her eyebrows shot up. "Oh?"

I pointed to the watch on my right wrist. "Lunch."

My partner, Drew Morales, chuckled beside me. His muscled forearms were crossed, and his expression was the amused smirk of a cop watching a crook hang herself with her own rope.

The fortune-teller narrowed her kohl-smudged eyes. "I see secrets on you, girl," she said in a low, knowing tone that pinned my stomach to my spine.

My smile dissolved. I reminded myself that psychics were frauds. She didn't know my secrets. "And I see you haven't posted a permit to perform Arcane acts in public," I said, hoping the shame in my gut didn't seep into my words. "You want to talk about that?"

She aimed her left forefinger and pinkie out like horns. "Devil."

I forced a dismissive laugh, like the curse hadn't hit me directly in the conscience. "Lady, you have no idea."

"It's not worth it, Kate. Let's go." Morales plucked my sleeve.

A few stalls later I sidestepped a rug rat in a SpongeBob SquarePants costume and pretended not to notice my partner's speculative glance.

"What's eating you today?"

"I thought once I'd made detective I'd be able to put the bunions of patrol work behind me." I glanced around the square at the kids in costumes running from stall to stall collecting candy.

"At least now that you're on the task force, you can wear

jeans instead of being stuck in a uniform." He nodded toward a pair of BPD officers in their blues standing by one of the ticket booths. "Besides, the covens have been quiet lately. If we weren't out here, we'd just be stuck behind desks with our thumbs up our asses while the BPD got to have all the fun wrangling the moonies."

I looked at him like he might be one of the lunatics in question. "You might want to look up 'fun' in the dictionary."

He ignored my sarcasm and took a deep breath. "Least we're getting some fresh air."

I took an experimental sniff and sneezed from the hay they'd brought in for the Halloween Festival. Normally the city held the event closer to the actual holiday, which was in two weeks, but with the Blue Moon bearing down on Babylon, the city council moved it up so kids could trick-or-treat safely. Pioneer Square had been filled with what seemed like a million jack-o'-lanterns, and local businesses—both Arcane and Mundane—had set up booths to pass out candy for the kids and sales pitches to the adults.

Before I could respond to my partner's uncharacteristic glass-half-full comment, flute music filled the square. A shirtless man wearing goat horns and woolly pants with fake hooves wove his way through a crowd on the steps of City Hall. Like many of the people at the festival, he wore a black mask that obscured the upper half of his face.

"What's this guy's costume?" Morales asked.

"He's a satyr."

He shot me a look like I'd spoken in tongues.

"What?" I said. "I know shit."

Morales and I paused on the edge of the group to watch. I crossed my arms and scowled at the performer. He had a thick beard, and tattoos covered every inch of his arms and much of

3

his chest. The families around us bopped along with the melody, but their smiles were forced from hours of wrangling rug rats buzzing off high-fructose corn syrup.

I started to tell Morales we should move on, but the goat dude danced our way.

He river-danced around us a couple of times. I could feel his gaze groping my ass. When he came back around, I shot him a keep-away scowl. He paused in his flute playing to blow me a kiss before skipping away to bother someone else.

I turned to Morales. "Guess I should enjoy the boredom," I said, nodding toward the retreating satyr. "The closer we get to the second full moon, the crazier these assholes are going to get."

We started walking again before he answered. Despite our casual conversation, our eyes were scanning the square for any signs of trouble. "C'mon, it won't be that bad."

"Just you wait," I said.

"I was in LA once during a Blue Moon," he said. "Except I was undercover, so I got to help raise hell instead of keeping it under control. How many times have you worked a beat during moon madness?"

I glanced toward the rusted statue of a steel factory worker in the center of the square. "Enough to wish I had vacation saved up to get out of town."

Another crowd had gathered near the statue, but I couldn't see what attracted them there. Still, something kept my gaze locked on the spot. I couldn't put my finger on what was bothering me. Call it cop intuition. Call it woman's intuition. Something was—

"Something's wrong." Morales went on alert like a hunting dog.

Danger sounds different. It has a distinctive pitch. Sound

crystallizes, air tightens. The herd gets spooked, and an invisible wave of metallic energy permeates the air.

We pushed through a crowd of clueless parents and their agitated children. It took a full minute to make our way to the statue. Two uniformed cops with hawthorn defensive wands beat us there.

I assumed they'd take care of the threat. But in the next instant a halo of energy flashed through the square. My nostrils flared at the acrid scent of ozone.

My protective instincts tightened my muscles for action. Someone was hexing the crowd with dirty magic.

Morales and I burst into the clearing. The first thing I saw was one of the cops humping the statue like a stripper on a pole. The other officer's chest was bare and he was just a zipper away from flashing his little wand to the crowd. A woman undulated around the circle, her hands raised high above her head as if in surrender. A couple writhed on the ground. Hands groping. Mouths hungry. Pelvises grinding.

And standing over them all, holding a black plastic cauldron, was a motherfucking leprechaun.

His costume—too short for his five-foot-and-spare-change frame—was a green double-breasted blazer, matching tights, and two black shoes with shiny silver buckles. A bowler hat on his head tipped jauntily forward over greasy brown hair. And on each cheek, he'd painted a jagged black lightning bolt.

He turned to face us, and a small plume of glittery golden powder spilled from the cauldron's wide mouth.

I had my weapon in my hand before you could say *Erin go Bragh.* "Stand down!" I shouted in my best or-I'll-shoot tone.

A single black brow disappeared under the brim of the hat. His gaze went to the salt flare gun in my hand. Every criminal in the Cauldron knew that the rock salt's purpose was as much about inflicting pain as it was neutralizing magic.

Beside me, Morales aimed his Glock at the guy. "Put down the cauldron!"

As it turned out, fake leprechauns are surprisingly fast runners. One second he was staring down the barrels of our guns, and the next the bastard took off. The tails of his jacket flapped in the breeze, and it was a miracle of physics that he managed to keep his hat attached to his head. Morales and I exchanged shocked looks and took after the little shit.

"We need EMS at Pioneer Square," I yelled into my phone. "Two officers down and several civilians hexed."

"Ten-four, Detective Prospero," the dispatcher replied. "On their way."

"Stay with him," Morales snapped. "I'll cut through the alley and head him off at the intersection."

He veered off to the left. I dug in and ignored the burning in my thighs. My gaze locked in on the sequined clover mocking me from the back of the leprechaun's coat.

A high-pitched, potion-mad giggle taunted me. "Ye can't catch the Leprechaun Man!"

I considered shooting the asshole in his pot of gold.

Franklin Street curved around and for a split second I lost sight of my green prey. When I came around the bend, I got an eyeful of my six-foot-tall, muscle-bound partner squatting as if to catch a runaway toddler. The next instant Morales was flat on his ass with a green blur retreating in the distance.

"Come on!" I yelled and kept running.

Ten seconds after I passed him, Morales caught up. He didn't look as winded as I felt, but judging from his expression he was definitely just as pissed off. "What kind of potion is this guy on?"

Instead of answering, I grabbed my salt flare again. "I'll spray, you slay."

After his quick nod, I stop running. Exhaled. Pulled the trigger.

A starburst of salt rocks exploded from the gun. Half the crystals hit the pinged off cars parked along the street. The other half shredded the leprechaun's coat and tights, streaking the green fabric red with blood.

He stumbled, a hand sweeping toward the pavement for balance. But before he could regain his stride, Morales tackled.

The pair rolled through the streets. Morales's deep grunt playing off the squeaky protests of our short, belligerent friend.

The fall didn't faze Morales, who quickly got two fistfuls of green coat and pegged his prize to the brick wall.

"Put me down!" the perp yelled with a fake Irish accent.

"Or what, tough guy?" Morales said. He was barely winded. Not surprising. I'd seen glimpses of the illicit muscles he was smuggling under his shirt.

The leprechaun jutted his face forward. "Or I'll hex ye!"

"How you going to manage that?" I asked. "You lost your pot of gold."

He struggled in Morales's hold. *"Feisigh do thoin fein!"*

I exchanged a WTF look with my partner. "You catch that?"

"What's your name, Lucky Charms?" Morales asked.

"Sean Patrick Finnegan-O'Lachlan."

I blinked. "That's a mouthful."

"Aye, lass." He motioned toward his crotch. "I'll give ye a mouthful."

Morales dropped the guy on his ass. "Watch your manners."

O'Lachlan scrambled up quickly and tried to take off again. I caught him by the collar. "Not so fast." Grabbing his left hand, I wrenched it behind his back. A tattoo on his arm depicted a cup and, underneath, the words IN VINO VERITAS.

"In wine, the truth," I translated.

"Odd," Morales said. "I thought leprechauns loved beer."

"That's racist as shit," he said, dropping the Irish accent.

I pushed him toward the ground. Once his ass hit the concrete, I said, "Stay."

"Please," my partner said. "Irish isn't a race. It's a nationality."

O'Lachlan scraped Morales with a bitter glare. "Whatever, Cheech."

I sucked in my cheeks and glanced at Morales. He stared down at the guy like he was an ant in need of a boot heel.

"Hey, asshole," he said in a surprisingly even tone. "I prefer wetback."

"Gentlemen," I said, "can we get down to business?" I waited until both shot me grudging looks to continue. "What's in the potion?"

The perp spat at my feet. "I ain't tellin' you shit, lassie!" The guy pressed his lips together, twisted a finger in front of them, and mimed tossing away the key.

"I'll call a squad car." I turned away from the pair to call it in. Since we'd run several blocks during the pursuit, I glanced around to get my bearings. Back when I was still in uniform my beat had been the Cauldron, across the Bessemer Bridge from the downtown square where the Halloween Festival was held. The muted bite of sirens in the distance didn't give me a lot of hope we'd get a car. But I tried anyway because I didn't want to get stuck pushing this turd through booking at the precinct.

"Wear you out, did I?" O'Lachlan said to Morales behind me. "You should cut back on the donuts."

I snorted and looked back over my shoulder. The leprechaun slouched on the ground with a torn jacket and one missing shoe. Thanks to the tussle with Morales, one of his lightning bolts was smeared across his cheek like shit.

My partner on the other hand loomed over the small man like some sort of vengeful Aztec god. "Cops eat donuts." He pulled his wallet out of his pocket and flipped it open. "I'm MEA. We prefer a nice Danish."

"Magic Enforcement Agency?" O'Lachlan's eyes widened. "Thought you guys went after the big wizes."

"Apparently, we also go after little assholes." Morales used his left hand to rub his eyes. The scars webbing across the knuckles were from a fire that had killed his Adept father and little sister when he was a kid. After that trauma, he'd chosen to leave the Lefty world behind and present himself as a Mundane. Usually he did everything with his right hand—until he got stressed or overtired. Then he forgot he wasn't naturally a Righty.

Dispatch came on, so I turned back around and gave her our approximate location. "We need a squad car to pick up the perp from the Pioneer Square attack."

"Hold on a sec," she said, "I need to see if I can find a free car."

"Can't you reroute one from the festival?"

"After your perp hexed those cops, a riot broke out. It's under control, but every available car in the area is there for all the arrests."

"Shit."

"Amen, sister. Gonna get worse the closer we get to Halloween, too. My advice?" she said.

"Yeah?"

"Take him in yourself. Gonna be an hour, two maybe, before we can get someone to you."

I hung up and turned back to Morales. "We're gonna have to take him in. This fucking Blue Moon is a pain in my ass."

O'Lachlan crossed his arms and grumbled something like, "Ain't seen nothing yet."

"You want to hang here while I go get the car?"

Morales shook his head. "I'll get it."

"Understood." I jerked my head back toward the square. "See you in a few."

An adrenaline-spiked cop plus a shit-talking perp made a dangerous enough combination. But when you added a hefty dose of full-moon-batshit energy to the mix, you had yourself a recipe for a real shit sandwich. As a lapsed Adept, Morales was more susceptible to the erratic energies of double full moons than other Lefties. Better for me to babysit O'Lachlan than to put my partner in the position of facing a battery charge because he kicked the wannabe leprechaun in the shamrocks.

After Morales jogged off, I grabbed O'Lachlan off the ground. "Why did you hex all those people?" I spun him around and pressed him against the wall for a frisk.

"You owe me two hundred bucks."

I tilted my head. "Like hell I do."

"Your fuckin' partner tore my jacket when he tackled me. I'll never get my deposit back now."

"Oh yeah?" His tights had large holes and runners from the asphalt. "Maybe you should be more worried about coming up with bail than paying the costume shop." I made quick work of patting down his undercarriage.

"Don't be shy, lassie," he said, falling back into his unconvincing brogue. "That clover's lucky, if ya know what I mean."

I didn't rise to the bait. "You didn't just decide to hex cops at a carnival for shits and giggles. It took some planning."

"Hmm."

In his right jacket pocket, I found a lump. Sticking my hand inside, I grabbed the item and pulled it out. "Well, lookie here." I turned him around and held up an ampoule of glittery golden powder so he could see. "Who sold it to you?" Since he was right-handed and high off a potion when we first saw him, I already knew he wasn't an Adept. Mundanes couldn't cook real magic, and from the spectacle I'd witnessed in the square, this magic wasn't just real—it was real dirty.

"Would tellin' ye help my case?"

"Maybe I'll put a good word in if I think you're honest."

He lips made a sound like a fart. "Bullshit you will."

"Try me." I raised a brow.

His expression tightened into something approximating wounded pride. "I'm no snitch."

"Maybe some time in the can will help you tune your singing voice." I pushed him back to the ground. "Stay."

I looked at the powder. An overwhelming, forbidden urge rushed through me to skip the red tape altogether and read the potion. Not all Adepts could read energy signatures, but it was one of my gifts—or curses depending on your perspective. Still, evidence gained through Arcane processes wasn't admissible in court. Besides, when it came to magic, I was supposed to be firmly on the wagon.

But it would be so easy to just open that bag. So easy to read the potion's secrets. So easy to target the guilty coven.

Despite the chill in the air, my left palm was slick and trembling. Something in my gut opened, like a black hole that wanted filling.

A throat cleared next to me. "You all right, lass? You're looking kind of . . . off."

I jerked my head up, realizing too late I'd been about to take a running leap off the wagon.

Again.

The sound of an engine signaled Morales's impending arrival.

Time to remind myself that magic might be easy, but it was never simple.

My pulse did a little soft-shoe in my chest. I stuck the ampoule in my pocket and swallowed to cleanse the tarnish of guilt from my tongue. I grabbed O'Lachlan's arm and pulled up and toward the curb. "C'mon."

Since his hands were bound I had to hoist him up into the SUV. He wriggled across the seat, and I followed him. Morales glanced back over the seat. "Everything okay?" He was frowning like his instincts were telling him otherwise.

I wiped my damp palm on my jeans. "Yep. Why?"

"You're all flushed."

I tilted my head and prepared to verbally punt. "Morales, I just spent the last fifteen minutes chasing down a leprechaun. Sorry I'm not looking spring fresh."

I worried I'd overplayed my sarcasm. But he blew out a breath. "All right then." He turned back toward the steering wheel. "Settle in, Mr. O'Lachlan, we'll have you at the Hoose-gow Hilton in no time."

The perp spat on the floor. "May the devil cut the head off ye and make a day's work of your neck."

"First of all, don't spit in the car. It's disgusting," I said. "And second, the devil can do his worst so long as he buys me dinner first."

O'Lachlan looked me directly in my eyes. His own had lost the fevered glow from the potion he'd taken earlier, but, even sober, his irises retained the icy-blue hue of a dirty magic addict. "Once the Blue Moon gets here, you'll all be praying for the devil, bitch."

Chapter Two

Later that evening, I pushed my way through the kitchen door with a grocery bag in my right hand and my gun rig in my left. The mail was clamped between my teeth.

Arriving home to play house after a day of chasing down scumbags makes for an uneasy transition. Back when my brother, Danny, was little, I usually had to hide in the bathroom for five minutes and do deep-breathing exercises to release the pent-up adrenaline before I could face putting on my nurturing, maternal mask for the kid. But now that he was older, I found the same cop's instincts that allowed me to handle criminals were also pretty handy in dealing with a sixteen-year-old.

"What'd you get?" Danny was at the table pretending to do homework in the hopes I wouldn't notice the game device on his lap.

I swung the grocery bag up onto the tiled counter. "Come unload the bag and you'll see for yourself."

He sighed from deep in his gut, as if helping me was a burden only a saint could bear.

I began flipping through the mail while he unloaded the bag.

"Oh eww!" He turned and shot me an accusing look.

Setting down the private school tuition bill I couldn't pay until after my next MEA overtime check cleared, I went to investigate the problem.

Grabbing the rotisserie chicken and sides from the grocery had seemed like a good idea at the time. Better than fast food, but not as time consuming as an actual home-cooked meal. But the container Danny held aloft like a gun at a murder trial held a pale-looking carcass swimming in a pool of congealed lemon-pepper-flavored grease.

I shrugged and took it from him. "It's not that bad."

"Like hell—"

He cut off the words when I pointed to the curse jar by the sink. I'd told him it was my way of maintaining a level of respect in our home, but the truth was, I added more money to it than the kid. I considered it a sort of savings account. Some people pulled pennies from couch cushions or sold plasma for extra scratch, but I paid for splurges with *shit*s, *damn*s, and the occasional *fuck*.

Danny shoved a buck into the jar before continuing. "I'm going vegetarian." He turned and pulled a bottle of soda from the fridge.

"If you don't want the chicken, you can have rolls and potatoes and—"

I realized with a start I hadn't grabbed one green thing to serve with the meal. A salad or whatever. The little burst of heat in my stomach was the familiar sensation that accompanied the reminder that I was a failure of a role model. Didn't matter that I hadn't asked for the job. I took care of my responsibilities. It's just that lately it felt more and more like parenting was a riptide I couldn't outswim.

"And what?" he said, a challenge in his tone.

I put down the knife and turned to face him. "What do you want from me, Danny? I spent three hours at the precinct this afternoon trying to get one guy through booking. And that was after Morales and I had to chase the guy down. You don't want chicken that's your choice, but I'm not going to apologize for not catering to your refined palate with money I worked my ass off to earn."

"Fine," he said softly, "I'll have the freakin' chicken."

The corner of my mouth quirked. I may not be a real mom, but I'd somehow managed to master the martyred tone my own mother had employed to guilt me into good behavior. I hated having to use it on him, but it got results. Pasting a June Cleaver smile on my face, I turned to set two full plates of food on the table.

We both sat and dug in. The kid had been right, the chicken was too greasy, but it helped counterbalance the overly dry mashed potatoes, so that was something.

A few minutes later I realized Danny was unusually quiet. He seemed to have recovered from the chicken discussion, so it couldn't be that. Also, the electronic squawks and beeps that created our typical dinner soundtrack were conspicuously absent. Plus, he was staring into his mashed potatoes like maybe they held the secrets to the universe.

"What's up?"

He jumped a little, like he'd forgotten I was there. "Nothing."

I frowned and turned fully toward him while I wiped chicken grease off my hands with a paper towel. "Something happen at school?"

"What?" His brows lowered and he shook himself a little. "Yeah."

I tamped down the flare of worry in my gut and tried to look not-too-judgmental. "Should I expect a call from the principal again?"

"Nah. Nothing like that." He took in a deep breath and leaned back. "I—uh, well—there's this thing."

"What kind of thing?"

"There's this new club at school I want to join."

I blinked at him a couple of times. "A club? You?"

His face crumpled into an offended frown. "What? I do stuff."

"Just surprised is all. You've never really been a joiner." Off his deepening frown, I realized I was probably offending him. I swallowed and tried again. "What kind of club is it?"

His eyes widened, like he was surprised he'd gotten this far with the discussion. Guilt hit me upside the head. I'd always been protective of Danny—overprotective if you asked Baba—especially after almost losing him six weeks earlier. So it was no wonder he expected me to refuse outright without hearing details.

"Well, remember how that girl Pen was helping died a while back from the diet potion?"

Pen was my best friend, Penelope Griffin. She was also the guidance counselor at Meadowlake, the private school Danny attended. The girl he mentioned had gotten in trouble for taking the potion at school. Turned out her mother had been making her take it to lose weight, but before Pen could get the authorities involved, the girl overdosed. The mom was now in jail, but the incident left its scars on the Meadowlake community.

"One of the teachers started a group to promote kids staying off dirty magic."

I didn't point out that the girl in question had died from a completely legal potion sanctioned by the Federal Drug and Potion Agency, not some dirty brew cooked by a junkie wizard in the Cauldron. Instead I focused on my surprise over him wanting to join this type of organization. "You want to join an antimagic group?"

"Yeah. Why?"

"It wasn't all that long ago you were begging me to let you learn how to cook."

"This is different. The club is about preventing kids from becoming addicted to *dirty* magic. Jeez. I thought you'd support me in this."

"I do—"

"Especially after what happened."

I snapped my mouth shut. Those four little words were deceptively innocent considering he was referring to spending several days in a coma. Ramses Bane, the Grand Wizard of the Sanguinarian Coven, had dosed my kid brother with a dirty potion hoping it would make me drop off the case. Instead I'd shot the asshole with a salt flare and cooked dirty magic after a ten-year abstinence to save Danny's life. Now Bane was being kept in a secure location while he awaited trial, and I was getting shit from Danny, who had no idea what I'd done to save his life.

Swallowing the knot of remembered fear in my throat, I readjusted my approach. "I support you joining an anti-dirty-magic club. Of course I do. It's just I wasn't expecting it, is all. We haven't really talked about…what happened in a while. I wasn't sure how you were feeling about it all."

His young face hardened. "How do you think I feel? If it hadn't been for John, I'd be dead right now."

My hand tensed into a fist on my lap. John Fucking Volos. Letting him take the credit for saving Danny had been the only way to ensure no one found out I'd fallen off the magic wagon. Over the last several weeks there had been so many occasions when I'd wanted to scream the truth. Without the help of my ability to read potions, John never would have been able to finish the antipotion that eventually saved both his and Danny's lives. But I hadn't told anyone because in addition to lying about cooking dirty, I'd also failed to report evidence that fingered my uncle Abe as the mastermind of the entire scheme.

But I couldn't very well contradict Danny's praise of Volos with getting some probing questions I was nowhere near ready to answer. So I swallowed the bitterness and forced a smile. "So when does this club meet?"

He pulled back, like I'd surprised him. "Every Tuesday and Thursday until about six thirty."

My brows rose. "The meetings will be two hours?"

"Mr. Hart said it would be longer in the beginning because we have a lot of work to do to get the club going." He toyed with his cell phone. "Making posters and stuff, I guess."

"How will you get home?" Normally, Pen dropped him off after school.

"I'll get a ride from one of the other members."

"If not, I bet Baba would come get you." Baba was our septuagenarian Wiccan neighbor. With my crazy hours, she often stepped up to keep Danny company if I had late nights.

His face screwed up. "I'll definitely get one of my friends."

"What's wrong with Baba getting you?"

"Her car, for one thing."

I grimaced. It's not that her old Cutlass Supreme was horrible, even though the avocado green made it look like some sort of '70s time machine. The real problem was the bumper stickers she'd plastered all over the back. As a witch, she felt the need to broadcast her support of her fellow Mundane magic users in the form of messages like WITCHES DO IT IN CIRCLES. There were also stickers with slogans like HONK IF YOU LOVE NAKED BINGO and TOM JONES MAKES ME FEEL LIKE A WOMAN.

So, yeah, I couldn't exactly blame the kid for not wanting to ride in her hooptymobile. I didn't want to be seen in it, either.

"All right, ask your buddies. We'll use Baba as a last resort for rides."

His face cleared. "Thank you."

My center warmed at the rare gratitude. "When's your first meeting?"

"Next week. Mr. Hart said the permission forms need to be in by Monday."

"Who is Mr. Hart again? I don't know if I've met him."

"He's the new chemistry teacher. The form's in my room."

"Go grab it and I'll sign it." He was almost at the door when another question occurred to me. "Wait!"

He froze and turned slowly in that teenager way of telling you they couldn't wait to get out of your company.

"What's the name?"

"Huh?"

"Of the club? Like DARE?" He stared at me blankly. Sometimes I forgot he wasn't yet born during the days of neon and cocaine. "It was a movement in the 'eighties that stood for Drug Abuse Resistance and Education."

"Oh." He didn't look impressed. "This one's Don't Use Dirty Elixirs."

I frowned. "The acronym is DUDE?"

He nodded slowly, as if he found nothing funny about it.

"That's kind of awesome, actually. You should tell that Mr. Hart what I do. Maybe he'd have me in to speak about the dangers of dirty magic."

He shot me a look like I'd just taken a dump on the linoleum.

"Mr. Hart said we won't be having speakers for a while since we'll be busy recruiting for the club."

"But having speakers might attract new members."

"It's not my call." Danny shrugged. "Can I go get the form now?"

I waved him off, trying to pretend his reaction to my suggestion hadn't taken the air out of my sails. At some point I'd gone from being the cool big sister he worshipped to the annoying nag who said unbearably embarrassing things.

"I bet none of your friends' moms knows how to apply a proper choke hold or reload a Glock in under ten seconds," I said to the empty kitchen.

I'm pretty sure none of his friend's moms ever had a feud with a dirty magic wizard end with her kid in a coma, either.

And with that cheerful thought, I turned to grab a beer. At least this development meant I was off the hook on my promise to teach Danny the basics of magic. I'd been waiting for him to bring it up ever since he recovered, but he hadn't brought it up. I leaned back and took a long swallow of cold brew, satisfied that everything seemed to be under control for a change.

Chapter Three

October 18
Waxing Crescent

The next morning I pulled my old Jeep, Sybil, into the gym's parking lot at eight sharp. The lot sat next to some abandoned train rails that used to carry steel from Babylon's mills to the rest of the country. Now the tracks were rusted and choked with weeds. Sort of like Babylon's justice system.

I walked across the lot toward the front door of Rooster's Gym. Downstairs, the building housed a bodega that sold cold drinks, cheap smokes, and titty magazines. Upstairs, though, was the space the MEA task force used as our office. It used to be one of those old-school boxing gyms before the steel bubble burst and the economy dried up faster than flop sweat on the mats.

Climbing the steps up to the gym, I inhaled the scent of body odor on stale vinyl and old varnish on scarred wood. Sun streamed through huge steel-framed windows, casting an ethereal glow on the old boxing ring that dominated the center of the huge room.

In the center of the ring was a large whiteboard covered with a map of Babylon, where Gardner kept track of calls we responded to on behalf of the BPD. Technically, we were only supposed to lend a hand in the Cauldron, but with the double full moons that month the circuits had been so overwhelmed with calls, we sometimes had to venture into the Mundane parts of the city, too. I was the only local cop on the task force; the map helped the rest of the team find their way around.

At that moment Morales ducked a head from behind a wall of the makeshift lab our team wizard, Kichiri "Mesmer" Ren, had erected to separate his work from the investigative side of things. Mez cooked up defensive weapons for us and broke down potions to help solve cases there, but the space also served as the coffee room. I went to join them.

The two men stood over the coffee siphon with mugs at the ready. Morales stood about half a head taller than the wizard. Mez's long dreadlocks were their natural brown this morning, but the sunlight caught the small bells and magical amulets he'd woven into the strands. A lab coat covered the top of his outfit, but the distressed jeans and motorcycle boots were visible below. In addition to basically being a magical genius, he was also the team's snappiest dresser. Technically, he was a civilian employee of the MEA instead of a sworn officer, but he was as integral to our success on cases as any of us cops.

The coffee contraption looked like something out of a mad scientist's lab. A glass siphon sat on a metal stand holding another glass bulb of water. Using gravity and the alchemy of heat, water, and strong coffee beans, the machine turned out a brew that wasn't a potion, but sure tasted like magic.

Neither spoke to me as I approached, but I didn't mind. Watching the coffee percolate through the contraption was something of a morning ritual. As usual, Morales had his favorite SEMPER FI marines mug. Mez's had a picture of Sir Isaac Newton and the quote I CAN CALCULATE THE MOTION OF HEAVENLY BODIES, BUT NOT THE MADNESS OF PEOPLE.

I went to the cabinet over Mez's collection of Erlenmeyer flasks and pulled out the WORLD'S BEST SISTER mug Danny had given me for Mother's Day a few years earlier.

"Aha!" Mez said, suddenly. "It's ready." He started to elbow Morales out of the way.

"As ranking agent I should get the first cup," Morales said.

A throat cleared from the doorway. We turned to find Special Agent Miranda Gardner standing at the entrance of the lab. That morning she wore simple brown pantsuit with an ivory shell. Her shoes bore a no-nonsense inch-tall heel, also in brown. The only jewelry she wore was a tiger-eye cabochon ring she never seemed to take off her middle finger.

"My office, two minutes," she said. She had that look on her face. The one that meant she either hadn't had her coffee yet or had just gotten off the phone with Captain Eldritch. In her hand she held a simple white mug half-full of the instant coffee she preferred, so it was safe she wasn't about to pull rank at the coffeepot. "And Morales?" she added.

He raised his brows. Mez took advantage of Morales's distraction to fill his own mug.

Gardner smiled tightly. "Make that second highest ranking."

Morales grinned. "Yes, sir."

Without another word she turned on her heel and marched back toward her office. I jumped in front of Morales, grabbing the second cup from the special pot. Judging from the look on his face, the offense ranked up there with making fun of his

23

mama. I stuck my tongue at him and filled his cup for him. "There, you big baby. Let's go see what the boss lady wants."

Gardner's office wasn't anything to write home about. A simple metal desk, a filing cabinet, and an ancient office chair. A couple of thin wooden planks that served as bookshelves. Single window cloudy as milk glass offering pitiful light. On top of her desk were a blotter, a phone, and a sign that read, NO BULLSHIT BEFORE FIVE P.M. I knew from personal experience she wasn't too fond of it after five, either.

"Sit down." She took her own seat. "Captain Eldritch will join us momentarily."

I frowned. "He's coming here?"

Eldritch used to be my boss before I joined the MEA task force. He was the captain of the Cauldron precinct of the Babylon Police Department. He specialized in Arcane crimes and political maneuvering, not necessarily in that order. He'd encouraged me to take the gig with the MEA in the hopes I'd be his insider gal, but once he realized I was more interested in solving crimes than earning brownie points our professional rapport had suffered. Still, he hadn't argued about granting me a promotion to detective after my first case with MEA resulted in the arrest of one of the Cauldron's most powerful wizards.

She nodded to the phone. "He's on his way up."

Morales shot me a grimace. A call from my former boss was usually bad enough, but a personal visit? Could only mean trouble.

The sound of footsteps trudging up stairs from the other end of the gym announced Eldritch's arrival. A few seconds later Mez called out a greeting that was met with a grumble. A good sign. If he'd been in a shitty mood, he wouldn't have responded at all.

Two seconds later the door to Gardner's office was filled

with the bulk of Captain Robert Eldritch. There was a coffee stain on the wide belly of his off-white dress shirt. His forehead shone with beads of sweat from the exertion of hefting his bulk up the steps. The brass clip on his navy-blue tie had been given to him by the mayor himself when Eldritch had been promoted to captain several years earlier. Now he was angling for the gold tie clip and sweet pay-grade increase a promotion to chief of police would earn him.

"How well you know Aphrodite Johnson?" This was his only greeting and when he said it, he was staring right at me.

My shoulders lifted even as my hopes plummeted. Here we go, I thought, back in the shit. I self-consciously tugged my left sleeve down to cover the Ouroboros tattoo on my wrist that marked me as a made member of the Votary Coven. I'd never had it removed because the snake winding around my flesh was a reminder of the viper pit I'd escaped a decade earlier.

"Hold on," Gardner cut in. Clearly she wasn't going to let Eldritch stroll in and take over. "You mean the head of the O Coven?"

"I'm impressed you've done your homework on the covens, Gardner," he said.

Her eyes went all cold steel on him. "I've been brushing up on Cauldron politics when I'm not busy picking up your precinct's slack."

Eldritch's eyes narrowed.

I stepped in to defuse the tension. "Yes, Aphrodite is the Hierophant of the Mystical Coven of the Sacred Orgasm."

Morales perked up the instant he heard the word *orgasm*. "Since the O's are a sex magic coven, does that make the Hierophant like a madam?"

"Something like that," I said. *Pimp* also worked, depending on the day.

"How well do you know Aphrodite personally?" Eldritch pressed me.

When you call yourself Aphrodite, you have to have either some serious confidence or a well-developed sense of irony. Judging from my dealings with the Hierophant of the O Coven, Aphrodite Johnson was in possession of both.

I sighed. "More than I'd like, honestly. The Hierophant was an old ally of Uncle Abe's." Aphrodite also knew my mother very well, but I didn't want to get into my mother's scandalous associations at the moment.

"How did she escape getting caught up in the net when he was arrested?" Morales asked.

I didn't bother correcting his presumption of using the feminine pronoun with Aphrodite. We'd get to the Hierophant's gender situation eventually.

"The O's are a special case," Eldritch said with a scowl. "Back in the 'seventies the Hierophant's predecessor, Matahari Jenkins, figured out how to get the coven registered as a religious organization on account of them using sex magic as a form of worship, which is why they call Aphrodite a Hierophant instead of just a wizard. Anyway, now they get to skirt all sorts of pesky laws and avoid paying taxes."

Morales laughed. "That's actually kind of brilliant."

"It would be if it didn't mean that a lot of their members get away with everything from prostitution to human trafficking and rape," I added. That wiped the smile off Morales's face. "Why are you asking about Johnson, sir?"

Eldritch crossed his arms. "It seems one of the O's 'houses of worship' was robbed last night."

I frowned. "Okay? What does that have to do with us?"

"She claims the thief got away with about fifty thousand dollars' worth of sex magic potions."

"Again," Gardner said, "how is that our problem?"

Eldritch sighed and dropped the combative expression. "Look, I'm up to my ass in potion freaks who think the full moons are excuses to raise hell all over the city. I don't have enough detectives on staff to deal with Johnson right now, especially with Prospero on your team."

Technically, I still worked for the BPD. The MEA paid for my overtime, but the city of Babylon still cut my paychecks. The task force model had been pioneered by the MEA a few years earlier to get more local law enforcement involved in bringing down large covens. It helped the feds navigate around some pesky jurisdictional issues, and allowed local cops like me to get experience and major federal busts under their gun belts.

My brows rose. "In other words, you suspect this is another vengeance stunt."

"Something like that." Eldritch nodded.

"Explain," Gardner said.

"Aphrodite is famous for holding grudges over the slightest insult. S/he's called the cops a couple of times after framing enemies for crimes they didn't commit."

"If you knew she was framing them, why isn't she in jail?" Morales asked.

"She's slippery," Eldritch said. "And has a lawyer that's a crafty son of a bitch."

"So let me see if I understand. You don't have the manpower to send on a wild goose chase, but you're more than willing to send federal agents on one? We're already saving your ass by backing up your patrols. And, by the way, we're still waiting on those extra officers we were promised to help my team bring down the covens."

"You were cleared to have Detective Duffy from the First Precinct."

The First was the main precinct in the Mundane areas of Babylon. Despite being an Adept, Duffy had managed to work his way up to a reputation as one of the best homicide detectives in the city. In Gardner's opinion, the more Adept cops she could get fighting the covens, the better the MEA's chances of closing some major busts. Problem was, most Adepts in law enforcement went into forensics or lab work. We tended to be pretty scarce on the investigative side, since most cops distrusted Adepts to solve cases without employing magic.

Upon hearing Duffy's name, I grimaced, bracing for Gardner's explosion.

Instead of yelling, she gritted her teeth. "You know damned well Duffy turned us down."

Eldritch shrugged. "Yeah, I heard that. Too bad," he said, sounding anything but disappointed. "Since you couldn't convince him, you're just going to have to wait until my crews aren't working overtime to keep the Blue Moon bullshit contained." Gardner opened her mouth to respond, but Eldritch wasn't done. "And as for building cases against the covens, wouldn't working on a case involving one of the covens be right in line with your mission?"

"Not if we're busy tracking down false leads on the Hierophant's behalf!"

Eldritch's lips curved. "Shall I call the mayor and ask him to send you an engraved invitation?"

She blew out a sigh. As it was the MEA's presence in Babylon was tenuous at best. We were coming up on an election, and Mayor Owens wanted to ensure the feds didn't steal any of the credit for high-profile arrests. We already had one strike against us after a raid went awry during the Bane case. To be seen as uncooperative with the BPD when the Blue Moon was causing so much havoc would be a second strike we couldn't afford.

"Fine. Morales and Prospero will go interview Johnson, but once we close that case, I expect at least one new head count the instant the Blue Moon passes and not a day more."

Eldritch sucked his teeth for a moment. The move made his mustache dance on his top lip. "It's a deal. But I expect to be kept in the loop on this."

"No dice. You came to us. That makes this an MEA op. I'll let you know if we need BPD assistance, but otherwise I'll be making all the calls."

It was clear Eldritch wanted to argue, but a smart leader knew when he'd gotten his way and didn't push for more out of ego. "Fine. I have a meeting with the chief for lunch." He glanced at his watch and then at Gardner. "I trust that as we get closer to the Blue Moon, your team will continue to be available to back up their brothers in blue?"

"And sisters, yes," Gardner snapped. "Agent Pruitt is out with your Arcane squad as we speak."

He nodded and tossed a file folder on the desk. "That's the initial incident report from the unis who responded to the call. They didn't find much."

"As long as they didn't fuck with the scene so our team wiz can do a thorough forensics search."

He ignored that. "Just be sure you get this Aphrodite case closed fast. We'll need more manpower, not less, the closer we get to Halloween." With that Eldritch hitched up his pants and walked out of the office without so much as a good-bye.

The three of us remaining sat there until we heard his steps start down the staircase. Since he was finally out of range, Gardner let out the frustrated sigh she'd been holding. "Asshole."

I bit my lip. Not because I disagreed, but because agreeing too vehemently was also a mistake. The relationship between those two changed depending on who needed favors, so it was just as likely that tomorrow she'd be singing his praises if he came through on one she needed.

"All right, Prospero, are you ready for this one?"

I nodded. "SSDD." Translation: Same shit different day.

"Mez!" she called. A muted response filtered through the gym, which I assumed meant he was on his way.

"You two go in first with the interview," Gardner said. "Mez will handle forensics."

"Great," I mumbled.

"What's wrong?" she asked.

"Aphrodite considers herself somewhat of a sexual guru. I'll probably spend most of the interview defending Morales's and Mez's honor."

"Defend my honor from whom?" Mez said, sticking his head through the door.

Gardner quickly filled him in on the situation.

"Doesn't sound so bad, if you ask me," he said with a smirk.

"Whatever you do, act natural when you see her/m," I said.

"Did you say 'herm'?" Morales's eyebrows shot up.

"It's short for 'her/him,'" I explained. "Aphrodite's a sacred hermaphrodite."

"Oh shit," Mez said. "Why didn't you say that to begin with? I'm totally in."

"I thought the term *hermaphrodite* was politically incorrect?" Gardner said.

"Technically it's only incorrect to use for Mundanes born with both male and female androgens," Mez explained, his voice rising in excitement. "But sacred hermaphrodites are created by wizards using powerful alchemical magic that makes a person exactly half-male and half-female."

I nodded. "They're the ultimate symbol of unity between the male and female energies of the universe. So they're basically revered among Adepts and rarely challenged once they reach high levels within covens."

"So they're both sexes?" Morales asked, slack-jawed. "At the same time?"

I shook my head. "Usually there's one in the lead, but Aphrodite likes to keep people off guard by switching in the middle of conversations. The trick is to watch for clues. If the male half is in the lead, you address using male pronouns. If the female is in charge, you use female."

"How will we know?" Mez asked.

"Aphrodite's voice and posture change according to who's in charge."

Morales blew out a breath. "This case is gonna be a real kick in the balls, isn't it?"

I nodded. "Pretty much. S/he's about as cuddly as a black widow on a good day, which of course today is not seeing how the temple was violated and some asshole stole the Hierophant's potions."

"Oh yeah, and don't forget we're less than two weeks away from a monster Blue Moon," Mez said helpfully. "So s/he'll be feeling the effects of that shit."

Morales rubbed his hands together. "I don't know. Considering how dead it's been around here lately, it kind of sounds like fun."

"Remember those words later," I said, "so you can regret them."

◆ ◆ ◆

On our way out to Morales's car, he and I ran into the fifth member of the task force, Shadi Pruitt.

For the last week or so, she had been assigned to help the BPD's Arcane unit do raids on corner boys to stem the flow of potions. With the moon's unstable energy in play, the fewer people out there freaking on potions, the better.

Normally she moved like a petite bull looking for a china shop, but now she looked like she was pushing a freight train uphill. The circles under her eyes and pale cast to her normally dark complexion bore testament to the late nights she'd been serving to help out the patrol units.

"You look like someone beat you with a bag of dicks," Morales called by way of greeting.

She flipped him the bird with her right hand. "Bite me, jackass." Her words lacked any heat. "Where's Mez?"

"Getting his kit ready," Morales said. "He's meeting us at a crime scene."

"How's it going out there?" I asked.

She sighed and pushed all her weight to her right hip. "Motherfuckers be trippin' like usual." She shrugged as if this was standard operating procedure, which, given we were working in a magical slum, it kind of was. "But it beats the hell out of patrol."

We all nodded because it was true.

"What crime scene you headed to?" Shadi asked.

"Someone stole some sex potions from a sacred hermaphrodite," Morales said.

If his announcement surprised her, she didn't show it. "All right, I'm going to go check in with the boss lady and then head home for some shut-eye." She yawned so big her jaw popped. "But I'll see ya tonight."

From the corner of my eye, I caught a flash of movement coming from Morales, but when I looked up at him he looked clueless. To Shadi, I said, "Actually, I've got AA tonight." I didn't mention that I had no intention of attending the weekly Arcane Anonymous meeting, just as I'd skipped the previous six.

Shadi's face changed into an expression I couldn't read. Almost a cross between confusion and guilt. "Oh, uh. Yeah. Cool."

After that, she left quickly. I shot Morales a look. "What was that about?"

He slipped on his aviators. "No idea. She's probably just tired."

I knew bullshit when I smelled it, but blew it off. Probably Morales and Shadi had plans to go grab a beer or something and hadn't invited me. Wouldn't be the first time. I didn't take it personally. Those two were pretty tight, and, besides, they never invited anyone else, either.

I glanced at Morales as we walked toward his car. Part of me wondered if those two had a thing going on. They never showed any romantic interest at work. Sure, they teased each other, but it always seemed more like two siblings giving each other shit than the way a couple teased each other.

"What?" my partner asked suddenly.

I jumped, guilty at having been caught staring. But, hell, I thought, might as well ask. "Are you two—you know?" I made a vaguely obscene gesture with my fingers.

He stopped walking so fast I was shocked he didn't get whiplash. "What?"

I waved toward the building. "You and Shadi."

Instead of answering, he threw back his head and brayed like the jackass he was. I crossed my arms and tried to ignore the heat searing my cheeks. When the laughter finally slowed into chuckles, he gasped for breath. "Jesus Christ, Prospero, that's the best laugh I've had in weeks." He swiped at his eyes, even though I knew he hadn't laughed *that* hard.

"So no?" I snapped.

He stilled and cocked his head at my overly pissed-off tone.

"Wait, you're serious?" At my look, he crossed his arms and narrowed his eyes. "You mean you had no idea Shadi bats for Team Sappho?"

"Fuck off. No she doesn't!"

"You're like the worst detective ever." He shook his head sadly. "That woman sees more snatch than an ob-gyn."

My face mashed up into a grimace. "Charming."

He grinned. "No? I thought that was kind of clever, myself."

"You would."

"Anyway," he said, clicking the button to open the SUV's doors, "not that I'm not into lesbians or whatever—I mean, what heterosexual man isn't?—but Shadi's like my sister."

I climbed into the passenger's side. Bringing this topic up had been a huge mistake. "Got it," I said, hoping he'd let it drop.

He buckled his seat belt and put the key in the ignition, shaking his head the whole time. "You're a trip, Prospero. Me and Shadi. Ha!"

"I said I got it."

"Besides," he continued as if I hadn't spoken, "dating a fellow cop is bad news." He looked across the car at me. Something shifted in the atmosphere. "Right?"

"Of course," I said quickly. "I was just making conversation."

His gaze held mine for a few more seconds, like it was an interrogation and he wanted me to admit something. "Conversation," he said, finally, "sure."

"Just drive, jackass."

Chapter Four

Morales pulled up in front of the building and stared at the facade. "Are you sure this is the right place?"

"Yep." I set down the unhelpful incident report Eldritch had left us and pointed to a small brass plaque discreetly set beside the revolving doors.

"Temple of Cosmic Love?" Morales read. "Jesus."

To the uninitiated, the sex magic temple looked like a typical Babylon office building. Four stories of brick and windows that looked like every other office building on the corner of Hope and Bleaker Streets. As it happened that corner was smack in the center of the border between Sanguinarian and Votary territories. That was because Aphrodite Johnson, among other things, was a shrewd strategist. Unlike the blood magic wizards and bathtub alchemists, s/he refused to choose sides in the street magic battles. S/he ensured the O Coven remained the sexy Switzerland of the dirty magic world. But even though the Hierophant kept the coven out of turf wars, that didn't seem to stop her/m from creating enemies as if it were a hobby.

As I passed through the revolving door, I felt static in the air that indicated some sort of magic detection system was scanning us. It was like a metal detector, only it was trying to catch people bringing potions into the temple. Usually I was annoyed by such invasions. But this time I found myself enjoying the tingle of energy across my skin and the adrenaline surge from the contact with magic. Since neither of us was wearing a protection amulet, we passed through without incident. When I emerged from the doorway, I cleared my throat, hoping Morales wouldn't notice the slight flush to my cheeks.

A security guard dressed in a sharp business suit met us by the front desk. "The Hierophant is expecting you in the garden," he said.

"Our task force wizard will be arriving shortly to begin the forensics," Morales said. "His name is Kichiri Ren."

He nodded. "I'll show him to the room where the potions were taken, and you can join him after you speak to Her Holiness."

I glanced meaningfully at Morales, so he'd take note Aphrodite was presenting as female that morning.

As the guard walked away, I hung back to give my partner some last-minute advice. "Whatever you do, don't touch anything while we're out there."

"That's a good rule of thumb in most whorehouses, isn't it?" Morales asked with a cocked brow.

"True," I said, "but I was talking about her garden." I used the feminine pronoun since we knew Aphrodite was presenting as female that day.

He paused and shot me a sardonic grin. "I definitely never touch whores' *gardens*, Prospero."

I gave up. He'd see what I meant soon enough, anyway. "Whatever. Just try to behave."

A few moments later we stepped out into a large courtyard in the center of the building. According to local legend, this space had served as the setting for many an orgy for Babylon's rich and famous, but it was also home to the madam's famous collection of poisonous plants, which was famous in Cauldron lore.

Aphrodite herself stood at the rear of the courtyard, bathed in a shaft of sunlight. I was pretty sure she'd planned the position for effect. When we entered the courtyard, she looked up and flipped the long side of her hair back over her shoulder. The left half wore a formfitting red wiggle dress with red stiletto, while the right half wore half a collared shirt, slacks, and a single black wing tip. As she moved forward, she led with the left side and a femme fatale smile.

"Kate— Oh, excuse me, I mean, Detective Prospero," she said, giving me a once-over that left me feeling like I'd come up lacking. Her seductive voice twined through the room like smoke. She sashayed toward us on one high heel and one thick-soled men's dress shoe.

When I'd told Morales that Aphrodite was half-female and half-male, I'd meant it literally. The left side of the face was perfectly made up with a shimmery nude eye, bold black eyeliner, and half a mouth lacquered in bold red lipstick. The other half bore carefully cultivated stubble, a bold, unwaxed brow, and not a single lick of makeup.

The weird part was that her lady side was as beautiful and conventionally feminine as her right side was ruggedly handsome and conventionally male. The gender differences extended down her entire body from the clothing to the body hair to the way she was graceful on the feminine left and confident on the masculine right. But to me, the most disconcerting feature was how the voice would change depending on which gender the Hierophant chose at the time.

When she caught sight of Morales, her cat eyes flared with prurient interest. "Who's your friend?" she asked me in a feline tone, but she kept her eyes on him.

Morales took her hand and bent over it like a chivalrous knight. "Special Agent Drew Morales, MEA."

Aphrodite's eyes flared and her lips jutted forward into a pout. "Whatever have I done to deserve the interest of the Magic Enforcement Agency?"

"Nothing yet," I said. She looked over at me grudgingly as she continued to hold Morales's hand. "The BPD is backlogged with the Blue Moon coming, so we're taking the case to help out."

She shot a terse glance at my partner as he not-so-subtly pulled his hand from her grip. "I must admit the idea gives me some comfort. Forgive me, Detective, but I've had somewhat disappointing dealings with Babylon's finest in the past."

"Uh-huh," I said.

"You also remember I was friends with your mother?" she asked with a sidelong glance.

My mom and Aphrodite were whores together back in the day. Then the O's were still controlled by Matahari Jenkins from a temple closer to the center of Votary territory. Word on the street was she and Uncle Abe had been sort of an item. Aphrodite had been Matahari's top moneymaker, and my mom had been number two. As far as I knew there hadn't been much competition between the two—Aphrodite's sacred status had given her a huge edge over my mom. So they had been friendly, but not best buds, either.

Anyway, Mom died a decade ago, and since then Aphrodite had taken over for Matahari and built this new temple.

"You were also friends with my uncle," I added.

"Still am. Poor dear," she said, batting her lashes. "How is he faring in prison?"

"I wouldn't know."

Our eyes met and held. Despite the somewhat disconcerting experience of looking into one heavily made-up eye and one naked one, I held her gaze steady. The look seemed to communicate that without her fondness for my mother, whom she respected, my poor standing with Uncle Abe would have prevented this conversation from happening at all.

"I appreciate you speaking with us," I said diplomatically. "This shouldn't take much of your time."

She seemed to accept that. "So let's get to it, shall we?"

Morales pulled out his pad to take notes. "Ms. Johnson—"

"Aphrodite, please."

"We'd like to ask a few questions about the break-in?"

"Of course," she said, motioning to a seating area arranged around a fire pit on the perimeter of the courtyard.

To get there, we skirted the large pergola, which dominated the center of the courtyard. Underneath it was Aphrodite's infamous garden.

Leafy moonseed vines with their deadly bright red drupes climbed up pergola's wooden columns. Oleander shrubs, with their white flowers and fatally toxic leaves, dotted the borders of the bed. The purple petals of devil's cherry and wolfsbane added deceptively cheerful spots of color. The green and purplish starbursts of castor bean leaves with their fuzzy red pompoms added depth to the display, as well as access to the deadly poison ricin. And in the very center, the wide branches of a *Brugmansia* plant with its large, drooping angel trumpet flowers. Those celestial petals contained a triple punch of the toxins atropine, hyoscyamine, and scopolamine.

As we passed, I gave the garden a wide berth, not wanting to accidentally prick myself on the deadly thorns or get any poisonous sap on my skin. But Morales stopped next to a plant bearing bright red berries. He reached a hand toward it, but I slapped it away. "That's a rosary pea," I hissed under my breath.

"So?" He frowned.

"The seeds contain a poison called abrin," Aphrodite explained. "It causes severe vomiting, liver failure, bladder failure, bleeding from the eyes, and convulsive seizures before it kills you."

"If it's that deadly, why do you have it in your garden?" he demanded.

The corner of her mouth lifted. "So your partner didn't already tell you about my revenge garden?" She glanced at me with a raised brow. When I shook my head, she chuckled.

Morales frowned. "Revenge garden?"

She leaned forward, allowing the bodice on the left side of her body to show an impressive amount of one-sided cleavage. "Every plant in that bed is lethal. I nurture that garden like a child to warn my enemies of what will happen if they cross me."

I slapped my hands together. "All righty, then. Let's get to the robbery, shall we?"

Aphrodite crossed her arms. "I already filed a report with the officers who responded to the call last night."

"Yes, we have that." I held the report file up for her to see. "But they were working it as a regular robbery. We're MEA, so our concern is making sure the potions that were stolen don't end up on the streets."

She frowned. "What can I tell you to help?"

"First, we'll need a list of all the potions that were taken," Morales said. "Including their formulae, if possible."

She laughed. "I can give you the list, but I'm not about to reveal the recipes for my formulae."

"Without the recipe we won't be able to know if any potions we find are the same as the ones taken."

She pursed her lips. "Just read the energy signature."

"Not possible," Morales said. "We don't have an Adept who can do that on the team."

Aphrodite's eyes snapped toward me. "Why not have Kate do it?" My stomach dropped. "Back in the day she was famous for being able to read the signature off any potion."

Morales's gaze snapped toward me, but he covered his reaction to this news smoothly. "Detective Prospero's talents not withstanding, the testimony of an Adept gathered through Arcane means won't hold up in court. We'll need the ingredients for our forensics wizard to be able to prove the potions are yours."

She sighed. "Fine. All of my potions contain fiery cinnamon and virgin copulins. Surely your agents are capable of doing simple chemical tests to detect those ingredients."

Morales glanced at me for confirmation. "I'm pretty sure our team wiz can identify cinnamon and copulins, but there's no test to confirm they were extracted from a virgin."

"If your wizard is any sort of professional, he'll know how," she said.

Morales raised a hand. "Dare I ask what a copulin is?"

Aphrodite raised a brow in challenge, but I nodded to her to go ahead. "Copulins are pheromones." She looked at Morales with a black widow smile. "Did you know a woman's pussy contains magical properties, Special Agent?"

I squirmed on the inside. I don't care if you're a seasoned cop or a rode-hard-and-put-up-wet prostitute, there's something electrifying about hearing *that* word spoken aloud. She knew it, too, which was why the Hierophant's gaze stayed on Morales's face when she enunciated it.

But Morales, God love him, did not even blink. "I'm well acquainted with the magical powers of pussy, ma'am."

I bit my lip to cover my amusement. Aphrodite laid her hands on the armrests and leaned back, eyeing my partner like a Serengeti lioness watches a juicy gazelle.

"Have you had any personnel problems lately?" I asked. "We'll need to see those files, too."

Aphrodite looked up sharply at me. I simply raised my brows.

Something in her face changed. As if the power center of her being shifted from left to right. Her shoulders squared and her jaw muscles engaged, as if the body instinctively felt the need to take up as much space as possible to command more authority. That sly smile dissolved into a neutral expression that gave nothing away. And when the half-painted mouth opened to speak, the voice that emerged was no longer the seductive purr of a madam, but the baritone of a pimp. "My files are not public record, Detective."

This wasn't the first time I'd seen the Hierophant morph between genders, but I'd never get used to the unsettling shift. "They could be with a simple phone call, Mr. Johnson."

When I didn't back down, that mouth tightened into a thin line, and that's when I knew I'd made it onto his shit list. I had a feeling it wouldn't be the last time.

"Surely you keep some sort of information on your followers," Morales said, playing the mediator.

"I'm not the MEA, Agent Morales. I don't keep dossiers on my congregation. They're not criminals. I've already said all this to officers who responded last night. So if there's nothing else I am quite busy—"

"Keep your wig on," I snapped. Not my coolest moment

ever—the Hierophant would see any reference to the feminine when the masculine was in charge as a direct insult. "For someone who was robbed you're awfully reluctant to help."

The wig comment earned me a death glare, but the implication got me a dismissive snort. "Why would I rob my own temple, Detective?"

"Beats me," I said with a shrug, "but if you continue to stonewall us it's an option we'll be forced to investigate further."

He squinted at me and sucked his teeth for a moment. He was wondering if the years had dulled the infamous Prospero stubbornness out of me. I smiled to let him know they had not. If anything, being on this side of the law had only solidified those tendencies.

"Now that I think about it," Morales said to me conversationally, "Mr. Johnson does seem awfully composed for someone who was just robbed of thousands of dollars' worth of potions."

I crossed my arms and glanced at him, playing along. "You may be right. Maybe we should call Judge Dread after all and ask for a search warrant. I bet we'd find all sorts of interesting things in those files then."

The Hierophant cleared his throat. "What do you want to know?"

I was impressed at how smoothly Morales digested the victory. His face betrayed none of his emotion, didn't give anything away that Johnson could use against us. Like it or not, the guy was a pro. "For starters you can tell us which of your enemies was most likely to do this."

He pursed his lips. "It could be any of a dozen wizards."

"The report the officer filed said there was no sign of forced entry," Morales said. "Any idea why?"

He shrugged his right shoulder. "Beats me."

I leaned forward. "Look, if you're concerned about us arresting any of your girls for solicitation, don't. We're just here to find the thief."

"Detective, most of the girls and boys that find their ways to my door are trying to escape something." His voice lowered even further into what I assume he felt was a sincere tone. "Abuse, poverty, discrimination. I give them a safe place to practice their skills and find a higher purpose. Very few happy individuals walk away from their lives for this kind of tough spiritual work."

Morales's brows shot up. "I'm surprised to hear such a fatalistic summary of what you do."

"I may be a believer, Agent Morales, but I'm also a realist. We do real work here. Work that helps people. But I am not in the business of selling sunshine and rainbows."

"Understood," Morales said.

"What I don't get is why you called the BPD in the first place if you're so set against helping us find the thief?" I asked.

"I have to provide a police report to give the insurance company."

My eyes narrowed. "Ah. I get it. You've got your own people on this, right? Guess finding out the MEA was getting involved put a crimp in your plans."

"The MEA is way more than a crimp, but as it happens, yes, I do have some of my personal security team investigating the matter. If they find anything, I'll be sure and pass it on."

I laughed. "Don't bullshit us. If I find out that you're keeping evidence from us, you'll be in jail alongside the asshole who robbed you."

"It's so optimistic of you," he drawled, "to assume he'll live long enough to go to jail."

I sighed. The truth was I couldn't blame him for not trusting us to get the job done. In the Cauldron, the wizards were the law. Plus, no kids grew up in the magical ghetto feeling like the BPD was there to protect and serve them. Aphrodite had grown up a decade or so ahead of me, but I was willing to bet I wasn't the only one who grew up watching relatives being taken away in cuffs. Hard, then, to grow up and trust a cop to settle what you saw as a personal offense. Especially when you had your own ready supply of poisons for just that occasion.

"Look." I sighed. "I know you want to go after this guy, but you need to leave this to us."

"You haven't been out of the game long enough to have grown that naive," he said. "If I get a chance at this asshole, I will fertilize my night plants with his blood."

"You do realize that if the guilty party shows up dead," Morales cut in, "the statements you've made today will make you the lead suspect."

"The city labs are so overworked and under budget that without strong evidence that poison was used, most won't do the specific tests for common poisons when another cause of death could be used." He smiled tightly. "Besides, you'd have to find a body in order to charge someone with murder."

"You seem to have done your homework on how to beat the system," I said.

"Let's not play coy, Detective. I make my living selling sex as religion. It's in my best interest to know how to work around the laws."

Morales looked at me. "He has a point."

I shot him a look. "You're not helping."

My partner shrugged.

I glanced back at the hermaphrodite. "It would be nice if you could provide us a list of your enemies."

The air shifted again, and suddenly Aphrodite was back.

Now she was a Lefty again with her graceful gestures and serpentine smile. She licked her lips, as if tasting the air. "The list of allies would be shorter, Detective," she purred.

Pressing my lips together to ensure I didn't speak the curse that would push me further up her enemies list, I changed tactics. "We'll also need to speak to those who were at the temple at the time of the robbery."

"I suppose I could allow you to speak to the priestess who was on duty last night."

She'd just thrown us a bone, so I didn't mention again that with a couple of calls I could get a warrant to gain access to her client roster. She was smart enough to know that herself. I just hoped for both our sakes her employees could give us some concrete leads so the warrant wouldn't be necessary. "That would be great. May we speak with her now?"

She made a pout. "So soon?"

I tilted my head. "You do want your property back, correct?"

She rolled her eyes. "I suppose." She snapped her fingers at the guard who was standing sentinel near the door we'd entered through. He came over and listened as she whispered instructions.

"Gregor will take you to meet her. If you need anything, she can help you."

"Thank you," Morales said.

She raised her left hand and pointed a single dragon-lady fingernail at him like a gun. "Of course, handsome."

I didn't bother suppressing the urge to roll my eyes. While I did that, Morales leaned forward and handed her his business card. "You think of anything else that might assist us, don't hesitate to call us."

She dragged her eyes from my partner with great reluctance to shoot me a resentful glance. "Is this your personal number?" she asked.

"It's the main number to our office," he said. "Anyone who answers will be able to reach us."

"I'd feel better if I had your direct line," she said, looking up at Morales.

He smiled wide, flashing his teeth. "Sure thing." He took the card from her, and I noted she managed to fit a brief finger-to-hand caress as he took it. In a flash he'd jotted down a number and handed it back.

I stood to end the meeting and made quick work of excusing us from the hermaphrodite's revenge garden. It wasn't until we'd returned to the lobby that Morales executed a full-body shiver. "She didn't even buy me dinner before she fucked me with her eyes."

I snorted. "You didn't seem to mind the attention when we were in there."

"I was playing good cop."

"Seemed more like you were playing horny cop," I teased.

"Trust me, Cupcake, when I'm horny you'll know it."

I grimaced. "Ignorance is bliss, Macho."

He chuckled and looked around. "So where's this other girl?"

The elevator on the other end of the lobby dinged. The doors opened. Gregor emerged first, but I caught movement behind him. I assumed it was the whore Aphrodite had told us about. I nudged Morales, who turned to look that direction.

At that moment trouble emerged from behind the bulky guard. Piles of glossy black hair piled on top of her head in an intricate updo. A red silk corset hugged her torso, and her bottom half sported a pair of ruffled black underpants on top of fishnets and a pair of sky-high red stilettos.

It took me a second to recognize her through the sugar skull makeup all of Aphrodite's girls wore when working. But once I realized who she was, I groaned.

"Shayla King," I spat like a preacher cursing the devil's name.

She paused with one hip jutted to the side. "Katie Prospero."

"Kate," I snapped. "As in *Detective* Kate Prospero."

She pointed a thumb at her ample bosom. "And I am *Priestess* Shayla."

Morales cleared his throat beside me. I shot him a look that I hoped indicated how unhappy I was with this turn of events. His smile told me he was going to enjoy watching me squirm almost as much as he liked eyeing the whore's revealing getup.

Turning away from me, he went to introduce himself to our tour guide. Her gaze took in his height like she was a monkey looking for a new tree to climb. But when he held out his hand to shake hers, she paused.

She looked down, shocked he'd offered it. A lot of cops would never deign to touch an O Coven whore, but Morales wasn't most cops. He might have an edge to him, but he wasn't a prick. Despite my obvious bad history with the girl, he was going to treat her with respect until her actions dictated otherwise. After a second's hesitation, she finally put her palm into his and gave it a lingering shake. "Wow, Prospero," she said, "you hit the jackpot."

I grimaced. "Where's the crime scene?"

She reluctantly released Morales's hand and turned toward me. "Your other colleague is already up there dusting for prints."

Morales shot her a smile that had a little too much dimple to be professional. "Can you show us the way, ma'am?"

"Of course. This way, please." With that she turned and sashayed back toward the elevators. I couldn't keep my eyes from wandering to the black ruffles and the twin red seams that licked her legs from ankle to ass.

An elbow nudged my ribs. I glanced up to see Morales

shooting me a pair of raised brows, as if to ask what the story was. I shrugged and shook my head. I wasn't about to explain my history with Shayla King right in front of the bitch. There'd be time enough for that later. For now, I needed to focus on the case.

"Ready?" Shayla called in a syrupy voice from the elevators. Gregor stood in the rear of the car like a statue.

"To the sex chambers," I said under my breath.

Morales's smile was back. "Oh goody."

Chapter Five

Once we were in the elevator, Morales started in. "On which floor did the robbery occur?"

Priestess Shayla turned toward him, which meant her back was to me. "The fourth." She turned to me. "So, Kate, you talked to John lately?"

My jaw clenched so hard I think I felt a couple of teeth crack. "No." I tried to talk to John Volos as rarely as possible.

She pouted. "That's too bad. He really was so upset after you left." A dramatic pause. "Luckily I was there to console him."

"Oh yeah?" I said, keeping my tone bored. "How much did he pay you to be his consolation prize?"

"John Volos doesn't have to pay for sex." She laughed. "Unless you count all the orgasms he gave me."

A warm hand touched mine—a gentle reminder from Morales to keep my cool.

I pushed a hot breath through my nostrils. "Did the intruder come through the lobby?"

She pulled back and pressed her lips together like she was savoring the flavor of victory. "All of our visitors who registered at the desk last night have been cleared."

"Cleared how?" Morales asked.

"We have security cameras in all of the treatment rooms. We were able to trace when each client entered and left the rooms, as well as when they exited the front doors, since there's only one entrance and exit. Everyone who arrived through the front door last night also left through it, and they did it without any detours to the fourth floor. In addition, the camera in the foyer shows the floor readout on top of the elevator. Not once last night did it go to the top floor."

My eyebrows shot up and I glanced at Morales, who was frowning. "Roof?" he asked.

She nodded. "We believe so. All of the buildings on this block are connected. It would not be difficult for a person to jump from roof to roof."

"How do you know they didn't go to another floor and just take the steps to the fourth?" I asked.

At that point we'd almost reached the third floor. Shayla stepped forward quickly and punched the button. The elevator doors didn't open. "All the floors require special key and code to access." She held up a key card and slid it into the slot. She turned her back, and the keypad beeped as she entered numbers. Two seconds later the doors whooshed open.

The elevators opened to a dark hallway lit only by dim red lights. It stretched out from the elevator like a long throat. Several doors led off the center hall. We stepped out of the car at Shayla's insistence. "It is possible without a key card. But you cannot enter the fourth floor without one. Which is why we think they entered from the roof."

She beckoned us with a hand as she started down the

hallway. About halfway down, a door opened. Another woman in the skull makeup emerged. She had long blond hair, but instead of a corset she wore only a thin silk robe bearing a red hexagram in the center of a spiral. The spiral represented the kundalini energy of the root chakra. The hexagram, however, is an alchemical symbol for the unification of opposites—a nod to Aphrodite's dual nature.

When the whore saw us, she hesitated in the doorway.

Shayla backtracked. "It's okay, Priestess Fiona. They're here to find the thief who threatened the sanctity of our temple."

The woman instantly bowed her head and pointed her gaze to the floor. With a quick nod, she ducked back inside the room. But not before I caught a glimpse of a middle-aged man getting pegged by another skull-faced priestess wearing a strap-on. By the time the door shut, I felt like I'd been punched in the face.

"What's wrong, Detective?" Shayla said, laughter slithering through her words.

I shook my head. She thought I was being a prude, but the sex hadn't shocked me. Any innocence I'd come to the force with—which wasn't much—had dissolved within a week on the job. Working the Cauldron was a crash course in all the depraved shit humans do to one another. But I was fine letting Shayla believe I was a prude. Because the alternative was to admit that the scene I'd just witnessed brought back a memory from my childhood. One I'd forgotten—or suppressed.

A different door had opened at the wrong moment. A different woman, one I knew all too well, in *memento mori* makeup had engaged in a sexual act with a different man I didn't know. That time, the woman had quickly pushed the man's face away from her crotch. The candles the priestess had lit for the ritual glistened off the wetness on his face. As I stood in shock, staring up at them, my mother strode to the door in the nude and slammed the door in my face.

I'd been five years old at the time.

Just like that door slamming twenty-two years earlier, I shut down the memory. I'd come to terms with my mother's profession a long time ago—long before she'd died, even. The memory was only coming up now because we were in a temple similar to the one where she worked.

"Prospero?" Morales nudged me.

I looked up. The teasing smile I expected wasn't there. Instead his stubbled face held an expression of genuine concern. "You okay? You look like you've seen a ghost."

I guess I had, in a way. "Yeah, I'm good." I looked over at Shayla. "Where are the stairs?"

Her smug look made me want to punch that makeup off her face. She thought she'd somehow discovered a weakness. She was wrong, though. Weakness came from shame, and I was not ashamed of my mom or my past.

And maybe if I kept repeating that over and over in my head, I'd finally believe it.

Shayla pointed farther down the hall, where a red EXIT sign indicated the stairwell's location. This one didn't have a keypad like the elevator did. Looked like even the powerful Aphrodite Johnson couldn't circumvent the fire marshal's laws.

I nodded, catching up. "So the perp could have used these stairs to access the lab."

She nodded. "But I already told you the video doesn't show anything."

I crossed my arms. Her patronizing tone made my spine tighten.

"And you said you verified all the people who came and went through the front?" Morales said.

Her eyes skittered sideways. That's when I knew they had a suspect. Probably someone they saw on the tapes, but they didn't want to tell us in case we got to him first. Morales had been wrong. Aphrodite didn't need us for shit.

"Where's the tape?" I said.

"I already told you—we already checked them."

Morales smiled tightly. "Regardless, we'll need a copy."

"But—"

"We could get a warrant, but then the theft will be public knowledge. I'm sure many of your clients would be distressed to learn about such a major security breach."

I clucked my tongue. "Might even be a few lawsuits."

Shayla crossed her arms. "I'll get you the tape," she said through clenched teeth. "But I'm telling you, there's nothing there to help with the robber's identity."

"If it's all the same, we'll leave that up to our audiovisual forensics specialist."

I shot Morales a quick glance. I assumed he meant Shadi, but she wasn't exactly the specialist he claimed. More like she got the surveillance duty by default. Either way, the fib got the desired result.

"Come on," she said. "Maybe your forensics wizard has found something."

Telling, I thought, that she didn't sound hopeful.

Now that we'd called her on the bluff Aphrodite told her to pull, her demeanor was different. As she walked up the stairs, her ass twitched with each tense step.

When we reached the fourth floor, she made quick work of getting through the security and threw open the door. She stood to the side so we could precede her. As I passed, her eyes were twin shards of ice.

54

Mez was standing at a lab table covered in an assortment of cooking supplies.

"How's it going?"

He put down a beaker he'd been dusting for prints. "Best I can tell, whoever did this came through the window." He motioned Morales and me toward a pair of tall windows set into the brick wall.

"You found a print?" Morales asked, inspecting the jamb, which was covered in gray powdery residue.

Mez twirled the small feather applicator he used to apply the powder. "Not a one."

I raised a brow. "You check the exterior?"

"Not yet." He used his gloved hands to open the window. Then he bowed like a butler, offering me access to the outside. "Why don't you look for yourself?"

Grimacing, I ducked out and turned, resting my butt on the windowsill. Morales put a steadying hand on my knees to ensure I didn't perform a backflip to the street below. I took the brush and small vial of powder Mez offered and applied it all over the surface—the glass, the wooden frame, the bracers, the brick surround. Nothing. Not even a partial.

"Damn it," I said, ducking back inside. "Wait, you sounded pretty sure they'd used the window. Why?"

"Elementary, my dear." The wizard smiled like I'd just walked into a logic trap. "When I came in, the window was open."

I glanced at Shayla for confirmation. "It was open when we discovered the robbery this morning."

I rolled my eyes. "Information you could have mentioned sooner."

She shrugged and yawned. The move distended her jaw like

a boa constrictor's. The image more disturbing on account of the *memento mori* skeletal makeup.

Dismissing her, I turned back to Mez. "What else?"

Mez pointed across the room, and my eyes followed. Someone had spray-painted symbols all over the wall, like a mural. I hadn't noticed it when we came in because it shared the wall with the door.

"What's that?" I asked.

"Oh," she said, "whoever broke in did that."

My brows rose. "If they took the time to do something like that, they knew enough about the alarm system not to expect someone to come busting in on them."

She frowned. "I guess so."

Morales and I moved closer to inspect the symbols. It was hard to mistake the central image—a three-foot-tall phallus.

"Are those veins?" Morales asked.

I shook my head. "Vines, I think. See? They're green." There were also two bunches of purple grapes at the bottom in lieu of testicles.

Whatever they were, they wove around the shaft of the penis. In the left-hand corner, a large blue circle that could only stand for the upcoming full moon. And on the right, a large pentagram.

A lot of Mundanes associate the pentagram with satanic cults, but the symbol had a long and complex tradition in a lot of different magical traditions. There were no obvious reasons to assume the image was some sort of threat—yet.

Morales frowned. "Not exactly original to paint a penis in a whorehouse."

I took out my phone and clicked a few pictures. Mez's first step when he'd arrived would have been to catalog the room, including taking official photos, but I wanted some for my own use, too. You never knew when you'd be stuck without a file on the run.

And we'd definitely be running on this case. If my hunch was right, Aphrodite already had a major head start on finding the thief.

I turned toward Shayla. "Where was the potion that was stolen?"

She pointed toward a large cabinet on the other side of the room. The bottom was a refrigerator unit—like a big horizontal freezer—and the top was row after row of shelving. Some shelves had vials and bottles of liquids and herbs. Others were marked with symbols or names identifying the premade potions.

Sex magic didn't just encompass the ritualized harnessing of sexual energy through chakra work. It also involved using potions to help people access their kundalini energy—the coiled power stored in the pelvis root chakra. The O's also made a pretty penny selling love potions. The kind that the lovesick paid through the nose for to help attract the affections of their crushes. But there were others. Potions to enhance sexual performance, ones for multiple orgasms, et cetera.

Sometimes the lines between sex magic and the other traditions got blurred, too. Like when someone wanted a vanity potion. Usually vanities fell under the heading of alchemy, but sometimes sex magic potions were employed to increase a user's attractiveness. Same went with blood potions, since the energies that influenced both blood and sex came from the same kind of chthonic power sources. All of this was to say, of course, that sex magic was big business, which was why Aphrodite put so much money into the setup. Also why she'd be so determined to find the offender and make him pay for daring to violate the sanctity of her lab.

I approached the wall-to-wall lab setup with Morales, while Mez continued to take notes at the table.

About three feet back from the shelves, I threw out an arm to stop Morales. He looked up with a frown. Instead of answering, I pointed to the floor. Several small shards of glass glittered on the concrete floor. A dried, sticky patch lay under the glass. I looked back at Mez. "You see this?"

He frowned and came over. "I got images, but haven't had a chance to test it yet."

"You think our perp was in a hurry and accidentally dropped one?" Morales asked.

I nodded. "Lack of prints indicates he was wearing gloves, right? Probably grabbed this bottle off the shelf and it slipped from his hand."

Morales knelt down and inspected the patch. "You got a black light in there?" he asked Mez.

The wizard nodded and removed a portable light wand. He glanced at Shayla. "Go close the blinds on all the windows."

While she scurried off, I stepped around the area and approached the shelves where the guys were working. "What are you doing?" I asked.

"Looking for a shoe print," Morales said.

The room dimmed as Shayla finally closed all the window treatments. While Mez waved the wand over the floor, I used a flashlight tilted sideways to cast a glow on each shelf just in case there might be a print. "Hand me the camera, will ya?" Mez asked Morales.

My partner grabbed it for him and brought it over. Mez messed with the controls for a moment before clicking several shots in a row. As he worked, I squinted at the spot on the ground. Sure enough, there was a mark in the ethereal blue pool cast by the black light off the spilled potion.

"That doesn't look like a shoe print," I said.

Mez put down the camera and looked up. The black light made the charms in his dreads glow. "I'll need to analyze the images under a magnifier back at the lab, but we definitely got a partial print of some sort."

I nodded. "Good." My phone buzzed on my hip. "One sec." Pulling the phone out, I answered it without looking at the ID. "Prospero."

"Hello. Katherine Prospero?"

I frowned, not recognizing the staticky female voice. "Yes, who is this please?"

"This is operator five-four-nine from the Crowley State Penitentiary. Prisoner six-six-six-four-two, Abraxas Prospero, would like to speak with you. May I patch him through?"

The blood in my arms and legs went frigid. "What?"

"Prisoner six-six-six-four-two, Abraxas Prospero, has requested to speak with you. Do you accept the call?"

"No," I snapped. "Take me off his call list." With a shaking finger, I punched the End button before the operator could say anything else.

I stood in shock for I don't know how long with that phone clutched tight in my hand. The hard plastic dug into my palm, and I had to resist the urge to throw it at the brick wall.

"Kate?" Morales called from across the room.

I swallowed the panic and shock, pushing them deep down where they couldn't interfere. Shoving the phone in my pocket, I turned. "Yeah?"

My partner was standing next to the graffiti penis. Mez was packing up all his supplies while talking to Shayla about getting the tape she'd promised us earlier. "Everything okay?"

"Fucking telemarketers." I feigned an annoyed shrug. "We done here?"

He watched me for a couple of seconds longer before nodding. "For now. What say we go visit the Wonder Twins? See if maybe they've heard of anyone trying to fence some sex potions."

The twins he mentioned were named Mary and Little Man. They were my best snitches, and the ones most likely to know if there was chatter on the streets about Aphrodite getting robbed.

Ignoring the nausea and the fist of worry in the base of my throat, I nodded. "Let's go."

Chapter Six

Fifteen minutes later we were at an intersection near the construction site for Volos's pet project, the Cauldron Community Center. The groundbreaking had been six weeks earlier, and the crews already had the foundation poured and the framing up for the walls. We'd just passed the sign announcing that the center would open by Thanksgiving when Morales tapped the brakes. "Hey, Prospero?"

I pulled my gaze away from the side window I'd been glaring out of for the last five minutes. "Yeah?"

He was pointing out the windshield. "Isn't that Mary?"

I squinted in that direction. Sure enough, a six-foot-tall lumbering hulk of a woman was crossing the street about a block up. As always, Little Man was strapped in a baby carrier on her chest. "They're usually at the park this time of day."

"Nice of them to save us some time by meeting us halfway." Morales pulled the SUV to the corner closest to where Mary had just crossed.

I rolled down my window. "Yo, Mary."

She glanced back over her hunched shoulder, and her eyes widened. Instead of stopping, she lumbered away faster, her lanky brown hair swaying like oily fringe at the back of her neck.

I frowned. "Mary?" I called. She shot a worried glance over her shoulder and picked up the pace even more. I threw open the door and hopped out to follow.

They were far enough away that I couldn't hear, but I could see Little Man waving his arms and shouting instructions to her every time she turned to look back.

Mary and Little Man had been my snitches for going on five years. They'd also met Morales a couple of times, so she had to have recognized him, too. In other words, there was absolutely no reason for her to be afraid of us. My instincts forced my legs into a jog. "Mary, wait!"

Morales caught up with me and we fell into a run together as Mary turned the next corner. "What the hell?" he snapped.

I shook my head. A second later we both skidded around the corner in time to see Mary duck into a city bus. The large vehicle belched away from the curb. I kicked up my speed, pulling my badge from my pocket. "BPD, stop!" But the grinding of the bus's gears drowned out my demand.

"We lost 'em," Morales called.

I stopped running and bent over with my hands on my knee. "Damn it! What the hell was that about?"

Morales put his hands on his hips. "Guess they weren't in the mood to talk."

I rose and cast one last annoyed glance at the bus's rear end as it grew smaller in the distance. "Something's going on."

He shot me an ironic look. "This is the Cauldron, Cupcake. Something's always going on. C'mon, let's grab some grub before we get an update from Mez on the evidence he gathered at the temple."

I stood watching the space where the bus had been a few moments earlier. Even with the Blue Moon fast approaching, my day thus far had been...strange. Given I worked in a magical slum, that was saying a lot.

Chapter Seven

Several hours later I was dragging my tired ass toward the house and groaning with each step like an unoiled hinge. Despite my exhaustion, I hadn't wanted to leave the office. But Gardner had all but kicked me out about half an hour earlier. "You're not going to break this case tonight," she said. "Go home."

At the time, I'd considered arguing, but she'd been right. After our aborted attempt to talk to LM and Mary, Morales and I had headed back to the gym and hit one brick wall after another on the case. Mez had been called away to assist in a crime scene on the other side of town, which meant he didn't have time to process the evidence from the temple. I'd made several fruitless calls to other snitches, but no one knew anything—or else they weren't in a talking mood. I'd also called some old patrol colleagues to see if they'd heard of any crimes similar to the MO of Aphrodite's robbery and got a whole lot of nothing. So I'd packed up and headed out, promising the team I'd see them early the next morning.

Halfway to the front door, a sense of foreboding scratched at the back of my scalp. Nothing concrete, really, just a tingle of awareness. Pausing at the base of the porch steps, I peered back down the street. The neighborhood was dark, and except for a couple of dogs barking a few streets over, there weren't any discernible noises. No unusual vehicles were parked along the curb. I chewed on my bottom lip and tried to put my finger on what was different. I swiveled my head back toward the door. That's when it hit me.

The house was dark.

It was almost seven, which meant Danny should have been up and watching TV with Baba in the den. But every light in the place was extinguished. It wasn't just quiet and dark—it was ominously quiet and dark, as if the house were holding its breath.

My holster dangled from my hand. I removed the weapon and laid the leather rig on the porch. Crouching low, I tested the doorknob and found it unlocked. The door swung in quietly, and I stopped it before it could bump off the wall. With cautious steps I crept inside, careful to avoid the squeaky parts of the old linoleum. A quick scan of the kitchen revealed nothing but the usual shadows. I placed a hand on the oven and found it warm. Someone had been cooking. Baba often cooked dinner for Danny. But if she'd been cooking, where were they both now?

Behind me, the sound of a car door closing filtered in from the street.

I skirted the bistro table and headed toward the opening that led to the den off the kitchen. My left hand gripped the gun tighter with each step, but I tried to stay calm. Freaking out and imagining all sorts of horrible things wouldn't help. Best to stay focused on one foot in front of the other and keeping my senses open for clues. Closer to the opening now, I heard a slight intake of breath. Not a gasp. Just a stifled breath.

I paused, gun at the ready, and opened my mouth to issue an order to stand down. But before the words could leave my mouth, light flared like a sun in the room. I squinted and fell back a step. Shapes moved in the light, and noise emerged from the forms. "Surprise!"

It all happened so fast it took my brain a couple of seconds to register what I was hearing and seeing.

At about the same moment I realized I'd walked in on a party, the couple of dozen people in my den realized I was holding them at gunpoint. I froze. They froze.

"Jeez, Kate." Danny emerged from the crowd and frowned at me like I'd just embarrassed him. "Put the gun away."

My cheeks heating, I lowered the weapon to my side. "What the hell's going on?"

Pen came to join my little brother. She looked more amused than alarmed.

"Surprise!" Pen said. "We knew you'd never agree to an official group celebration so we brought one to you."

"For what?" I frowned, praying it wasn't for my Arcane Anonymous anniversary.

"Your ten-year anniversary of sobriety!" Danny announced. He thrust a can of soda in the hand that had held a gun.

The words entered my ears and promptly sank to the bottom of my gut where they corroded in my stomach acid. I bit my tongue to keep from uttering a curse that would make a hardened criminal blush.

Danny bounced on the balls of his feet like a little kid at a birthday party. The pride in his face at pulling off the surprise made me keep my expression neutral. But inside I was raging. Instead of taking that out on the kid, who didn't know better than to ambush me with a party I didn't want, I glared at my best friend.

She grabbed me and pulled me in for a hug. "Smile," she hissed into my ear, "they put a lot of work into this."

Before I could tell her where to shove that suggestion, a warm hand landed on my shoulder. I pulled away from my best friend and rounded to find Morales standing behind me wearing a gotcha smile.

"You knew about this?" I snapped.

Shadi walked up behind him, with Mez and Gardner not far behind.

My partner shot me a guilty grin and nodded. "We were sworn to secrecy."

Shadi laughed. "I really thought I screwed the pooch this morning when I mentioned tonight."

My mouth fell open. "Wait, this is what you were talking about?"

She tipped her head. "Yeah, what'd you think I meant?"

Morales cleared his throat, a subtle reminder of the stupid question I'd asked about the nature of their relationship. Ignoring him, I said, "I wasn't sure."

She moved on to go say hi to Pen and Danny. Morales hung back. "So you really were surprised?"

I made an angry sound deep in my throat.

"Whoa. Not a fan of surprises, then?"

"Ambush, you mean."

"Well," he said, "you stopped using magic, but you obviously haven't given up *bitch*craft."

I pressed my tongue to the roof of my mouth and tried to get a harness on my anger. Morales didn't know the reasons why I didn't want this party. Actually, no one did. "Sorry. It's just—touchy."

He laughed and replaced the soda with a beer. "Drink up, Cupcake. Try to enjoy your own party."

At that moment Baba shuffled forward with her cane. "Ha! We got ya!"

I forced a smile. "Sure did."

"Hey there, hot stuff," she said to Morales.

My seventysomething-year-old next-door neighbor had taken a shine to my partner the first time she'd met him. He endured her flirtations with humor, and never complained when she pinched his backside.

"Hey, good lookin'," he flirted back. "Is that a new dress?"

"This old thing?" She pointed a black orthopedic shoe like a Rockette. "Why don't you come put those muscles to use and pass around some drinks?"

He shot me a grin before offering her his arm like a real gallant. She giggled and grabbed his bicep, giving it a squeeze as one might a ripe melon. As the pair moved away, I saw the perfect opening to get the hell out of Dodge.

"Kate?" Rufus called, preventing my escape.

Rufus Xavier was the leader of the Arcane Anonymous group I'd belonged to for the last decade. I hadn't talked to him in about a month, since I'd been skipping our weekly meetings. He'd been calling me at least once a week, though, and giving me shit for my lack of attendance. The man's middle name was "Tough Love," and he looked for any opportunity to call us on our bullshit.

I took a deep breath and forced some new life into my false smile. "Wow, this was unexpected."

"Shouldn't be. The way you been playing hooky?" He speared me with a knowing glare. "How long you think I was gonna let it go?"

My hands shoved into my pockets, I looked away from the

man I considered both a mentor and a friend. "Wasn't playing hooky," I muttered. "We've been swamped with the double moons."

"Mmm-hmm," he said. "Tell that to some muh-fucker ain't already heard every excuse in the damned book, girl."

I looked down at my beer, willing it to turn into something stronger. Nearby, Danny turned on some music, which filled the room with a booming bass line.

"What's going on with you, Kate?" Ru said, leaning in to be heard.

Ru was the kind of man you wanted to trust. Everything about him invited sharing secrets.

From the corner of my eye, I saw Gardner chatting with Mez, Danny, and Baba.

But my secrets weren't going to be shared in that room with that crowd. Or ever, if I had my way.

"I've had some stuff on my mind I'm not ready to talk about."

"Ah," he said, nodding. "It's no wonder after what happened to the boy." He patted me on the arm. "Tonight's for celebrating, but soon enough you're going to have to purge those demons before they eat you alive."

I swallowed and nodded. His words struck too close to the truth for comfort. "Maybe once things quiet down. After Halloween."

His mouth tightened, a sure sign he was about to start one of his lectures. I held up a hand. "Listen, I need to go grab something. I'll be right back."

"But—"

I turned away before he could continue. I escaped through the kitchen and into my bedroom. The instant the door closed behind me, I slid down the plane until my butt hit the floor.

For weeks, I'd been waking up from dreams of cooking.

Sometimes it was an orgasm that woke me, other times, bone-shaking sobs. I'd known my choice to use magic was wrong, but the surge of power that came with manipulating that kind of energy was seductive. Cooking was a lot like masturbation. Doing it had left me feeling dirty, but I couldn't stop thinking about wanting to do it some more.

The worst part had been knowing it was only a matter of time until the choices I'd made that night in the factory with John Volos came back to bite me. Arriving to a house full of people I cared about who had no idea they were celebrating a lie was too much to bear.

I put my head in my hands and squeezed my eyes shut. How had I gone from a clean-and-sober cop with a great record to a liar who got off on cooking dirty potions in abandoned factories?

A soft knock sent vibrations through the wood at my back. "Kate?" Pen whispered.

I rubbed my hands over my eyes, as if maybe I could wipe away the traces of guilt. With a groan, I pulled my ass off the ground and opened the door just enough for her to slip through.

"Hey," she said with an exaggerated smile. The kind moms give their kids when they're trying to pretend nothing's wrong.

I leaned back against the dresser. "Hey."

"What's wrong?" she asked, looking genuinely perplexed.

I shot her a look. "Seriously?"

She sighed. "I don't get why you're being so stubborn about this—"

I slashed a hand through the air. "You don't have to understand it. You just needed to respect my wishes."

"Rufus thought since you hadn't been to group in a while—"

"I haven't been to group because I've been fucking busy!"

Her face morphed from confusion to anger. "Jesus, what is your problem? You're acting like this anniversary is something to be ashamed of."

"That's because it's not a real anniversary. I've seen what real junkies go through and my challenges didn't even begin to compare."

After my mother died from using a potion I'd cooked, I'd realized that magic had poisoned my life and I'd be better off without it altogether. I'd joined AA to have a visceral reminder of why I'd quit cooking in the first place. Seeing all those sad cases trudge into meeting every week reminded me that there are real human costs to messing with magic in any form.

She frowned. "You have to know what an accomplishment it is. You walked away from one of the most powerful covens in the Cauldron and turned your back on your own magic to give yourself and Danny a better life. *That* is what's worth celebrating. It's not about who had the hardest road to travel. It's about all of us being so grateful you're in our lives."

Those words should have warmed me. Made me thaw enough to admit maybe she was right. Instead, they simply added another layer of frigid self-loathing. "You wouldn't be grateful if—" I stopped short and redirected. "Look, I'm just tired and I had a shitty day."

She stepped forward. "Wouldn't be grateful if what?"

"Just tell everyone to go, okay?" Panic made my voice rise.

"You want them to go?" She stabbed a finger toward the door. "You want to disappoint them and tell them you don't give a shit that they care about you? Do it your damned self."

Pen crossed her arms and gave me her best probing stare. The one she normally used on the teenagers she counseled at the school. I was used to interrogating hardened perps who lied as easily as they breathed, but Penelope Griffin had her own methods for applying the screws to stubborn teens—and recalcitrant best friends.

I could feel my temper unraveling. If I didn't end this soon, I would attack her and say things I didn't mean but wouldn't be able to take back. "Fine," I gritted out through clenched teeth.

I pushed past her, but she grabbed my arm.

All pretense disappeared from her expression. "What are you hiding?"

Cold fear swam under my skin. She had the look in her eyes. Pen wasn't an Adept, but sometimes she had scary intuition. Maybe it was a skill she'd honed after years of studying human nature, or maybe the ability to read people was what had led her to psychology in the first place. Regardless, that look told me she wouldn't let me out of that room until I came clean.

I looked her directly in her eyes. "Nothing."

"Bullshit." She laughed in my face. "You think I don't see it?"

My gaze strayed toward the door. "See what?"

"The drinking, for one."

Frowning, I looked at her. "Please. It's not that bad."

She pursed her lips. "Denial, defensiveness. Something's been eating you for weeks."

I opened my mouth to argue, but she slashed a hand through the air. "And don't blame it on the moons again. This started before that. After Danny's accident."

"Gee, Pen, maybe I'm still dealing with the fact he almost *died*. Ever think of that?"

"Try that misdirection bullshit on someone who'll fall for it, Kate."

I closed my eyes. I'd been soaking in my secret for weeks. Marinating in guilt until my fingertips were pruney. That was the problem with lies. The only cure for the guilt that came with them was to tell the truth. But the consequences of coming clean were usually worse than the guilt, which is why you lied to begin with.

I'd planned to keep lying to Pen when she walked into the room. But when I opened my eyes and saw the determined tilt of her chin and the hardness of her eyes, I knew that lying to her face would cause more destruction than coming clean.

She was inviting me to jump off the cliff, and I was too exhausted to keep clinging to the edge. "I cooked."

She blinked. "What?"

"I *cooked*, Pen."

Her mouth worked open and closed for a moment. "Wh— when? Why?"

"When Danny was in his coma. With Volos." My heart should have been pounding and my palms swampy, but they weren't. I was too numb.

"But— You mean you let Volos cook, right? He said he could cook the antipotion. You were just going to pick it up. Not cook."

I shook my head. "When I met him at the old brewery, he admitted he couldn't finish the potion. He—" I cleared my throat because it suddenly felt clogged. "Without knowing who cooked the recipe for Gray Wolf, he couldn't finish it. So, I—I *read* it. And then after Bane hexed John with Gray Wolf, I had to do the final processes to finish the antipotion alone."

The sounds of music and laughter from the living room crept under the door to fill the silent space growing between us. Pen's normally dark complexion was pale, and her eyes were showing too much white.

The silence shouldn't have gotten to me. I'd used it as a tactic against criminals for years—too long to fall for it myself. But Pen's silence wasn't some sort of interrogation tactic. I'd shocked her, and now that the words had left my mouth I wanted to snatch them back and push them back down into the dark place inside me.

I swallowed and crossed my arms. "Aren't you going to say anything?"

Her numbed expression hardened. "What do you want me to say, Kate?" She sounded soul-tired.

I blinked. All these weeks of hiding this secret, I'd played out what would happen when I was discovered over and over. Fired from the force, shunned by friends and family—the works. But never in all that time had I imagined what would happen if I came clean, much less what I'd want to hear.

While I grappled with that, Pen rubbed at her eyebrows. "Christ. Why couldn't you have told me this yesterday? Or a month ago?"

That brought me up short. It wasn't the complaint so much as the lack of something in her voice. "Why don't you sound more surprised?"

She crossed her arms and leaned back against the door. "Because the instant you told me, everything made sense. Plus, for real, Katie, this job's been a kick in the ass all the way. It was only a matter of time until you had to use magic."

I blinked. "This isn't about the job."

She arched a black brow. "No?"

"I did it to save Danny."

"Who was in a coma because of that fucking case."

Pain punched me in the chest. It was one thing to see the disappointment in her face, but something else to hear damning words come from the one person I'd hoped would understand. "Screw you."

"You have a lot of fucking nerve being mad at me," she said, her voice rising. She pointed a finger toward the shut door. "There are thirty people out there ready to celebrate your abstinence from magic and you choose now to tell me you've been lying to us for weeks?"

Confusion kept me silent for a few moments. I had expected anger, sure, but I had not expected to be bitched at about my timing.

"Why the hell do you think I told you I didn't want a party?"

She threw up her hands. "Well, that's just fucking fantastic." Pushing away from the door, she began pacing at the foot of my bed. I crossed my arms and watched her, cursing myself all the while for not bringing a bottle of hooch into the room with me. When she finished her debate with herself, she stopped and speared me with an ultimatum-glare. "You're going to have to play along."

My mouth fell open. "What? You can't seriously expect me to go through with this."

She tapped her foot. "You'd prefer to go tell everyone out there what you just told me?"

Cold fear sucked the blood from my face. Tell Danny and Baba? Or worse: Gardner and Morales? "Hell no."

"Then you're going to march your skinny white ass out there, take the fucking medal, and then never tell anyone what you did." She took a menacing step forward. "And then you and I are going to have a nice long chat about your life choices."

I frowned. "Wha—"

"Ever since you joined that team you've been different."

"No I haven't." My gaze went south, unable to stand the knowing look in her eyes.

"The drinking, the lies, using magic—how much of yourself are you going to surrender for this job?"

I took a deep breath and tried to keep my tone reasonable. "I told you, I did magic to save Danny. It had nothing to do with the team." Which wasn't the complete truth. Eventually Bane might have admitted my uncle had been behind the Gray Wolf case, but I probably wouldn't have believed him without seeing the truth in the magic, so to speak.

"Denial," Pen singsonged.

"Don't pull that AA bullshit with me, Pen. You would have done the same to save Danny's life."

She nodded reluctantly. "Maybe. But don't you see? It's not just that you cooked. It's that you cooked and then lied about it. That's not healthy behavior, Kate. I'm telling you, this task force assignment is bad news."

I sucked air into my lungs and let out a shaky breath. "I just have to be more careful going forward. Volos got the better of me. It won't happen again."

"Keep telling yourself that, Katie." She put her hands on my shoulders. "But it's only a matter of time until you're required to use magic on a case. What will you do then?"

I felt like she'd slapped me. My head shook back and forth in denial. "I had the chance to read a potion yesterday and I didn't do it," I argued. "I have it under control."

That was what I said on the outside, but on the inside a small voice told me she was right. Eventually I'd have to choose, but not that night. That night, I had to focus on putting on a convincing act in front of everyone I loved and respected so they wouldn't know I was a liar.

Pen blew out a big breath, as if surrendering this particular battle in order to win a different one. "We can discuss your choices later, but for now you need to go play like you're clean."

The implication that one slip-up had suddenly rendered me dirty in her eyes filled me with shame. "Are you sure I can't just sneak out the back door?"

"Take a deep breath, put on your game face, and go do the damned thing," she said.

I couldn't believe my best friend was encouraging me to go along with this farce. Receiving a ten-year sobriety token was a huge deal. When she'd received hers, we celebrated into the morning hours with most of the people in my living room. I remembered being so proud of her that night. The exact opposite of how she felt about me right then. Hell, it was the exact opposite of how I felt about myself. "I don't feel right—"

"It's too late for that," she said. "If you refuse the anniversary token, everyone will want to know why. Normally, the group would support you through a relapse, but if your team finds out what you did, you're toast." She pulled herself up straighter, as if she was trying to convince herself as well as me. "There's no choice but to play along."

With that, she must have decided the discussion was done, because she was already opening the door and pushing me out into the lion's den.

The sounds of music and laughter from the living room made my steps falter. Pausing by the kitchen table, I saw Gardner and Mez chatting with Rufus and Sarah by the fireplace. Sarah was one of the girls who'd recently joined the recovery program. The first time she'd come to a meeting, her face bore the mottled red sores of a long-term dirty magic user. She'd been too pale and her hands had tremored. But now her skin was clear, and when she reached out to shake Morales's hand as he approached, her grip was steady. She even smiled, though it was the unsteady expression of one unfamiliar with happiness.

In the last ten years I'd met dozens of former freakers like Sarah. Junkies who'd decided to change their fates and get clean. The zeal of conversion fueled them those first few months. But eventually, once their minds cleared and they started working deeper through their steps, the problems morphed from the physical challenges of detox to the emotional ones of putting your life back together without the help of potions. Let's face it, most people don't start using potions because they're well adjusted. Magic helps people create a sort of artificial wall between them and their demons. And once that wall comes crumbling down, the demons emerge bigger and more pissed than ever.

I didn't know what Sarah's particular demons were. Didn't much matter, really. Everyone's got some and everyone's got to figure out how to battle them on their own. Problem was, lots of times those in recovery discovered that battling demons was a lot harder than hiding behind that wall.

"Kate!" Rufus called above the party noise. He waved me over, his demeanor one of someone about to make a grand gesture. "Everyone, your attention please!"

I pressed my lips together to hold in the curse stabbing at my teeth. When I reached him, he pulled me into the center of the room. Everyone circled up.

Directly in front of me, Danny fell in with Pen on one side and Sarah on the other. Pen wouldn't look at me, preferring to stare at the floor.

"We've gathered tonight to celebrate a milestone for our good friend Kate." He glanced at me with a paternal smile. "Ten years ago, when Pen dragged her to group, I have to admit I had my doubts."

A titter of amusement trickled through the crowd. My gaze strayed toward Pen. She still wouldn't look at me.

It had been six months after I'd left the coven. I was so poor it was getting harder and harder not to think about how much easier life could be if I sold a couple of harmless potions to help ends meet. I'd mentioned this to Pen one day, and that night she'd dragged me to meet Ru and the gang.

"But Kate quickly proved she was committed to working the

steps. And before long she was encouraging other lost souls to keep the faith."

That first night Rufus had spoken about his own experiences with recovery. How he'd had a promising career as a baller and pissed it all away for the quick fix of a speed potion. Even getting kicked off the Babylon Enchanters team hadn't convinced him to get sober. The thing that finally did him in was his girlfriend finding his stash one night when he'd crashed after a weeklong bender. By that time he'd been on the junk so long that he was shooting up a seriously concentrated dose.

He'd found her dead on their bathroom floor with his syringe sticking from her arm.

"It's hard to believe it's already been ten years," Rufus continued. "Despite my initial doubts, I have to say I've seen few people dedicate themselves so totally to leading a clean life. I'm sure we've all heard Kate's lectures on the dangers of everything from potion-fueled cars to crops grown using drought-resistance potions."

More laughter. I forced a smile because it was expected. But inside, I was picturing my dead mother's body, blue and bloated from the potion I'd cooked.

That first night I'd heard Rufus speak, I knew I'd met someone who understood the pain I'd lived with since the day my mother died. The acidic guilt eating at your stomach lining until you prayed it'd just consume you whole. He made me feel hope that someone could fuck up and experience heart-crushing loss and still go on to have a good life.

Rufus grabbed my hand and squeezed it. When I looked up, he winked at me. My stomach dipped. I was a grade A asshole for playing along with this farce.

But Rufus was always saying that rituals and symbols mattered. Joining a program like Arcane Anonymous provided structure and support for the battles. Rituals provided focus. And the symbols of recovery could be potent talismans against temptation.

Despite my misgivings about my dishonesty, I knew that stopping the ritual would have consequences beyond exposing me for a liar. The truth was, the tradition of earning anniversary tokens wasn't just about celebrating the accomplishment of one person staying clean. It was also about giving everyone else faith that they, too, could stay sober. If I came clean and refused the token, I'd be depriving Sarah and the others of their hopes for a long recovery.

Rufus reached into his pocket and removed a small black box. I'd been to a few anniversary events and knew what was inside, but it wasn't until that moment that it hit me I'd be receiving one. I glanced up, uncertain. Behind Ru, Baba had tears in her eyes, and Danny looked so proud it broke my heart.

Ru opened the box. The room's lights sparked off a silver chain and pendant inside. He removed them and held them up for the assembly's inspection. A few appreciative *ooh*s and *aah*s filtered through the room. My eyes zeroed in on the pendant.

The ten-year token was triangular in shape with a Roman numeral X on one side and the chemical formula for salt— $NaCl$—engraved on the other. Since salt was used to banish magic, the symbol was a reminder to stay clean. The triangle stood for the three pillars of sober living—making good choices, maintaining healthy relationships, and learning gratitude for the Mundane.

He motioned for me to turn around. As I did as instructed, I felt as if I was turning to face a firing squad without a ballistics vest. Clearly unaware of my sudden panic, the members of the team all had smiles, except Morales, who looked uncharacteristically solemn. A couple of neighbors Baba invited smiled politely but looked ill at ease to be witnessing such a private moment. Most of the rest of the faces belonged to members of the group. Darla, the former vanity-potion-addict homemaker, stood beside Jacob, a very large bald man with tattoos, who spent his days crafting delicate sculptures out of scrap metal. The only member I didn't see was Callahan, who only attended the meetings because a judge ordered it after he exposed himself to a busful of schoolkids while freaking on a sex potion.

But it wasn't until I'd turned completely around that I saw the last face I expected to see in my living room.

Our eyes didn't just meet—they collided. The impact ricocheted through my midsection.

I knew instantly who'd invited the devil into my house. Danny's admiration for John Volos was vocal and mind-numbingly repetitive. I'd stopped trying to mitigate the hero worship because it was a waste of breath. As far as Danny knew, his life had been saved by the Cauldron's version of King Midas.

He wore a three-piece suit, but I wasn't egotistical enough to believe he'd dressed up special for the occasion. He always looked like he'd stepped off the cover of *Handsome Millionaires Quarterly*.

On some level I was aware of Rufus speaking again. Felt his hands brush my neck as he put the necklace around it. His fingers fumbled with the clasp. The metal was cold on my skin. John's eyes were hot.

"There," Ru said in a triumphant tone. His hands rested on my shoulders. They urged me to turn around again. Not having to look at John anymore was a relief, but I could feel his gaze on my back like a visceral touch. "Let's all give her a hand, folks!"

The next five minutes were a blur of applause, hand shaking, and hugs. Danny threw himself at me, like he used to when he was five and hugs weren't yet embarrassing. "I'm proud of you, Katie."

"I'm proud of you, too, kid," I whispered, holding him tight. Deflecting the compliment was self-defense. If I let myself wallow in the guilt, I'd combust.

"Isn't it cool John showed up? He said you wouldn't want him here, but"—he pulled back—"you're fine with it, right?"

My smile froze in place. "Sure."

Pen cleared her throat beside us. "Congratulations." Her tight smile looked more like a grimace. With all the expectant eyes around us, she reluctantly pulled me in for a tense hug. "We still need to talk," she whispered.

I didn't respond. Not because I couldn't speak, but because I knew if I let myself give voice to the words gathering like bile at the back of my throat, I'd never be able to take them back.

Her grip tightened for a second before she pulled away, turning her back on me.

Danny watched her go with a confused expression. "What crawled up her butt?"

"It's an emotional night." I forced a casual shrug. "I think I need a little fresh air."

" 'Kay," he said. "I need to go help Baba get the cake ready anyway."

I nodded and smiled what I hoped was a reassuring smile. "I get cake, too?"

His smile was so bright it hurt my eyes. "Of course! It's your big night." He gave me another impetuous hug and skipped off toward the kitchen.

I turned away with a boulder pressing on my chest. Moving

across the room, I avoided looking in the direction where I'd last seen John. I smiled and waved at well-wishers but avoided getting trapped in any conversations. On my way out toward the back patio, I grabbed a bottle of wine. If I didn't get outside, all the pressure building up behind my eyes would explode.

Chapter Eight

The screen door's squeaky old hinges announced his arrival. As the first fine leather loafer stepped onto the cracked concrete step, I had the wine bottle tipped back like a wino. Since I was sitting on the steps, the position allowed me an upside-down view of his face. But that's usually how I felt around John Volos—disoriented.

In the last decade, time had polished his features into a distinguished but brutal handsomeness. His dark-blond hair was slicked back in the style preferred by sociopaths masquerading as CEOs. He'd shucked his suit jacket and loosened his tie, but I didn't for a minute think his appearance wasn't about business.

The stems of two wineglasses were tucked between his fingers. "Thought you might like a glass."

I pulled the wine away from my lips with a small gasp and smacked my lips. "Prefer it this way. Bye now."

I turned away and licked the cheap red from my lips.

Movement to my left as John lowered himself onto the step beside me. His broad shoulder brushed mine as he got settled. "Well, pass it over, then."

I shot him the side-eye. "What?"

He set down the two glasses and held out a hand. He didn't repeat himself. Just raised a brow in challenge.

I licked my teeth. "Get your own bottle."

"Ah."

My eyes narrowed. "What's that mean—ah?"

He sighed and shrugged, moving his eyes over my backyard, like he was taking stock. "Let me guess: You're drinking because you're feeling guilty about lying to them."

My eyes shot toward the door first to ensure no one heard him. Through the open door, the sounds of the party filtered down, but I didn't detect anyone on the lower level where Danny's room was located. I turned back to John and leaned in. "You don't know shit."

His lip twitched. "Does this mean you're still angry with me?"

"You give yourself way too much credit if you think I care about you enough to get angry."

He grabbed the bottle from my hand and took a long swallow before I could snatch it back. When I wrenched it from his hands, a few drops of red landed on the pocket of his pristine white shirt. "Oops, sorry," I said, not bothering to sound like I meant it.

"I have others."

I was sure he did. Dozens and dozens of dress shirts. Probably handmade by tiny Bangladeshi children in a run-down factory without air-conditioning or sanitary restroom facilities. Or hand-spun by blind Irish women who worked their fingers to the bone to produce shirts good enough for Babylon's Golden Hope.

"Why are you looking at me like that?" he asked, suddenly wary.

"Because I hate you." I shrugged.

I hated him for being in my home. I hated him for blackmailing me to lie to my team. I hated him for tricking me into cooking that antipotion. But most of all, I hated myself for feeling *anything* for John Volos.

His eyes widened as if it hadn't occurred to him that I could possibly hate him. "I came tonight because I thought it was important to maintain the facade that we are on good terms since everyone believes I saved Danny's life alone. I asked you to lie because we both know I have a better chance at making Abe pay for siccing Ramses Bane on Danny. And I blackmailed you because I knew it was the only way to ensure your cooperation."

My mouth fell open at this last part. In John's world ends always justified means. Even if the ends themselves were immoral or illegal. "Get out."

"One of these days my reasons for blackmailing you will become clear and you will forgive me for what I had to do."

"Get out."

"That's two," he said, "what are you going to do on the third strike? Go get your team and tell them I'm bothering you?"

I shook my head. "No, I'm going to arrest you for trespassing on private property."

"I was invited."

"Not by me, you weren't."

"Have you heard from Abe?"

The question caught me off guard, just like he'd hoped it would. I lowered the bottle and looked at him. "Why? Have you?"

John snorted. "Please. The only way that man would contact

me is by inscribing a message on a bullet." He leaned over and took the bottle. Took a sip before asking again. "So have you?"

Here's the thing. I couldn't tell the team about the phone call because it would open the door on all sorts of questions I wasn't prepared to answer. But John already knew the story. Hell, he'd been the reason there was a story to begin with. Even though I didn't trust the guy, I was genuinely curious to see his reaction to my answer. I took the bottle back. "He called today."

John's entire body stiffened. "And?" He kept his voice calm, but I could feel the anger coming off him. The heat of it made the scent of his expensive cologne—a heady mix of chypre and sandalwood—stronger. "What did he say?"

I took a casual swig from the bottle, making him wait for it. Enjoying it. "I refused the call. Told the prison's operator to take me off his call list."

John relaxed a fraction. "He won't stop trying."

I nodded. "Of course he won't."

"Do you think he knows you know he was behind Bane's plot?" When John and I had taken Bane down for his crimes, the wizard had admitted that the plan to frame John for unleashing the dangerous potion Gray Wolf had been Uncle Abe's idea. But when the team figured out the plot to frame John, Bane had gone after Danny to try to derail the investigation. John wanted Uncle Abe to pay for trying to frame him, and I wanted him to suffer for instigating the events that led to my brother almost dying.

I shook my head. "Who knows?" I glanced at him. "You decide what you're going to do there yet?"

When John had asked me to keep Abe's involvement a secret from the BPD and MEA, I'd been so angry with Abe that I agreed. I knew that if anyone could make my uncle suffer, it was John. But in the time since then, I'd also realized that I'd made a colossal mistake—and not just because John had proven to be a lying snake himself since we'd made our agreement.

"Now's not the right time," John said. "Abe's expecting retribution. Suspect that's why he's calling. He wants to find out if you know what he did and plan to make him pay."

I sighed. "He can keep waiting. Between the Blue Moon bearing down on the city and this new case, I don't have time to think about Abe." I handed the bottle to John. He hesitated, then took it without a word. I'm not sure why I decided to share it freely, except it felt nice to have the call off my chest.

"What case?" he asked, taking a drink.

"You haven't heard?" I looked at him with wide eyes. When he shook his head, I made a surprised sound. Surely the great John Volos knew everything that went down in the Cauldron. "Someone knocked over Aphrodite's temple."

John grimaced. "That's why I haven't heard. Hermaphrodite and I aren't exactly friendly."

"Ah," I said, "s/he's mad at you for turning Abe in to the cops."

He smiled behind the mouth of the bottle. "Among other things."

The detective in me wanted to press him for more details, but I didn't want him thinking I was interested in his life.

He handed over the bottle. I took it and polished off the last mouthful. "Well, I wish I could say this has been fun, but, well—you know." I pushed my hands against my thighs for leverage and rose to stand over him. Standing made me finally feel the effects of the wine, and I swayed a little. John rose quickly to try to steady me, but I pushed him off. "I'm fine, I'm fine." I took two steps away from him. "Stay away from Danny or I'll break your kneecaps."

"How about you, Katie?" He crossed his arms and smiled. The way the porch light hit his face, he looked like a devil standing on my back porch. "Do I have to stay away from you, too?"

The problem is, as devils went, he was one I knew all too intimately. In my life I'd seen that look in his eyes more times than I could count. It was the expression he wore when he'd decided to prove me wrong about something. The only thing John Volos loved more than power or money was being right.

I took a step forward and poked a finger into the wine stain over his heart. "You come near me and I'll put a bullet right here."

He captured my finger and pulled me in closer. I could smell the wine on his breath when he whispered, "You already did that ten years ago, sweetheart."

Chapter Nine

October 19
Waxing Crescent

The next morning Morales and I were driving around looking for Little Man and Mary again. I was nursing a wicked wine hangover, so I wore dark shades and clung to a bucket of coffee like a life raft.

After the conversation with Volos the night before, the party had wrapped up pretty quickly. Pen had slipped out while I was outside, so I hadn't had to deal with that awkwardness, but I knew it was only a matter of time before we had a real come-to-Jesus.

After the party ended, Baba had stuck around to help clean up. She's been so enthusiastic about reliving every second of the event that I'd resorted to drinking another bottle of wine. By the time she'd waddled back home, it had been one in the morning. What's worse, after only getting about five hours of sleep, I'd had to drive Danny to school when Pen didn't show up to take him. I'd tried calling a couple of times, but she hadn't answered. It was unusual for her to ditch the kid like that, but I figured she just needed some space after our argument.

The fact we weren't having much luck finding the Wonder Twins didn't do much to help my disposition. "Where the hell are they?" I said after about an hour of driving by all their usual spots.

Morales shot me a sharp glance, but before he could call me on my mood, both of our phones buzzed at once. I read Gardner's message out loud: "Get your asses to the gym ASAP."

"That doesn't sound good," Morales said.

"You do anything to piss her off recently?" I asked.

He shook his head. "You?"

"Not that I know of."

"Guess this means some other shit has hit the fan."

I groaned and winced from the flare of pain in my head. "Next time I decide to drink a bottle of wine, remind me of this moment, okay?"

Morales made a clucking sound. "Serves you right." He shot me a sideways glance as he turned the car back toward the office. "What were you and Volos talking about out there anyway?"

I kept my head down and sent Gardner a quick text that we were on our way.

"Kate?"

"Hmm?" I said, looking up.

"Volos?"

"What about him?"

"What gives?"

"He wanted to ask me how Danny was doing."

"You two were outside talking for a good hour."

I filed away the knowledge that Morales had been paying

enough attention to time our talk. "Oh, then I asked him if he'd heard any gossip about the Aphrodite break-in."

Morales's shoulders relaxed a fraction. "And?"

I shook my head even as I patted myself on the back mentally for the evasive maneuver. "Hadn't even heard about it. He and Aphrodite aren't on good terms after John testified against Abe." I paused to glance over and see if Morales looked suspicious. When he merely nodded, I continued. "I told him he might want to make sure his security is tight just in case."

"Why? Do you have a reason to think he's a target?"

"Just a precaution. Last time we had a Raven in the Cauldron, we almost had a turf war break out. Figured it was better to warn him in case someone was dumb enough to target him, too."

"What's a Raven?"

"That's what we call rogue wizards who steal from other wizards' labs."

"Ah," Morales said. "In LA we called them Scavengers."

I nodded. "Right. Anyway, we don't have proof the guy who knocked over Aphrodite is a Raven, but if all the coven leaders are on the lookout for one they might see something useful."

Morales laughed. "That'd be great if we believed for a minute a wizard would call the cops to report suspicious activity."

He had a point, but I wasn't really trying to argue a case here. Mainly I just wanted to cover my ass so he didn't keep asking about my conversation with Volos.

You did that ten years ago, sweetheart.

What game had John been playing anyway? Like I was supposed to believe he'd been heartbroken all this time? Give me a break.

Luckily, it was about this time that Morales turned his car into the lot outside the gym, so I was saved having to analyze that train wreck of a thought.

Moments later we walked up the steps to find Gardner tapping her sensible low-heeled pump. "What the hell took you so long?"

I paused with one foot hovering above a riser. "We came straight here."

She pressed her lips together like she wanted to tell us that wasn't good enough, but thought better of it. Gardner was tough, but she was fair. "In my office," she snapped and walked away, obviously expecting us to follow.

As I trailed her, Mez poked his head from behind the walls of his lab. That day, his dreadlocks were deep purple, which made the metal charms and beads shine like stars in his twilight hair. "Come see me after," he called. I nodded and continued on.

"Sit," Gardner said when we walked in. Morales and I took our seat and waited for her to shuffle through some file folders. "Just got off the phone with Mayor Owens," she said without preamble.

My stomach sank. I glanced at Morales, but he only shook his head, like he couldn't think of any reason we should know why the mayor was calling, either.

"Seems His Honor got a call from an attorney this morning." She stared at me while she said this.

"Why?" Attorneys never called with good news.

"Not why—who." She slid a piece of paper across the desk. It was one of those pink phone message slips. I'm no handwriting expert but my boss's chicken scratch looked like a cross between a doctor's and a serial killer's scrawls.

Despite the incomprehensible symbols, my eyes managed to make out a pair of words: *Abraxas Prospero.*

"What the hell?" I whispered.

"Seems your uncle's attorney called Owens this morning claiming Abe had important information regarding the Aphrodite Johnson case." She paused to let that sink in like poison.

"Naturally, Owens hadn't been briefed on the case, which was the first thing he chewed my ass out about when he called me an hour ago."

"Why the hell would he call Owens?" Morales asked.

"The attorney said Abe didn't trust Eldritch to act on this lead so he went right to the top." She paused, but something in my gut told me the other shoe had yet to drop. I didn't have to wait long for that feeling to get confirmed. "Which is also why he'll only speak directly to you."

Morales muttered a curse. Gardner was silent, but she watched me closely, like she didn't want to miss one flicker of my reaction to this news. I focused on trying to control my physical signs of distress. Just last night Volos had predicted Abe wouldn't stop at one ignored phone call. I had assumed then he was right, but I had no idea Abe would resort to such extreme measures to force me into this corner.

"Why would Abraxas Prospero want to help the MEA?" Morales asked. I got the impression my partner was trying to buy me some time, and I appreciated the hell out of it.

"Only one way to find out," Gardner said. "I already called Abe's lawyer to arrange the meeting. You're booked on the first ferry to Crowley in the morning."

My mouth fell open. "Sir, you can't seriously expect me to go there." Cold sweat bloomed on my chest at the thought of sitting across a table from my uncle. The closest I'd come to seeing him in the last decade was watching his trial on TV, and even then I'd squirmed in my seat as if he somehow could see me through the screen.

She frowned. "Why the hell not?"

"You have to know this is a setup. Abe doesn't do anything to help anyone but himself. He's got an angle and I guarantee it's got nothing to do with helping us."

"We can't ignore this. If he really does have information and something goes down, the mayor will have us on the first bus back to Detroit." By "us," she meant the rest of the MEA team, who were based out of a regional office in Michigan. I, however, would be stuck in Babylon with Eldritch and the mayor making my life a living hell.

"Shit," I said. "This is bullshit."

Gardner's face softened, and she leaned forward. The compassion in her expression looked out of place, like she was trying on a tight pair of shoes she rarely wore. "I know it's not going to be easy, but at least you'll have the upper hand. He'll be in shackles and you're a detective now on an MEA task force."

"That's the problem, sir," I said. "As long as we need him for information, he'll always have the upper hand."

Her face hardened again. "Sorry you're uncomfortable, but you will go to Crowley tomorrow and you will interview him."

My stomach dropped. Pen's angry words from the night before echoed in my head. *How much of yourself are you going to surrender for this job?*

I'd dismissed the question as ridiculous when she'd asked it. But that was before my boss decided my mental well-being was less important than not pissing off the mayor. I could face down junkies and stand up for myself against just about anyone—except my uncle. He'd been a surrogate father to me growing up, then he'd been my mentor, and finally he'd become my enemy. Going there wasn't just dangerous to my equilibrium but a threat to everything I'd built. Chances were good Uncle Abe knew I'd found out he was behind Gray Wolf. If he brought it up in front of Morales, I was toast.

I raised my chin. "And if I refuse?"

Gardner's expression hardened. "Then you won't even have your old patrol job to go back to."

It wasn't just a line in the sand. It was a crater opening at my feet. If I refused to fall in line, I'd lose it all.

"I'd advise you to think before you speak, Prospero," Gardner continued. "I know this won't be easy for you, but are you really willing to throw your career away because you're afraid to spend five minutes in a room with your uncle?"

It was the word *afraid* that hit me like a sucker punch. If I walked away from this, I'd be admitting that I was scared of Abe. All the work I'd done, all the sacrifice and the struggle, would have been for nothing. And worse, Abraxas Prospero would get the last laugh.

Because no doubt about it: This was a test. He knew I'd be nervous about seeing him. He wanted to find out if I had the balls to stand across from him and ask for help with the case, or if I'd run away like a spooked child.

Pen's concerns aside, I refused to throw away my career for Uncle Abe. "Fine," I snapped, finally. "I'll go." I stepped forward and made sure Gardner was looking into my eyes when I continued. "But you're fooling yourself if you believe that Abraxas Prospero would ever help the cops. He's setting us up."

"And you're fooling yourself if you believe I am naive enough not to know that." She threw down the pen she'd been holding and rose from her desk. "When you're done, you will file a detailed report to both me and Captain Eldritch."

And with that, we were dismissed. As I turned to leave, my movements felt mechanical and a cold numbness descended over the part of my brain that allowed me to regret decisions.

"Don't look so glum." Morales nudged me with his elbow. "I'll be there with you."

I tried to force a smile, but knowing my partner would witness the shit show at Crowley accounted for a large portion of my dread.

I wanted to go hide in a bar and drink until alcohol poisoning gave me an excuse to delay the meeting the next day. But cases don't care about your feelings. They don't wait for you to find your nerve. They move forward, leaving you no choice but to keep up or get out of the game altogether. I had to just put one foot in front of the other and hope that Mez had some good news to share to brighten up this shitty day.

"What's up?" Morales asked when we entered the lab.

Mez's dreadlocks were pulled back into a ponytail and topped with a pair of goggles. Pair that with his lab coat, embroidered vest, and dark gray trousers, and he looked like an Asian mad scientist, which, the more I thought about it, he kind of was.

"I got the initial chem reports ready for the potions we found at the temple."

Relieved to have a distraction from worrying about the impending meeting with Abe, I leaned back against one of the counters that didn't contain any bubbling beakers or Bunsen burners. "And?"

"As expected, it's definitely a sex magic potion. The bad news is it's not your typical libido enhancement elixir." He waved us over to look at the printouts in the folder. I scanned the list of active ingredients.

"Holy shit, why would they combine yohimbe and dulse?"

"Explain," Morales said, squinting at the list like it was written in hieroglyphs.

"They're often mixed into beverages to incite lust. Alone, each is powerful. But combined?" Mez shook his head. "It's like pouring gas on a fire."

Morales grinned. "Okay, so this potion gets people really horny. So?"

I shot him an annoyed look. "Morales, this potion won't

just make people horny. It will make them incredibly sexually aggressive."

He glanced at Mez for confirmation. "Super rapey." The wiz nodded. "Plus, yohimbe is toxic in high doses, which means this potion could also be deadly if it's not administered with care."

"Shit," Morales said. "Anyone want to guess why Aphrodite might be developing a rape potion?"

I sighed. "As far as we're concerned, the issue isn't why she would make one, but what our perp intends to do with it."

Mez shook his head. "Nothing good."

"This would worry me on a normal month, but with the Blue Moon coming…" I trailed off as my mind provided a lovely horror movie of what a rape potion would do to a population of Adepts high on lunar madness.

"I think we need to go talk to Little Man," Morales said. "Assuming we can find him."

I nodded. "Mez, can you do me a favor and research if there are any known sex magic rites that require a potion like this?"

"Sure. You thinking another sex magic coven might have stolen it?"

I shrugged. "I'll be shocked if some upstart is making a run for Aphrodite's territory, but at this point anything is possible."

"I'll let you know what I find."

The cell phone buzzed at my hip. The number on the ID was Babylon General Hospital. Frowning, I answered, "Prospero."

"Is this Kate?"

I frowned. Almost no one involved in my job called me Kate. "Yeah."

"This is Nurse Smith, from Babylon General—"

"Oh, hi!" She was the nurse who took care of Danny when he'd been in a coma. "How are you?"

"Wishing I was calling with better news, actually."

My stomach dipped. "What happened?" My brain flashed up a montage of Danny in all sorts of horrifying accidents.

"Your friend was brought in a little while ago." There was some shuffling of papers. "Penelope Griffin?"

My heart was suddenly busy trying to bust its way through my rib cage. Beside me, Morales reached out a hand and touched my arm, as if to silently ask if I was okay. I shook my head. "Is she okay?"

"Traffic accident. She's stable but she's pretty banged up. Once we got her triaged, she asked that we call you."

My pulse slowed a fraction. "If she could ask for me, then she couldn't be too bad off, right?"

"She's been in and out of consciousness due to a concussion. We're keeping her overnight to monitor her status."

"It happened this morning?"

"Actually, the police who responded said the accident must have happened last night."

A frigid chill crept across my skin. "What?"

"From what he could tell on the scene, the other car hit her and then both vehicles rolled into the old McLeod Quarry. A commuter spotted the wreckage this morning on the way to work."

I closed my eyes. "Jesus." The abandoned quarry site was about a mile from Pen's apartment. She'd almost made it home last night, but instead she'd spent the night hurt and alone in a fucking ditch. "I'm on my way."

It took three tries to disconnect the call. By the time I managed it, I was shaking so badly Morales had to take the phone from me and set it down.

Mez stood on the other side of me, so the two of them created a sort of human shield. "What happened," he urged.

I told them what I knew, my voice an autopilot monotone.

When I finished, Mez nodded, like he was choosing his words carefully. "The nurse said she's stable, right?"

I nodded jerkily.

"So why do you look like you just got the worst phone call of your life?"

I swallowed hard. "Because she said Pen got into the accident late last night. On the way home from my house."

Morales frowned. "Had she been drinking?"

I waved a hand. "No—I mean she'd had maybe two beers." I huffed out a frustrated sigh. "I need to get going. Do you think you can continue to look for Little Man and Mary without me for a couple of hours?"

He shook his head. "I'm going with you."

"But—"

"Don't *but* me, Prospero. I'm taking you. Once we're sure she's really okay we can continue our search for the twins."

I blinked. "Thanks."

"Why do you sound so surprised? Pen's your friend. That means she's family."

"You guys go on," Mez said. "I'll let Gardner know the situation."

"Thanks, Mez."

With that, Morales turned me by my shoulders and urged me toward the door. "Don't worry, Kate. She's going to be all right."

I nodded, but I wondered if I would be. Because my first thought after Smith told me Pen was stable was that if I'd told the truth about cooking with Volos, that party never would have happened and Pen wouldn't be in the hospital. Karma was a fucking bitch.

Chapter Ten

My heart raced my sneakers down the white corridor. Nurse Smith had assured me that Pen would be okay, but on the drive over my adrenaline had spiked to dangerous levels.

In my head, I was remembering the day six weeks ago when Danny's body had been wheeled in after Gray Wolf turned him into a monster and we'd had to shoot him with a salt flare to stop him from killing me.

"Kate!" Nurse Smith called. As I moved toward her, I tried to find some solace in the fact that she was assigned to Pen. Back when she'd treated Danny, I appreciated that the nurse didn't candy-coat and she never lost her nerve when shit got tense.

"Special Agent Morales," the nurse said in greeting to Morales. They'd met when Danny was in his coma.

"Thanks for calling," I said. "Is she okay?"

Smith rubbed her eyes and stretched her back, indicating she was well into a long shift. "She'll live, but she might not be happy about it for a while. In addition to the concussion, her left wrist is sprained, and she has a couple of broken ribs, contusions all down the left side of her body, and a nasty case of whiplash."

"Any idea how the wreck happened?" Morales asked.

Smith jerked her head toward a uniformed cop loitering by the coffee machines. "That's the responding."

I nodded. "Is she awake?"

"She's having her dressings changed." She gave me the number of a room about four doors down the hall. "By the time you're done getting the story they should be done and you can check on her."

"Thanks, Nurse Smith."

She smiled genuinely. "If there's anything you need..."

Morales and I approached the uniform a few moments later. "Excuse me?" I held out my hand. "I'm Detective Kate Prospero and this is my colleague Special Agent Drew Morales, MEA. I'm Penelope Griffin's best friend."

The officer swallowed his mouthful of coffee hard and his eyes widened at hearing our titles. The guy couldn't have been old enough to have outgrown wet dreams. "I'm Officer Murphy. I responded to the wreck?" When I nodded and waited expectantly, he shuffled on his feet. "Can we discuss your friend's wreck someplace private?"

I was torn between annoyance and pity. The kid was obviously fresh out of the academy and just trying to do a good job. But his deferential demeanor struck a chord in some jaded part of me that had forgotten the days when I had that same ambitious shine in my eyes. Back when I thought I could make a difference. Back when I still believed there were good guys and bad guys, and it was always clear who deserved to win.

"Detective?" he said hesitantly after I didn't respond.

I snapped myself out of the dark spaces and cleared my throat. "Yes, of course. Sorry."

"Totally understandable, ma'am."

It was the "ma'am" that spelled his doom. "In there," I snapped, pointing to a small consultation room off the main waiting area.

Murphy, Morales, and I entered the empty waiting room. My partner shot me an odd look, like he'd seen something on my face that concerned him. I shot him a dismissive frown.

The door wasn't even closed when the kid started in. "Does Miss Griffin use illegal Arcane substances?"

I paused in the process of shutting the door behind us and then slowly snapped it shut. Talk about choosing the absolute worst question to lead with. I turned to face him, my back against the closed door. "Are you sure that's what you meant to ask me?"

He frowned. "Yes?"

I pushed away from the door. "Really? Did you have any evidence from the scene that might implicate her in potion use? Further, was there evidence that the wreck was her fault?"

"Err—no. I'm just trying to cover my bases."

I narrowed my eyes. "By putting the interview subject on the defensive before the conversation even starts? Bad form, Officer."

"Kate," Morales said under his breath. I ignored him and continued to stare down the rookie.

His mouth worked for a second. I let him flounder on the end of the line for a few seconds before I continued. "If you want someone to be open and honest with you, you need to first establish rapport. Most of the people you will talk to in this line of work are emotionally distraught and/or hiding something. If you come at them head-on you're going to hit one brick wall after another."

His expression became wary. "Okay?"

"May I see the initial accident report," Morales asked. The guy shrugged and handed it over.

I made a disgusted sound. "How long have you been on the force?"

He pulled himself up straighter. "Six months, ma'am."

My eyes narrowed. *"Ma'am* is something you call your Sunday school teacher or your mother, not a goddamned detective, son. When you're talking to a superior female officer, you call her *sir* or by her rank. Got it?"

He nodded slowly and backed up a step, like he was worried I was mentally unstable. I suppose I was in a way. Unhinged. Yeah, I felt about two screws away from becoming totally fucking unhinged. "Now, as to your question: It's pointless to ask me if Pen's had a history of Arcane because even if she did and you tried to pin a DUI on her, the evidence wouldn't hold up in court because her lawyer would have it dismissed as hearsay."

"According to this," Morales said, holding up the paper, "Pen's car was T-boned by the other vehicle, which means she is not at fault for the accident."

My eyebrows shot to my hairline. "Seriously?" I grabbed the report from Morales. "In addition, the car that hit her was a potion-fueled vehicle that was in hover mode. With the two full moons this month, owners of those cars have been cautioned to drive in Mundane fuel mode so as to avoid collisions caused by the unstable lunar energy."

The kid nodded. "I—"

"Why don't you cut the shit and tell me where the other driver is?"

He blinked once, twice. Cleared his throat. "Um, the other

party didn't survive the accident. That is documented if you'd kept reading, *sir*."

I sucked on my teeth and glared at the smart-ass.

He grimaced. "Look, I'm sorry I got this off on the wrong foot. It wasn't my intention to insult your friend." He sounded so sincere that I lowered my hackles. "I asked if she had a history because she had on one of those recovery token necklaces."

I glanced down to be sure my own necklace was tucked inside my shirt. "And that made you suspicious?"

"No offense, Detective"—he nodded toward my own necklace—"but being in dirty magic recovery doesn't mean she's clean."

That took a lot of the wind out of my sails. "I see." I quickly pushed the necklace back inside my collar. "Was the other driver freaking on anything?"

Murphy nodded. "As it happens, yes. There were two empty ampoules with traces of Arcane substances found in the car, and the ME said preliminary signs indicate the deceased had been using some sort of Arcane substance. Said he likely wouldn't test it, though, since the cause of death was obviously the collision."

"How does he know the guy didn't have a heart attack or stroke while driving?"

Murphy shrugged. "Suppose he doesn't, but as it happens the guy lost his head." He mimed slicing across his neck. "So I guess the ME figured that was good enough for the death certificate."

Not long after that exchange, Murphy escaped to go file his paperwork at the precinct.

"Went a little hard on him, don'tcha think?" Morales said.

I grimaced at him. "He deserved it."

He raised a thick brow. "Did he?"

I sighed. "Maybe I rode him a little hard, but he was lucky I was a cop and not some hysterical civilian leading with that question."

"Mmm-hmm."

I was saved by Nurse Smith, who called across the way, "She's awake."

I swallowed the last dregs of frustration from my conversation with Murphy. The last thing I wanted when I saw Pen was to walk in lugging a chip on my shoulder. I'd already dumped one of those on her during our argument the night before. I cleared my throat and ran my hands through my hair.

"Be right back," I said to Morales. He nodded and leaned on the counter like he planned to work his mojo on the nurses. Three of them had found excuses to linger and make doe eyes at him.

Leaving him in their capable hands, I walked to Pen's room. Because of her crappy health insurance plan, she was stuck in a joint room with three other patients. A TV droned from the wall, and the chatter of the other patients and their families rose from behind the partitions. The curtain was pulled around the bed marked as Pen's, but a couple of weak coughs came from the other side. I poked my head though the panels.

It had been one thing to hear Smith's list of Pen's injuries. Seeing her battered face was a shock to every protective instinct in my body. Her left eye was totally swollen shut and her right was surrounded by abrasions. The anger threatened to erode my intention to put on an upbeat facade. I wanted kill the asshole who'd done this all over again. While I was at it, I also wanted to kick my own ass for being the reason she'd been at that sham of a party in the first place.

"Hey," I whispered.

"Hi." The sound was a barely audible scrape of words against air.

"Next time you want to clean the street try to remember not to use your face," I joked lamely.

The corner of her lips lifted but immediately dissolved into a pained grimace. "Ow."

I moved forward to comfort her, but she was so banged up I was afraid to touch her. Instead I settled on adjusting her pillow a little. It wasn't much but it was movement, and it made me feel a little less useless.

"You here alone?" she asked finally.

"Morales is out in the lobby. He insisted on coming after I got the call at the gym."

She frowned. "I'm sorry—"

I shook my head. "No, that's not what I meant. I just— Look, it's no big deal. He wanted to come to make sure you were okay."

She nodded but looked down at her bandaged hand. According to the nurse, when her car flipped, her left arm was trapped between her body and the door. An image of her unconscious and unprotected in that car for hours made my stomach turn with fear and guilt.

I shuffled my feet. "I'm sorry."

Her head jerked up, but the move made her wince. "Why?"

"That you're in pain. That I'm a dick. That we fought last night. Lots of things, I guess."

Her eyes widened. "It's not your fault, Kate."

I snorted out a breath. "Like hell. I—"

She held up her good hand. "Stop it, okay? I'm not going to let you make this about your guilt. I'm the one in the hospital, and frankly I don't have the energy to try to make you feel better about that."

My mouth fell open at the unusual bitterness in my friend's tone. "I—" But then it hit me that she was absolutely right. I should be comforting her, not the other way around. Which was also why I wouldn't be bringing up my surprise visit with Uncle Abe the next day. Normally, Pen was my sounding board and best advice dispenser, but now she needed me—not the other way around. "Do you need anything?"

She opened her mouth to answer, but a nurse whipped the curtain back. She rolled a cart ahead of her that was filled with a bunch of tiny plastic cups and potion vials. "Time for your pain potion, Miss Griffin."

Without thinking, I spoke for Pen. "She doesn't take potions."

A hand slapped mine. Hard. I turned to see my best friend frowning at me like I'd kicked a puppy. I hesitated. "What?"

The nurse answered for her. "Your friend has a sprained wrist, two broken ribs, and whiplash. She needs pain relief."

I put my hands on my hips. "She's also a recovering potion addict, which should be in her file."

The nurse's brows rose. "So? This is a clean potion."

I crossed my arms and pinned her with a glare. "Clean or not, it's still common for people to become addicted to pain potions, correct?"

Her eyes shifted. "Occasionally, but—"

"But nothing. If she needs pain relief, surely there are Mundane remedies."

"Kate—" Pen's voice was small.

I turned. "Do you want to throw away ten years of sobriety because you're in a little pain."

Her eyes went all squinty. It took me a second to realize her expression wasn't from pain, but from irony.

I pressed my lips together. "Do what you want, then."

Pen's gaze flicked from me to the pills in the nurse's hand and back to me.

"It's up to you, Miss Griffin. I can give you some high-dose acetaminophen and ice for the swelling, but it's not going to do as good a job as a potion would."

Indecision was sketched clearly into her features. Part of me wanted to relent and tell her to just take the damned potion already. But what kind of friend would I be to enable her like that?

A small voice in the back of my head reminded me that she'd encouraged me to accept Volos's help with the Danny situation. But I'd like to think if she'd known that decision would have ended up with me cooking, she would have helped me find another solution.

Anyway, I hated the idea of dooming her now to live with the same guilt that had been eating me alive for weeks.

"It's not worth it, Pen." She paused, looking me directly in the eyes. I shook my head to underline my plea. Finally, she sighed.

"I'll just take the aspirin and an ice pack." She certainly didn't look or sound happy about it. In fact, she looked pretty pale and her movements were too careful, like any sudden gesture would jack up her pain level.

And then I really felt like an asshole. Because deep down I had to admit that I hadn't talked her out of using potions to keep her from feeling guilty. I'd done it to save myself guilt.

But by the time I realized this, the nurse had shrugged, muttered "Suit yourself," and walked away shaking her head.

Chapter Eleven

October 20
Waxing Crescent

To get to Crowley Penitentiary for Arcane Criminals, we had to take a ferry to the center of Lake Erie, where a small island called Crook's Point squatted near the border between the United States and Canada.

As the main correctional facility for magical criminals on the eastern seaboard, the prison's location was no coincidence. The beaches on the island were laced with iron sand and salt to dampen magical attack. Plus the magnetic properties of the magnetite crystals acted like a sort of organic metal detector. But the island's location also was effective for one far more mundane reason: No sane person would swim across the frigid five-mile expanse separating the island from the mainland. In fact, in the penitentiary's hundred-plus-year history, only a few less-than-sane men had tried and met tragic ends.

There weren't many boats in this part of Lake Erie. The penitentiary forbade any unapproved watercraft from coming within a mile of the island. But I could see a couple of sailboats and barges crawling along the water's surface closer to the mainland. Overhead the sky was heavenly blue and the few billowy clouds conspired to make one think of sheep frolicking. And the sun glinted off the skyscrapers of downtown Babylon like it was a golden city where dreams came true and paupers could become kings. But I knew the effects were just tricks of light—illusion. I knew Lake Erie bore monsters in her belly, and I was more than familiar with the nightmares that plagued Babylon.

I didn't mind the slow boat trip because it gave me time to practice my approach. Abraxas Prospero had already served five years of a fifteen-year sentence for distribution of illegal Arcane substances, as well as conspiracy to commit murder via Arcane means. So why contact us now? I didn't believe for a second the iron bars of his cell prevented him from knowing everything that went on in the Cauldron, but I couldn't imagine what he'd know that could help with the Johnson case.

"You glare at that water much longer the whole lake's going to boil." Morales nudged me with his shoulder.

I clenched my jaw and turned that glare on my partner. "I'm so glad you're enjoying this."

He chuckled. "Aw, c'mon, Prospero. It won't be that bad."

I bit my tongue. Not only was the meeting with Uncle Abe going to be bad, it might very well end up being disastrous. Uncle Abe hadn't maneuvered me into this situation to do me any favors.

Instead of retorting to Morales's claim, I used a fingernail to chip away at some flaking paint on the boat's railing. "You ever been to Crowley?"

He shook his head. He'd only been in Babylon for a few months. "You?"

I shrugged. "Not in an official capacity, but I went some when I was little. Mom had some cousins get collared for cooking charges."

He just nodded.

I glanced up at him. "What, no cracks about my fucked-up family?"

He raised a brow. "Aren't all families fucked up?"

My lips quirked. "I guess so." Morales and I hadn't been partners long, but what little he'd told me about his own past supported his point. "Still, I'd feel a lot better if I knew what Abe's angle was."

He nodded and turned his gaze out toward the water. Then we both fell silent as we nurtured our own theories about the reason for the meeting. It wouldn't be any good to compare notes because we both knew whatever Abe had planned was something we'd never see coming anyway.

"You ever seen the Lake Erie Lizard?" Morales asked out of the blue.

"How do you know about that?"

He shrugged. "Been reading a book on the city's history. They mentioned it a couple of times."

I chuckled at the unexpected turn of conversation. "I haven't thought about that old wives' tale in years." He raised his brow as if he was waiting for a real answer. I shook my head. "Nah. Lots of kids in the Cauldron claimed they saw it growing up, but I never did."

"What do you know about him?"

I shot Morales a rueful glance. "How do you know it's not a girl?"

"Please, all the best monsters are dudes: Mothra, Godzilla, King Kong."

"What about Nessie?" I asked, raising a brow.

He grimaced. "*He* probably hates that sissy nickname. Admit it—males are superior at the whole monster thing."

I knew he was just trying to distract me, but the very real monsters I'd known in my life came in all genders and sexes. If I wanted to get into an argument, which I didn't, I'd have told him it wasn't men who made the best monsters, but humans. But I didn't want to start an existential debate, so I told him what I knew about the Lake Erie Lizard.

Back before a Chinese alchemist and some unfair trade laws destroyed the American steel industry, the city of Babylon was hardly a mecca of progressive thinking. There was lots of money, sure, but it was earned at the expense of the area's abundant natural resources. Factories churned chemicals into the Steel River unchecked—which incidentally is why the damned thing caught fire several times over the years—and into Lake Erie.

Once the factories closed down, most of the city's pollution was caused by neglect instead of apathy. Buildings sat like empty, rotting shells. Mother Nature started reclaiming the buildings on the outskirts of town; in the center of the city the structures became rabbit warrens filled with the homeless, the strung out, and the clinically insane. It was only in the last decade that major efforts had been made to revitalize the city's lagging economy and culture.

As for the waterways, there was a pretty determined effort by the city to clean up the river. Eventually you hardly ever saw rats riding rafts of garbage down the canals anymore and the fires stopped altogether—with the exception of the occasional floating alchemy lab explosion.

Despite that cleanup effort, some damage couldn't be undone. A lot of the pollution's legacy could be seen in the animal population, especially in the lake. Every couple of years, there was the inevitable news story about some kid who managed to hook a three-eyed fish or a bird born with a leg sticking out of its head. But no story got as much play in the annals of Babylon folklore as the Lake Erie Lizard.

"The first stories started back in the sixties," I began. "According to the legend, a man was out fishing alone one night. When he was pulling the hook out of his final catch, the hook pricked his finger. He rinsed it off in the lake, but it wouldn't stop bleeding. He started rowing back to shore because his wife would worry if he was too late getting home. Apparently he was about two hundred yards from shore when something bumped his boat. It was dark, so he couldn't see anything, but he assumed he'd just rowed over a large log or something."

I shook my head and smiled, remembering the fevered accounts of the monster whispered by kids in my neighborhood. They always involved some variation on someone cutting themselves in the water, as if the monster was some sort of shark-like creature that could detect a few drops of blood in the trillions of gallons of water that made up Lake Erie.

"What happened next to our fisherman depends on the teller," I continued, "but most versions involve a large lizard-like creature rearing up over the boat and forcing it to capsize. The man had to swim for his life back to shore, but the monster swallowed his boat whole."

"I take it you find the tale suspicious."

I shrugged. "You ask me, it's just a story parents made up to keep their kids away from the water. Rip currents can get pretty bad."

Morales leaned his forearms on the boat's edge and peered into the steel-gray water. "I dunno, Cupcake. This lake's gotta be what—a hundred feet deep?"

"Two hundred in some places."

"Right. Just saying, maybe there's things down there we don't want to believe in."

"One time Uncle Abe told me he had summoned the lizard using a potion he cooked with blood and dew gathered from a rose petal under a full moon." I rolled my eyes.

"Did it work?"

"He said it did, but Abe said lots of things."

Unbidden, a memory rose from the depths like the Lake Erie Lizard. Me at age five, sitting on Uncle Abraxas's lap.

"Mama says I don't have no daddy."

Abe laughed, making his belly jiggle. "Darlin', you don't need a daddy."

"Why not?"

"Because you'll always have your old uncle Abe." He chucked me under my chin. "I'll always take care of you."

"And my mama?"

When he smiled, his eyes twinkled like he knew all my secrets. "Yes, Katie Girl. I'll take care of your mama, too."

A cold wind rose up off the lake. Goose bumps spread over my arms, but they had more to do with the memory than the temperature.

"Hey?" Morales said. "You're not gonna get seasick, are you?"

I shook my head. "No."

"Good, because we're almost there." He pointed over the bow.

The black shores of Crook's Point rose out of the lake into steep cliffs. On the far rise, the gray stone walls of the prison loomed like a storm-shrouded castle out of an old faerie tale.

But the inhabitants of the prison weren't warmongering goblins or dragons guarding faerie gold. They were hardened magical criminals—rapists, murderers, criminally insane masterminds who'd hex you dead for your last smoke.

I leaned against the ferry's railing and ignored my sudden urge to tell the captain to turn back around. To call Gardner and tell her I'd give up my task force role and return to patrol, but then I remembered that she'd said I wouldn't even have that shitty job to go back to.

Morales leaned in and whispered, "Don't let him see your fear."

I looked up to see hundreds of small windows facing out from salt-blackened walls. My gut was churning like the Great Lake before a midwinter storm. Without a doubt, I knew Abraxas Prospero watched me from behind one of those thick, bulletproof panes.

Cold spray from the gathering waves hit my face like a slap of sanity. I stood straighter, shoving my anxiety down to the deepest recesses of my psyche. Morales was right. Abe Prospero was like a snake—he'd taste my fear on the air. Then he'd use it against me by spewing venom from that forked tongue.

I pasted on a smile and looked up at Morales. "What fear?"

The corners of his lips rose and he tipped his chin as if to say "Atta girl."

I turned back toward the shore, where a contingent of prison guards had already gathered to escort us to the main gates. Morales was wrong to assume it was the distant past that had me worried. Instead it was more recent events—just six weeks earlier to be exact—when I betrayed my family and my team by cooking a dirty potion and then covering up the secrets the magic had whispered in my ear.

"Kate?" Morales called from the dock. I shook myself,

realizing he'd exited the ferry without me noticing. I raised my chin and climbed out of the boat without accepting his offered hand. If Abe had invited me to my doom, I damned sure was going to go down fighting.

◆ ◆ ◆

The guard showed me into a white room. A single white table with a chair on either side. There was also a pane of two-way mirrored glass next to the door, so we could be observed. There were no handles on the interior of that door. Prison guards waited on the other side to open it if there was trouble. Two fluorescent bulbs buzzed overhead behind steel cages. But mostly the room was just a white box.

Before I'd been allowed in, they'd made me empty my pockets and check in any Arcane substances or magic defense weapons. I didn't balk at any of these demands. An alchemical wizard as powerful as Abraxas Prospero could MacGyver a magical weapon from little more than some pocket lint and a discarded paper clip.

He stood in the dead center with his hands bound at his waist, his ankles chained, and his back ramrod-straight. His jumpsuit was blinding orange, like a street sign warning of a need for extreme caution. His white hair was combed neatly back, and his sharp blue eyes glinted like shards of glass behind simple wire-framed glasses. To someone who'd never met him before, he'd probably look like a mild-mannered accountant or someone's grandpa. But I knew him better than most, and was well acquainted with the monster that lurked under that placid facade.

"Katie Girl." Hearing my name so casual on his lips took me back to a time when I was small and he seemed larger than life. Even bound and trapped in prison, he exuded a power that made memories rise up to haunt me like hostile spirits.

"Detective Prospero," I corrected in an even tone.

Those X-ray eyes narrowed, as if I'd taken him off guard for the first time in my life. "My, my—look how far you've come."

I raked a scornful gaze down the jumpsuit and simple canvas sneakers on his feet. "And look how far you've fallen."

"Smart to attack my vanity." He chuckled, but the sound was more menacing than amused. "I trained you well."

"You didn't train me to attack at all, Abe. You taught me to take orders like a good girl."

He raised a single steely brow. "Fat lot of good that did me, eh?"

I ignored that and sauntered toward the table. "You look like shit, Abe. The prison chow not agreeing with you?" It was true. He looked thinner. Not more fragile, but sharper, like a blade.

"If I look poorly, it's because I'm troubled over recent events." He shuffled toward the table, making his chains scrape against the concrete. He settled himself in his chair before continuing. "How is dear Danny?"

I froze. If my name on his lips made me uncomfortable, listening to that poison mouth uttering my little brother's sent a spike of icy fear and hot anger through my core. "Better now, no thanks to Ramses Bane."

Abe's eyes narrowed and shifted toward the two-way mirror behind the table, where Morales watched our conversation. I could practically feel him trying to puzzle whether I knew of his own connection to Bane's crimes. "I assure you," he said lightly, "Ramses Bane is no friend of mine."

A quick flare of relief sparked in my chest. He'd decided to wait for me to outright accuse him of being involved. Which, of course, I'd never do with Drew Morales—or any member of my team—listening.

"Whatever alliance Bane and I had in the distant past," Abe said, "was severed when he went after my blood."

"I'm relieved to hear that," I said in a flat tone.

He could try to distance himself from Bane's blunders all he wanted, but I'd never forget the role he played in concocting the plan to begin with. Still, best to let him believe I wasn't holding that grudge. At least until it benefited me to do so. Guess the old man had taught me a few lessons that stuck, after all.

"Although I must admit," he continued with a heavy sigh, "I was disappointed to hear Bane didn't manage to rid the world of that traitor John Volos."

I could practically feel him trying to bore into my head. I might be intimidated by the man, but I knew better than to invite an emotional vampire like him inside. "I'm surprised to hear that, Uncle. After all, without Volos's discovering the key to the antipotion, Danny would have died. Ironic, no?"

"Volos rarely helps anyone without expecting a boon in return, niece." He leaned forward and pointed a finger. "Remember that."

"What I remember is you're the one who taught him that lesson."

"True enough." He dipped his chin. "Tell me, Katherine, how did you reward him for his help?"

There was a challenge there, and also, I thought, an accusation. One I wouldn't give him the satisfaction of answering. I leaned back and crossed my arms. "Why am I here today?"

I watched him quickly file my evasion away to analyze later. Instead of answering my question, Abe leaned to his side with a sly smile. "You still smoke?"

I shook my head. "Quit when I was twenty."

He raised his eyebrows. "Impressive. I've never been able to kick the habit, myself."

I shrugged. "It was a breeze compared with giving up cooking."

Those lips pressed together in a thin line. "You say that like you're proud of turning your back on magic, but you ask me, it was the worst decision you ever made."

I laughed out loud. "Says the man in prison for magical crimes."

A thundercloud passed behind his eyes. Abe cleared his throat, and the threat of a storm passed quickly. "Don't suppose you could rustle up a coffin nail for your old uncle?"

I stared him down for a few seconds. Part of me wanted to tell him I wasn't his damned errand girl or nicotine dealer. But I also knew he'd never share his bombshell until I'd jumped through some hoops. "Hold on."

I went to the door and knocked, sure to keep my body turned to the side so I could keep on eye on Abe the whole time. Not that I expected him to attack me physically—mental anguish was more his style—but you could never be too careful. The door opened, and I found Morales standing on the other side. He shoved a pack of cigarettes and a lighter through the crack. "You okay?"

I shot him a look. "Peachy." I snatched the package of cigs from him and closed the door before he could offer any advice.

Returning to Abe, I tossed the pack across the table. "There."

"Old Goat Ultra Lights?" he said with distaste. For years the old man's brand had been Viceroyals, with their purple rolling paper and golden filters. In a place like Crowley the "king of cigarettes" would be more precious than diamonds.

"You're not exactly in a position to be picky here."

He smiled as he made a show of packing the smokes against

the table with his bound hands before selecting the perfect specimen. He looked up expectantly for me to do the honors. The damned lighter was stubborn and took five flicks to catch. On the outside, I probably looked annoyed. But inside, I was counting to ten over and over and reminding myself to keep it together.

Finally, he leaned back and exhaled his first drag in a plume of gray smoke. "Blue Moon's coming." He'd said it too casually to be idle chitchat.

"I'm well aware."

He paused with the cancer stick jutting from his mouth. With the fiery tip and the smoke spilling from between his lips, he suddenly reminded me of a dragon. The comparison was apt, I thought, because one wrong move would definitely get me burned.

"Freaks keepin' you busy?"

All he got was a tip of my chin in response.

He raised his cuffed hands to remove the cig from his lips. "Gonna be a lot busier soon enough."

I sighed. If I let him, he'd play this game all day. "Which begs the question, why am I here when there are criminals back in the city I could be arresting?"

"Because I want to do you a favor."

With a snort, I leaned forward, glaring. "Sell that load of bullshit to someone who doesn't know you." I glanced at the digital clock over the two-way. He'd already wasted fifteen minutes of my time. "Start talking or I'm out of here."

He tilted his head down. "As you wish. It may surprise you that even in this prison, I still receive updates from some of my previous business associates—"

"You mean the midlevel potion cookers who can barely hang on to their corners now that the coven's disbanded?"

121

"Don't interrupt me, girl!" His hands slammed down on the table so hard the cigarettes flew to the floor.

The outburst was so unexpected and violent, I reared back. When I was younger, I'd known how to tiptoe around the land mines of Abe's temper. But the years and distance had dulled those old protective instincts, and I'd clumsily tripped over the wire that was his obsessive hatred of disrespect.

But I wasn't an awed teenager anymore. I was a grown-assed woman who'd stared down her share of psychos as well as loaded guns. Abe's temper was as hot as the barrel of a discharged gun, but he couldn't hurt me anymore. At least not with his fists.

"If you speak to me like that one more time, I will walk out of this room and never return," I said in an ice-shard voice. "Am I clear?"

His jaw clenched and unclenched, like he wanted to chew me up and spit me out. But as much as my refusal to bow down and show my neck to him pissed Abe off, he still needed me for something. So he unclenched his hands and set them in his lap, and the anger on his face cleared as quickly as a summer shower.

He cleared his throat. "As I was saying," he continued in a quiet tone, "my associates have informed me there is a new player in the Cauldron."

"What kind of player?" I hooked an elbow over the back of my chair to portray a casualness I didn't feel. My heart was still thumping from the outburst. I might have called him on the bluster, but the shadowy part of me that remembered the sting of his fist had flinched.

"Raven."

My brow rose and my heart quickened from something much more optimistic than fear. Morales and I had just talked about the possibility that Aphrodite's thief might be a Raven. They weren't usually strong potion cookers themselves, so in addition to money, they stole potions from coven stashes to sell for even more profit. As one might expect, they were considered the bottom feeders of the magic world. And if the Cauldron had a new one in play, things were about to get interesting.

"So?" I said to Abe, not wanting to betray my interest. "What's one more vulture in the ecosystem?"

"During a Blue Moon?" He raised a brow and pursed his lips to challenge my casual attitude. "Especially one this psycho." Abe leaned forward, pointing the cig at me for emphasis. "Calls himself Dionysus on account of he thinks he's the reincarnation of that deity."

My brows slammed down. "Dio—the Roman god of wine?"

"Greek," Abe corrected. "Regardless, he's crazier than a shithouse rat. And you know what happens when you mix reckless with crazy, right?"

"Yeah," I said, shooting him a pointed look. "I'm pretty familiar with that particular combination."

"Please, Katie. You can do better than that. Besides, I am many things, but I am never reckless."

He had a point. Everything Uncle Abe did was calculated to impose maximum pain. Which begged a question. "Why are you coming to me with this? You could have contacted the coven leaders."

He shrugged. "Yes, Aphrodite in particular would surely pay handsomely for this information."

I kept my features poker-straight, but inside I was wondering how on earth he'd heard about the robbery so fast. "So why not approach her instead?"

Abe took another drag of his cigarette and blew out a succession of rings. I couldn't help but imagine them as little nooses.

"As it happens, I seem to have developed a troubling condition since I've been in prison."

I frowned. If he'd been diagnosed with some sort of disease, surely I would have been informed. "What's that?"

"A conscience." He chuckled, but the insincerity made it sound rusty. "As I get older and the days grow shorter, I've had to come to terms with certain truths."

"Such as?"

"One day I'm going to die. And when that happens, what will I have to show for my time on this planet? Since you and the boy left, I have no blood family to speak of." He shook his head sadly. "The regrets compound with each passing day." He at least made an effort to sound sincere, I'd give him that. I briefly wondered if he'd even practiced that look in the scrap of polished metal that passed as a jail cell mirror. Either way, I wasn't buying the expression or this performance.

"I'm gonna save both of us some time." I held up a hand to stop him when he made as if to continue his line of bullshit. "There is no way in hell I am ever going to believe that you called me here for a reconciliation. Further, I'm not naive enough to believe you'd hand me a lead on a case out of the goodness of your heart."

He had the nerve to attempt an offended expression. "Why not?"

"Because there is no goodness in you—or heart, for that matter." I stared at him with a challenge to try to convince me otherwise. When he remained silent, I said, "So stop insulting me and tell me what you want in return for this information."

He crushed the cigarette out right on the table. Then he took his time, brushing any stray ashes off his pant legs. Once he was settled again, he looked up. All traces of remorse were gone. Now his eyes gleamed with the calculating light of a sea-soned criminal.

"Naturally, if the lead I'm giving you results in a major arrest for the MEA, I'd expect a good word with the parole board."

The words hung there between us for a good thirty seconds before I responded.

"It's now my turn to teach you a lesson." I leaned forward. "You listening?"

He narrowed his eyes, but he nodded.

"The day I put a good word in for you with anyone is the day I put my Glock between my teeth."

His smile was tight, restrained. "You keep disrespecting me like that, little girl, and I'd be happy to help you pull the trigger."

Silence crouched between us for a good minute before I responded. Even as I tried to keep my calm, Gardner's voice kept rolling through my head. If I stormed out and this Raven caused big trouble, it would be my badge that got melted down for scrap metal.

"You want help, I'm going to need something more traceable than an assumed alias."

"Does this mean you'll talk to the parole board?"

"It means I'll tell my supervisor about your request. I don't have power with the board."

Abe pursed his lips and watched me for a moment. Whatever he thought during that time, it must have convinced him to take the gamble and play along. "All I know is he escaped from some mental institution in New York."

I pulled out a small pad and wrote down a couple of notes. "Anything else?" I asked, looking down at the words I'd written. When Abe didn't immediately respond, I looked up.

A grave expression had taken the place of his calculating smile. "My associate had reasons to believe this guy has plans for the Blue Moon."

"What kind of plans?"

Abe raised his cuffed hands in a helpless gesture. "Don't have anything concrete, but this came from a guy I trust."

"What's your associate's name, then?"

"That I definitely can't tell you."

"Won't, you mean."

He shrugged, as if to imply I was splitting hairs.

"Why do you care if this Dionysus has some dire plans for the city?"

"I'm not a good man, Katie Girl. We both know that. No sense pretending otherwise." He nodded toward the pack of cigarettes on the ground. With a martyred sigh, I threw them back on the table. He removed one and waited for me to light it before he continued. "But my ambitions have always been about money and power." He looked up to see if I agreed. I nodded. He chose to believe the move was agreement, but I meant it as encouragement to continue. "Ravens? Those assholes have no honor."

I snorted.

"Laugh all you want. Least I live by a code. Take care of my people, my family, and I give a man a chance to prove I can trust him. But Ravens are a different breed. They get off on chaos. Ain't no more chaotic time than the Blue Moon. I'm tellin' ya, there's some dirty shit coming, Katie Girl."

I narrowed my eyes and stared at him hard. "Why should I believe you?"

"Says the girl who turned her back on her family to go work with the Mundane pigs." He let feigned hurt seep into his words. I didn't take the bait, simply stared at him without a lick of remorse on my face. Finally, he shrugged. "Think of me what you will, but the Cauldron is mine. Always has been. Cops thought that would change if they stuck me on this island." He blew out a plume of smoke. "They were wrong." He licked his lips, and the resulting shine reminded me of venom. "I won't let some fucking Raven destroy everything I built."

Unlike Gardner, I could put up with some bullshit in my life. But there was a limit to how much I was willing to wade through from my uncle. He'd overplayed his hand with the martyr routine. "And we're done here." I scooted the chair back. "I'd say it's been nice chatting with you, but I'd rather have spent the last hour getting a root canal with a rusty hook."

"You remain a delight, Katherine," he said in a tone that made it clear I was anything but. "I wish you luck on this case. It's not going to be easy on you."

I frowned at him in the process of gathering my coat. "What does that mean?"

He slipped another cigarette between those lying lips. "Once the smoke clears and you find yourself the big hero, you're going to realize you couldn't have done it without me." He leaned forward with the cigarette hanging from his lips. "You're going to owe me."

I snatched the smoke and broke it in half. "I will never owe you a fucking thing."

"You owe John Volos." He sat back and raised a brow. "How's that feel?"

"The only thing I owe either of you is a bullet."

"Give him my regards when you see him." He was trying to get a reaction. To see if I'd show my hand. But I'd learned how to play poker from the best.

I looked my uncle directly in his glittering eyes. "Why don't you ask Mayor Owens to tell him now that you two are such pals?"

He smiled. "Why waste Owens's time when you'll run straight to John to deliver my message yourself. You always were so needy where he was concerned. Panting over him like a bitch in heat."

I pivoted on my heel and marched toward the door. He was quiet until the guard opened the door. I could see Morales standing in the hallway. Just before I cleared the doorjamb Uncle Abe called, "Kate?"

I stopped and turned. "What?"

"You said you walked away from magic."

I turned fully and raised my brows. "So?"

His eyes narrowed. "It's still there around the edges."

My stomach dropped three stories.

"But it's weak." He made a dismissive noise with his mouth. "A pity. You could have been a formidable wizard."

I lifted my chin. "Like you?"

His lips tilted up. "Indeed."

I looked around the room. "And look where you ended up."

Abe leaned back in his chair and clasped his hands on the table. "These shackles won't be on me forever, Katie Girl." He smiled wide, showing off his large, white teeth. "I'll be waiting to hear from you once you catch Dionysus."

"Don't hold your breath."

The corner of his mouth twitched. "Say hi to Danny Boy for me."

I saluted him with my middle finger and slipped through the door before the manipulative bastard could launch another parting shot.

Chapter Twelve

Morales was quiet the entire ferry ride back. As much as the guy liked to tease me, he also had the good sense to know when to shut the fuck up. My hands gripped the railing until my knuckles ached. For a few moments I indulged in a fantasy of imagining it was Uncle Abe's throat.

Once we exited the ferry and were back by his car, Morales pulled out his phone and held it up to the sky to check the signal. I guess he found one because next thing I knew, he was speaking to Gardner through the mouthpiece. Leaning against the SUV's bumper, I listened as he gave her a nuts-and-bolts version of what had happened. He left out the embarrassing details that made me look like an emotional wreck, bless him.

Instead of watching the water spread out like a stainless-steel ocean, I raised my face to the sky. The midday sun stabbed at my corneas, seagulls shrieked like banshees, and the cold wind felt pushier than it had earlier. Despite the less-than-idyllic scene, I realized it was worlds better than the sliver of sky visible through Abe's cell bars. He might be the king of Crowley State Penitentiary, but I was a pauper with access to the whole world. That freedom gave me the upper hand. I had choices. He did not.

And since I was the one with choices, I decided to take the meeting with Abe at face value. As far as the Johnson case went, he'd offered very little in the way of convincing evidence. Sure, we'd check out his story about Dionysus, but I didn't plan to take his story as gospel.

Morales nudged me. I glanced up, ripped out of my thoughts. "She wants to talk to you?"

I cleared my throat and put the phone to my ear. "Sir?"

"What's your read on this?"

I chewed on my lip for a moment. "He's fucking with us."

"That's my gut reaction, too." The sound of her chair creaking back cut through the line. "Unfortunately, the mayor has called a meeting. You and Morales need to meet me at City Hall in an hour so we can debrief him."

I closed my eyes. What I needed was a stiff drink, not a meeting with the fucking mayor. "Any way we can put him off?"

"Not a prayer."

◆ ◆ ◆

An hour later Mayor Owens slammed a newspaper on the desk. The headline shouted the news about Aphrodite Johnson's temple being robbed by a criminal they dubbed the Aphrodisiac Bandit. "Anyone want to explain to me why I had to hear about this asshole from Abraxas Prospero instead of my own fucking police force?"

The Honorable Skip Owens, mayor of Babylon, Ohio, was not an attractive man. His nose was too big, his chin too weak, but what he lacked in looks, he made up for with charisma and sheer force of personality. He had salt-and-pepper executive hair and wore a nice navy suit with a tie as red as his Republican blood. On his right hand he wore a signet ring depicting the seal of the city of Babylon. On it, a lion with two emerald eyes guarded a gate bearing the city's name. Judging from Owens's proud posture, he considered himself the king of this particular concrete jungle.

"Sir, with all due respect, we've been briefing Captain Eldritch of the situation almost daily."

Owens turned to glare at Eldritch. "Well?"

"Sir, I handed the Johnson case to Special Agent Gardner but she has not provided updates as promised." He shot a glance in the direction of his boss, Chief Stanley Adams.

Chief Adams sat stoic as a statue beside his employee. As near as I could tell, the man rarely got his hands dirty with Cauldron politics, preferring instead to court the favor of wealthy Mundane citizens in the nicer parts of Babylon. He'd even lobbied to have the Cauldron's violent crime statistics kept separate from those for the rest of the city because, he claimed, they were an anomaly due to the high percentage of Adepts who lived in that part of town. Not surprisingly, like all the brass in Ohio state and local law enforcement, he was a Righty.

Gardner's posture stiffened. Standing next to Morales and at the back of the room, I shot him a worried look. Watching a bunch of power brokers play political hot potato wasn't my idea of fun. Especially since we didn't have the luxury of time. With less than a week remaining until the Halloween Blue Moon and the threat of a possible Raven at large, we needed action, not the blame game. Not that I was going to be the one to point that out to the four people in Babylon who could guarantee I'd never find work again.

"All right, let's try another tack. What did Abe Prospero have to say today?"

All eyes turned toward me. I cleared my throat and stepped forward.

"Mr. Mayor," I began.

He held up a hand. "Who the hell are you?"

I blinked. "Detective Kate Prospero, sir."

The man's eyes widened. "Abe's niece, right? I do not appreciate being your messaging service, Detective."

I nodded. "Sorry, sir."

His eyes narrowed. "You were in the middle of the Ramses Bane case, as well, correct?"

Grimacing, I nodded again.

"Why do you keep coming up in all the cases that cause a pain in my ass lately, Prospero?"

I shrugged. "Just talented, I guess."

The corner of his mouth twitched. "Proceed."

"According to my uncle, the theft was perpetrated by a man who believes he is the modern incarnation of the god Dionysus. He's a Raven—a wizard who robs other wizards."

Owens frowned. "So he's insane?"

I nodded. "It would certainly seem so, if Abe's telling the truth."

He tilted his head. "You don't believe your uncle, then?"

"Not especially." I shook my head. "He's not exactly known for his honesty, you know?"

Owens pursed his lips and crossed his arms. "I'd agree with you if I hadn't received correspondence from this Dionysus myself."

My mouth fell open. From the corner of my eye, I saw that everyone else had stiffened like pointer dogs on the trail of a juicy squirrel.

"He contacted you, sir?" Eldritch asked carefully.

The mayor nodded and went to retrieve something from

his desk. He shuffled something around in the drawer before removing an envelope. "This letter arrived this morning."

He brought it to me. Not wanting to get more fingerprints on it than necessary, I pulled the cuff of my shirt up to cover my fingers as I took it. Moving toward the meeting table in the middle of the room, I placed the envelope on the surface. "Morales?" I asked, looking up. "I have a pair of gloves in my pack. Can you bring them to me?"

He nodded and brought them over while everyone else circled the table. With the gloves on my hands, I opened the envelope and pulled out the sheet of paper. A Polaroid fell out on its face, but I ignored that for the moment.

The missive itself resembled a ransom note, with each letter cut out of a magazine. Not sure why the guy bothered when any computer and printer would suffice, but he obviously loved a little drama.

Mayor Owens,
   The Blue Moon's coming. Are you ready for a party?
I'll bring the refreshments.

                        Sincerely,
                        Dionysus

My stomach flip-flopped in my gut. Not because of the threat, but because that short note confirmed that Uncle Abe hadn't been lying. And for some reason, knowing he was telling the truth about wanting to help me scared me more than the idea he'd been lying.

I shook off that thought. First matter of business was finding Dionysus. I'd deal with being in Abe's debt once we'd arrested the asshole.

"How did this arrive?" I asked.

Owens shrugged. "Through the mail."

I flipped over the envelope; there was no postmark. I showed it to Gardner. "Planted it in the mailroom, probably," I said.

"Sir," Gardner said, "we'll need to take this and have our lab wiz look it over."

"Not so fast," Chief Adams said. "This is a BPD case."

Gardner's eyes widened. "If it's a BPD case, why did your captain hand it over to my team?"

"That was when we thought the case was about some potions being stolen. That letter is clearly a threat to the entire city, which means it's a BPD matter."

All eyes turned toward Owens. He rubbed his lower lip with his finger. "What did he take from Aphrodite Johnson?"

I exchanged an anxious glance with Gardner. Once this was out, there was no way the case wasn't going to become a media circus. "He took a large stash of a potion we believe makes the user sexually aggressive. Extremely so."

The mayor's face paled. "So this man who just threatened my city has a stockpile of rape potions?"

"I'm afraid so."

The bad news hung in the air between for a good thirty seconds while Owens considered the angles. Probably he was wondering how to play this so he came out looking like the hero. Finally, he snapped at Eldritch, "I want an APB for this asshole and his name plastered on every TV set and street corner in the city."

The captain shifted uncomfortably. "That's going to be a problem, sir."

"And why is that, Captain?" Owens crossed his arms.

"Because we don't know what he looks like," Gardner offered. "We don't even know his real name."

Without answering, Owens flipped over the picture I'd

forgotten about. He handed the picture to Eldritch. He showed it to the chief and Gardner. The three of them exchanged a worried look.

"May I?" I asked, taking it in my gloved hands.

The image was grainy, like it had been taken with a vintage camera. In the center, a shirtless man whose torso, neck, and arms were littered with tattoos stood with his arms spread like Jesus on the cross. His head was back but his eyes were aimed at the camera, daring you to look away. His black hair was wild, and a large beard clung to his jaw. Despite the unkempt appearance of his hair and beard, his torso was toned with muscle and a pair of suspenders lay over broad shoulders and down to the waistband of his low-slung jeans. He wasn't traditionally handsome by any means, but he exuded untamed sensuality and recklessness.

I shook myself. The last thing I'd expected was such a visceral response to a simple picture.

Morales pulled the photo from my hands. "He looks familiar."

I looked again and shrugged. "Maybe." Something tickled at the back of my brain, but I couldn't access it.

"Now you have the picture," the mayor said, "I want to know who this asshole is. I want to know why he's picked my city. But most of all, I want every available law enforcement agency in this town working to find this Sinister son of a bitch."

Sinister. Hearing my city's mayor use such a derogatory slang for Adepts made me cringe. Granted, Dionysus wasn't exactly a stellar example of my kind, but still, Owens's attitude reflected that of so many of the city's officials. According to too many Mundanes in power, Adepts were to be either controlled or feared. Usually both.

Eldritch stood. "Yes, sir. We'll have his photo plastered all over the city within the hour."

"And you," Owens said to Gardner, "find out what he intends to do with that potion."

"Yes, sir," she said, ignoring a glare from Eldritch and the chief.

"All right," Owens said. "Keep me updated on progress. And make no mistake about it: I expect progress yesterday, am I understood?"

Chapter Thirteen

October 21
First Quarter

The next afternoon I was sucking down the last of a soda from the late lunch we grabbed on our way to the park. Even though we were sitting on a tight deadline until all hell broke loose, I was trying to enjoy the abnormally sunny weather with the windows down. Morales looked at ease, too, with the wind ruffling his hair as he drove along the river.

"Yo," he said over a mouthful of fries. "You ever wonder what it would have been like if you hadn't left the life?"

I paused with the straw halfway to my mouth. "What? You mean the coven?"

He nodded and shot me a side glance.

I shrugged. "Probably be dead, most likely."

"I don't know. You're pretty smart, Cupcake. Maybe you would have been running the whole show by now."

"That had been the plan," I muttered.

"Huh?"

I sighed and looked at him. "I said, that had been the plan. Abe was grooming me to take over the coven."

Morales whistled low. "But you left anyway?"

I nodded. "Like I said, I doubt I would have survived long enough to put my management skills to the test." I shook off the heavy feeling the conversation lowered over my skin. "Besides, if I hadn't left I never would have had the pleasure of dealing with your annoying ass."

He flashed me a sideways grin. "You love my ass."

I glanced toward the ass in question. "It has certain charms. Too bad you insist on talking so much and ruining it all."

He laughed then, crumpling up his trash and stashing it in the bag. With a jolt, I realized this hastily gobbled lunch was as close to a date as I'd had in months. The last official date I'd had was with a mortician named Barry Finkleman, whose idea of a good time was taking me to a funeral trade show to ogle embalming equipment. That thought was depressing enough to make me wish I had some whiskey to add to my soda.

"What's wrong? You've got that frown that usually means you're thinking too much."

I gave him a dirty look and chugged the rest of my drink. "After that meeting with the mayor, I'm just hoping LM's gonna have something to help us find this Dionysus guy."

Morales pulled the car toward the side of the road and pushed the gear into P. "Only one way to find out." With that he shut off the ignition and hopped out. As he jogged around the front of the SUV, I took a couple of seconds to admire the rear end we'd just discussed. It really was a world-class ass.

In the next instant Morales stopped and turned toward the

car, staring at me from the curb. He tapped his watch. "Tick-tock, Cupcake."

I grabbed my bag and climbed out of the car. "You got cash?"

He frowned. "Remind me to introduce you to reimbursement forms when we get back."

"Hey, you're the higher pay grade here. It's up to you to deal with that bullshit."

He shook his head and turned away like he knew pushing the issue was a waste of time. Smart guy.

I jogged to catch up with him in time to walk through the gated entrance to the park. Well, *park* is a generous term for what was really just a dirt lot dotted with a few benches and bent metal structures that used to be swing sets and seesaws. Back in the day, it used to be the playground for the families of those who worked at Babylon Steel. Now it was a nighttime recreation area for potion junkies.

But we'd arrived during the day, so all the hex-heads were passed out in their rabbit warrens waiting for night to fall so they could get their next fix. The only people we found there that afternoon were the very ones we'd been looking for: Little Man and Mary.

While they technically were two people, the pair came as a single unit. Mary was a six-foot-tall tank of a woman with the intellect of a child, and Little Man was the size of a baby with the intellect of an adult. Their mother had been a fertility potion junky, but her dealer had fucked her over by giving her an experimental potion. Unfortunately, baby Mary had grown too large in utero and killed her mama on the way out.

About the time Mary hit puberty a large mole on her chest had grown into her brother, Little Man. He never grew larger than a baby so she could easily carry him around in a carrier strapped to her chest. One time I asked if they ever thought about having surgery to separate. Mary's reaction to the question was...violent, so I never brought it up again. But I knew from experience she was fiercely protective of LM, and there was no way he could survive on his own in this world, and Mary could never survive the mental rigors of living without his guidance, so in a way their relationship was symbiotic.

Morales had met the pair before during our last big case a few months back. Still, his shoulders tensed once we spotted them on their normal bench. The last time he'd met them, Mary had had a negative reaction to an offhand comment my partner had made, so I couldn't blame him for his caution. Especially since the last time we'd tried to talk to the pair, they'd run like frightened animals. Still, it was odd to see such a big guy get freaked out by an intellectual cripple and a homunculus who would have lost a wrestling match against a toddler. "Relax," I said. "As long as you don't do anything to make her think you're a threat to Baby"—Mary's pet name for Little Man—"it'll be fine."

"That's the problem. That little fuck loves to stir the shit."

"Then keep your mouth closed and let me do the talking." It had taken me a while to trust Morales enough to introduce him to my snitches. But now that I had I didn't want him doing anything else to jeopardize my relationship with them. As tricky as it was to deal with LM and Mary, they tended to give me good intel most of the time.

"Is that bacon I smell?" A bored voice floated back over the bench toward us. I wasn't sure exactly how he knew we were there, since Mary's back was to us and LM couldn't see over her shoulder. Still, I'd learned not to underestimate LM because of his size.

Mary didn't get up or turn to address me. Instead, she waited for Morales and me to come around the bench. When we did, I stopped and gaped. "What the fuck happened?"

Little Man had a busted lip, and one of his wrists was swollen and purple. Mary had her left hand in a cast and a large bandage across her forehead that bore smears of blood that had seeped through the gauze. LM chuckled, but the noise morphed into a pitiful cough. "Had a little trouble."

"No shit," Morales said, coming forward. "Who did this to you two?"

The move earned him a menacing growl from Mary.

LM raised his uninjured right hand. "Careful, Macho. Sissy's a little more protective than usual ever since the attack."

Morales shot a worried look at the woman and backed away. "Sorry," he said to Mary.

"Tell us," I prompted. "Is this why you ran from us the other day?"

His gaze scooted left, as if he'd been hoping I'd have forgotten about that. "Had a misunderstanding with a business associate is all." LM sighed and leaned back, like he was enjoying sharing his woes with an audience. "The fucking moon. Got people acting a fool."

"Which people?" Morales asked.

LM shrugged, his eye skittering to the side. "Forgive me, Special Agent, but I'm not at liberty to share details about our confidential business with an officer of the MEA."

Morales rolled his eyes. It's not like we didn't know that LM and Mary were tits-deep in the magic trade in the Cauldron. It's just that by comparison they were relatively small fish in a filthy pond full of bottom feeders. Arresting them for their small-time potion deals would be like capturing a tadpole when there was a school of barracuda swimming past.

"If this business of yours has anything to do with the case

we're working," I said, "it'd be in your best interest to give us some names."

LM shook his head. "This ain't none of your business, Prospero." His tone was so serious it gave me pause. Little Man wasn't ever Mr. Happy Good Time, but he usually enjoyed busting my balls during our meetings. Something was up. He knew I'd go to bat for him if it was in my power to do so, but for some reason he believed I either wouldn't or—more likely—couldn't help him with this one.

I nodded. "I hear you. Just make sure you two watch your asses. I don't have time to train new snitches."

That finally earned me a chuckle. "Ah, shit, girl. You're a trip, you know that?"

"That's funny. I thought she was just a pain in the ass," Morales added.

LM laughed again. "I hear that, Macho." He held up his uninjured hand. Morales paused only a fraction of a second before he leaned in to slap the homunculus some skin. When he pulled back I held my breath, worried he might do some stupid thing like wipe his hands on his jeans, but he didn't.

"Anyway, don't worry about us," LM said. "This busted lip is a fucking pussy magnet."

Vomit rose in the back of my throat at the mental image conjured by his words. I felt rather than saw Morales shudder next to me. LM cackled and raised his hand for another high five, this time in my direction, but I sidestepped it verbally. "Anyway, we were wondering if you two heard anything about this asshole calls himself Dionysus."

Mary, who'd been staring off into the middle distance, as was her habit, suddenly became very alert. Her massive melon head jerked up and she stared at me like I was her enemy. LM felt her go tense and started patting her arm. "Shh, Sissy," he whispered. To me he narrowed his eyes. "Who told you?"

I froze. "Wait. He did this to you?"

The small face scrunched up with confusion. "You mean you didn't bring him up like that to see how we'd react?"

I frowned and shook my head. "No, we're investigating him for real. I had no idea you were connected to him."

LM crossed his arms over his tiny chest. "Well, fuck. I knew we shoulda skipped out of town before this fucking moon got its claws in the city."

"Why didn't you?" Morales asked.

LM's posture changed. His movements hesitant, as if he was worried about giving away too much. "That's the thing. This business I mentioned, it came up last minute right before we was gonna leave."

"Wait," I said, "Dionysus approached you?"

Mary stiffened again at the mention of the name. LM shushed her and then reluctantly looked at us again. I raised a brow. "Fuck," he said. "Fine. What's-his-name came to me couple weeks back—just after the last full moon. Said he heard I was the man to talk to for information."

I nodded because that much was true. No sense asking how Dionysus figured out LM was the guy. It was common knowledge in the Cauldron that the homunculus knew everything. The only thing keeping the little shit alive was his sister's reputation for violent overprotection and that most people were just plain freaked out by the pair. "What kind of information?" I asked.

"Said he wanted to know who the key players in town were. Paid real well for a list of the top wizes and their specialties."

"Was he after something particular?" Morales asked.

LM shrugged. "At first no. He just took the list and paid me. But last week he comes back demanding to know why I didn't list all the Cauldron's wizes."

I frowned. "Who'd you leave off?"

The homunculus looked me in the eye. "Aphrodite and Volos."

"Goddamn it." I felt Morales shoot me a look but ignored him. "What about them?"

"I left the Hierophant off the list because I was afraid it'd get back to her/m and s/he'd poison our asses." Little Man crossed his arms with a huff. "And I didn't put Volos on the list 'cause he's all legit and shit."

I raised my brows to indicate I didn't believe Little Man was naive enough to think Volos was really out of the game completely.

He shrugged. "Leastwise, ain't nobody knows of any new potions he's produced in a few years." He waited for me to acknowledge that.

Truth was Volos had put a potion out in the last few months, but it was the legit antipotion he'd created with my help to battle the dirty potion Ramses Bane put on the streets. Still, LM's point held up because all that aside, Volos still hadn't been a player in the Votary Coven in years—not since he betrayed Uncle Abe and testified against him in court in exchange for a clean slate.

"So Dio"—Morales shot a worried glance in Mary's direction—"err, the asshole came back demanding to know why Volos wasn't on the list specifically?"

LM shook his head. "No, he came back saying I had to have left someone off. Got the impression he'd checked out all the other alchemists on the list and didn't find whatever it was he was looking for. So he figured I musta left someone off."

"Did you figure out what he was looking for?" I asked.

"Said he knew a wizard in Babylon had ordered a large shipment of calamus root recently. That's what he was after, see? When he checked out the others and didn't find those barrels, he knew I'd left someone off."

"Calamus root?" Morales asked.

"It's used in some Hoodoo traditions to gain control over someone's will," I explained quickly. "I didn't see it listed as an ingredient for Aphrodite's potions."

"So it was Volos." Morales didn't sound surprised, and frankly neither was I. He was developing a bad habit of getting himself tangled in my cases. A bad habit I was going to have to cure him of ASAP before it got more people hurt—or worse, cost me my job.

I turned back to LM. "Is that how you ended up hurt? He beat you until you gave him their names?"

The silence was the only affirmation I needed. "Son of a bitch." I scrubbed a hand over my face. "So what happened after you gave up the names?" I didn't even bother to ask how a lone man managed to rough up Mary, but the fact he'd done it spoke volumes about what we were up against.

"He told me if I left anyone else's name off the list he'd be back. He said if I went to the cops, he'd be back. He said if I so much as thought about him, he'd be back."

"That's why you ran the other day?" Morales asked.

He nodded. "This asshole wasn't no joke."

The fear in his tone shocked me. Little Man was usually full of piss and vinegar. I'd never heard him admit to being intimidated by anything.

"Anyway, I heard he already hit up Aphrodite's joint," LM said. "That asshole better hope the herm doesn't catch him before you guys do."

I chuckled despite the bad feeling swirling through my abdomen. "I'd actually pay for ringside seats to that show."

Morales crossed his arms and gave LM a hard look. "Hold up, so you've known for a while that this asshole was gonna knock over wizes and it didn't occur to you to call us?"

LM shrugged. "He paid better. Plus"—he pointed to his face—"I was pretty sure if he found out I was snitching to you bitches, he'd come back to finish what he started."

Morales opened his mouth to deliver what was no doubt a meathead threat to the only source we'd spoken to who'd had contact with our suspect. I elbowed him in the ribs before he could deliver it. I ignored the glare it earned me. "Did he give you any indication what he was planning to do with the stuff he took?"

LM shook his head. "Just said something about how he had some fireworks planned for the city of Babylon to celebrate the Blue Moon."

Something dropped in the pit of my stomach. LM had just confirmed both Abe's predictions and the letter the mayor received. "He said that? Fireworks?"

LM nodded. "Yeah, so?"

I shook my head because there was no sense giving him more rumors to spread on the streets. "Is there anything else you can give us? Any detail, no matter how small, that might help us find this guy?"

LM leaned back against Mary's flat bosom. "I might be convinced to call you if I hear something." He raised his little left hand and brushed his thumb across the tops of his fingers.

"You fucking got to be kidding me," Morales said. "If you'd called us earlier we could have arrested the asshole and saved that ugly mug of yours. But now you want us to pay?"

LM grimaced. "I might be an asshole, but I ain't your bitch, Macho. Pay up."

I nodded at him. He jerked his wallet from his back pocket and threw a twenty at them. The wind caught the bill and whooshed it up so it landed on Mary's large noggin. Despite her catatonic look, her hand had no trouble snatching the bill and stashing it quick as lightning.

Little Man leaned back with an elbow on Mary's bosom. "It's been nice doing business with you."

Morales looked like he wanted to strangle the homunculus, but I tugged his sleeve. "Let's go."

Little Man pursed his split lip and blew Morales a kiss. "Bye-bye, Macho."

Chapter Fourteen

October 22
First Quarter

"All right, people," Gardner said, "if you got ideas about how to find this asshole, I want to hear them."

We were gathered in the old boxing ring back at the gym. Gardner stood next to a large whiteboard pasted with the picture of Dionysus we'd gotten from the mayor and a list of facts we knew about him—not many—as well as information I'd gotten from Abe—very little—and facts about the crime scene at Aphrodite's temple—slightly more, but not nearly enough to inspire confidence that we'd get this guy.

Even though Mez and Shadi hadn't had the pleasure of getting their asses chewed out by the city's mayor, they'd been fully briefed on the shit show. The instant we'd left the mayor's office, Gardner had called Shadi in off patrol so she could help.

But like the rest of us, she sat silent, totally stumped about how to track down a madman armed with a rape potion.

"Eldritch is working the robbery now, right?" Morales said.

Gardner nodded. "He's sending some of his guys over to go over the crime scene in case we missed anything," she said, her tone dripping with rancor.

Mez's posture stiffened with pride. "They won't find shit."

"Of course not," Gardner said. "Not our issue anymore. Our goal is to track down the potions."

Morales leaned forward, resting his elbows on his knees. "How about the other covens?"

She tilted her head. "What do you mean?"

He shrugged. "Maybe they've been robbed, too, but aren't too eager to get a visit from the BPD."

"It's possible," I said. "Little Man said he gave Dionysus a list of all the top wizes in the city."

Gardner crossed her arms and thought it over. "I'm pretty sure we don't have the manpower to interview every wizard in the Cauldron."

"If Dionysus has the balls to go after Aphrodite Johnson, he's not going to waste his time with two-bit sorcerers selling snake oil on the corner," I said. "He'll go after the other big dogs."

"Volos," she said.

I paused before nodding. The thought of having to interview John made my skin feel too tight. After our talk at my party I wasn't too eager to spend time with him anytime soon. Especially when it was because I needed his help breaking another case. "Harry Bane, too," I said, trying to redirect focus. "He'd be an excellent target for a Raven since he only just took over his daddy's coven."

Hieronymus Bane had turned on his own father to escape jail time in the Gray Wolf case. According to my snitches, Harry was now running the Sanguinarian Coven out of a junkyard.

Gardner nodded. "Wouldn't be a bad idea to check in with him anyway with Ramses's trial coming up soon."

"We'll go talk to Harry, then," I said quickly.

Morales blinked, as if he'd been expecting me to volunteer to talk to Volos instead. I shrugged.

Luckily, Gardner didn't find anything weird about me asking for Harry duty over Volos. "Shadi, you go have a chat with Volos. Even if he hasn't been targeted, he might have heard something on Dionysus that might help."

"Fine by me," she said. "Interviewing a suit like Volos in his sweet office beats chasing stank assholes down by the river."

"Can I get that embroidered on a pillow?" Morales asked.

"Embroider this." Chuckling, she flipped him the double birds.

"Okay, you guys have a place to start. Mez, what's your next move?"

The wizard rose and stretched his arms over his head. "I'm going to call Val over at BPD and see if she'll share what she found on the letter the mayor received from Dionysus."

Val was my friend in CSI at the precinct. Despite Mez's constant flirting with her, she sometimes helped us on the down low when we needed information Eldritch wouldn't want us to get.

"And if she refuses?" I asked.

Mez smiled at me like he was humoring me. "Then I'll start working on a new super-strength protection amulet just in case we don't find this asshole in time."

Gardner's jaw tightened. "And I'm going to call in some favors to see if I can get us access to the mental hospital databases. If we can figure out who this guy is, we might stand a chance of catching him before he can make good on his threats." She looked around the room, meeting each of our gazes directly. "I don't care what games Eldritch is playing, we're going to do our jobs and protect the people of this city."

◆ ◆ ◆

You could smell the junkyard long before you saw it. Squatting on the edge of Lake Erie in an old industrial area that used to be full of steel factories, Harry Bane's new headquarters made Rooster's Gym look like the Four Seasons.

"Least he's aboveground now," Morales said with unusual optimism. I nodded absently and kept my eyes on the eight-foot-tall chain-link-and-barbed-wire fence that surrounded the place. Before Harry's dad, Ramses, was arrested for trying to frame John Volos with his crimes, the Sanguinarian Coven was run out of the abandoned subway tunnels that ran under the Cauldron. But not long after Ramses was arrested—thanks to Harry turning state's evidence on his father—the city condemned the tunnels and filled all the entrances with concrete. Luckily for Harry, before his dad's arrest Ramses had diversified the family's crime empire to include waste management.

Morales steered the SUV to the ancient call box at the front gate. When he punched the black button, the machine crackled with static and high-pitched electronic sounds. Finally, it cleared enough for a voice to come through. "The fuck you want?"

"Need to speak to Hieronymus."

"He's indisposed."

"Tell him it's Morales and Prospero."

Silence. We waited a good thirty seconds.

Morales glanced at me. "How long you think he's gonna make us wait?"

"Long enough."

Morales scooted down in his seat and closed his eyes. "Good, I could use a nap."

It took another two minutes before the intercom buzzed again. "You got a warrant?"

Morales opened his eyes and took his time leaning back out the window. "Don't need one. We're here as a public service."

The speaker made another squawk and then the first voice was replaced by Harry's more familiar one. "Bullshit. You're here to plant some evidence like you did last time."

I rolled my eyes and leaned across Morales. "Open the gate, Harry, or I'll have my friend at the waste management department come down here for a surprise inspection."

Ten seconds later the gate screeched open on automatic rollers. Morales laughed. "You even got a friend at waste management, Prospero?"

"Of course not."

He flashed those white teeth. "You're a trip, Cupcake."

The car started rolling toward the opening, slowly just in case Harry decided he was clever enough to ambush us. I had a hand on my pistol the entire time. Once we cleared the gate, we were surrounded by a mountain range made out of rusted metal. A road wound through hills of discarded diapers and empty milk cartons and aluminum cans. Soon we came upon a double-wide that served as the yard's office. Two mangy-looking rottweilers were chained up out front. When we got out, one of the dogs farted, but neither lifted their chins off their paws.

The door to the trailer burst open. Harry emerged with a sneer. His long white hair flowed in the shit-stench breeze coming off his trash kingdom. His pale coloring combined with the black ankh tattooed on his forehead made him look sinister. However, the effect was ruined when his watery blue eyes squinted at the sun. He snapped his fingers at a flunky just inside the trailer and a second later a pair of dark sunglasses appeared in his hand. He stowed the Ray Charles numbers on his face before swaggering down the steps.

The black suit and leather boots he wore probably cost more than my car, but the dust from the junkyard made him look like a dirty crow instead of the grand wizard of a blood coven. The only affectations that actually worked in the entire ensemble were the single red rose on his lapel, which symbolized the sacred blood of his coven, and the walking stick he swung forward with each step. The top of the cane had a crystal skull on it with ruby eyes. I hated to admit it, but it was pretty badass, even when wielded by an utter douche like Harry Bane.

As he came forward, two equally pale assholes emerged from the trailer with suspicious bulges under their shirts. One picked at his few teeth and plentiful gums with a switchblade, while his partner cracked each of his knuckles like a walnut.

"Love what you've done with the place," Morales called.

Harry's narrow face pinched like an anus. "You've got five minutes to state your business."

"Won't take that long," I said. "You heard what happened to Aphrodite Johnson?"

Harry's smile was genuine. "Best news I got all month."

I tipped my head. "Back in the day one coven leader got hit and all the wizes would circle the wagons."

He spit on the ground. "Case you haven't noticed the He-bitch is the last of the old guard still in the game. This a new era, where the strongest wiz wins."

Morales raised a brow. "Wait, just so we're clear, by 'strongest' you're referring to yourself?"

Two white brows pulled together like angry caterpillars. "Of course."

"I can see how the capable assistance of Tweedledee and Tweedledum would convince you of that."

The guy with the blade sucked loudly at his front teeth.

Harry's frown was back. That was always the worst thing about him. Mean, I could handle, but mean and stupid was a lethal combination. "Anyway," I said. As much as I enjoyed watching Morales deliver insults that flew over their heads, it was kind of like watching an armed gunman threaten children. "Turns out Aphrodite's break-in wasn't an isolated incident. There's a new Raven on the streets, and we have reason to believe he might target other covens."

Harry's chin came up. "Let the asshole try. He gotta be suicidal to come after the Sangs."

I barely managed not to roll my eyes. Harry was only weeks into his leadership of his daddy's coven, so he made the perfect target for a Raven. Mercenary wizards loved to strike fragmented covens, because they had the weakest infrastructure. My guess was, despite Harry's bravado, he had his hands full of pissing matches among his lieutenants on down the chain as everyone scrambled for position under the new leadership.

"Yeah, yeah," Morales said. "We get it. I'm sure you got lots of new blood potions some Raven would love to steal."

"That's—" Harry caught himself and narrowed his eyes. "That's bullshit, man. You can't entrap me."

"All right," I said. "Look, this Raven goes by the name Dionysus." I pulled out a photocopy of the picture Owens had shared.

"Looks like a fag." He crumpled the image between his pale fingers. "This asshole steps up to me or mine, I'm a put a bullet in his mercenary ass and throw the body on a trash trawler."

I sighed. "Look, tough guy, I'm gonna give you some advice for free on account of you helped us put your daddy in the can—and in exchange we kept you out of it, I might add. You ready?" At the mention of how we'd blackmailed him into turning state's evidence on his father, his cheeks flared red. "Threatening to murder someone in front of cops is bad juju."

"Fuck off, bitch."

"Watch yourself, asshole," Morales said, his voice low and mean.

I shook my head at Morales. "How's your dad doing, anyway?" I asked, going for the jugular in my own way.

Harry's eyes narrowed. "I wouldn't know. They got him locked away someplace safe while he waits for trial." He shrugged. "Not that he'd talk to me anyway."

"Maybe once he's in Crowley," Morales said, "you can sneak him in some cigarettes and buy back his love."

"I don't give a fuck, man. The old man wouldn't even be in this position if he turned on Abe like I told him."

I froze. From the corner of my eye I saw Morales's muscles flex like he was about to pounce on that information like a dog on a juicy steak. "What's your dad got on Abe?"

Harry snorted. "Shit, man, some cop you are. Everyone knows Abe was the one put Dad up to framing Volos."

If I didn't think quick, Morales's investigative instincts were going to take over and cause a lot of fucking problems for me. "Guess your dad doesn't have enough evidence to frame Abe for the crime or he already would have done it."

"Frame him?" Harry laughed. "Ha!"

"Evidence against Abe would be a get-out-of-jail-free card," I said. "If he had it to use, Ramses would already be out of jail."

I chanced a glance at Morales. He looked less intense, but not exactly convinced, either. Harry just shook his head like we were both naive, and I was content to let him go on thinking that. "Look," I said, "you see Dionysus around or hear anything about his plans, just call me, okay?" I handed him a business card.

"Detective, huh?" He glanced down at it. His lips made a mocking sound. "They let just any bitch be one of those these days, I guess."

"A pleasure talking to you as always, Harry."

"Fuck off." With that he tossed the card in the dirt and walked back toward the trailer.

"Well," Morales said, "that guy's about as useful as a knuckle on a dick."

I shrugged. "Better than dealing with Volos."

We started walking back toward the car. Morales's head was down, a bad sign since it meant he was probably thinking. "You think Abe's getting away with murder on the Gray Wolf case?"

I kept my stride even and my reaction cool so he wouldn't see how much this topic affected me. "I think Abe's gotten away with a lot of murder, both metaphorical and literal. But I know the last thing we need is to chase down hearsay from a blood wizard when we've got a different psycho threatening the city."

He paused, thinking it over. I tried not to look like I was praying he'd let it drop. Finally, he shrugged. "Maybe Harry's right. If Ramses has proof Abe was behind Gray Wolf he would use it to plea-bargain."

I let out a breath. "You're probably right."

He smiled that Morales smile. " 'Course I am, Cupcake."

I smiled back. Not because I thought he was right, but because I was happy to let him go on believing I was wrong.

Chapter Fifteen

That night Danny and I went to visit Pen. She'd been discharged from the hospital the day before. Baba had been hanging with her during the day, and her neighbor Lavern took night duty. I'd been so busy chasing down foul-mouthed homunculi and douchebag albinos that I'd not spent any quality time with her since the accident. To make up for that, I'd picked up a couple of containers of soup from Pen's favorite Vietnamese place in downtown Babylon.

"Do we have to stay long?" Danny asked on our way to the building.

After spending part of my day interviewing the brat prince of the blood coven and then ten minutes hunting down a parking spot outside Pen's building, I was in no mood for teenager drama. "We'll stay as long as we need to stay. Your video games can wait."

His eyes rolled so hard I worried he might pull something. "I have some posters to make for tomorrow's DUDE meeting."

"Oh," I said, "we're just staying for supper. Should have plenty of time after."

Baba answered the door. That night she wore a black house-coat with purple cats embroidered along the hem. She even had a broom in her hand to complete the domestic witch look. "Come in, come in," she said, waving us inside. "What took you so long? I'd punch a priest for a pizza right now."

I raised the bag. "How about some pho instead?"

She sniffed at the brown paper and scowled. "What she needs is a bowl of my mama's *homemade* chicken soup."

"This will have to do until you can kill a chicken on the full moon, Baba." I was too damned tired to bother trying to disguise the sarcasm from my tone.

She took the bag by the corner and started for the kitchen. "Pen's in the living room."

I shed my coat and turned left to the tiny den. The instant I walked into the room, I got a noseful of lavender's soft purple scent and vetiver's earthy green musk. I looked around until I spotted a small ceramic container of the oils sitting over a tea light on the coffee table. Definitely Baba's handiwork. She was always spouting the virtues of aromatherapy for everything from anxiety to headaches to PMS.

Dismissing the oil diffuser, I focused on the mound of yellow blankets huddled on the denim-covered couch. "Pen?" I whispered, not wanting to disturb her if she was asleep.

The blankets moved and a groan emerged. When her face popped out, I saw that her complexion was gray and dark shadows weighed down her lower lids. "Kate?"

I lowered myself onto the foot of the couch, careful not to jostle her too much. "Hi," I whispered. "How you doing?"

Behind me, Danny was telling Baba about a test he'd had that day. Why hadn't he told me about it on our way over?

Maybe because I was so busy seething about the traffic and the frustrating meeting with Harry Bane. Tuning them out, I leaned forward to help Pen sit up. When she moved, her hand went protectively to the right side of her rib cage. A thick brace cupped her neck, and a bandage wrapped around her sprained wrist. Her right eye wasn't as swollen as it had been the last time I saw her, but the bruises had mellowed into a sickly green-yellow color.

"Owowow," she panted through clenched teeth.

I grimaced in sympathy. "Sorry, honey. Do you need anything?"

She opened her mouth, but behind me Baba rushed in bearing a tray. "Time for her arnica pellets!" The old woman used her hip to nudge me out of the way. Arnica was a common homeopathic pain remedy and a cheaper alternative to aspirin now that big pharmaceutical companies had all focused on magical therapies. "Poor dove," she said to the patient. Pen's eyes were glazed over with pain. "We'll have you fixed up in no time."

I backed up and joined Danny by the coffee table. Together we watched Baba hand the arnica to Pen, who placed the tablets under her tongue to dissolve. While that happened, Baba turned back to ready the tea. A small brown bottle with a dropper lid sat next to the teacup. The old woman carefully measured out three drops of orange liquid into the tea she'd already poured.

"What's that?" I asked.

Baba's eyes shot to me and then away. She turned to hand the tea to Pen and watched to make sure she downed it before answering. "Bergamot and birch bark tea." Her eyes wouldn't quite meet mine.

"And the stuff you added to it?"

Baba sighed deep, like she'd been expecting the question but hoped I'd forget to ask it. "It's tea, Detective, not poison." She glanced over her shoulder. "Why don't you make yourself useful and dish out supper."

Rather than take the bait, I retreated into the kitchen.

" 'It's tea, Detective,' " I echoed mockingly to the stovetop. "My ass." I'd bet my Glock the witch put some sort of Spagyric compound or philtre in that tea.

"Kate?" Danny called from the den.

"What?" I snapped.

"When are we gonna eat?"

When I'd arrived I couldn't wait to eat the delicious beef soup from the Vietnamese restaurant, but now I would have traded my left ovary for four fingers of bourbon.

I blew out a deep breath. I knew I was being overly touchy, but I was having a harder time than usual lately tamping down my annoyance. Opening the cabinet above Pen's sink, I sorted through the bottles until I found what I wanted. Shoved behind the coconut rum and peach liqueur and vanilla vodka for the fruity cocktails Pen preferred was a fifth of Bulleit rye whiskey I'd given her for Christmas the year before in the hopes her taste in hooch would improve.

I broke the seal on the lip and tipped the bottle back to my mouth. The wood smoke and sweet fire flavor hit my tongue. The sliding burn was a baptism of sorts, cleansing stress and fear and guilt from my throat.

Rufus would have called this behavior self-medicating. But shit, if Pen could use suspicious tinctures to deal with her pain, then why couldn't I experience the delicious sorcery of rye whiskey?

"Kate?" Danny called. I heard Baba say in a low tone that she'd check on me.

I shoved the cap on the bottle and stowed it in the oven. By the time the old woman made it into the cramped kitchen, I was unloading soup.

She pursed her lips and cocked her head to the side, as if she was measuring up my mood. "It wasn't any of your dirty magic."

I raised a brow. "Then what was it?"

"Before I tell you, I need you to understand how hard the last few days have been on her."

"What did you do?" I lowered my voice instead of raising it, despite the panic welling in my chest.

"It's the broken ribs," she said, as if I hadn't spoken. "Terrible pain. And the whiplash is causing migraines."

I closed my eyes. "What. Did. You. Give. Her?"

Baba's chin lowered and she looked up at me through her graying lashes. "It's kind of like sun tea." She wouldn't meet my narrowed gaze.

"Sun tea?"

"Calendula, Saint-John's-wort, chamomile, and a few juniper berries."

"And what did you use to brew this sun tea? A chalice? Or a cauldron?"

She made an offended face. "One of my mama's crystal pitchers."

"So you're telling me it wasn't a philtre?"

Her eyes shot to mine. "Maybe? But even if it was a philtre, that's not really magic."

I crossed my arms. "Did you chant over the herbs? Did you let it steep in the sun's rays from dawn to dusk?"

She nodded reluctantly.

"Then it's magic." Mundane magical energy was weak compared with the kind wielded by a trained Adept, sure. Baba's kind of kitchen witchery was powered by intention and wishes. But it was still magic. And to an addict like Pen, it could be a gateway back to the personal hell of dependency.

Anger was a hot fist in my gut. "I can't believe you gave her a fucking potion," I hissed.

"You're always telling me I'm not capable of real magic." Her arms crossed, and that chin came up. "If so, then it wasn't a potion but a simple home remedy."

My eyes narrowed. "You can play word games all you want, but you know damned well that part of what gives magic its power is intention. The sun energy contains incredibly potent magic whether it's gathered by an Adept or a Mundane. You know that."

"That girl's been in real pain. Pain so bad she's not sleeping at night and spends most of her days in tears." Baba's face jutted forward, her eyes glassy with anger.

I sighed. "Regardless, giving a recovering potion addict a philtre is irresponsible."

"I gave a friend relief from her suffering," she corrected. "It's not even addictive magic."

"It's a slippery slope, Baba. One you seem far too eager to slide down."

She reared back. "What's that supposed to mean?"

"Please," I said. "You're always trying to give me your special teas and brews even though I've repeatedly told you I don't want to ingest anything that even smacks of magic."

Her expression morphed into one of offended pride. "So I'm only allowed to help on your terms."

"Yes," I said, my voice rising. I flinched and cast a guilty glance toward the den. "Yes," I repeated in a less shrill tone. "That's the whole point of help, right? If you're going against the person's wishes then it's just interfering."

The instant the words left my mouth, I wanted to snatch them from the air and gobble them back down. But it was too late. Because those hateful words had already crawled inside Baba's ears and planted inside her brain like some of Aphrodite's poisonous plants. Her eyes narrowed and her arthritic hands curled into shaking fists.

I raised my chin as she leaned forward. "You think I don't see what's happening? You think I don't know?"

"I—" I began, but stopped when I realized I had no idea how to answer. How could I when fear was tightening my ribs in a cold grip?

"You're jealous that your boy and your best friend lean on me instead of you."

I gritted my teeth. We were getting off track and I needed to rein it in before we went totally off the rails. My own guilt over falling off the wagon was making me act unreasonably. If I wasn't careful, the old woman would have me spilling my guts out about my own sins.

"It's not that," I said, looking her in the eye to show I was sincere. "And I'm sorry I gave you grief. I know you were trying to help."

She sighed, as if willing to give a couple of inches in this battle of will. "But what if she asks for it? She's in real pain, Kate."

"She'll be in worse pain if she gets hooked on magic again. We have to be strong for her." It was too late for me to take back my own mistakes, but I could make sure Pen never had to deal with the guilt of a relapse.

Her lips pursed as she thought it over. "All right, I'll stick to Mundane pain relief."

"Thanks, Baba. Believe it or not, I really appreciate everything you're doing."

She pulled me in for an uncharacteristic hug. "I know you

163

do, girlie. Just take care of yourself, too." She pulled back with her hands on her shoulders. "I can smell the devil water on you."

I jerked away. "Don't act like you don't have a flask in your bosom, old woman."

Her mouth broke into a wide smile. With one hand, she reached between her pendulous breasts and withdrew a metal flask. "Guilty." She cackled. "You know what I always say, though, right?"

I shook my head. With Baba there was no telling.

"The skeletons in our closet are proof of a well-lived life."

Chapter Sixteen

October 23
First Quarter

The next morning I was talking to Mez about the potions Dionysus had taken from Aphrodite when Shadi popped her head into the lab. "Got a minute?"

I glanced at Mez. "Try running the samples through ACD."

He shrugged. "Worth a try."

ACD was the Arcane Crimes Database. Sometimes you could find a potion that was used in more than one crime. If Dionysus had sold Aphrodite's formula to a wiz in another town, we might get a hit. Or not. Either way, it was worth investigating with every tool at our disposal.

Leaving him to that, I went to join Shadi. "What's up?"

She nodded toward her desk on the other side of the boxing ring. "Got that research you asked me to look up."

"Cool. But first, how did your meeting with Volos go?"

She shook her head. "It didn't. He was out of town. Some big meeting in Canada."

I frowned. "Did his secretary say when he'd be back?"

"Few days. I left my card and asked her to have him give me a call."

"He won't," I said.

"Guess I'll just have to keep calling until I get him, then." She had a determined look in her eye that reminded me of a bulldog who'd spotted a juicy bone.

I nodded because that's exactly how I would have handled it, too. "Good. All right." I leaned a hip on the desk. "What you got on Dionysus?"

She popped open a folder on the top of the table she used as a desk. "There's tons of myths about the god, so I'll focus on the basics. He was the god of wine, parties, and ecstasy. He had these half-goat dudes who were his followers, called satyrs, and a cult of sex freak women, called the Maenads, worshipped him."

Something niggled at my brain. "Satyrs," I said. "Huh."

"What?"

"Maybe nothing, but there was a guy dressed like a satyr at the Halloween Festival."

"Did he do anything unusual?"

I tilted my head. "You mean other than dress like a half-goat?" I laughed. I tried to think back to the moment I'd seen him. "He just kind of danced around and played a flute. And"—I stopped myself from thinking to the moment when he blew me the kiss—"he flirted with me."

"Sounds like the god Dionysus, all right. He basically spent his time drinking and fucking."

"So he was basically every man's hero?" Morales called from his desk nearby where he was going over recent arrest reports.

166

Ignoring him, I nudged Shadi. "Hey, do you still have that picture of Dionysus the mayor gave us?" She shuffled through a folder and handed it over. Staring down at the image, I realized with a start that if Dionysus had on a mask he'd look a hell of a lot like the satyr from the square.

And then there were the eyes. In the mayor's picture they were heavy-lidded and issuing a challenge. When I'd seen him in the square I remembered a glint of something off in the two eyes looking at me from behind the mask. "Shit, Morales," I breathed, "it was totally him." I looked up, my eyes wide and my stomach tight. "He was right there in front of me."

Shadi's eyes widened and she took the image from me. Morales's chair creaked. Two seconds later he was taking the picture from Shadi. "Well fuck me," he said, "I thought this asshole looked familiar when the mayor showed it to us, but I figured I was just remembering some perp I'd arrested." He glanced up. Whatever he saw in my face made his expression soften. "Whatever you're thinking, stop it. We both let him go."

I knew he was right. Unlike the gypsy who'd taunted me that day, I didn't claim to have the gift of prophecy. But damned if it wouldn't have been a really fucking handy skill. "Regardless, it's clear we need to revisit everything that happened that day—" I froze, the events of the rest of the day coming back to me. I grabbed Shadi's folder. "The god of wine," I whispered. "Morales, what was it that leprechaun prick said right before we took him to the precinct?"

My partner looked up, his eyes narrowing as he tried to recall. "Something about the devil fucking your neck?"

"What?" Shadi asked.

I waved a hand and grimaced. "No, after that. He warned us about the Blue Moon, right?"

"So?" he said.

"So, don't you find it odd that two minutes after we saw Dionysus in the square, a fucking leprechaun hexes two cops and then starts spouting bullshit about the Blue Moon?"

"Not especially." He crossed his arms. "No offense, Cupcake, but I think you're reaching. The moons are making people do all sorts of crazy bullshit right now."

"Hold up," I said, ignoring his doubt. "Shit, Morales, that tattoo."

Something shifted in my head, like the tumblers of a lock clicking into place before the safe opened to reveal its secrets. My eyes met his and I could see the memory spring up behind his eyes, too, and then quickly shutter.

"*In Vino* Fucking *Veritas*," I said.

"Someone fill me in," Shadi said.

I turned to her. "The leprechaun we arrested at the festival had a tattoo that translated to 'In wine, the truth.' And the potion he hexed those cops and people with made them dance around and hump everything in sight."

"You think the leprechaun worked for Dionysus," she said, frowning like she was considering it. However, Morales's expression was closed as tight as a bank vault.

"Come on, Morales. It's worth a trip to county to talk to the little shit at least."

His nostrils flared as he expelled a rush of air. "Even if you're right, he's not going to tell us crap."

I raised my brows in challenge. "He's a potion freak who thinks he's a leprechaun, and he's been locked up in county for almost a week. I'm thinking he'll jump at the chance for a plea bargain in exchange for information on Dionysus."

"He's facing assault with an Arcane weapon on two cops, Kate. The DA will never go for it."

"He doesn't have to know that. He just has to think it's

possible." I tugged at his shirtsleeve. "C'mon. It's the best lead we've had in days."

His lips screwed up into a martyred grimace. "I'll do it if you buy me a burger on the way."

I awarded him with a wide, bright smile, the kind I reserved for people who were smart enough to let me have my way. "Deal. I'll even throw in a shake to sweeten your disposition."

Shadi shook her head at us. "You two are a trip."

"What's that supposed to mean?" Morales asked.

"Oh, nothing." She chuckled like she was laughing at a private joke. "Enjoy your interrogation."

◆ ◆ ◆

Two hours later Morales had a full belly, but his attitude hadn't improved much. We'd been sitting in the interview room for thirty minutes already waiting for Sean O'Lachlan to grace us with his presence.

Morales slouched in the metal chair beside me. Clearly he'd decided to play "ambivalent cop," which left me to play both good and bad. He'd made no secret of his doubts about getting intel from the leprechaun. But I figured that was just his pride talking, seeing how O'Lachlan had gotten such a rise out of him last time. Honestly, I was fine taking lead on this one. Especially since of the two of us, the leprechaun seemed to favor me, which meant I was the more likely one to get intel from him.

The door cracked and a detention officer ushered our friend inside the cramped interview room. I didn't react to the way the guy looked, but I was cringing on the inside. The green suit was gone and replaced with a bright orange jumpsuit. The legs and sleeves were too long for his short legs and arms, so he'd had to roll them up a couple of times. But it wasn't his ill-fitting uniform that grabbed my attention when he walked in. It was his face. Or what was left of it, anyway.

Judging from the way his right eye swelled and the large bruise on his jaw, his time inside hadn't exactly been relaxing. Not surprising since the cells at county tended to be less civilized than some zoo pens I'd seen. Weakness of any kind was sniffed out, targeted, and exploited with vigor. "Someone take exception to your charms, Leprechaun Man?"

He launched up a middle finger to let me know what he thought of my sense of humor. "The fuck you want?"

"Sit down." I nodded to the uni to "help" our friend comply. Once he was seated, I waved the officer off to go wait outside.

O'Lachlan watched the guy leave with a placid expression. Despite the bruises and abrasions, he had the scent of a guy who prided himself on not being a snitch. Prisons were full of these assholes. Criminals don't follow society's moral codes, but that doesn't mean they have no code of conduct at all. Rule number one was no snitching, which made my job a pain in the ass sometimes. Trick was you had to find some sort of currency to use against them. Or, failing that, you had to locate their weakness and apply the screws until they broke. That part could be really fun.

He propped his cuffed hands on the tabletop. "So?"

I glanced at Morales, who raised his brows in challenge. Looked like I was the only one in the room convinced I could break this guy. "We have a few follow-up questions for you."

He sighed. "Yes, you're both assholes. Happy?"

I grimaced at him. Sometimes it really was too bad police brutality was frowned upon. But the worst thing I could do at that point was show the guy he was getting under my skin. I tipped my head toward his hand. "What's that tattoo mean?"

He frowned and pulled his hands off the table into his lap. "Nuthin'."

"Did you know there's a god of wine?" I asked casually. "His name is Dionysus."

"I don't know nuthin' about myths and shit." His eyes narrowed. "I just happen to enjoy a fine box of rosé every now and then."

"I'm sure by now you've heard there's a new Raven in the Cauldron. Calls himself Dionysus."

"Everybody hears things." He shrugged. "Don't make 'em true."

"This thing is true, I assure you."

"So?" His eyes met mine in that practiced stare that criminals perfect because they think looking you in the eye will prove they aren't lying.

"So if you know anything about this Dionysus, now's the time to mention it."

"Oh yeah? Why's that?"

"Because if you are connected to him, you will be charged with being an accessory after we find him."

The guy snorted. "You won't find him."

I watched him without speaking for a full ten seconds before his expression registered that he'd realized what he'd done. He shifted in his seat. "I mean—if this guy's a Raven he's probably a bad motherfucker, am I right? 'Specially if he's crazy and shit."

"We've already tied him to thefts from one of the most powerful wizards in the Cauldron. If we don't find him first, Aphrodite will," I said. "Do you think the Hierophant will hesitate to track down his associates?"

His eyes flared a little. "I didn't have nuthin' to do with those thefts."

"Do you honestly think Aphrodite will believe you when she catches you?"

His face went white as spoiled milk, and a slight tremor shook his hands. "I-I—she can't get me in here."

"These prison walls might as well be vapor as far as the Hierophant is concerned," Morales said. I smiled inwardly at how naturally he slipped into his normal role despite his earlier protests. A cop's instinct to get answers is pretty powerful. "Or maybe we'll just cut you loose and let it slip to Aphrodite you're out."

O'Lachlan swallowed hard. "I don't know nuthin' about the covens getting robbed."

"But you do know Dionysus, correct?"

He looked down at his hands and nodded. "He paid me to create some chaos at the festival, is all."

"How did he approach you?"

"I work at a club over on Exposition—the Cock and Bull?"

My eyebrows shot up. "The gay dance club?"

"I'm a go-go dancer there," he said, nodding. "Anyway, he comes up to me after my shift and says he's got a proposition for me. I tried to tell him I didn't turn tricks anymore, but he said it wasn't like that. He bought me a drink and told me he'd pay me five hundred bucks if I wore a costume and raised a little hell at the Halloween Festival. Then he gave me a sample of this potion that made me feel seven feet tall and bulletproof. Said if I did what he asked, he'd give me all I wanted."

Morales and I exchanged a look. "What does he look like?"

"He was wearing a hat and sunglasses, so I didn't see his face real well, except he has a beard and there were tattoos on his hands."

"What kind of tattoos?"

"Tarot cards and shit. And some of them pinup girls with the big ol' titties."

"Did you see him again?"

"Couple other times. He came back to club once more. Then he had me meet him at an apartment to give me the potion I used the other day."

I perked up. "Where? Do you remember the address?"

Sean sighed. "Yeah, but I doubt he's there anymore. He said he had to keep moving so the cops didn't catch him."

"We'd still like to check it out."

He rattled off an address in the shittiest area of the Cauldron. "Look, I don't know what all he's into, but he didn't strike me as a bad guy. He just wants to spread his message."

Morales leaned forward. "What message?"

Sean adjusted his ass in the chair, which made his short legs swing like tiny pendulums in the air. "He thinks society is an artificial construct designed to keep humans enslaved. The masks we wear are like handcuffs. We pretend we're normal but deep down we're all freaks. He just wants people to start being real."

Morales snorted. "How does using dirty magic make people more real? The whole point of potions is to escape reality."

Sean crossed his arms. "You don't get it. Look at you." He scraped a scornful gaze over Morales. "I bet you've never had a problem fitting in, have you? You play the game so well you've convinced yourself it doesn't even exist." He leaned forward and pointed a stubby finger at my partner. "But guess what? Dionysus knows you have secrets just like everyone else. You're just better at hiding them."

I rolled my eyes and glanced at Morales, expecting him to laugh at the asshole. Instead his fists curled up on the tabletop. In a low, mean voice, my partner leaned in and said, "The only thing I'm hiding is my weapon, but that could be changed."

I shot him a warning look. I rarely saw him ruffled, but for some reason this guy had managed it twice.

Sean laughed. "Too close to home, huh? Don't worry. By the time Dionysus is done with this city, all your secrets will be exposed like raw nerves."

I rose from my chair and went to pound on the door before the asshole could taunt Morales into doing something stupid. "We're done here. If you think of anything else that could help us find Dionysus, get in touch."

"Tick-tock, Detective." Sean leaned back and crossed his arms across his chest. "Your time's running out."

"We got more than a week until the Blue Moon. No sweat."

He smiled. "Your first mistake was assuming he'd wait until the full moon. The stunt he paid me to pull at the festival was just the beginning of his plans."

The uniform came in to take the guy away. I held up a hand. "Hold on. What else do you know?"

O'Lachlan shook his head. "I know he's too smart to trust me with information you could blackmail out of me before he wants you to know it." The guard led him to the door, but just before he walked through he paused and looked back with a smile. "If I were you, I'd get as far from the city as I could before Halloween. Because the devil's coming to settle accounts with the sinners of Babylon."

Chapter Seventeen

October 24
First Quarter

Morales's biceps bulged. He hesitated at the top of the arc. Then... *boom*! Wood shards exploded everywhere. A chorus of shouts. "MEA!"

Guns poised, we crashed into the small space like a force of nature. What probably looked like chaos was actually a carefully orchestrated maneuver. We each had a job to do. Morales was the ram man, and Shadi and I were the second wave, pushing forward through the apartment to clear rooms. Normally we would have had more backup go with us on a raid, but Gardner hadn't been too eager to ask Eldritch for favors.

After the meeting with O'Lachlan, we'd put together the raid as quickly as possible. Gardner handled calling US Attorney Stone about securing a warrant for Dionysus's place. The mayor's dictate that Dionysus was enemy number one in Babylon greased the wheels, but it still took a few hours to get everything in place. We opted for an early morning raid because we were more likely to catch Dionysus at home at the butt crack of dawn than during prime night hours. We were at the door bright and early with a signed warrant and enough weaponry to take down an entire coven of junkie wizards.

Off the front door was a long, narrow hallway. I hated hallways because it meant there were usually lots of doors for perps to jump out of, like that FireArms Training Simulator at the academy. Any second a masked gunman or a five-year-old could pop out of those doors and I'd have to make a hair-trigger decision whether they lived or died.

The first door revealed a small bedroom that contained no furniture. The walls, however, had plenty going on. Every inch of wall space was covered in a pornographic collage. Interspersed among the T&A display were headlines about the incident in Pioneer Square, as well as pictures of Mayor Owens, John Volos, Aphrodite Johnson, Harry Bane, and several members of the city council.

While Shadi got my back at the door, I looked in the closet. There I found overturned boxes with nudie magazines, dildos, and lots of electronic devices I couldn't immediately identify. What I didn't find was Dionysus. "Clear!" I shouted.

She rolled out the door to move on to the next room. I followed, gripping my gun tighter. With each space we cleared, the chances of finding our guy in the next room rose.

The second bedroom was a mess. The mattress was overturned and the stuffing spilled out like entrails. The bedside table held an overflowing ashtray and empty wine bottles. The drawer hung out from the front and its contents were piled on the floor. The closet here held the satyr costume I'd seen

Dionysus wearing at the festival, plus a few boxes of ammo and empty potion ampoules.

Morales joined us when he moved back into the hall. While we advanced toward the living room at the back of the hall, my brain buzzed. Keeping an eye out for attackers, in my head I was cataloging the scene for clues about what we might find farther in.

Up ahead, the living room and kitchen area were accessed through an archway. Light from two windows on the far wall sparked off dust motes. The couch's cushions were askew, like someone had wrestled on them—or spent a restless night sleeping there. To the left a breakfast bar separated the living room from the small galley-sized kitchen. Every cabinet in the place was open, and all the contents lay on the linoleum. An overturned distilling apparatus dominated the counters below. It wasn't a professional setup by a long shot, but a quick glance told me this guy knew his way around a cook.

"Clear!" Morales called. He lowered his weapon a fraction and cursed. "We missed him."

I sighed and used the back of my hand to wipe the sweat off my brow. "Maybe O'Lachlan was telling the truth about Dionysus moving out?"

Morales shook his head and executed a fuck-if-I-know shrug. He spoke into his vest mike. "Mez! We need you up here to sweep for potions!"

"Ten-four," came the reply.

We wanted Mez to sweep before we touched anything because sometimes wizards booby-trapped their homes with potions to incapacitate police in case they got raided. The kitchens and bathrooms were usually especially vulnerable to these booby traps because wizards liked to protect their cooking areas. Given what we'd seen so far, Dionysus seemed the type.

Shadi let her assault rifle slide down to hang from the strap from her shoulder. "Anyone else thinking this place is a little too messy?"

Morales crossed his arms and shrugged. "The guy's a slob."

She shook her head with a frown. "Nah, you didn't see the bedroom. Mattress was cut open."

I paused and looked around the space with new eyes. Now that she mentioned it, I realized the couch cushions weren't just sloppy, but also could have been hastily thrown back on. Walking toward the furniture, I used a gloved hand to lift one of the pillows. "I'll be damned."

"What?" Morales snapped.

I held up the pillow with one hand and pointed to what I'd found with the other. "It's been cut open, too."

He and Shadi came to take a closer look. "Someone's been looking for something," she said.

I dropped the pillow and looked around again. This time I noticed a gateleg table sitting beneath the bank of windows. Moving closer, I realized there was a slip of paper and a small bunch of flowers lying in the sun.

"Guys," I said. I didn't touch the paper, but the words written on it were clear: *Ravens who fly too close to the sun always get burned.*

"Looks like we weren't the first ones to find this place," Shadi said.

"Any idea what the plant is?" Morales asked me.

The plant beside the message had little starburst clusters of white flowers. I didn't recognize the species, but I was willing to bet six months' pay I knew which garden it had come from.

"No, but I bet Mez will know."

Shadi crossed her arms and leaned against the windowsill. "So Aphrodite found the address, searched the place, and then left a message for our boy in case he comes back."

I nodded. "Looks like. But O'Lachlan claimed Dionysus said he planned to vacate this place more than a week ago."

"What I want to know is why would this asshole risk incurring the wrath of Aphrodite Johnson if he's a wiz himself?" Shadi asked.

"Lots of reasons," I said. "Maybe he didn't have the scratch to buy the materials himself. Or maybe he's not very good. Or—"

"Or he just enjoys fucking people over," Morales said impatiently.

I frowned at him. He'd had a bug up his ass for a couple of days. Initially I figured he'd just been stressed about the case and jacked up on adrenaline for the raid, but now that the worst of the danger was over, he should be back to joking like he always did. But as it stood he looked like he was spoiling for a fistfight. "What's your problem?"

He paused and turned the full force of his scowl on me. Maybe that shit would make a lesser person back down, but I'd seen Morales in all sorts of moods and this one didn't intimidate me more than any of the others. "Shit, I don't know, Prospero. We've got a rogue wizard stirring up a shitload of trouble with a fucking Blue Moon bearing down on our asses like a loaded gun. Sorry I'm not more chipper." His tone dripped with venomous sarcasm I'd never heard from him before. I tilted my head.

"Morales?"

"What?" he snapped.

"What sign are you?"

He looked like he was worried I was a few grams shy of a kilo. "Why?" His eyes narrowed.

"Just humor me, jackass."

"Taurus," he grunted.

I nodded. "Oh. I get it now."

He crossed his arms. "What the fuck does that mean?"

"The Blue Moon is also in Taurus, which means you'll be feeling its effects especially strongly." I shrugged. "Which is why you've suddenly developed an intense case of PMS."

He gritted his teeth so hard that I swear I heard them grinding all the way across the room. "Shut the fuck up, Prospero."

I raised both brows at Shadi. Her corresponding sour expression told me she didn't appreciate me egging him on. I sent her one back that told her to lighten the fuck up.

Before I could continue to give either of them shit, Mez came busting into the room. His dreadlocks were alternating strands of red and black that day, but his normally composed look was disheveled as he lugged his potion kit into the living room.

"On my way in, I checked the bathroom. Didn't find any signs he cooked in there but he's definitely working on an impressive mold colony." The wiz made a pucker of distaste. As he passed, I caught the telltale cucumber-melon scent of his favorite hand sanitizer. In addition to being a fastidious dresser, Mez was a committed germaphobe. I once saw him go through an entire bottle of that antibacterial stuff in a day, and that was when he was working in his own lab.

"Hey, Mez," I said, waving him over to the table. When I pointed to the flowers, I asked, "Look familiar?"

He set down his leather doctor's bag and leaned over the table for a better look. "Hmm. White snakeroot, I think. Nasty."

"What's it do?" Morales asked.

"Vomiting, tremors, delirium," he said, as if reciting days of the week. "Used to grow in pastures. Cows would eat it and then anyone who drank the milk or ate the meat would fall sick. Back in the day, entire towns died from milk sickness. Killed Abe Lincoln's mom."

I frowned. "Sounds like Aphrodite's work for sure."

Mez raised his brows and I realized he hadn't been caught up to speed on our new theory. I quickly told him that we thought Aphrodite had tossed the place.

"Hmm," he said, approaching the kitchen. "She would have been looking for her potions. But we need to figure out what he's planning to do to the city. And judging from the rig in the kitchen, I'm guessing he wasn't trying his hand at beer making." He made some waving motions for the three of us to back away from the kitchen so the master could do his work. He set his large tackle box on the counter and opened the lid. He took his time placing rubber gloves on his hands while he surveyed the contents for the supplies he needed. I'd never watched Mez clear a scene before, so I moved forward to get a better look, but far enough back that he wouldn't feel I was invading his space.

He removed a small wooden box. From where I stood I couldn't identify the type of wood but I did catch some glyphs painted on the top and sides. He used a small key from around his neck to open it.

Unable to curb my curiosity. "What's that?"

He smiled, keeping his eyes on the item in the box. "A little something I cooked up to help detect magic." With his fingertips, he lifted a small round object from the box. He held it up for us to see. A glass orb with a spindle through its center hung from a copper frame. It looked more like an antique pendant for a necklace than an Arcane investigative tool.

"What's it do?" Shadi asked, her tone suspicious.

"Watch and see." Mez smiled like he had a secret and raised the amulet over the distilling pot. Almost immediately the orb glowed red and spun rapidly on its axis.

Morales, who'd apparently forgotten he was being a prick that day, moved forward and emitted a low whistle. "Damn. That's awesome."

"Oh stop," Mez said with a grin that encouraged us to keep going.

"Will it pick up magic on anything?" I asked.

He glanced over and nodded. "For the most part, there are some variables that might throw it off, like a lot of salt in the vicinity or if there's some other particularly powerful magical energy."

"Like the full moon?" Shadi asked.

He shook his head. "Like a potion-powered machine or something." Moving toward the opposite side, he waved the detector over the stove and the microwave. The amulet remained quiet until he waved it in front of the oven. Then it started spinning like it was going to fly right out of Mez's hands and glowed redder than the devil's ass.

The wizard whistled low. "Everyone stand back."

He didn't have to tell us twice. Shadi, Morales, and I retreated toward the doorway. Mez shot us a disgusted look.

"No offense, man," Shadi said, "but if there's a potion trap in there I'd rather you get hexed than me."

She had a point. As a powerful wizard, Mez had the best chance of surviving a magical attack. I was second in line, but since I didn't actively practice the craft, my ability to equalize magical energy was limited.

"Okay," Mez said with a sigh, "here goes nothing."

I pulled my emergency canister of saline from my raid rig just in case we needed to douse him.

Mez ducked down, hidden behind the breakfast bar. The oven's hinges emitted a loud squeak. I held my breath and listened hard.

"Huh." The wiz's voice was muffled.

"Was that a good huh or a bad one?" Morales demanded.

"Well, there's a bomb, so...bad, I guess."

I started, unsure whether to run toward Mez or the door.

"Mez," Morales said in a too-calm voice, "should we be running?"

"Nah." His head popped up from behind the counter. "It's not live."

"How can you tell?" asked Shadi.

"There's a digital timer on the front that doesn't have any power and, well, it hasn't gone off yet."

Morales glanced at Shadi. "Call BPD and have them send their bomb squad."

"Hold on," I said, "BPD doesn't have a bomb squad. You'll have to call it in to the tactical wizardry unit at the sheriff's office."

He nodded at Shadi. "While she does that, I'll call Gardner. Kate—"

"Uh, guys?" Mez was frowning down at the oven. "I think we need to get out of here now."

When a wizard with knowledge of potion bombs tells you to go, you don't question it. The four of us ran out of the apartment. As we did, Mez, shouted, "The magic detector must have set off the timer. We have five minutes."

Among the four of us, we were able to knock on the doors of the other three units in the building. I pulled a woman who looked to be about Baba's age out of her place, and Morales carried a three-year-old and hustled his worried mom ahead of him. By the time we got outside, Shadi was already there with the apartment's super, a middle-aged woman with a cigarette hanging out of her mouth. Mez ran out last, his leather bag in one arm and the other around a man whose pale blue irises, unwashed hair, and arm and neck lesions indicated he was several days into a bender.

We guided everyone to an empty lot across the street from

the apartment building. Morales was already on the phone with Gardner. Shadi was on hers, too, trying to get in touch with the county tac wizes. I glanced at my watch. The entire evacuation had taken less than four minutes.

Luckily, the apartment building sat at the end of a dead-end street and the building next to it was abandoned, so there weren't any bystanders to worry about.

"Gardner's on her way," Morales said. The kid was clinging to his mom and crying. The piercing wails ramped up the tension of waiting for time to tick down. I glanced at my watch again. Fifteen seconds left, give or take.

"Everyone back up some more," I said.

Our raid gear was designed with salt slabs built into the antiballistic vests. If the explosion was large, we'd be safer than the others. The four of us gathered in a circle around the residents to form a shield. My back was to the building. I lowered my head and held my breath to brace for the explosion.

A loud pop sounded. Breaking glass. And then the whirring siren of a smoke alarm.

Frowning, I looked over my shoulder. Green smoke rolled out of the three broken windows of the apartment we'd vacated. I exhaled my breath and lowered my arms. "Well, that was anticlimactic."

BOOM! A wave of heat and energy slammed into me. My body was tossed forward by the concussion, slamming me into the potion freak Mez had pulled out of the building. We fell forward in a heap.

My ears weren't working. They hurt and there was a buzzing that sounded like it was coming through several thick layers of wool. The back of my neck stung and my forehead ached where it had slammed into the guy's chin.

Groaning—I couldn't hear it, but the pain in my chest was

pretty obvious—I turned my head. Shadi lay a few feet away, the mother and child under her. The kid was squirming. The mom was not.

Rough hands on my back, turning me over. Morales's face monopolized my vision. He had a gash on his forehead and blood on his hands. His lips were moving. I think he was saying my name, but he kept shaking me so I couldn't tell for sure.

He pulled back to shout something to his right. When he moved back, it expanded my field of vision to reveal a wall of fire behind him. Those flames made something in my body flip like a switch. I reared up with a gasp. The movement made me dizzy, but it was suddenly crucial that I stand up and move. Morales grabbed my arm and helped me rise. I leaned into him for a second while I regained my equilibrium. My eyes wanted to close so I could take a nap against his chest.

Sound rushed back with a vengeance. A sudden onslaught of roaring sirens and shouts of firemen and the whimpering child made me wish for the silence's sweet relief.

"Look at me," Morales said, lifting my chin. I blinked because the concern on his face felt too intimate. "How you doing, Cupcake?"

I opened my mouth to say I was fine. But I knew it was a lie. Another lie in a string of half-truths and white fibs and outright falsehoods. "Shitty," I said.

His lips curled up into a smile that felt like a reward.

I pulled away, hoping it didn't seem too much like retreat. "What's our status?"

"Everyone's banged up but alive. Med wizes just pulled up. They're patching up the mother and Shadi."

I let out a relieved breath. Last thing I remembered was seeing those two motionless on the ground. "Good," I said, "that's good."

"C'mon. Let's have them look you over."

I waved a hand that felt heavier than it had ten minutes earlier. "I'm okay."

He paused and narrowed his eyes at me. "Kate, you're covered in blood."

I looked down. My hands were slippery with red slick. The skin looked like it belonged on someone else. "Wh—how?"

"Looks like the glass got you." He touched my head gingerly. The contact stung my scalp, and the movement made the back of my neck come alive with pain. "Let's go."

He led me toward the three ambulances at the curb. A medical wizard came forward immediately. I dropped onto the bumper of the ambulance while he cleaned the wounds with saline. Morales stood over me as if he expected me to bolt, but I wasn't going anywhere. Exhaustion had its own force of gravity, pinning me to the bumper.

A black car screeched to the curb near the ambulance. Gardner emerged and I could have sworn that for a split second her face registered complete panic. The emotion was quickly doused as she put on her cop mask. She flashed credentials to the firemen working the scene and beelined for Morales and me.

"Everyone okay?" Her hawkish eyes moved over the streaks of watery blood running down my arms.

"It's just flesh wounds," I said. "We're all okay."

Her shoulders lowered a fraction. "Good. Now what the fuck happened?" She said this to Morales, who as ranking agent had been in charge of the raid.

"Mez found a bomb in the oven. Best guess it was a booby trap left by Dionysus, but"—he sucked in a deep breath, as if bracing himself—"we found evidence that Aphrodite Johnson might have tossed the apartment before we got there."

Gardner's eyes widened. But before she could comment on that revelation, her phone rang. She looked at the screen and cursed. "Shit, it's Eldritch. Be right back."

She put the phone to her ear with as much enthusiasm as if it were a gun. "Captain— Yes, I— No, that is absolutely not—" By that point she turned away to take the rest of the ass chewing in private.

"What a shit show," I said.

Morales nodded sagely. "Totally FUBAR'd."

The med wiz applied a bandage to the back of my neck. "I'm going to dose you with some saline intravenously just in case."

I nodded my consent. The pinch of the needle paled in comparison with the thrum of pain behind my eyes. "So our next step is to go get Aphrodite, right?"

Morales's head tilted. "Correction: My next step is to get Aphrodite. You're going home."

"Like hell—"

He held up a hand. "Don't even try it, Prospero. Go home and get some rest."

He probably hadn't meant the comment as judgment, but I was raw as an exposed nerve. "Don't pull that fragile-woman-needs-protecting crap with me, Morales. I'm fine."

He looked at me like I'd stepped in dog shit. "This has nothing to do with you being a chick, Prospero. I need you in fighting shape for the Blue Moon."

I deflated. "Sorry." Rubbing my temples with my hands, I closed my eyes. "Jesus Christ, this case."

"We still have a week until the Blue Moon. We'll get him."

I opened my eyes and looked my partner in the eye. "Of course we will. I just hope we can do it without getting blown up, shot, or poisoned."

Morales's smile was weary. "Just another day in the MEA."

Chapter Eighteen

When I arrived at Pen's apartment that night, I took a deep breath before exiting the car. The last thing I wanted to do was walk into her place with the weight of the day hanging around my shoulders.

Even after a shower and some grub, I still felt like shit warmed over. It didn't help that I'd forgotten Danny had a sleepover at his friend Aaron's house that night. I'd tried to follow Morales's orders to relax, but after half an hour in that silent house I'd been ready to punch myself in the face just for something to do.

That's when I decided it was time to visit Pen again. I knew Baba had her weekly romance novel book club at the senior center that night and Lavern was working night shift, so Pen would be alone. Didn't call ahead because I knew she'd tell me not to bother.

Grabbing the bag of food I'd brought, I exited the car and jogged across the street to the building. The building's facade was the color of a rotten peach. Back during Prohibition, the Mundane gang bosses had stashed their mistresses in the tiny apartments there. Pen loved it because she said she enjoyed living someplace with a scandalous history. As I climbed three stories of stairs—no elevator—I wondered what she'd think about the history once she was mobile and had to navigate those steps with her healing injuries slowing her down.

I used my key to enter the apartment. The living room was clean and held the lingering scent of Baba's aromatherapy oils. I turned right and took the bag of sandwiches to the table in the pass-through that pretended to be a dining room. The galley kitchen was also clean. I briefly eyed the cabinet where I knew the bottle of rye waited to be violated, but decided to hold off until I found Pen.

A tiny hallway jutted off to the left from the kitchen. I ducked around the corner, expecting to find Pen asleep in her bed. The double mattress took up almost the whole room, but it was empty.

"Pen?" I called softly. A quick look confirmed the bathroom behind me was also empty. I stayed calm because I knew panicking never helped anyone. Moving quickly, I went back through the living room to the bedroom on the other side of the apartment. Pen had converted this room into a sort of office/closet. Guess the mobster's dolls hadn't had much use for clothes, because the apartment only had a tiny linen closet near the bathroom for storage. Besides the large portable clothing racks lining three of the room's walls, there was a tiny writing desk wedged next to the door leading to the apartment's balcony.

I was about to duck back out the room and go call Baba when I saw something move out on the balcony. Frowning, I went to investigate. While the rest of the apartment was roughly the same square footage as a shoe box, the balcony was surprisingly spacious. It formed an L-shape that stretched from one bedroom to the other.

I opened the door and poked my head out. At first, all I saw was a red-winged blackbird sitting on the railing. When I burst through, the damned thing didn't fly away or move in surprise. Just turned those black-bead eyes on me as if I'd disturbed it.

My heart sank as I realized Pen wasn't out there, either. But then a soft cough reached me.

Turning, I finally spied a bundle of blankets huddled on a chair over by the other balcony door. "Pen?"

The bundle froze, and then a hand emerged to push the blankets back from Pen's face. I blew out a relieved breath. Rushing over, I knelt beside her. "What are you doing out here?"

I looked her over, as if expecting to find new wounds. But all I saw was the same neck brace and the cast on her arm. The bruises on her face were less puffy and mellowing into a dull yellow instead of the green they'd been a few days before.

But it wasn't the bruises around her eyes that worried me—it was the eyes themselves. Her pupils were dilated as hell, and when she looked at me her gaze was glassy and unfocused.

"Honey?" I whispered. "Why are you out here?"

"Hi, Katie," she slurred.

"How did you get out here?" Surely Baba wouldn't have moved her out here and then left.

"Wanted some fresh air."

I looked down to the trash containers three stories down. There was definitely air out here, but it wasn't particularly fresh. "Pen, can you look at me?" She had to move her whole head to manage the task. Dread weighed down my stomach. "Sweetie, when did you take the potion?"

"Din't."

I took a deep breath and prayed for patience, even though impatience and worry made me want to shake her. "Yes, you did," I said. "Where is it?"

She smacked her lips like they were numb. Then she smiled like she'd just noticed I was there. "I love you, Katie."

"I love you, too," I snapped. "Tell me where the potion vial is."

She vaguely waved a hand toward her bedroom.

"Stay here." She was so loaded I'm not sure she even heard me.

Inside the bedroom, I found an empty potion vial sticking out from under the bed. The label on the front identified it as Maslin's Tincture and noted that the user should take three dropperfuls every six hours as needed for pain. The good news was that Maslin's was the most commonly prescribed pain elixir on the market and was about as clean a potion as you could get. The bad news was that the vial was totally empty.

Back on the balcony, I held the vial up for Pen's unfocused inspection. "Did you take the entire vial today?"

She just chuckled. With a curse, I pulled my phone from my pocket and punched a couple of numbers. "Baba, it's Kate—just be quiet a sec and listen, okay? Did you fill the pain potion prescription the med wiz prescribed for Pen?"

"Of course not," Baba said, sounding insulted. "Why?"

"Because she's higher than a kite right now and there's an empty vial of Maslin's."

The old woman spat out a curse that would make a sailor blush. "That's my potion. I take it for my arthritis." The sound of rustling came through the phone. "She must have taken it from my purse. I'd set it on the bed before I went to use the restroom. Shit, Kate, I'm so sorry."

I sighed. "It's not your fault. Look, I need to call her doc. I'll call once I know more."

Luckily, I had Nurse Smith's number in my phone. When she answered, I quickly told her what had happened.

"Relax, Detective. She just needs to sleep it off. She'll be fine."

I let out a relieved breath. But the nurse wasn't done.

"Just in case, though, don't leave her alone. If she stops breathing, call me back."

"What?"

"Just a precaution. There have been a few, rare cases where the potion worked a little too well and a patient's lungs shut down."

"Shouldn't I bring her in just in case? Or is there an anti-potion we could give her?"

The nurse sighed like she'd reached the end of her patience. "Look, you can bring her in if you want, but a bus wrecked on Interstate 71, so we won't be able to see her for several hours anyway. It's up to you, let her rest comfortably in her bed or drag her here to sleep it off in a waiting room."

"Got it," I said through teeth clenched so hard they creaked. "Thanks so much for your help."

When I punched the End button, I let out a frustrated growl. I wasn't really mad at the nurse. It wasn't her fault. It wasn't Baba's fault, either. Hell, I couldn't really blame Pen, for that matter. I knew her pain levels were off the charts. Add to that the addiction demon that constantly sat on every recovering addict's shoulders for the rest of their lives.

No, it wasn't anyone's fault, but that didn't make it suck any less. The only solution was to get her inside and let her sleep it off, like the nurse suggested. Having some sort of game plan helped me feel better.

"All right, sister," I said, standing. "Bedtime for you."

♦ ♦ ♦

My eyes felt like someone had buffed them with sandpaper. The siren Sleep had been trying to lure me into her welcoming arms for two of the previous four hours, but I'd managed to resist her by calling Morales every fifteen minutes for an update on his progress tracking down Aphrodite. He'd finally threatened to come over and take my phone away if I didn't leave him alone. After that I stayed awake by pouting that he was out having all the fun chasing down the Hierophant while I was stuck watching Sleeping Beauty.

The other thing is, the longer I sat there, the angrier I grew. Initially, I was just relieved I'd shown up to keep an eye on her rather than her being alone and potentially hurting herself. But then the more I thought about it, the more I resented the entire situation. I was pissed at the selfish asshole who'd hit her with his potion-fueled car. I resented Baba having arthritis. I resented my job for making it hard to help Pen before she resorted to magic. But mostly I resented Pen, herself. There were plenty of nonmagical options for pain relief. Maybe nothing strong enough to take it away entirely, but surely enough to make her more comfortable.

"Kate." A groggy voice came from the bed.

I hopped up and went over. A small bedside lamp was lit, but even that dim light made her blink as if in pain. I didn't turn it off because I needed to see her to reassure myself she was okay. I also needed to see her reaction as I read her the fucking riot act in a few minutes.

"Hey," I said softly. I handed her a glass of water and sat on the edge of the bed. She lifted her head enough to take a sip and then surrendered the glass.

"What time is it?"

I glanced at my phone. "Almost nine."

Her eyes widened. "Last I remember it was four."

"Yeah, potions tend to make one lose track of time."

Her gaze skittered from mine, as if looking away would protect her from the judgment in my tone.

"Don't start on me." She rubbed her eyes and yawned.

I tilted my head. "Start on you? Why in the world would I do that? I mean, it's not like I just spent the last four hours of my life watching you sleep in case you stopped breathing."

She froze and looked up from beneath her lashes. "I'm sorry," she said in a small voice.

"Sorry don't cut it, sister. What the fuck were you thinking?"

Using her good hand, she pushed herself up into a sitting position. But she moved too fast and ended up swaying. I reached out a hand to steady her but she shied away. "I got it," she snapped. Then she settled herself back and looked at me. "I was thinking that I was in pain, Kate. For the last week, I've been in constant pain. I can't sleep, I can barely eat, and I was so fucking exhausted."

"You could have—"

"What?" she snapped. "Arnica didn't do shit and you told Baba to stop giving me the philtres."

"So the solution was to steal an old woman's arthritis potion? Jesus, Pen."

She blinked at me but didn't respond for a long time. Just watched me like she was seeing me clearly but didn't like what she found. "You've got a lot of fucking nerve judging me."

Gut check. This time it was my turn to look away. With those words, she hit on the thin vein of guilt that I'd been suppressing ever since I got the call she'd been injured. If I hadn't hidden my magic use from Pen in the first place, that damned party never would have happened and she never would have been in that car for that asshole to run into her.

Recriminations rose like bile in the back of my throat, but I wouldn't let her off the hook completely. "Me cooking to save Danny's life is light-years different from you stealing an old woman's arthritis potion." I was being nasty and I knew it, but defensiveness added venom to my tongue.

"I tried to fight it," she snapped. Off my doubtful expression, she looked me in the eye. "Really, Kate. I tried. But when Baba left her purse on the bed, I saw the apothecary bag sticking out. I told myself to just ignore it. The pain was bad but I wasn't dying or anything. But then this little voice in the back of my head starting whispering about how one little potion wouldn't make me fall off the wagon. About how I could just do it this once and no one would have to know. Baba was going to be gone all afternoon. I could have a little relief and then I'd never take it again. I guess it's what Rufus always talks about—the bargaining?"

I nodded. I knew that seductive voice all too well.

"Anyway, before I knew it, my hand was grabbing that bag and hiding it under my pillow. And then, once Baba was gone, that same hand was opening the vial and lifting it to my mouth. The weird thing was, it didn't even feel like it was me taking it. It was like watching a movie of someone falling off the wagon."

I grabbed her uninjured hand in mine and squeezed. "This doesn't have to be you falling off the wagon. Maybe it's just a wake-up call. You tried it and it sucked. Now you know and can never try it again."

She looked down at our hands. Her teeth worried her bottom lip for a second. Then she whispered, "That's the problem." She looked up, and her eyes were bright with fear. "It didn't suck, Kate."

I closed my eyes and cursed. A memory elbowed its way to the front of my brain. Holding the Gray Wolf potion in my hand. The tingle of energy zinging up my arm. The rush of adrenaline making my pulse sprint. The surge of power that bordered on lust. No, I agreed silently, it didn't suck at all.

Let her off the hook, my conscience begged.

But I couldn't. In my gut I knew it was a mistake to enable

her just to ease my own guilty conscience. "This ends today," I said. "No more."

Her expression morphed from regretful to rebellious. "Don't take that tone with me, Detective. I'm not some freaker strung out on a five-dollar dirty magic potion."

I raised a brow. "Not yet."

She paled as if I'd struck her. "What are you gonna do, report me to your precious team? Send Morales over to put me in cuffs?"

I sighed. "It's not like that and you know it. I'm worried about you, Pen. Have you forgotten the last time you got hooked on potions?"

Her gaze skittered away from mine. "This is different."

I stared her down. "The pain you're experiencing isn't easy, but it won't kill you. But we both know an addiction will. Your heart is still weak from the last time."

A decade earlier, Pen had been a stressed graduate student who fueled her studying binges with an energy potion supplied to her from one of her classmates. On her twenty-third birthday, she had a massive heart attack.

A wave of emotion rose like a tide in my chest. I blinked quickly before I lost my ability to deliver the tough love she needed. "If I find out you've taken another potion, I won't be coming back around."

My words lay between us like a bomb. In the other room, the sound of Baba bustling through the front door echoed through the tiny apartment. "Kate? Pen?"

Pen ignored her. "In here," I called, glancing toward the bedroom door.

"I want you to leave."

I swung back around, my mouth open in shock. "Pen—"

She jerked so suddenly, I was worried she'd hurt herself. "Get out!"

Baba appeared at the door, a worried expression on her wrinkled face. "Kate?"

I held out a hand to quiet her for a moment. "Think real hard before you tell me to leave again," I said in a low tone. "Because it won't be easy to get me to come back."

She looked me directly in my eyes. "Go back to your precious team. That's where you'd rather be anyway."

Her words were like jabs to my gut.

"Girls?" Baba said.

Instead of responding to either of them, I rose with as much dignity as I could muster. I collected my coat and shrugged into it on my way toward the door.

"Pen? Tell her to stay."

I shook my head at the old woman. "She made her decision."

Baba paled. Clearly she believed this fight was all about Pen's potion use. I wasn't going to be the one to correct that assumption. "Make sure you check your purse before you leave. If she steals anything else, I suggest you file charges."

"Bitch," Pen hissed.

I looked back at my best friend. Her hair stuck up in spiky tufts, and her skin was pale. Dark circles made her eyes look like black holes.

"Get well soon, Pen."

With that I turned and walked out the door with the echo of my best friend's sobs chasing me all the way out of the apartment.

Chapter Nineteen

October 25
Waxing Gibbous

The next afternoon I rolled into the gym feeling like I'd spent the night sleeping on rocks. Frustration and anger over my argument with Pen had pushed at my pressure points until I was tossing and turning like the princess and the fucking pea. I'd finally given up trying to sleep before the sun rose.

I'd been a cop for five years. In that time, I'd heard every excuse in the book from potion junkies. My life would have been a hell of a lot easier in some ways if I'd never quit magic. I certainly would have had more money. Most likely, I'd be the head of the Votary Coven, assuming no one put a bullet in me and I hadn't gone down with Uncle Abe.

I had walked away not because it was the easy thing, but because it was the right thing. So my tolerance for other people's excuses for weak behavior was pretty much zero. Especially people I knew were capable of being strong, like Pen. She'd put herself through college and created a nice life for herself despite a very troubled past. If she thought I was going to stand by and watch her throw all that away, she was sorely mistaken.

"Yo, Prospero!" Shadi called the instant I walked into the gym.

"What?" I snapped.

She paused and widened her eyes. "Who pissed in your cereal?"

"How much time you got?"

She laughed. "Might have something here could change your luck." She waved a file folder like it was chocolate or a bottle of good whiskey.

"What's that?"

"I spent my night going over the information we got from Dionysus's landlord."

"And?"

"I found him, Kate."

I went very still, praying she wasn't fucking with me. *"Found him* found him?"

"The name he used on his lease matched an alias used by an escaped mental patient from New York."

"Holy shit, Shadi." I couldn't help it. Despite my best efforts to be in a pissy mood, a smile broke out across my face. "Tell me everything."

She waved me over to a desk and opened the folder. Inside were several printed pages that looked like hospital forms.

"His real name is Scott McQueen."

"Scott McQueen." I sampled the name on my tongue. "Seems too... Mundane."

Shadi nodded. "Figure that's why he decided to call himself Dionysus."

"What else you got?"

She pulled out some forms. "Called in a favor from some MEA agents who called in some of their own favors to get access to his files. I was worried we'd need a warrant, but turns out the MEA in New York already had his records on file."

I frowned. "They're looking for the same guy?"

She nodded. "Scott was arrested five years ago for murdering his parents. The guy went nuts at trial, claiming his father had been abusing him for years and his mother turned a blind eye."

I frowned. "Did the jury believe him?"

She shook her head. "His father was a judge and his mother was on the board of every charity in their town. Real upstanding folks." She shrugged. "Anyway, didn't matter really because his behavior was so erratic everyone believed he'd just gone insane and killed them. What did him in was one day in court he tackled a guard and got ahold of the S and P spray the guy was carrying. Before anyone could stop him, he sprayed himself in the face with the stuff."

I whistled low. "Ouch."

She nodded. "No shit. Anyway, they sentenced him to a prison for the criminally insane. And that should have been the end of it."

I crossed my arms and leaned back against the desk to wait for her to continue.

"About six months ago, there was a riot among the inmates." She looked up. "Several guards were injured. A few inmates killed. Took a full day to lock the place down. But when they did, guess who wasn't accounted for?"

My brows shot to my hairline. "Scotty McQueen."

She nodded. "Before he left, he raided the prison's infirmary and stole all of the potions in their stockroom."

"How did the MEA get involved?"

"The agent I spoke to said he first hit their radar in Boston.

Local wizes started reporting thefts. Thought they had a new Raven in town. After a few weeks, though, the activity died down. But then the MEA in Chicago had similar reports. Same MO. Near as they can tell he's been moving from city to city funding his moves by robbing the top covens in each city."

"And now he's in Babylon."

She nodded. "But his moves here haven't fit the pattern."

"Why?"

"First of all, he stayed under the radar before. Didn't taunt cops or city officials like he's done here. The Dionysus thing is new, too. Reports we have out of the other cities don't show any mention of a name."

"So why put on a special show for Babylon?"

She shrugged. "Could be this was his destination the whole time. He seems too organized for this to be a random place to pull off the Blue Moon plan."

I chewed my bottom lip and thought it over. "What do we know about his parents?"

"I need to do some more digging," she said. "I did see some notes from the mental hospital that he kept up the abuse story even after he was sent away."

"Nothing new for a criminal to deny guilt."

"Yeah, but one of his therapists seemed to believe him."

"You got a name?"

Shadi glanced down at the report. "Dr. Flamel."

"Hmm," I said. "According to O'Lachlan, McQueen is preaching to his followers about stripping society of its masks. Might be a connection to his parents putting on a front." I shrugged. "Or he's just batshit insane."

"Clearly he's that. Question is why'd he bring all that crazy to our town?"

"See if you can track down Flamel. Maybe he can give us some insight about why McQueen chose Babylon. Also ask if there's any specific connection to the full moon."

"I tried and couldn't find anything specific, but I'll try to get in touch with some of our agents in New York." She nodded and slapped the folder shut. "Anything else?"

"Is Gardner around?"

She shook her head. "She was here earlier, but she got a call and ran off in a hurry."

I frowned. "All right. I'll catch her later." I paused and smiled at her. "Thanks for finding this intel."

She grinned back. "I just hope it helps us nab this SOB."

"Amen, sister." While she returned to her bloodhounding, I went to my desk and set down all my things. About that time, Morales came out of the door that led to the old locker room. His hair was wet, which meant he'd gotten to work early to make use of the old punching bags and grabbed a shower after. "What's up, Prospero?"

"You talk to Shadi already?"

"Yes, ma'am. Odd, ain't it, that he chose Babylon?"

"That's what I said." I sat with my hip perched on the edge of my desk. "She's looking for a local connection."

He nodded, as if he'd made the same call when he'd talked to Shadi. "How's Pen?"

My lips twisted. "She's fine."

"I hope you weren't too hard on her."

My mouth dropped open. "You're joking. Of course I was hard on her."

He shook his head. "You ever have a broken rib, Cupcake?"

"No, but I've broken other bones."

"All I'm sayin' is she's been through a lot. Taking one potion to ease the pain doesn't mean she's going to start riding the magic dragon again."

"Whatever," I said, crossing my arms. Before I could change the subject to one less likely to get me yelling, his phone buzzed.

He checked caller ID first. "What's up, sir?"

Whatever Gardner's response was, it made Morales's brow slam together. "Got it," he said in a clipped tone that could only mean trouble. "We'll be there ASAP."

He punched the End button and looked up at me. "Let's roll, Cupcake."

◆ ◆ ◆

The luxury apartment building stood out like a garish rhinestone in a pile of rust. Volos had built the Phoenix along the Steel River as part of his plans to revitalize the Cauldron's dying neighborhoods.

When the call came from Gardner to meet her at this address, she'd been sketchy with the details. Just that we needed to meet her there ASAP. When we'd arrived, the entire block was cordoned off and police lights flashed like strobes.

Morales and I ran into Mez on our way toward the building.

"You know what's happening?" I asked the wizard. His dreads were their natural brown color that day. Instead of his normal vintage-inspired uniform, he wore a pair of faded jeans and a concert T-shirt from the alchemical band Spirit of Vitriol's *Solutio* tour.

He held up his phone. "Just got a text to meet her at this address."

"Judging from the production out here, we're not looking at another theft."

In the city of Babylon, personal theft was categorized as

a felony, and any calls coming in for those sorts of crimes required four units to respond. But there had to be ten uniformed cops just outside the building, and through the glass doors of the building I could see dozens more milling around the building's lobby.

"Murder?" Morales said.

Thinking about Aphrodite's potions, I countered, "Or sexual assault."

At that we all fell silent. We flashed our credentials at the police tape. "Special Agent Gardner around?" I asked the shift supervisor near the front doors.

"Top floor."

Morales froze beside me. "Isn't Volos's apartment up there?"

The blood rushed from my face. I nodded and took off toward the building with the guys on my tail.

We took the stairs to the fourth floor because the CSI team was busy dusting the elevator for prints. On our way up we passed several other officers, who all wore the stoic expressions cops get at particularly gruesome crime scenes.

By the time we reached the top floor, my heart was pounding in a way that had nothing to do with the stairs we climbed and everything to do with worry. All the signs so far indicated a violent crime had occurred. The thought that the victim might be John scared me more than I was comfortable admitting to myself.

Once we reached the hallway, I expected to turn right, toward the door I knew to be John's. Instead, all the action was centered on a door on the opposite end of the long hallway. Momentarily disoriented, I veered left and stopped in my tracks. About halfway down the hallway, a female uni was taking a statement from none other than John Volos.

The tightness in my chest eased a fraction, but before relief could totally claim me, a hotter emotion reared up. Deep down

I knew the anger was directed at myself, but I wasn't evolved enough to claim it. Instead I spun it around and aimed it directly at the man I'd been worried about two seconds earlier.

"Watch yourself, Cupcake," Morales said under his breath. "You're glaring at Volos like he killed your best friend."

I realized that my hands were clenched into fists and my jaw was tight. I forcibly relaxed my muscles.

A quick glance down the hall revealed that John was watching me. His eyes were narrowed with concern. A silent question passed from him to me—*What's wrong?*

I shook my head. I didn't want his concern. I didn't want to talk to him about how I was pissed at myself for caring whether he was alive or dead. And I certainly didn't want to focus on the fact that in his faded jeans, mussed hair, and bare feet he looked a lot like the old John I used to love.

"I'm fine," I snapped at Morales. "Let's go."

I marched forward, studiously avoiding Volos's probing gaze. I heard Morales greet the tycoon and saw Mez nod a greeting from the corner of my eye. I barely spared him a glance and kept walking.

"Hello, Kate," he called. I waved a hand over my shoulder and kept going.

The CSI supervisor, a real hard-ass named Perkins, greeted us at the apartment's door and insisted we all don booties and gloves. "What's the deal?" I asked him.

"Homicide. You might want masks, too. It's pretty ripe."

I shook my head. It's not that I enjoyed the smell of death, but the ability to handle a rotting corpse was somewhat of a mark of honor among the BPD. Only rookies and pussies wore masks, and God help you if you yakked. Especially in front of one of the CSI guys, who'd give you holy hell for contaminating the crime scene.

Morales and Mez refused masks, too. Guess things weren't all that different in the MEA, either. But we all put on the booties and took gloves.

"They're waiting for you in the master bedroom," said Perkins. "Down the hall. Try not to touch anything, m'kay?"

Once inside, the traffic was sparser. I had a feeling if Gardner hadn't specifically requested our presence, we wouldn't have been allowed inside at all.

The apartment was a mirror image of John's on the other side of the top floor. Wide floor-to-ceiling windows spanned the living room, offering a breathtaking view of the lake. The seating area, dining room, and kitchen were open-concept, which made the space feel massive. But the place was empty except for a couple of fingerprint techs working their way around the room.

We found Gardner inside the massive master bedroom with Eldritch, Detective Pat Duffy from the First Precinct, and my old friend Medical Examiner Thomas Franklin.

The bedroom was designed with a sort of seating area; an archway divided it from the sleeping area beyond. On the far end, massive windows overlooked Lake Erie.

"Prospero!" Franklin raised his hand for a high five, but when I saw the rubber glove on it I settled for a wave.

"What's shaking, Franky?"

Before he could answer, Eldritch stepped forward. He pulled the mask covering his mouth and nose down to speak. "Oh good," he said in a less-than-thrilled tone. "They're here."

Ignoring the jab, I nodded at all assembled. "What we got?"

Duffy turned toward Eldritch, ignoring us completely. "Sir, I'd like to go on record—"

Eldritch held up a hand. "The mayor was clear that he wanted the BPD to cooperate with the MEA."

"Not like he can get pissed at us for ignoring that order now," Duffy said under his breath. His reluctance to have the MEA involved had to do with more than a jurisdictional pissing match. A few weeks earlier, Gardner had approached the Adept detective about joining the MEA, but he'd shut her down completely. None of us understood why he'd rejected the opportunity, but whatever it was obviously colored his attitude now.

I frowned at Gardner. "What's that supposed to mean?"

Franklin jerked his head toward the arch. "See for yourself."

Shooting a frown at his uncharacteristically grave tone, I moved forward. Morales and Mez were on my heels as I approached the opening. My first impression of the room beyond was that it was decorated like a bordello. Red silk slithered around the columns of the canopied bed. The walls were covered in paintings of naked, blindfolded women. The mattress itself was covered in black rubber sheets. From my vantage point, all I could see was the top of a leather cap or something on the body's head.

I moved forward to see around the bed hangings. The male was upside down on the rubber sheet—his head was where the feet usually went. From my vantage point at the foot of the bed, I looked down the body at his pale torso, flaccid penis, and legs. The face was obscured by what I realized was a leather mask. The zipper over the mouth was open, allowing the blackened tongue to flop out like some kind of alien larva. I wasn't real eager to do a closer inspection with the smell of expelled fluids and vomit permeating every molecule of air in the room.

"Who is that masked man?" Morales said, deadpan.

Gardner's voice came from the archway. "Check out the right hand."

Frowning, I peered over. My mouth fell open. A large signet ring with the seal of Babylon winked at us from the body's right ring finger.

"Motherfucker," I breathed. My stomach flip-flopped. I turned toward Gardner. "No fucking way."

Her expression was solemn as she nodded.

"Um," Mez said, "Someone want to clue me in?"

"That," Morales said, "is the honorable mayor of Babylon, Skip Owens."

"What the fuck?" Mez exclaimed.

"Our thoughts exactly," Eldritch said, joining Gardner.

"Apartment's registered to a dummy corporation. Probably to make sure Mrs. Owens didn't know about it."

"Someone want to fill us in on what we know?" I asked, turning my back on the dead man. Even with the mask, it was hard to look at the body of someone I'd spoken to only a few days earlier. Not that I was Owens's biggest fan, but you had to have some pity for the indignity of his final moments.

"Anonymous call came in reporting there'd be a murder at this address. Volos said he was home at the time, but didn't hear anything unusual. There weren't any signs of forced entry, either."

"So it was probably someone he knew," Morales said.

Duffy nodded. "You could say that." He held up a Baggie containing a photograph. "We found this sticking out from under the bed."

I took it from him. It took me a minute to realize what I was seeing because the shot had been taken at such an odd angle. Apparently the photographer was standing over the subject. The subject, of course, being Mayor Owens with his face buried in a crotch. One side of the torso in the image had a large breast and the other had a clearly defined pectoral. "Shit," I said, "that's Aphrodite Johnson."

"How can you be sure? Aphrodite isn't the only hermaphrodite in the Cauldron," Duffy argued.

I pointed to the tattoo on the left wrist, which was visible on top of Owens's head. "The red spiral and hexagram is Aphrodite's sigil."

"That image isn't enough to implicate anyone in the murder," Duffy said.

"Of course," I said. "What do we know about the body, Franklin?"

He stepped forward with a clipboard. "Cause of death is TBD, but if I had to guess it's poison."

Morales's brows shot up. "Another argument in favor of Aphrodite."

"Explain," Duffy snapped.

"Oh right, the Cauldron isn't normally your beat," I said pointedly.

"Detective Duffy was kind enough to come over from the First. I requested him specifically because of his decorated history in homicide."

I nodded. "Okay, so Aphrodite has this revenge garden. It's famous in the Cauldron." I glanced at Franklin. "You'll be testing for plant-based poisons, right?"

He nodded. "It would help if I knew which ones the Hierophant had access to."

"I was just there a few days ago. Would it help if I wrote down all the ones I can remember?"

"Might." He grimaced. "But there's something else that's off about this scene."

"What is it?" Eldritch snapped. He was a little green around the gills now that he'd removed his mask. The man had been out of the field so long he'd lost his edge when it came to dealing with the day-to-day realities of solving crimes.

"The forensics team also said it appears the leather mask was put on postmortem," said Franklin.

I frowned. "Seriously?"

He waved us over. Closer now, the proof of poison was even more apparent. There was blood mixed in with green vomit all over the bed. "See anything odd?" he asked.

Mez tipped his head. "You mean besides the dead mayor wearing a gimp mask in a puddle of his own sick?"

"Yeah, Einstein." Franklin rolled his eyes. "The mask is clean."

I looked again. The leather didn't have one speck of vomit on the outside.

"And is it me or has the body been posed?" Morales asked.

We all stepped back for a wider look. Sure enough, the mayor's body had been arranged to look like—

"Hold on," Mez said, "that's the hanged man!"

I squinted at the body and realized he was right. In tarot, the hanged man was the twelfth card of the major Arcana. In it a man was depicted as hung by one foot from a tree, which corresponded with the body being oriented with the head at the foot of the bed. Also like the card, his hands were bound behind his back and his left ankle was tied to the headboard. Meanwhile his right was bent and the foot tucked behind the left knee to form a number 4. Even the spray of green vomit under his head was reminiscent of the halo of light around the figure in the card.

"I don't see it," Duffy said. "You're stretching."

I shot him a look. "Really, Detective? Do you make a habit of dismissing possible clues without further investigation?"

His eyes narrowed. "No, I make a habit of not trying to complicate cases that are cut-and-dried."

"Maybe that works in the Mundane precincts of this city, but you're in the Cauldron now. When chances are good the perp was an Adept, you can't discard magical evidence outright like that."

"All right, Miss Wizard," Eldritch said, "why don't you tell us what it means."

Duffy crossed his arms and shot me a challenging look. On the other side of the room Gardner and Mez looked at me expectantly. I cleared my throat, damning myself silently for walking into this. "All right," I hedged. "It's been years since I studied the tarot in depth, so I might be a little rusty. However, I remember that the hanged man represented sacrifice or martyrdom to the greater good." I glanced at Mez for confirmation. He winked and nodded for me to continue. "It can also mean surrender, I think."

"Don't forget it can also mean to beware a traitor," Gardner added quickly.

I cringed. "Oh right."

"And its a card ruled by Neptune, so it's associated with water," Mez continued. "It tells us not to fight against the current, to let it take you wherever it's flowing."

Duffy clapped slowly. "Holy shit, that explains it all, then."

I grimaced at him. "Don't be a smart-ass. We're just saying it's not something to dismiss outright."

"All I need to know is that we have proof the mayor was involved in illicit dealings with a known prostitute who is known to grow poisonous plants," Duffy countered, "and he was found wearing accessories common in sex play, dead from apparent poisoning."

It was hard to argue with that logic, but from what I knew of Aphrodite s/he was too smart to leave such obvious clues around if s/he was to kill someone. The Hierophant's words from the other day came back to me: *They'd have to find the body first.*

"You don't think Aphrodite is too obvious?" Morales said suddenly. During the tarot discussion, he'd been standing to the side with his arms crossed, looking over the entire scene. Now that he spoke, he had everyone's attention. "I mean, we seem to be forgetting that the mayor received a threatening letter from Dionysus less than a week ago."

Duffy's brows rose. "What are you talking about?"

Eldritch made a dismissive sound. "Rogue wizard robbed Johnson last week and then sent a vaguely threatening letter to the mayor. From it we gathered he plans to attack the city on the Blue Moon."

I held up a hand. "Hold on. Dionysus robbed Aphrodite." I glanced at Morales. His eyes widened, as he came to the same conclusion. In stereo we both said, "He stole the poison from her/m."

I looked at Gardner, who'd gone still. "He's trying to frame her/m for this," she said slowly. "Why?"

"Aphrodite's been on his trail ever since he robbed her/m," I said. "This might be about getting her/m off the streets so s/he can't put heat on him while he carries out his plans."

"Plus, didn't the leprechaun say that Dionysus had several tattoos of tarot cards?" Morales asked.

Duffy's clapping was slow and sarcastic. "That would all be very convincing if this were a cop show. But this is the real world where we need actual evidence to convict a person of a crime. And right now, all the evidence points to Aphrodite Johnson."

"Not yet, it doesn't," Franklin said. "I still need to get the samples back to the lab to test for the poison."

"What are you waiting for?" Duffy snapped.

His jaw clenched tight, he started gathering his things together. "Call me," I said under my breath. He paused in the process of putting a set of calipers in the bag and nodded slightly.

Once he was gone to let the boys in the meat wagon know it was okay to remove the body, Eldritch turned to Duffy. "I'll have a detail stationed on Aphrodite. If that freak tries to leave town before we have those labs back, they'll stop her/m."

"We've been looking for Aphrodite for two days now," Morales said. "There's no evidence s/he left town, so we think s/he's hiding out."

"The BPD won't have problems tracking down the city's most famous hermaphrodite," Eldritch said in an insulting tone.

Duffy nodded. "In the meantime, I'll have the unis get statements and review the security footage in the building."

"What can we do to help?" Gardner said.

Eldritch frowned at her. "You can stay out of our way. This is a BPD matter."

"Then why did you ask us to come to the scene."

Eldritch's chin lifted. "I needed you to see what you cost this city by dragging your feet on the Johnson case."

With that the captain stormed out of the room, shouting orders at the remaining unis on the premises.

Mez, Morales, and I stood quietly in the wake of the captain's parting zinger to Gardner. She cleared her throat, straightened the jacket of her pantsuit, and turned to address us. "Well," she said, glancing toward the bloated body of the dead mayor, "I don't know about you guys, but I need a fucking drink."

Chapter Twenty

Hours later, we had all gathered at a pub called the Irish Rover. It was a favorite watering hole of the BPD, but that evening there weren't any cops in the place besides us since all the city's officers were busy hunting down Aphrodite Johnson.

The place smelled like beer and wood polish and blue chalk from the pool cues. The dark-paneled walls and low light made it feel like a cave. In other words, it was the perfect sort of place for drowning our frustrations in dollar pitchers of beer.

We were on our third round when Morales challenged Shadi to a game of pool. Mez got up to go put some blues on the jukebox and then went to provide color commentary for the pool match.

I leaned my head back against the cracked vinyl of the booth and let the smooth Mississippi currents in Muddy Waters's voice wash over me. Gardner nursed her beer across from me and seemed as content as I was sharing a companionable silence.

Eventually, though, I opened my eyes and leaned forward to take a sip. As I did, my gaze landed on the tiger-eye cabochon on her left hand. "Where'd you get that?" I asked, nodding toward her hand.

She held up her hand and looked at the large gold-and-brown-streaked stone. "Bought it from a street vendor in Mexico. I was on vacation after a tough case and it just kind of spoke to me. Helps me stay grounded."

I nodded. "You were with the MEA then?"

She nodded and leaned back. I wasn't sure if the move was deliberate or if the retreat was meant to distance herself from my questions.

"You don't have to talk about it," I said. I knew from Morales that there was some drama in Gardner's past that risked her job with the MEA. According to him, this task force was her chance at redeeming herself.

"No, it's fine," she said on a shaky breath. "I'm surprised Morales or Shadi didn't tell you already."

I shook my head.

Her eyes widened, as if she'd expected me to admit the opposite. "It happened four years ago. We were working a long-term case to bring down a big-time wizard in Miami. The guy was smuggling weapons, young girls, and rare rain-forest flowers into the country. The weapons sales and the human trafficking funded his lab, where he was trying to develop a new super potion. We'd heard from an informant, he was trying to develop the elixir of life."

I chuckled. Every wizard boasted about trying to find the elixir at some point.

"Anyway, we had a big task force going—ATF, FBI, Postmaster, you name it. But we were in charge of things. It was our guy undercover in the gang, see?"

I nodded. "Which gang?"

"A Morte."

My eyes flared. "The Brazilians? Holy shit." In Portuguese, the name meant "the Death."

Back in the '80s, when narcotics were the substances destroying the moral fabric of America, the Colombian cartels had dominated the drug trade. But once magic had usurped narcotics as both the bigger threat and the bigger money-maker, the Colombians had been dethroned by the Brazilian shamans. These powerful wizards controlled access to certain rain-forest plants the United States now controlled due to their use in dirty potions. Uncle Sam preferred to sell those flowers, herbs, and plants to Big Magic companies. Not only did that net the government healthy tax incomes, but the FDPA also earned tons of money vetting all the legal potions for sale in government-run apothecaries and through med-wiz practices.

Anyway, when it came to potion cooking in the southeastern United States, especially, the Brazilian covens were to be feared because they controlled the substances wizards all over America wanted to get their hands on. They controlled the flow of controlled ingredients in and also had their hands in almost every arms deal and human trafficking outfit from Florida up to New York.

"So what happened?" I asked.

She leaned forward. "Our guy on the inside got word to us that he was getting a bad feeling. There had been rumblings among *A Morte* that the leader suspected a snitch." She adjusted in her seat, as if the memory made her physically uncomfortable. "So I went to my ASAC and said we needed to call off the sting. He called a meeting of the heads of the other groups in the task force to discuss it. Naturally, they all agreed too much money and manpower had been invested to back out based on rumors."

"Shit."

"Right. In their defense, we were close to having what we needed to make the case. We had one of the *A Morte* guys willing to testify and a judge ready to issue a warrant under the RICO statutes." She exhaled a shaky breath. "What we didn't know was that one of the ATF guys was in the coven's pocket. Somehow he found out the identity of the undercover and told the coven leader."

I closed my eyes. "Fuck, Gardner."

"No one becomes the head of a Brazilian coven without being pretty crafty, right?" Her tone was dripping with scorn. "So he came up with a sting of his own. Let it leak to our guy that a big buy was coming up. Naturally, our guy got word to me about it. I should have known better, but all I could think was that I wanted that case tied up quickly so I could get him out of there."

The clocked ticked in the background as she gathered her courage to continue.

"See, the guy who was undercover? He and I . . ." She trailed off. "Anyway, I let my feelings cloud my judgment. So I sent my team in while I sat in a fucking van a mile away with the ATF fucks and my ASAC and the other high-ranking agents." She swallowed hard. "The guns started firing almost immediately. By the time the rest of us made it across that unending mile, the entire team was dead and the cowards who killed them were gone."

Silence settled over us like a black shroud. My chest felt tight out of sympathy. I knew a thing or two about carrying around the guilt of causing someone's death. But I couldn't imagine carrying around the karmic debt of leading an entire team to its slaughter.

"Sir, I know it wasn't easy for you to share that story with me. But hindsight's a bitch. Makes you think you should have seen things you couldn't possibly have seen."

She sighed. "I guess you're right. Still, this stuff with the mayor? Got me wondering if we've missed something."

"Probably," I said, "but that's Eldritch's problem now, right?"

She shook her head. "Just because he says he's taking point doesn't mean we can't pursue the potion aspects of the case. After all, this Dionysus prick's violated about twenty federal laws."

A little dose of adrenaline had me shifting in my seat. "So what's our play?"

"Way I see it BPD's gonna have their hands full for a while with Aphrodite."

I shook my head in disgust. "That's bullshit, sir. I'd bet my left hand Dionysus killed Owens."

She raised a brow. "I don't disagree. The question is, how do we prove it?"

Morales's voice rose over the music. "Yo, barkeep, turn up the tube, will ya?"

We both glanced over to see the bald guy behind the counter punch some buttons on the remote. The jukebox went silent and the TV over the pool tables got loud.

On the screen, Captain Eldritch stood at a podium addressing media. "As many of you know, our beloved mayor was murdered earlier today. His loss is a huge blow for this community and we extend our sincere condolences to Mrs. Owens and the mayor's two sons, Chip and McKinley Owens."

An inset picture on the screen showed the entire Owens family smiling together in front of a church. Nice touch, the church. I wondered if Skip Owens prayed to Jesus with the same mouth he used to suck Aphrodite's cock.

"Obviously, bringing the perpetrator of this violent act to justice has become the sole focus of the BPD."

"Yeah that's just what Dionysus wanted, you idiot," Morales yelled at the TV.

The captain adjusted his hat and looked directly in the camera. "I am pleased to report that less than an hour ago, we arrested Aphrodite Johnson, a notorious Hierophant of a sex magic coven with a long history of lewd behavior and violence."

The picture-in-picture flared to life with footage of Eldritch himself escorting a bedraggled Aphrodite to a waiting squad car. I didn't recognize the building they were in front of, which meant one of Aphrodite's associates must have rolled over on the locations of the Hierophant's safe houses. The female side of the hermaphrodite's face had no makeup and the masculine right was covered in stubble, as if they'd dragged her out of bed.

Mez emitted a low whistle. "There's going to be hell to pay once she's cleared."

"Let's hope it's not too soon," Gardner said.

I frowned at her. "Why do you say that?"

"Because now Dionysus thinks the heat is off him for a little while. He'll get cocky. Maybe make a mistake."

"Let's hope so. That asshole's been one step ahead of us since this began."

Gardner chugged the rest of her beer, wiped her mouth with the back of her hand, and smiled. "Then we'll just have to make sure his next step is into a trap."

Chapter Twenty-One

October 27
Waxing Gibbous

Two days later Morales and I were on our way out of the medical examiner's office with a folder full of papers we weren't supposed to have about Owens's death. We'd spent a couple of days chasing down every possible lead on Dionysus. But so far we'd come up with a big fat goose egg. With each passing day Gardner was getting more and more pissed, which meant we were getting closer and closer to the edge of the law when it came to tracking down leads. Luckily the media circus surrounding Owens's death and Aphrodite's arrest was keeping the BPD too busy to pay attention to what we were doing.

Since Franklin is a tad touchy about things like cell phones going off in his morgue, I'd turned mine off when we arrived. But the instant we walked out with the illicit lab reports he'd given us, I fired up the phone again. A voice mail from Baba was waiting saying she couldn't pick Danny up from school since she had to take Pen to a follow-up with her doctor. A sharp spike of guilt speared me. Poor Baba had been working double duty with both Danny and Pen so I couldn't very well complain about the inconvenience. Still, stress was a constant aching burn in my gut, and the added complication ratcheted my cortisol a couple of notches.

I had Morales drop me off at my Jeep, Sybil. Before I got out, he said, "I'm going to go check in with Gardner and then see if I can get a bead on Aphrodite's guard. Maybe he can be convinced to share some information about what they found at Dionysus's apartment."

"Take Shadi with you."

He smirked. "You worried about me, Cupcake?"

"Nah. Just don't trust you not to beat that guy's ass when he lies to you."

He chuckled. "Fair enough. Give me a shout once you get the kid settled and I'll let you know where to meet up."

Thirty minutes later I pulled up in front of Danny's school. Despite the chilly air outside, my back was sweaty from sitting in traffic. I pulled up in front of the school with fifteen minutes left to spare before DUDE let out. Instead of sitting at the curb, I decided to go in and introduce myself to the teacher sponsoring the club. If he was cool, maybe I could arrange for the team to do a demonstration at an anti-dirty-magic rally or something. I knew Danny said they weren't going to invite guest speakers, but I figured I could talk this Mr. Hart into it.

A woman I'd never met was working the front office, and she informed me that the club met in the library on the second floor. Over the years I'd been in the school several times both as a parent and to catch up with Pen. Even though a lot of the parents who sent their kids to Meadowlake could be snobby and exclusive once they found out Danny and I were both Adepts as well as lower middle class—wasn't sure which ranked lower in their esteem—there were some cool ones, and I liked almost every teacher Danny had over the years. It helped that Pen was popular among the staff, and I knew she often smoothed things over for the kid.

The library was nothing like the one at the public school I'd attended in the Cauldron. My school basically had what amounted to a broom closet full of books. Mostly the shelves were taken up by musty-smelling encyclopedias and unused thesauruses. An ancient woman named Mrs. Strahan had been in charge of the "library." She was nice, but basically ignored by the kids and staff.

I have to admit that back then I was so full of myself for being the heir apparent to the most powerful coven in the city that I didn't think it was worth exerting much effort on book learning. It wasn't until I enrolled in night school at Babylon Community College that I realized how deprived I'd been not growing up a reader. Now I read most nights before bed to unwind. Nothing literary or anything. Just cheap paperbacks where I knew the good guys would always win the day or the couple would live happily ever after.

But this library? Double doors opened up into a two-story temple to books. The main floor held the circulation desk, rows of computers and study carrels, and dozens and dozens of shelves of books. Steps led up to the second-floor, U-shaped balcony that held shelves so tall, you needed a ladder to reach the top. Mrs. Strahan would have peed her adult diapers to see this place.

Since school was done for the day, there weren't a lot of students present. I glanced around and saw a group of kids gathered in an enclosed classroom off to the side of the circulation desk. Laughter echoed and when voices spoke, they sounded excited and passionate. I smiled, glad Danny had found a group that encouraged such a positive energy.

Moving toward the doorway, I peeked inside. At the front of the room, a tall guy who looked maybe three years out of college was standing in front of a white erase board. His sandy-blond hair flopped into his eyes as he jumped around. I suppose he was handsome in a white-bread-and-missionary-position sort of way. He wore a corduroy blazer, a skinny tie with a wrinkled white button-down, dark-washed jeans, and a pair of battered Converses.

Kids called out the names of famous dirty potions and he wrote them on the board. His movements were so animated, I realized this was a teacher who absolutely loved his job. Not one of those pruney government employees who never went off the script the state curriculum provided. This guy was too new to be cynical, and I liked him immediately.

"Yes, Josh, that's right," he was saying, "some people use vanity potions to impersonate other people. The stronger the potion, the more convincing the transformation, but those stronger ones are almost more addictive." As he turned back to write this on the board, his gaze blew past the door, where I stood. He paused and stood up straighter. "Oh, hi. Can I help you?"

"Sorry. I was early for pickup. Thought I'd come watch." My eyes scanned the young, eager faces for Danny's.

When I spotted him, he slid down in his seat as if he wanted the floor to swallow him. I frowned.

The teacher glanced at the clock. "Okay, everyone, time's up."

A collective groan of disappointment filled the room.

"I know, I know," the teacher continued. "But don't forget: Next week we have a very special speaker stopping by." He took a deep breath to draw out the drama. "We owe a huge thanks to Danny for inviting the one and only John Volos—"

He said more, but the instant he'd said that name, anger flared in my belly, like flames licking the inside of an alchemist's athanor. "I'm gonna kill him."

The room fell silent. "Pardon?" the teacher asked.

I jerked upright, realizing too late I'd said it out loud. "Nothing," I said with a lame chuckle, "carry on."

My gaze slashed toward Danny, who was busy smiling at his classmates' praises and studiously avoiding any glance in my direction.

"Remember to bring in your lists next week, too," the teacher continued. "Other than that, have a great weekend, guys!"

I ducked farther inside the room to get out of the way of exiting teens. The teacher approached with a hand extended. "Brad Hart."

"Kate Prospero," I said, returning the shake. "I'm Danny's sister." Who, I noted, was lingering at the back of the room, instead of coming to greet me.

He tilted his head. "The cop?"

"Guilty," I said, forcing a smile.

Hart smiled back. Something about the expression gave me pause. It took me a minute to realize there wasn't a problem with it at all. Instead, Brad Hart's smile was totally lacking in guile and his eyes were clear, like maybe his conscience was, too. In my line of work, it wasn't often you ran into anyone who didn't have some sort of secrets or ulterior motives behind their smiles.

"Is everything okay?"

"Yeah sorry, long day," I said.

He crossed his arms and leaned in a fraction. "Cleaning up the streets is tough work."

I gave him a sideways glance. Despite his fashionably shabby clothes, the guy didn't look like he'd spent much time on any street that didn't boast large houses with top-dollar alarm systems and security gates.

"Sure," I said. He was a nice guy. He didn't deserve my sarcasm or jaded comebacks. "Listen, thanks for putting this group together. Danny's very excited."

Hart beamed. "We're thrilled to have him. I have to admit, I was a little disappointed when he told me you wouldn't be able to be one of our monthly guest speakers."

If he'd knocked me upside the head with a two-by-four, I would have been less shocked. "Huh—"

"I understand you're busy and all," he continued, oblivious to my distress, "but I think these kids could really benefit from your stories from the front lines of the War on Dirty Magic."

My gaze sought Danny out like the red beam of an assault rifle's laser. The kid looked up and paled at whatever he saw on my face. "Yeah, actually," I said, holding my brother's wide gaze, "I could probably make some time if you think the kids would enjoy it."

Hart's expression opened up. "Really? That would be awesome!" He thought it over for a second. "We have Mr. Volos in this month, but maybe in November."

I shot a glance at my brother, who was working hard not to look like he was trying to hear our conversation from the other side of the room. I smiled real wide for his benefit. "I'd be happy to help." I pulled out my wallet and handed him my card.

He glanced down at my newly minted MEA business card. His eyes widened. "Wow. I'd heard you were a cop from some of the other teachers, but I had no idea you were a detective working with the MEA." He waved the card. "If it's okay, I'll call you soon to set up a date."

I frowned.

"To speak to the, uh, class and stuff," he finished lamely.

Something in my belly warmed. Brad Hart wasn't my normal type. He was more like a puppy dog than a guard dog. But, I thought, it's not like hanging out with the assholes I normally went for was getting me too far lately.

"Definitely do," I said with an encouraging smile that felt foreign on my face.

"Great." He smiled that sweet smile again. My poorly socialized inner voice whispered something about devouring him. I hushed her and reminded the minx it had been so long since we'd both had sex with something that didn't require batteries that we couldn't be too choosy. "In the meantime, try to behave yourself, Detective."

I looked up and paused. Those clear, guileless eyes had darkened to reveal the promise of a few intriguing shadows in Brad Hart. And on top of that, I was pretty sure he was flirting with me.

Well, well, I thought, things just got a lot more interesting.

"Ditto." With that, I walked away, careful to put a little English in my stride, and went to go deal with my disloyal little brother.

◆ ◆ ◆

By the time we burst through the back door of the kitchen I was a volcano ready to blow. The drive home was painfully tense and quiet. Danny spent the entire ride trying to curl himself into the smallest space possible and kept his eyes focused on the stained floor mats. I tried to focus on not wrecking the car and resisting the urge to go take my anger out on Volos for accepting the invitation to speak.

The kitchen door slammed shut behind us. I threw my purse and keys on the table. "Sit." Even to my own ears, my voice sounded too quiet, too full of banked rage.

On some level, I knew I was overreacting. Teenagers lie. They get embarrassed by their parents. But for this to happen so soon after my fight with Pen was just too much. It felt like everyone I cared about was slipping away, and deep down I was painfully aware of my own responsibility for that. What was worse? Pen was right. None of theses issues would exist if not for my job.

Needing something to do to put some space between me and my unpredictable, singeing emotions, I went to the fridge. Naturally, I was all out of beer, so I settled for a wine cooler Baba had left there after the party. The cap hit the floor with a ping. Two seconds later, the sickly sweet flavor of fake strawberry and malt liquor hit the back of my throat. But it was cold and fizzy and scrubbed the taste of guilt from my tongue.

When I finished every drop, I pulled the bottle from my mouth with a loud exhalation. The sugary liquid sloshed in my stomach, making me instantly regret chugging it.

"Kate?" said Danny's small voice.

I held up a finger. "I'll do the talking. You say nothing unless specifically asked to provide a response." I glanced out of the corner of my eye in time to see him nod. "First of all," I continued in a conversational tone, "when did you invite John to speak?"

He kept his eyes downcast. "At your surprise party."

"Have you two been in touch besides the night of the party?"

He nodded reluctantly. "But only to set up the time for him to come to the school."

I let out a little sigh of relief. Some part of me had been imagining a conspiracy between those two behind my back. "Okay," I said. "Now what about lying to Mr. Hart about how I couldn't speak? I offered to do just that the night you told me you wanted to join."

A teenager shrug.

"Were you embarrassed to have me speak in front of your friends?" My gut tightened at the thought. I kept forgetting that at some point I'd gone from being Danny's hero to his humiliating mother figure.

He shook his head. "Figured you wouldn't show," he mumbled.

"What the hell does that mean? I wouldn't flake on you, Danny."

His head jerked up then. "Bullshit." The word zinged round the room like a bullet.

I pointed to the curse jar. "Cough it up."

He slammed out of his chair and threw a five in the jar. My eyes widened, but before I could say anything he took off.

"You act like you're such a fucking selfless saint, but you're never around anymore. You don't care about me or DUDE. All you care about is looking good in front of your damned team and earning promotions. And the only reason you're mad at John is because you're jealous you're a shitty wizard and he's such a badass."

If he'd punched me in the gut, I wouldn't have been more in pain than I was from those hateful words. "First of all," I started in a slow, calm tone totally at odds with the lava simmering in my gut, "I don't act like I'm selfless. I act like a woman with lots of responsibilities. At sixteen, I can't expect you to understand the concept of having to worry about anything more important than when the update to your favorite video game comes out. But I assure you, it's no fucking picnic."

"Jar," he snapped.

"You had a credit left, so I took it." I shook my head. "Now, as for me not being around, that's only temporary. Once we get past the Blue Moon, things will even out."

He snorted. "Until your next big case."

I threw up my hands. "What do you want from me, Danny? I can't tell the criminals to stop killing people because my little brother needs some quality time."

His jaw set. "Jesus, sorry I'm such an asshole for wanting to see you."

I sucked a cleansing breath into my nose, hoping it might dispel some of the bitterness in my throat. "You're not an asshole." Neither of us commented on the profanity. From the looks of things, we'd both be bankrupt before midnight if we kept paying the jar.

He crossed his arms and folded his lips into a frown. "It's not just the late nights. You've always had a crazy schedule. It's just that since you started the task force, when you're here you're not really here, you know?"

I frowned at him. "Have you been talking to Pen?"

He shook his head, looking confused. "No, why?"

"Never mind." I waved a hand. "I'm sorry I've been bringing my stress home. I'll try to do better."

He nodded but didn't look convinced I'd be successful. Since I doubted it as well, I moved on.

"Now, about the other thing." I licked my lips to stall for time. This next conversation wasn't going to be as easy. "It pisses me off that you believe the reason I have issues with Volos has anything to do with who's better at magic. It has nothing to do with cooking and everything to do with morals."

Danny rolled his eyes. "Here we go again. You think you're all high and mighty because you don't cook. But you know what, Kate? If it weren't for John's use of magic, I'd be dead right now."

There. Right there. A tectonic shift. A rift exposed in the bedrock of our relationship.

"That's not fair, Danny."

229

"I don't give a shit," he yelled, that man-child voice cracking. "You would have let me die to save your precious principles."

My ribs got too tight to contain the hot, swelling, pulse of my shattered heart. How in the hell could this kid believe I'd just stand there and let him die? "I would never let anything happen to you."

He sat up straighter, looked me in the eyes, and delivered the deathblow. "You let Bane hex me."

"You don't know what you're talking about." My tone was so icy, even Danny shied away. "You wanted to hurt me? Congratulations. Mission accomplished." I tried to breathe over the pressure in my chest, but each inhalation felt thin and cold. "But if you think I'm going to let that distract me from the fact you snuck behind my back and lied, you're sorely mistaken."

His face fell. "I—"

I slashed a hand through the air. "I don't care about your excuses or your reasons. I don't care about anything except letting you know that you are grounded until further notice. No phone, no games, no TV, no fun, no freedom, no DUDE."

When his gaze jerked upward, it was sharp as daggers. "How are you going to enforce that, Kate?"

The bald rebellion in his expression stole my breath. This boy, this rebel, used to be a sweet little toddler who'd give me sticky kisses and bring me crushed dandelions he'd found in the sidewalk cracks. Now he was staring at me with the defiance of an enemy combatant.

"Watch yourself," I said in my best cop voice.

"I mean it," he said. "You're never here. I could invite an entire coven of wizards over and you'd have no idea."

My fist slammed into the tabletop like a gavel. "You spoiled little shit. You think you're tough? You wouldn't last five minutes in the Cauldron. Those wizards you admire so much would eat you alive and leave your bones for the Ravens to pick over."

"John isn't like that."

"Grow up, Danny. He's worst than most."

Danny stood up so fast, his chair flew back and skittered across the floor. "It's not like that! At least he talks to me."

My eyes widened. "You said you haven't been talking to him."

Danny threw up his hands. "I lied!"

"Well, that's just fucking great." I slammed my hands on the tabletop. "I've been out busting my ass to keep us housed and fed and you pay me back by lying?"

His eyes narrowed. "Sorry I'm such a burden. Say what you will about John, but at least he gives a shit."

His words were like fists attacking my most vulnerable spots—the ones where I kept all my insecurities about raising the kid. They also made it clear Danny had been lying about the extent of their interactions. "If I didn't give a shit about you, I would have started teaching you magic years ago. If I didn't give a shit about you, I would have let you stay in the Cauldron in Uncle Abe's care. If I didn't give a shit about you, I wouldn't be so angry right now that I want to punch something." I swallowed hard. "John Volos is not your friend, Danny. He wants you to think he is because he wants to use you somehow."

Danny crossed his arms and set his jaw in a stubborn angle I recognized from my own mirror.

"You can't trust a wizard, Danny. Especially not that one."

"You used to be one, too. Does that mean I can't trust you, either?"

Another crack. This time I felt it in my conscience.

No, he couldn't trust me, I realized. Maybe John had flattered the kid, but I'd lied to his face. But my sense of self-preservation reared up and reminded me that I'd lied for the kid's own good.

And your own, my traitorous conscience added.

I pulled out my phone. "Call him and tell him he won't be speaking at DUDE next week."

His teeth ground together with tectonic plates. Teeth I'd paid a fortune to straighten when he was eleven. "No!"

"Call him or I'll call Mr. Hart and tell him you're grounded from DUDE for the rest of the year."

"I hate you!"

"Join the club!" I shouted back. I wasn't sure who else exactly I included in that club, but my inner voice had an idea and I didn't like what it said about my mental state at all. I swallowed that uncomfortable realization and thrust the phone at Danny. "Call him."

He snatched the phone and punched the numbers so hard I was worried I'd have to raid the curse jar to buy a new one. Then the phone was at his ear and his toe tapped angrily against the linoleum. He sat there long enough for me to realize the call was going to voice mail.

"Hi, John," Danny said in the most put-upon voice I'd ever heard. "It's Danny. Can you, like, call me back and stuff? Bye." Then he punched the End button.

"Happy?"

No, I wasn't. I wasn't sure how long it would be until I was again, but it wasn't worth pointing that out to the little shithead.

"Go to your room until I call you for supper. We'll discuss the rest of your punishment then."

The look he gave me before he stomped out made my heart sink. A seismic shift had occurred in the foundations of our relationship, and damned if I knew how to repair the damage.

Chapter Twenty-Two

October 29
Waxing Gibbous

The call came just after midnight. One minute I was dreaming about swimming away from a beast with sharp teeth, and then next the shrill ring of my cell woke me. Getting away from the dream was a relief, but the information Morales called to tell me was not.

"Chaos at the college. Pick you up in fifteen."

"Wha—"

"Wakey, wakey, Sleeping Beauty. We've got an orgy to stop." With that he hung up.

I scrubbed a hand over my face. My brain wasn't working at full thrusters yet so I was basically moving on autopilot. I threw back the cover and went to pee and brush my teeth. I made it all the way to washing my face before the words really sunk in. I reared up, splashing water droplets all over the sink. "Orgy?" I said out loud. "What the fuck?"

I glanced at my phone for the time. Now I only had eight minutes before Morales came pounding on my door. I threw on a pair of cleanish jeans and a long-sleeved T-shirt with my boots. Over that went the leather jacket I'd snatched at a yard sale a few years back.

By the time Morales pulled up out front, I'd already gone to tell Danny. Music seeped out from under his door, but when I knocked he wouldn't open it. The only response I received was a grunt when I told him I was leaving. I'd called Baba, too, and she'd said she'd head over in a few minutes to stay with him.

"You don't have to do that," I said, my guilt rising once again.

"Nah, it's fine," she'd replied. "I haven't been sleeping well because of my arthritis. Besides, there's a marathon of *Blue Devils* on tonight."

Blue Devils was her favorite cop show. Since she didn't own a TV, she usually didn't mind hanging at my place—she could catch up on all her stories.

At fifteen minutes on the dot after he called me, I locked the kid inside and jogged out to Morales's car. When I climbed in, he handed me a large coffee and watched me gulp down a few steaming mouthfuls before he spoke. "Better?"

I gasped over my burnt tongue and nodded. "What's this about an orgy?"

In the darkened car his white teeth showed up like a Cheshire Cat's. "Yes, ma'am." He sounded way too excited. "According to Gardner, who took the call from Eldritch, a couple of sororities started an orgy on campus. When the campus cops stepped in, the girls began attacking them and all hell broke loose."

"By attacking them you mean—"

"Fucking them."

I nodded slowly. "Are you trying to tell me there is a sorority sex riot at U of B?"

My partner put the car in gear, rubbed his hands together, and hit the gas. "Best call ever."

As much as I wanted to find humor in the situation, I couldn't. "Morales? Dionysus stole a rape potion from Aphrodite, remember?"

His smile faltered as he pulled up to a red light.

I raised my brows and looked out the windshield at the fat moon overhead. "It's only a couple of nights until the Blue Moon."

"Fuck." All traces of amusement disappeared. He punched the window button and reached down to grab the siren from under his seat. A second after he slapped the light on the roof, he kicked the gas. "Get Mez and the others on the phone. We'll need backup."

◆ ◆ ◆

At University of Babylon, the sororities were all grouped together on a street called Sorority Row. Across the street from the line of McMansions was a large park with a playground, baseball diamond, and tennis courts. Every available surface was covered in naked bodies contorted into positions that made the Kama Sutra look like Dr. Seuss.

"Jesus H.," Morales breathed. He practically smashed his face against the windshield for a better view. Close to the road where we'd parked, some co-eds were holding down a campus cop. One girl was sitting on the guy's face and another on his crotch. The way the guy's legs were kicking and his arms strained against the delicate hands holding him down, he wasn't having the time of his life.

My phone buzzed at my hip. "Prospero."

"It's Mez. I called in a favor at the sheriff's department. They're bringing in a riot tank."

I watched five women chase down a pair of large frat boys and bring them down like sacrificial lambs to the slaughter. "That thing have a salt-cannon in it?"

"Yep."

"Good. Get here fast."

As I hung up, red and blue lights flashed on the perimeter of the park as some of our backup arrived. Once we'd told Eldritch that we suspected the city's most wanted was behind the scene, he'd pulled several black-and-whites off patrol to help subdue the crowds.

I looked over at Morales. The sense of wonder had disappeared from his face. Now he looked pale as he absorbed the reality of the situation. I'm sure most red-blooded heterosexual men would tell you they'd love to get gang-raped by sorority girls. But the scene before us wasn't sexy: It was grotesquely carnal. The air vibrated with masculine screams and the scent of violent arousal. And judging from the horror on Morales's face, he was having trouble reconciling the fantasy with the ghastly reality.

Over the years, I'd arrested my share of sexual predators. The thing was, rape was never about lust. It was about power. To an alpha male like Morales, seeing a group of young women exerting such power over an entire campus of men had to be unsettling as hell.

We'd already pulled on our bulletproof vests and loaded down with weapons—mostly salt flares and extra canisters of S&P spray. Our goal wasn't to kill any of the attackers, but to subdue them. Now that we were there, it was obvious these women were freaking on dirty magic. I nudged Morales. "Let's roll."

We climbed out and met up with the dozen unis Eldritch had sent us. Not nearly enough but better than nothing, especially since Mez was on his way with heavy metal. The fourteen of us formed a line—each about arm's length away from the next—and started pushing our way into the crowd. The only benefit to wading a group of naked people was that it was easy to see none of them was armed.

The first grouping I met up with was a pair of girls—one blonde and one redhead—who were using a sex toy to violate a boy who couldn't have been older than nineteen. Judging from the tears rolling down his face, he wasn't enjoying the ministrations. "Back away, ladies!" I said in my command voice.

The blonde looked up but kept her hands busy on the boy's shaft. She smiled and licked her lips. "Ooh look, Rachel, a lady cop."

The redhead pushed the sex toy deeper, eliciting a pained groan from the kid. "You can sit on his face."

I raised the S&P canister. "Stand down or I'll spray you with sodium capsicum spray."

The redhead laughed, a deep, throaty sound. Then she slowly pulled the phallus back out before slamming it home again.

The spray hit her right in her face. She sucked in a breath, forcing the stinging mixture deep into her lungs. She shrieked and fell to the side, her naked body convulsing in pain.

I turned the can toward her friend. "You want some, too, Blondie?"

Instead of answering, she lunged. Ready for her, I side-stepped and she face-planted into the grass. Removing a zip-tie from my waist, I made quick work of tying her wrists together. "Stay." The redhead got the same treatment. I left them to two unis who ran up to help and went to intervene elsewhere.

I didn't get ten feet before I ran into a cluster of bodies with pretzeled appendages. Diving in, I was grateful I'd had enough forethought to don a pair of gloves as I grabbed arms, hair, legs, whatever else I could get a handhold on and pulled people out of the pileup. Unlike the last encounter, I didn't bother to warn them before spraying them with the saline canister. The salt water wouldn't hurt them, which was kind of a pity, but I didn't have as much S&P spray to waste on noncombative perps. Besides, I didn't want to go overboard with the highly caustic spray and risk a lawsuit later from some spoiled sorority girl's parents.

I was almost at the bottom of the pile where a male and a female were performing an enthusiastic 69 on each other when the sound of music nearby grabbed my attention. I looked up to see a shirtless, goateed man traipsing through the naked, writhing bodies. He wore a pair of fake goat horns on his head and woolly chaps on his legs, held up with suspenders. While everyone around him tried their damnedest to create sparks by furiously rubbing their genitals together, this guy pranced and played a pan flute.

It wasn't Dionysus himself—this guy had blond hair and a potbelly. Plus he played the flute using his right hand, which made him a Mundane. Still, it didn't take a genius to put the asshole in the chaps together with the satyr/Dionysus connection and come up with a whole lot of adrenaline.

I jumped over the 69ers, pulling my salt flare from my belt as I ran. "Morales!" He was wrestling a blonde wielding a massive black dildo like an extremely flexible baseball bat. "With me!"

He ducked the weapon and shot the girl right in her perfect nose job with S&P. She fell to the ground behind him as he pivoted to join me. "What's up?" he called.

I pointed. "We got ourselves a satyr at twelve o'clock."

My partner's face hardened as he zeroed in on the satyr in question. Together we closed in on our prey, who had his back to us as he skipped around a particularly large moaning tangle of people. Morales lunged. The flute music cut off, quickly followed by an *oof.* The satyr and my partner were airborne for a second before they crashed to the ground.

I stood over the grappling pair with my salt flare ready for action. "Freeze!"

Unfortunately our goat-horned buddy was too busy hitting Morales with his pan flute to comply with my order. I reached down to grab Morales's shirt and wrench him out of the way. At the same moment, the goat-man launched a knee right at my partner's crotch. Morales sucked air and then froze before howling in pain and falling to the side.

"Freeze, asshole!" I shouted again. I didn't want to use the salt on him if I could avoid it. At close range, it was liable to take off his face. Normally I wouldn't have minded so much, but if he was indeed one of Dionysus's followers we needed him well enough to speak. Tough to do with no lips.

But men who dress as goats and gallivant through sex riots playing flutes tend not to be the most logical people. As if to prove this point, the guy launched himself off the ground and took me out at the knees. Now it was my turn to hit the dirt. I lifted the salt flare—because, seriously, fuck his face now—but before I could pull the trigger he covered one of the holes on his pan flute and blew hard into the mouthpiece. A plume of powder exploded from the end of the flute.

Directly into my face.

In shock, I sucked in, pulling the potion deep in my lungs. I choked on the odd sweetness. A moment of panic when I realized what had happened. Didn't last long, though, because a nanosecond later a curious heat began to spread through my veins. Not painful. A rush. Yeah, a major rush of adrenaline shooting straight from my heart to strike like lightning in my groin.

From somewhere that sounded far away I heard a confrontation—two males shouting, a loud grunt. Didn't care. I suddenly was very aware of a void in my center that longed to be filled. The need to swallow, to suck power from marrow. Take, take, take.

"Prospero?" came a deep voice close by. The delicious scent of sweat and heat and pheromones.

My eyes popped open and my vision filled with his face. A rock-hard jaw covered in scruff that I suddenly needed abrading my hot skin. Those full lips. The muscles. Good God, those muscles. I needed to feel them flexing under me.

Those chocolate eyes narrowed. A warm, calloused hand on my cheek. "Kate? Talk to me."

The next part was pretty crazy, so my memory is blessedly fuzzy. But somehow, I ended up straddling that big body. Somehow I ended up shoving my tongue inside that hot mouth. Hands tried to push me away, but I circled my pelvis and kept at the mouth, stroking the tongue until his resistance melted. I moaned and went deeper. I needed to swallow him whole. To make him beg and plead before I conquered him completely.

He groaned and those arms went around my back, trying to take control. I reared back and slapped him across the face. The voice that emerged from my lips was mine and yet somehow not mine at all. "Take it, bitch."

Everything shifted. The body beneath me wasn't so pliable anymore. Those hard hands, those heavy muscles pushed me off. I slammed to the ground. But the need to conquer had me up again in an instant. "Kate, stop!" he commanded.

Some small part of my brain wanted to obey his demand,

but my body was having none of it. It was like I wasn't behind the steering wheel at all. Instead some sex-crazed succubus was in charge, and she was going to consume Drew Morales whole.

My body launched at my partner. He caught me around the neck and pulled me back toward his front with a vise-like headlock. My ass ground into his crotch and a hand snaked around to tweak his nipple. "Jesus Christ, Kate. What the fuck?" He pulled his hips back out of grinding range. "Little help over here!" he shouted above me.

In my head I was ordering my body to stop this shit. My breath panted in and out of my heaving lungs. Lust was a fire that consumed every urge to follow my conscience. But the rational part of my brain kept whispering, This shouldn't be happening. I was an Adept. Getting hit with a potion shouldn't affect me this strongly. Besides, I was a civilized woman. I didn't use sex as a weapon.

I screamed like a frustrated banshee. The energy inside me yearned for sex. Being denied only urged the flames to rise higher until the lust threatened to consume me. I believed I'd die if I didn't have an orgasm.

Frustrated with the captivity, my left hand reached toward his crotch. But my captor was way too fast. "Goddamn it." He grabbed my hand. "Stop that!"

Another male voice from close by. My head perked up and Mez appeared. I licked my lips. Mez with his sexy dreadlocks and his large hands. I stared at his crotch and purred. "Bring that wand over here, wizard."

While I struggled to get away from Morales so I could dive for Mez's crotch, the two men were exchanging words I couldn't hear. Someone shouted a command. A mechanical sound.

Mez said something like, "This is gonna be cold."

"Do it," Morales said, his tone grim.

One second fire licked under my skin like acid. The next, a whooshing sound. Cold wetness splattered my skin. I screamed from the icy-hot pain of it. From the effects of what felt like gallons of salt water invading my mouth and nose. I was drowning. Choking.

Through it all, strong arms supported my weight. Later, I'd remember his encouraging whispers, promising everything would be okay—that I was safe. But as the salt did its job and consciousness returned, gut-wrenching shame surged through my midsection, dousing every spark of lust.

◆ ◆ ◆

My cheeks burned like twin coals, and my pride didn't feel much cooler. I was in the back of an ambulance while the med wizes worked on me to make sure I wasn't suffering any lingering or long-term effects from the potion. The back doors to the ambulance were open, which gave me a good view of the cluster of cop cars a short distance away. Morales leaned his arm against the roof of one of the black-and-whites while he listened intently to the guy who'd hexed me. The horns hung from a cord around his neck, and his waterlogged chaps dripped on the street.

In the distance several other ambulances were lined up as they treated victims. They'd separated the female attackers from the males they'd raped for obvious reasons, but everyone there was a victim.

After a few moments, Morales left the goat guy in the hands of the unis and jogged over to my ambulance.

"Anything?" I asked, keeping my eyes on the med wiz, who was removing an IV from my arm.

"According to the school, the sororities were hosting some sort of charity dinner tonight. Best guess is Dionysus had this asshole pretend to be a waiter and spiked all the wine with the potion they stole from Aphrodite."

"He say anything about how he got hooked up with Dionysus?" I asked. Talking was good. Kept my mind too busy to play the endless loop of me propositioning him.

"Dionysus has been recruiting people for a few weeks. Guess he promises them that after the Blue Moon, they'll run the city or some shit." He shrugged. "Classic cult tactics."

I nodded. "That research Shadi did on the god Dionysus said he had a couple of cults. One was a group of satyrs and the other was a gang of lustful women called Maenads. They were known for frenetic sex rites. Maybe this was our Dionysus's homage to those myths."

"I'd say this counts." Morales's expression was grim.

The med wiz took the cuff from my arm. "Your blood pressure has leveled out. I'm going to release you, but promise that you'll get plenty of fluids and rest for the next twenty-four. The saline drip should have cleared out any lingering potion, but the magic he used was pretty dirty. You need to take it easy."

"Thanks," I said with a nod.

He handed me a bottle of water. "Take your time. I'm going to go check on the others." With a parting nod to us both, he ducked out of the ambulance.

Sighing, I rolled my sleeve down and swung my legs over the side of the bed. The sudden movement made blood rush to my head. Morales was at my side in an instant.

"Easy there." He placed a steadying hand on my shoulder.

I shook him off. "Just moved too fast," I snapped. "I got it." My defensiveness was due partially to embarrassment, and partially to the lingering tenderness between my legs.

He grimaced like he wanted to argue but backed away.

I kept my eyes focused on my shoes so I wouldn't have to look directly at him.

"Kate."

"Yeah?" Eyes on the wall right behind his right shoulder.

He stayed silent until I was forced to look at him. The instant my gaze touched his face it ricocheted back to the wall. "What?"

"Look, if you're worried that what happened let your secret out, you shouldn't worry."

I frowned. "What secret?"

From the corner of my eye I saw those lips curl up. "That you're totally hot for my bod."

My mouth fell open and, all traces of embarrassment forgotten, I rounded on him with a glare. "You fucking—"

His laughter cut through the anger and cut me off. "Gotcha!"

I punched him in the arm. "Asshole."

"Relax. You were under the influence, right?" His mischievous eyes danced toward the gurney I'd just vacated. "Or did you want to bang right here and get it over with?"

"*Bang?* Really? What are you? Fourteen?"

He reached out and chucked me under the chin. "That's some of my best material, Cupcake."

The problem was I knew that if he ever dropped the charming rogue routine and got serious, most women—me included—would be pretty powerless to resist. Even though I didn't harbor a secret crush on Morales, it was hard to deny he was sexy as hell. An asshole, sure, but that's the kind of lover I preferred. Assholes were uncomplicated. They didn't get all emotional or confuse sex with promises. I didn't have room in my life for more feelings or complications. And somewhere deep in my gut—probably in the same spot the potion had lit up like a Roman candle—I knew that Morales would be one hell of a lot of fun in the sack.

All of these thoughts rolled through my brain while we stood in the cramped quarters of the ambulance. We were practically plastered against each other, each trying to pretend that we weren't both suddenly wondering what it would be like to give that gurney a workout. And I was suddenly very aware of the heat coming off him and the scent of his cologne and the sheer size of him. A man like Morales could make a self-sufficient woman believe she'd like being treated like a randy wench for a couple of hours of naked fun.

A throat cleared nearby. I turned quickly, leaving Morales at my back. Mez was standing on the ground by the ambulance's bumper. "Sorry, didn't mean to interrupt."

"You weren't," I squeaked. "I mean—we were just—"

Mez shuffled his feet. "Sure, yeah. Anyway, I, uh—they're taking the goat dude to the precinct for booking. Shadi's going to meet them there to make sure he doesn't get lost in the shuffle."

A warm hand landed on my shoulder. The shit of it was I didn't have any potions to blame for the heat the contact conjured. "Sounds good, Mez." His deep voice was so close to my ear that hairs stood at attention on my neck. "Thanks."

"I'll just be going then." Mez said.

A sudden realization hit me: If I let Mez go, I'd be stuck with getting a very awkward ride home from Morales. "Wait!" I all but leaped out of the ambulance after him. "Can you drop me?"

Mez frowned, and his gaze pinged back toward Morales. "You sure?"

"I don't mind—" Morales began at the same instant.

I turned, looking at his shoulder again instead of his face. "It's on Mez's way. Besides, I'm sure you need to hang out and wait for Gardner, right?"

He was quiet for a suspicious few seconds. Long enough that I chanced a peek at his face. "Yeah."

"And the med wiz said I needed to rest, so I'll just go home and get some sleep so I can be back in commission later today."

"Okay, yeah. That makes sense." Morales cleared his throat and shoved his hands in his front pockets. "Just let me know if you need some more downtime."

"I'm good," I said. "Just tired."

Mez had a pained expression on his face. "All righty, I'll just—uh—go get my car." With that he practically ran away.

Morales jumped down. When he stepped up, he was too close for my comfort. I stepped back a little. I knew I was acting like a skittish colt, but that potion had left me all raw and on edge. I didn't want to do something—well, more—that I'd regret the next day. When I backed up, he frowned. "You sure you're okay?"

I nodded too enthusiastically but didn't speak.

"Kate, listen—"

Mez's black sports car pulled up, offering me the perfect escape. "Gotta go. See you tomorrow!" With a quick wave, I left my confused partner standing in the middle of the road with his hands at his sides.

"That was awkward as hell," I breathed when Mez pulled away.

"No shit," Mez said. "You two really need to just get it over with."

I swung around. "What? No we don't."

"Please, Kate. The rest of us have a pool going."

I slapped his arm. "Shut up. You do not!"

"Yep." He smiled.

"Did you bet?"

"Of course," he said without a trace of guilt. "My money's on this month, too. So it'd be great if you'd get the show on the road. I got some new lab equipment I'm gonna buy if I win."

"Sorry, Mez, but I'm not going to fuck Morales just so you can get a few new beakers."

"You know you're gonna fuck him eventually anyway. Why wait?"

Chapter Twenty-Three

The sun was high by the time Mez dropped me off at home. My head hurt so bad my vision was blurred, and my skin was tight and itchy thanks to the brining I'd received courtesy of the tactical wizard's saltwater-cannon. Every step was a painful reminder of the synthetic arousal that had gone unfulfilled. So the last thing I wanted when I walked in was to find Baba waiting for me at the kitchen table.

She had a steaming mug of something grasped between her gnarled fingers. "We need to talk."

I dragged my ass across the threshold. "Not now, Baba."

She pointed at the chair. "Sit." The tone she used put my cop voice to shame.

I could have just ignored her, but she didn't deserve that kind of disrespect. Not when she helped us out so much, and especially now that my fight with Pen meant I wasn't pitching in on her care.

I plopped into the chair with a bone-deep sigh. "What are you drinking?"

"Hones-tea," she said. "One of my mother's recipes. You want some? It's very cleansing."

I grimaced. Even though Baba's magic was more folk remedy than actual magic, I avoided consuming her brews as a rule. Besides, a tea designed to encourage honesty would be a mistake given my brittle mind-set.

"I need something with a little more kick." With a grunt, I started to stand, but she held up a hand.

"Enough with the booze, Katie."

I froze and raised a brow. "Excuse me?"

"People drink heavily for one of two reasons: to hide or to forget." She leaned forward. "Which is it?"

I sat back and crossed my arms. After the night I'd had the last thing I needed was a fucking intervention in my own goddamned kitchen. "You don't like watching me drink, you're welcome to leave."

She crossed her arms to indicate she was staying put. Pursing my lips, I reached for the fridge handle. "The people I deal with day in, day out? They'd kill you for your last nickel." I glanced up from the door. "Being around that shit takes a toll." Returning my gaze to the fridge, I searched until I turned up one lone beer hidden behind a head of wilted lettuce. After popping the top and having a couple of long gulps, I wiped my mouth with the back of my hand.

"You've always dealt with those assholes, but the drinking is new. Ever since you joined that task force."

"Jesus, not you, too." I shook my head and took another pull from the beer.

She toyed with the spoon next to her mug. "What happened

between you and Pen isn't my business." She paused to give me the opportunity to fill her in anyway. I raised a brow and watched her with an unblinking gaze. Finally, she cleared her throat. "Anyway, it's not right, you two love each other too much to be acting this hateful."

"You're right," I said. Her face cleared. "It's not your business."

Her expression soured and she sat silent, watching me. Judgment came off her pale, wrinkled skin in hot waves.

I took another drink. "I got hexed this morning." I said it so suddenly it shocked us both. But I kept my gaze on the ground because I couldn't handle watching her eyes see through me. Almost out of instinct, my hand went to the AA token, as if I expected her to revoke it after that admission.

"Are you okay?" she asked quietly.

I nodded and picked at the label on the beer bottle.

"What kind of potion was it?"

"Lust," I said, looking up. My face was hot with shame. "I threw myself at Morales. They had to hose me down with a saltwater-cannon."

A shocked laugh escaped Baba's lips. I frowned at her. "It's not funny."

"Like hell," she snorted. "It's hilarious!"

I bit my bottom lip. My mind chose that moment to flash up an image of Morale's shock when I tackled him, followed by the consternation on his face after they'd doused us both with freezing water. My own laugh caught me off guard. But soon I was doubled over with it. On some level I was aware this wasn't actual humor, but a hysterical reaction to the stress of the night. I fell into my chair with tears streaming down my face. Baba's cheeks were red as beets, and her laughter whooped through the room like a large bird. We laughed until no noise escaped our mouths. And then the mirth subsided into watery chuckles.

"Woo," Baba said, finally, wiping tears from her cheeks. "I needed that."

I smiled, genuinely for the first time in what felt like weeks. "Me too."

She swallowed some tea and leaned forward. The mood shifted immediately. "Were you wearing a protective amulet?"

I shook my head. "Of course not. A potion like that shouldn't have affected me at all."

"Then why did it?" Baba asked.

"The damned Blue Moon." I raised my beer in a mocking toast.

"Ask me, the Blue Moon is a blessing, not a curse." She took a delicate sip of her tea.

"How can you say that? They make magical energy go haywire and everyone's emotions get all out of whack."

"Shaking things up isn't always bad, Kate." She stared at me in a way that felt like she could see through my skin. "You'll stop the Dionysus."

My chest tightened. I didn't bother pretending I didn't know she was talking about Dionysus. "What if I can't?"

"Is that what's scaring you? Why you're drinking?"

I made a noncommittal shrug.

"That reminds me. I got something for you." She reached into the pocket of her housecoat. She held up a tiny vial filled with a glowing blue liquid.

I frowned. "What is it?"

"Gideon's Dew. Found it at the apothecary yesterday when I went to refill my Maslin's prescription. I asked the wizard behind the counter about it. He said with the Blue Moon coming, lots of people want some sort of souvenir."

"It can't be true Gideon's Dew unless it's collected on a Blue Moon."

She waved this off as unimportant. "Do you know the story behind it?"

"You mean like the biblical story?" I shook my head. "They weren't too big on teaching scripture at Albertus Magnus High."

"According to the wiz at the apothecary, the story comes from the book of Judges. This guy named Gideon was a poor farmer living in a land filled with heathen tribes. God came to him and said, 'Hey, you need to kick those heathens out of Canaan.'" She leaned back, toying with the vial. "Naturally, Gideon was skeptical. How could one poor farmer beat an army? So he asked God for a sign to prove he would prevail. So God put some dew on a fleece." She crossed her arms like she'd just made a brilliant point.

I blinked, but I kind of got the gist of what she was saying. "In alchemy, Gideon's Dew is closely aligned with *aqua permanens*. It's used in potions requiring answers or solutions. It's a symbol of divine wisdom and the need for faith."

"Exactly. The point of the Gideon story is that you have to trust that answers will present themselves when you're ready for them."

I sighed. "Baba, that's great and all, but I'm afraid police work doesn't jibe too well with faith."

"You came down hard on Danny today." The comment was so unexpected, it nearly gave me whiplash.

"He lied."

"He did." She nodded and took a sip of her tea. "Volos hasn't called him back."

My brow rose. "I won't take the blame for that, too."

She shook her head. "No one expects you to."

I scrubbed a hand over my face. "Christ. Sometimes I wish I'd never taken this damned job." The words spilled out before I realized I said them.

Baba, bless her, didn't pounce on it like Pen would have. Instead she slowly set down her mug and looked me in the eye. "You're doing good, Katie."

I laughed bitterly. "By whose definition? Pen thinks the task force is going to lead me down a path of self-destruction."

"I'm not saying you haven't made some damned fool choices, but you're a smart girl. You'll do what needs to be done when the time comes." She raised her teacup at me in a toast. "Think about our friend Gideon. He probably had to make some sacrifices, too. But he fought the battles because no one else could." She reached across the table and grabbed my hand with her own. The cool touch of her papery skin felt like a balm. "You're doing noble work, Katie. Never forget that."

"That's funny," I said, polishing off the beer. "Sometimes it doesn't feel very noble."

"You tell that to all the mothers who don't have to bury their kids because you busted a potion ring. Tell that to the kids who don't have to go to foster care because their mamas didn't die."

A memory of my mom's funeral roared to the front of my mind like a phantom. The day had been sunny. The bright light glinting off Lake Erie in the distance had felt wrong, like the sky was mocking my pain. My skin had felt so tight, and my chest filled with a pulsing bruise where my heart used to live. I hadn't cried, though. Because standing next to me at that gravesite was six-year-old Danny. His hand had felt so small in mine. So fragile. I remember looking down at that sweet little face with the tear streaks and the heartbreaking loss of innocence in his eyes and vowing to protect him no matter the cost.

If I hadn't been old enough to take custody of him, we both

would have ended up in foster care. Most likely separated. Like so many other of the Cauldron's children, we probably would have ended up in homes with Mundanes who would have forced us to use our right hands so we'd fit in.

Kids like that? The lost kids Danny and I almost were? They were one of the reasons I kept fighting against the covens. Because I'd seen what almost was and it scared me more than standing up to bullies like Uncle Abe for the kids who couldn't fight for themselves.

"Thank you," I said, finally. "I needed that."

"You don't have to do it all yourself, Kate. We're here for you, too."

"Right," I said, bitterness creeping into my tone. "What would happen if I just threw my arms in the air and gave up?"

"Dunno, why don't you try it?"

I shook my head at her. "Stop, okay? Just stop. It's so easy for you to tell me to surrender, but you don't have the responsibilities I have."

"You mean like caring for a kid that's not mine?"

Ouch.

"Or helping my friend with an addiction keep off the potions?" She pointed an arthritic finger at me. "Or having to watch someone I care about self-destruct because they're in denial?"

"I'm not in denial." I set my jaw. "I'm exhausted."

Her shoulders drooped. "Then go to bed."

"Look," I said with a sigh, "I appreciate your concern, but I'm fine. It's just been a long night—hell, it's been a long month."

"Blue Moon's in two nights. It's almost over."

I blew out a shaky breath. "But when it is, who will be standing?"

Baba shook her head sadly, as if apologizing for not being a psychic. "Go to bed, Kate. This won't all feel so overwhelming after a long nap."

"I don't know what I'd do without you, Baba. Thank you for having my back even when I'm being an asshole."

She chuckled. "Ah hell. What else would I be doing with my time?"

"Harassing the eligible bachelors at the senior center."

She winked saucily. "Damn straight." She held out the vial of Gideon's Dew.

I sighed, but couldn't help a smile at her insistence. While she watched, I used the tiny loop on the vial's lid to add it to the AA token necklace. Putting magical dew next to an Arcane abstinence symbol felt a little sacrilegious, but it was also kind of fitting given my life lately.

"Good night, Baba. Thanks for kicking my ass."

"Anytime, doll."

Chapter Twenty-Four

I woke up feeling like a small animal died in my mouth. I washed away the funk with a liter of soda and a piece of cold fried chicken from the fridge. Danny watched my afternoon breakfast with a sneer. He must have gotten home from school at some point while I napped. But I was saved from having to talk to the kid when Baba arrived. She shooed me out the door to go do what needed to be done. I knew I'd need to have a reckoning with Danny eventually, but for the moment I needed to focus on making sure there was a city to hold that conversation in once Halloween was over.

Since I had no leads, I decided to check in with LM and Mary. A quick call to Morales confirmed he was busy chasing down leads with Shadi, so I told him I'd hit up the Wonder Twins alone. Frankly, it was a relief to know he wasn't going to be joining me. After the clusterfuck the night before, I wasn't ready to play the awkward-silence-all-day game with him—or worse, the let's-joke-about-it-all-day game.

I called ahead just in case LM and Mary were in a running mood again, and was told to meet them at an address on the east side of town instead of at the park. After our last meeting I'd demanded they give me a phone number in case they decided to pull a disappearing act again. I didn't question the change of location since they were already so worried about Dionysus finding out they were talking to the cops.

On my way across the Bessemer Bridge, I got a call from my good friend Val, who was a lab rat for the BPD. "Prospero, you got a minute?"

"What's up?"

"Got some labs back from items collected at that college thing last night."

I turned right off the bridge. "Okay," I said slowly. I'd left before the CSI team arrived, but I figured with the confession from the satyr and all there wouldn't be much to need processing through the lab.

"Eldritch said we're not supposed to share this with the MEA, but he's an asshole."

I chuckled. "Go ahead. I won't tell him."

"The unis from the scene brought me some of the wine bottles from the sorority party. I know the perp said he potioned everyone, but I tested the bottles just in case."

"And?"

"And from what I can tell, the potion was already in the wine before it was opened."

My foot lifted off the accelerator. "Are you sure?"

"Yep. There were traces of the same potion stolen from Aphrodite Johnson's temple inside the bottle and embedded in the cork."

"Could it have been added to the bottles by sticking a needle through the cork?"

"Definitely possible."

"Can you e-mail me the report and a picture of the bottles? Oh, and copy Mez so he can see it, too."

The click-clack of fingers tapping on a keyboard came through the phone. "Done and done."

"Thanks, Val. You're a peach."

"No problem. Just remember this next time I need some DNA run through your lab."

I chuckled and promised I'd pass that on to Mez. After we hung up, I parked down the street from the address LM had given me. I opened my e-mail to find the picture she'd sent. Squinting at the small screen, I tried to read the label on the bottle in the picture. It featured a dancing satyr playing a flute.

Chewing on my lip, I tried to figure out how Dionysus could have gotten that potion into those bottles. The labels could easily have been printed off any color printer and attached to the bottles. I cursed myself for not investigating the wine bottles at the college the night before, but I'd been too busy trying to shove my hands down Morales's pants to do any quality police work.

I pushed that thought aside and tried to see the clue Val had just provided as a blessing. It was more than I'd had an hour earlier, and hopefully I'd have even more to go on after talking to LM.

Blowing out a breath, I shoved the phone in my pocket and exited Sybil. The address led to an apothecary in the heart of Votary Coven territory. The storefront had a large plate glass window out front with gilded lettering that identified it as the Black Cat Commissary. I wasn't familiar with the place, but I knew the type. They specialized in filling prescriptions from med wizes and selling over-the-counter herbs and tinctures. I also knew plenty of these apothecaries also had a side business out of a back room or basement where a wizard with enough scratch could score some harder-to-find illicit ingredients for dirty potions.

I parked a little ways down the street from the store. The bell over the door dinged when I walked in, but the long-haired wizard behind the counter didn't look up from the potion he was cooking over a Bunsen burner. Judging from the bite of isopropyl alcohol on the air and the Soxhlet apparatus on the counter, he was making a Spagyric tincture.

The wall behind the counter was covered in rows of shelves bearing glass canisters of herbs and other components for homemade remedies. The rest of the store was filled with low shelving units bearing packages of arnica pellets, witch hazel, and various other legal herbal remedies for common ailments.

I took all this in quickly, noting as I did that Little Man and his sister were nowhere to be seen.

"Help you?" the guy behind the counter said in a bored voice. His hair was straight and black as an asphalt highway, and the butt-cut part harked back to a painted lane divider. His name tag identified him as Zane, but his ironic mustache labeled him as a total douchebag.

"Little Man around?"

He pressed his lips together. "You gonna buy something?"

I squinted at him. "No."

He crossed his arms and sat back on his stool. "Then I ain't seen him."

There was no use in getting pissed. The Cauldron was the kind of place where even the old ladies sweeping their front stoops were on the make. I grabbed a pack of clove gum from the display at the front of the counter and slapped it on the surface. "How much?"

"Two."

I fished two crumpled bills from my pocket and tossed them. "Well?"

He raised a brow. "Plus tax."

My squint became a glare. I shoved my hand in my pocket and came up with two quarters, which I dropped one after the other onto the counter. "Keep the change."

His eye roll told me he was unimpressed by my generosity. "Upstairs." He nodded toward the steps at the rear of the store.

"Thanks a lot."

"Whatever."

At the top of the stairs, there was a hallway leading to a door at either end. The one on the right had a simple welcome mat out front, and the one on the other end had two trash bags. The scent of dirty diapers permeated the air on that end of the hall, which told me I had the right place.

After a quick knock, a shadow moved behind the peephole. "Who is it?" a suspicious female voice shouted from inside.

"It's Kate, Mary."

The door opened quickly and I was pulled inside by a meaty hand. I stumbled in and blinked against the dim light. The hulking form in front of me helped me gain my balance. "Hi, lady."

I forced a smile despite the overpowering stench of body odor and something similar to dirty cat litter. Little Man wasn't in his normal baby carrier. Instead, Mary cradled him in her arms like a baby doll. He was shirtless and wore nothing but a diaper. The bruises from the beating Dionysus gave him had dulled into sickly green-and-yellow smears across his face. Seeing him look so vulnerable was unsettling. Instead of a street-wise homunculus, he looked like a battered infant.

I pushed that disturbing thought aside and tried to be thankful that Mary, at least, had a shirt on. She was not, however, wearing any pants. Luckily the T-shirt was long enough to cover her to midthigh.

"Yo, Prospero," Little Man said in a drowsy voice. "You caught us just waking up."

I glanced at my watch. It was five in the afternoon, but considering I'd only woken up an hour earlier myself, I couldn't really fault them. "Thanks for seeing me on short notice."

"Come on in." He waved to instruct Mary to move farther into the apartment. I followed more slowly, careful to breathe through my mouth and not touch anything.

The room they led me to had a single recliner, a TV tray, and a small television perched precariously on a two-by-four and a couple of cinder blocks. The walls were yellowed from cigarette smoke, and the carpet looked like a breeding ground for pubic lice.

Mary lowered her bulk into the recliner with a groan. Her legs fell open to reveal a pair of tighty-gray-ies. I forced my eyes upward to where Little Man leaned back against her chest. He crossed his bare legs at the ankle and rested his feet on Mary's impressive belly. "I don't know where he is."

I blinked. "I know."

"How?"

"Because you're smart enough to understand that if you did know where he was and didn't tell me, it would not go well for you."

He laughed. "You ain't as scary as you let on, Prospero."

"You haven't given me a reason to show you how scary I can be." I crossed my arms. "Yet."

"And I don't plan on it neither."

I raised a brow.

He waved a tiny hand. "Relax, Kate. You're too good a customer for me to fuck over."

I nodded. "So you don't know where he is, but you gotta know something."

He shrugged his thin shoulders. "Believe me, I wish I did. We barely left this shithole for days now."

"Why?"

His eyes widened. "You been out there? The moonies are going apeshit."

"Yeah," I said, "I been out there. Which is why I really need you to tell me what you're hearing. We have to stop this asshole."

Little Man heaved a sigh from his tiny chest. "Shit, Prospero. He's a ghost. Just ask your boy."

I frowned. "Which boy?"

The homunculus's smile bordered on evil. "Volos."

I pressed my lips together and let the jab lie like a pile of shit on the floor between us. "What about him?"

"What? You ain't heard?"

I shook my head.

"Motherfucker got robbed."

Shock prevented me from schooling my features in time. "You're fucking with me."

"No, ma'am." LM shoved a tiny hand in the waistband of his diaper.

I blew out a big breath. "When did it happen?"

LM smiled, obviously thrilled he knew something I didn't. "Last night."

In other words, while most of the police force had been busy dealing with a sex riot at the college, Dionysus had been knocking over one of the Cauldron's most powerful citizens. Problem was, the Raven obviously didn't know Volos well enough if he'd thought John's first move would be to call in the cops. He preferred to handle things himself. So my next question was, when was Volos going to make his move? And, more to the point, what did he know that I didn't?

"That's a huge help, LM. Thanks."

The homunculus cleared his throat. "You could show your gratitude in a more material way."

I cursed myself for not bringing Morales—and his wallet—along. Removing my too-thin billfold from my pocket, I pulled out a five-dollar bill. When I handed it to LM, he shot me a look like I'd offended him. Rolling my eyes, I removed the gum from my pocket, as well. "Here."

I half expected him to throw it in my face. Instead his face lit up like a kid at Christmas. "Ooh! Look, Mary. Clove!"

The silent partner's large paw snatched the gum from his hand with surprisingly agile fingers. "Mine." She tucked the package into her bosom.

I filed that little tidbit away for future use. If I'd known all it took was gum to make her happy, I would have been using that instead of my beer money all this time.

"Yo, Prospero," LM said after I turned to go. I looked back to see uncharacteristic candor and a touch of fear in his gaze. Or maybe it was just the shadows from the bruises around his blue eyes. "You catch this motherfucker, okay?"

I nodded and forced confidence I didn't feel into my smile. "Sure thing, LM. You stay loose, all right?"

He scratched himself and burped his acknowledgment.

"Later, Mary."

She pulled her gaze away from the grainy black-and-white images flashing on the TV. For a moment I could have sworn I saw shrewd brightness in the eyes lurking behind those heavy lids. "Bye-bye, lady. Don't get dead."

Chapter Twenty-Five

I hadn't called ahead to warn Volos I was on the way. I'd found it was best to keep him off kilter in order to keep an upper hand. The man was frustratingly hard to faze, so I'd take any advantage I could get.

I parked Sybil at the curb across from the luxury apartment building. Compared with the scene there a few nights before, the place looked quiet. There was a single cop car parked down the block. No doubt the uni was posted there to keep nosy citizens and even nosier journalists away from the crime scene on the fourth floor. I didn't bother stopping to say hi. I knew Eldritch had started pulling guys from the other Babylon precincts to pitch in on the Owens case since all the Cauldron guys were busy keeping up with the moonie freaks.

I also didn't stop to greet the guy because I wasn't real eager for it to get back to Eldritch I was on the scene. No doubt he'd see my presence as a threat to his jurisdiction, and that would prompt a pissing match between him and Gardner that would only result in me getting drenched.

By the time the elevator dumped me off on the fourth floor, I was wondering if I'd made a mistake going there alone. Probably I should have called Morales and asked him to come play mediator. But I wasn't real eager to drag him into the middle of the personal shit this conversation was bound to dredge up.

I took a deep, cleansing breath. The kind they teach in meditation workshops and 12-step programs to help you find your center. I took a few more because my center was getting harder and harder to access lately. But before I could exhale the third breath, the door opened and John was staring down at me with a curious expression.

"Why are you doing deep-breathing exercises in my hallway?"

I blew out the breath. "How did you know I'm out here?"

He jerked his head. "I have a video console that lets me see who's in the elevator."

I froze. "Does that mean you saw who came up to Owens's apartment?"

"As I told the cops, I was asleep and didn't hear or see anything during the hours the event occurred." His tone lacked the practiced cadence of a lie, so I let it go. He crossed his arms and leaned against the doorjamb. "You been talking to your favorite snitch?" He didn't sound surprised to see me at all.

I crossed my own arms and squinted at him. "You leaked the robbery to him?"

The corner of his mouth lifted. "No one has to leak anything to Little Man. I swear that tiny bastard is psychic." He hesitated. "But I'll admit I was hoping he'd tell you."

"Why not call me yourself? Or the cops?"

He stepped back in a silent invitation to come inside. I

walked into the hallway and waited for him to lead the way inside. It's not that I didn't want to turn my back to him. More that I didn't want to get into the habit of making myself at home in his place.

"I knew you wouldn't take my call." He shut the door and moved past me toward the living room. "And I didn't call the cops because I didn't want them involved."

I didn't bother asking why. Volos only used cops when he thought he could control the outcome.

He motioned toward the couch in the sunken living room. The U-shaped leather couch was the color of rich cognac and looked as expensive as everything else in the room. Through the large windows along the back wall, the sun was kissing Lake Erie. Dusk. Only two nights until the Blue Moon, and we were no closer to finding Dionysus than we'd been a week earlier.

"What happened?" I asked, praying he had something that might break the case wide open.

He pulled two glasses from the bar and poured a couple of fingers of Pappy Van Winkle bourbon in them. Only the best in the Volos house. He didn't bother asking me if I wanted any. I didn't bother pretending I didn't.

"One of my labs at Volos Towers was robbed."

I frowned. "After midnight, right?"

He nodded and handed me my glass before joining me on the couch. "My security guy called me about an hour after I got home to let me know."

"What was taken?" I took a gulp of the bourbon and savored the smoky sweet burn on its way home.

He grimaced. "That's where this conversation gets tricky, Detective."

I pursed my lips. "Been cooking dirty, Johnny?"

His jaw tightened at the nickname he'd always hated. "The

cook was clean, but the materials weren't exactly sanctioned by Uncle Sam."

Most legitimate magic labs had to use ingredients authorized by the Federal Drug and Potion Agency. The government claimed this kept clean magic pristine, but everyone knew it was so they could ensure they got every penny in tax revenue they could from Big Magic companies, like Sortilege Inc.

"All right, so you were cooking something that might not be exactly legal. You got reason to think the perp was our friend Dionysus?"

John set down his drink and rose. He retrieved a file folder from the long granite counter separating his state-of-the-art kitchen from the living area. When he came back he threw the folder on my lap. Frowning, I opened it. Two photographs fell out. The first showed overturned stainless-steel tables and broken glass and equipment littering the floor. On the wall, someone had spray-painted the phrase IN VINO VERITAS. The second shot showed a large walk-in freezer with empty and overturned shelves.

My heart kicked into overdrive. "I'd say this looks like his handiwork." I looked up at John. "How bad is the potion he took?"

John finished off his bourbon before answering. "About six months ago, a party contacted me needing a special package."

"Should I even bother asking who?"

He shook his head. "It's safer if you don't."

"Safer for me—or you?"

He smiled but didn't elaborate. "They wanted me to develop a truth serum."

I frowned. "That's what all the secrecy is about. Everyone and their brother tries to cook a truth serum at some point."

He shook his head. "They wanted something odorless, tasteless, and totally untraceable by all scientific and magical means."

My eye widened. "Jesus. And you said yes?"

He had the decency to at least grimace. "The price was right."

I sighed and shook my head. All along I'd suspected John had still been cooking. But hearing him admit to being what basically amounted to a magical mercenary made me sick to my stomach. Especially when he was cooking such dangerous shit. "You're a bigger asshole than I gave you credit for."

"Careful, Katie. It's a long fall down from a high horse."

I gritted my teeth and resisted rising to his bait. "So to recap: You made a completely untraceable truth serum, which has now been stolen by a fucking lunatic who plans to unleash some kind of weapon on the city in two nights."

He thought it over a second. " 'Bout sums it up."

"Not quite," I said. "Because now you want me to help you find him. Right?"

"Yep."

My laugh was bitter. "You got a pair of brass fucking balls. I'll give you that."

"Look, Kate, I know you're mad at me. I probably even deserve it."

I snorted. "Oh, you definitely deserve that and more."

"Regardless, we have the same goal where Dionysus is concerned."

"Not really. I want to stop him before he can hurt innocent people. You just want your property back."

He tilted his head. "Jesus, you're so jaded. What the fuck happened to you?"

I thunked my glass on the table. "Life happened, John."

"As it happens, I have just as much investment in protecting this city—more. Especially now."

Something in his tone made the hair on my neck stand on end. "Why now?"

He leaned back and looked me directly in the eyes. "Because I'm running in Owens's place for mayor."

The words were so incomprehensible and unexpected, they left me punch drunk. "Wha—"

He nodded. "The special election will be held in March."

"What the fresh fuck? You? Mayor?" I laughed out loud now that my brain had started working again. "That's fucking hilarious."

His face hardened. Not with doubt but with that look proud people get when they're doubted. "I don't see what's so funny about it."

"You can't be serious. You're a criminal."

An eyebrow rose. "With a sealed record thanks to an immunity deal."

I paused. I'd forgotten about that part. After John turned on Uncle Abe and testified against him, he'd gotten a clean bill of legal health thanks to the US attorney's office. "Hernandez isn't running?" After Owens died the head of the city council, Pablo Hernandez, took over as acting mayor until a special election could be held. Hernandez was one of Owens's longtime cronies. I'd just assumed the mayor's office was as good as his.

John picked at an invisible speck on his leg. "Mr. Hernandez has had a change of heart about his ambitions. He'll serve until the election is over, but he won't be running."

I frowned. "What about Rebis?" Anton Rebis came from old steel money. Despite his full coffers, no one had expected him to give Owens much of a problem in the election. But now Owens was dead. Would the city really pick an Adept, like Volos, over an old-money Mundane candidate?

"Soon Mr. Rebis will be busy doing some damage control over an unfortunate incident involving a minor."

I blinked. Owens was barely cold, but John had already managed to not only launch a bid for mayor, but also ensure any opposition would be destroyed. "Holy shit," I said. "You really want this?"

He nodded. "I really do."

"What's your angle?"

He shook his head. "Why does there have to be an angle, Kate? Why is it you're the only one allowed to serve this city?"

That brought me up short. "I didn't say that—"

"Anyway," he said, standing, "regardless of my motivations, I'm entirely too busy with the campaign to seek vendetta justice against Dionysus."

Something clicked for me in the subtext of his little speech. "Oh, wait. I get it." I stood, too, and went to stare out the windows overlooking the lake. "Now that you're running for mayor you need to keep your nose clean."

"Yes," he said, coming to stand next to me. "Plus, I would like to announce my candidacy on November first."

I looked up at him and laughed bitterly. "And displaying Dionysus's head to the masses will do wonders for your campaign."

His lips twitched. "I knew you were a smart girl."

I closed my eyes. A sensation of water closing in around me, rising up to cover my head. The moral part of me, the one that had principles, wanted to tell John to go fuck himself. To walk away and let the whole fucking city sink to the bottom of Lake Erie. But the cop part of me—the watchdog—couldn't surrender the henhouse to wolves like Uncle Abe and Dionysus. I knew which side of me would win. It was always the part that won despite the murky grayness of the choice. When I opened my eyes again, I found John watching me with a solemn expression.

"You hate me again." A statement.

"I never stopped."

Turning away, I went to go look at the pictures. I'd have to spin whatever information I got from John with the team. But I reminded myself that one more half-truth in a history of lies wasn't so much a sin as a means of survival. "What do you know that I don't about Dionysus?"

"That's the problem." John refilled his glass. When he held up the bourbon as if to ask if I wanted a top-off, I shook my head. Now that I knew the score, I couldn't risk it. He shrugged. "I'm not sure I know much more than you. This guy's good. Thorough."

I nodded. "He's been one step ahead of us this whole time. We only find clues when he wants us to find them."

"What do you know about his motivations?"

I looked up from the pictures. "The usual. Mom and Dad thoroughly fucked him up, so now he's making the world pay. Only he's charismatic enough to sell his revenge as a new sort of religion."

I started pacing around the living area. Helped me think better as I talked. "So far we know he's stolen a rape potion and a truth elixir. So it's a good bet whatever he's planning involves those two things."

"Nothing tears down society's foundations faster than truth and sex," he said. "What's his delivery method?"

Worrying my bottom lip with my teeth, I made a pass by the kitchen. "Water sources?"

"Lake Erie is the water source for the entire city. Too large."

"But he could dump it into one of the filtration tanks."

"Maybe, but that seems too quiet for his MO. He'll want fireworks."

I stopped and turned. "When we raided his last known residence, there was a bomb waiting for us. Probably more where

271

that came from." My heart picked up pace. *Two nights, two nights, two nights*, my mind chanted. I started pacing again.

"Considering how much potion he stole from Aphrodite and me, he's got to have a large facility to store all this stuff while he prepares."

My pacing trail took me past John's bar. With the cogs of my mind spinning, my gaze barely grazed each item I saw. "The BPD's already searched all the warehouses at the docks," I said. "And all the abandoned factories along the tracks. It could be any—"

I stopped in my tracks as a wine label on the bar captured my attention: a dancing satyr playing a lute. The name of the brand was Veritas. I grabbed the bottle and pointed it at him. "Where'd you get this?"

John shrugged. "A client sent it to me. Haven't had a chance to try it."

"When did you get it?" I looked down at the bottle and flipped it over.

"About a week"—he paused as if it had just clicked for him, too—"ago."

The label on the back held the typical jargon about alcohol percentage. The description said, "This sexy red should be consumed when you're ready to lose all your inhibitions." I held up the bottle and recited the name of the vineyard. "Dithyramb Winery—Babylon, Ohio."

John's eyes widened. "You're shitting me."

Dithyramb was the term for an ancient hymn to Dionysus.

I shook my head and handed the bottle over. My brain was busy thinking about the call from Val. Pulling my phone out, I checked the image she'd e-mailed me. "I'll be damned."

"Hmm?"

I looked up. "Last night, Dionysus hexed a couple of

272

sororities on campus with a rape potion. We arrested one of his followers on site thinking he'd slipped it into their drinks. But I found out earlier the potion had been in the wine when it was bottled. The labels of the bottles on the scene match this one."

John hefted the bottle in one hand. "Who else you think he sent these to?"

I glanced toward his door. "I'd bet our friend across the hall received some, or it was hand-delivered." I made a mental note to call my friend Val at the BPD CSI lab and see if they'd logged any opened wine bottles at the crime scene.

"Let's see what we can find on this winery." John walked over to the counter, where a sleek, silver laptop sat open like he'd abandoned it when I'd arrived. He quickly shut down a window filled with what looked like accounting spreadsheets. The only number I saw on it had so many zeros I couldn't count them.

He pulled up a browser and entered the name of the winery. Two seconds later we found it. "Jesus this guy's got a pair. Creating an entire online presence for his secret lair?"

The front page had a picture of a bottle of wine bearing the same label as the one John had received. Along the top were typical links: Home, About, Discussion Boards, Map.

The map showed a location on the far side of Babylon, along the Steel River before the city's pollution got ahold of the water. The area was a popular destination for Babylonians looking to get away for a weekend. Lots of charming bed-and-breakfasts and antiques shops. And, apparently, the headquarters of a madman masquerading as a winemaker.

"I'll be damned. I've driven by that place before. Back then it was called Babylon Cellars."

John clicked on the Discussion Board link. And immediately ran into a password-protected page. A large red warning claimed this area was for members only, but there was no place to request membership. "Wonder if this is how he spread his instructions to his followers."

I pulled my phone from my pocket and punched a number. "Gardner, it's Prospero, can you call the team together at the gym."

"We're all here," she said. I cursed realizing that while I'd slept off the potion from the night before, they'd been working all day to break the case. "You coming in?"

"I'll be there soon."

"Everything okay?"

"I found him."

"Get your ass here yesterday."

"Yes, sir."

I hung up. "All right. I'm headed in."

John stood. "You'll be careful, right?"

I grimaced at him. "Don't pretend you care about anything other than getting credit for breaking the case."

He put his hands on my shoulders. "Shut up. You can convince yourself I'm your enemy, but deep down you know it's because we have unfinished business." His hands kneaded my flesh and his pupils had that special light men's eyes get when they think you're going to allow them access to one of your holes.

"Thanks for reminding me." His lips started to curve into a charming smile. I removed it with my knuckles.

His head snapped back. Pain shot through my hand and wrist. When I pulled it back, blood coated the skin. John's blood. It was my turn to smile.

A rivulet of blood leaked from his left nostril. He didn't wipe it away. Instead he watched me with red-flushed cheeks. I couldn't tell if he was angry or turned on, but I suspected it was a little of both. I wasn't naive enough to believe John actually wanted me; more that he wanted to assert himself over me. "That was...unexpected."

"Shouldn't have been," I said, shaking my throbbing hand. "Stay away from Danny."

He stepped forward, lording his height over me. "Or what?" he whispered.

I made a gun out of my fingers and stabbed it just over his heart.

His eyes flared. He caught my hand with his larger one and pulled it up to his mouth. His tongue flicked against the sensitive skin, sending lightning from my hand down to my toes.

Snatching my hand back, I closed it into a tight fist. I told myself the unexpected spike of arousal was an aftershock from the night before. But my libido called me a liar. Like magic, John was a dirty vice I couldn't afford to indulge or I'd risk losing myself to it completely. Mixed in with the shameful attraction was a hefty dose of anger that left me unsure whether I wanted to fight him or fuck him. My breath coming faster, I pushed away. His eyes tracked me like a predator.

"This isn't over," he threatened.

I licked my suddenly dry lips. "It was over ten years ago."

"Like hell it was."

I shook my head. "You're poison. I don't want you in my life."

He raised his hands to the side. "Like it or not, I'm in it, sweetheart. Besides, you came to me—twice, now, isn't it?"

I clenched my fists. He was right. Like a junkie I kept coming back. "Won't happen again."

"We'll see." He smiled. "Good luck with Dionysus. I'm sure that partner of yours won't find watching your ass a hardship."

The spike of jealousy in his words pleased me. "He hasn't complained about it so far."

With that, I turned the ass in question toward him and walked away. "Good-bye, psycho."

"Good *night*, Kate."

Chapter Twenty-Six

An hour later Gardner slammed down the phone and marched out of her office. Mez, Morales, Shadi, and I were gathered around the whiteboard in the old boxing ring. I'd posted a map with a big red X over the winery onto the board. While she'd been on the phone with Eldritch, I'd been telling them everything I knew so far, which wasn't nearly enough to make this op a slam dunk.

"He can't spare the backup," Gardner said. "Some of Aphrodite's girls are staging a protest at city hall and there's a jumper on the Bessemer Bridge who's got traffic backed up for miles."

"Did you tell him this winery is the best and only lead we have on Dionysus?"

She shot me a give-me-some-credit look that prompted me to immediately mumble an apology.

"Okay, so we don't have BPD backup," Morales said. "What's our play?"

Gardner scowled and looked down at the floor. After a few tense moments, she shook her head. "We can't risk it."

"Sir—" I began, but she cut me off.

"Save your breath, Prospero. I understand the risks involved. I also know how close we are to the Blue Moon. That's exactly why I can't send you in. This guy's been one step ahead of us since the new moon." She shot a grave frown around the circle. "He'll for damned sure have the winery rigged in case of ambush."

"But—"

"No," she said. "He knew we'd eventually put this wine thing together. Didn't you say they found a bottle at Owens's murder scene?"

I nodded. On my way back to the gym, I'd called Val at CSI, who confirmed they'd collected a half-empty wine bottle from the scene with the same label. She'd tested it for the plant-based poison that had killed Owens. Naturally, it was a match. Since Aphrodite was their suspect, they'd used that information as justification for arresting her. But now that we knew the source of the wine, it was looking more and more like Dionysus had framed the Hierophant. However, even if Eldritch would listen to us, the fact remained that jail was probably the safest place for Aphrodite Johnson while Dionysus was still on the loose.

"Val said she'd take the information to Eldritch. But we still need proof Dionysus is the one who gave Owens that wine."

"We still have two nights until Halloween," Mez said. "We can go in tomorrow."

I shook my head. Deep in my gut—down by the place I stored my resolve—the cop sensor that told me I was close to nabbing the bad guy flashed like a homing beacon. I knew I was asking Gardner to ignore her own instincts to protect her team. I knew I was putting us all in danger. I also knew I didn't deserve their trust. But that's the part they didn't know.

So it was difficult to find the words to convince them to trust me. "Sir, may I speak with you a sec?"

Her eyes narrowed. "Speaking to me in private won't change my mind on this, Prospero. I won't let you get hexed again."

Panic pressed like icy air against my sternum. "I'll wear a protection amulet," I blurted. "And use Mez's new magic sensor."

The entire team looked at me like I'd just sprouted horns and a tail. I crossed my arms. "What?"

"But you never voluntarily use magic," Mez said.

I forced a casual shrug. "Whether I want to or not, the Blue Moon makes me twice as vulnerable to getting hexed, as we learned last night."

"You won't have to worry about it at all since I'm not signing off on this raid," Gardner said in her favorite because-I-said-so tone.

I looked her in the eye and went for her jugular. "If we do not stop Dionysus you can forget the team's safety, because the entire city will be on its knees. And it will be your fault."

She jerked back like I'd struck her. "You are out of line, Prospero."

"No she's not, sir." Morales stood. "She's right. It's our safety versus millions. We have to do this."

Thunder rolled behind her eyes. "You're going to risk your life based on evidence that is circumstantial at best?"

He shook his head and glanced at me. "No, I'm putting my life on the line because my partner believes it's the right play."

Gardner looked at the others to gauge their reactions. Shadi nodded that she was in, too. Mez sat back and hooked his elbows over the back of his seat. "Now or never."

My gut shriveled with doubt. They didn't know they were putting their faith in a liar. I opened my mouth to say—

Shit, I didn't know what to say. They'd just given me the answer I wanted. I couldn't very well try to talk them out of it now. Still, a small cluster of synapses in the back of my head was urging Gardner to pull the plug and send us all home.

She looked around the circle at all of us. I tried to keep my expression neutral, but the tension between my eyes told me I was failing. She walked over to the whiteboard and studied the map for a moment. Her shoulders were tense, and her hands clasped and unclasped at her side like a beating heart.

With her back to us, she finally spoke. "You will wear every anti-Arcane weapon at our disposal."

My heart lurched and then broke into a gallop.

"You will not split up. You will not be out of radio range for even a moment. You will abort the mission the instant there is a sign of trouble."

"Yes, sir," Morales said in a strong, true voice. Thank God he had one because I suddenly had a fist blocking my throat.

She turned to address us like a general speaking to troops. Her eyes burned with determination and something hotter than fear. "You will find this asshole. And if he makes one off move, you will shoot to kill."

Chapter Twenty-Seven

October 30
Waxing Gibbous

It was midnight by the time we made our way out of the city. The moon was at our back over Lake Erie, but in the rearview it loomed like a neon warning. Out here in the rural area east of the city, electric lights were scarce. The moon's light cast the fields and wooded areas bordering the highway in an otherworldly silver glow.

Before we'd headed out, I'd called Baba again to ask her to stay with Danny. She didn't ask why. She'd heard the tension in my tone. The promise of danger. "Watch your ass, Katie."

"Yes, ma'am."

Now we were speeding away from Baba and Danny and safety. Inside the SUV, the air was heavy and thick with tension.

"Shadi, what did you find out about the winery?" Morales asked.

She was in the backseat with her laptop, pulling up everything she could from online city records. I sat beside her while Morales and Gardner took the front seats. Mez was dialed into the car through the phone speaker. The wiz was in a van behind us that would serve as the command post for the mission. Gardner decided the wiz needed to stay back while we went in so he could monitor all of the sensors and amulets we had strapped to our bodies.

"According to the real estate records," Shadi said, "the place was foreclosed upon about ten years ago. A couple by the name of Daniels bought it three years back with the hopes of reviving the vineyards and restoring the buildings to serve as a bed-and-breakfast. They reopened eighteen months ago under the name Babylon Cellars." She clicked a couple more times. "I just pulled up the website and it has a banner announcing the B and B is temporarily closed for the month of October."

"Interesting," I said, "considering this should be peak time for them with the grape harvest and all."

"Question is did Dionysus kill them when he took over the place or brainwash them like he did the others?" I asked.

"Be ready for anything," Gardner said, her tone tight as piano wire. To Morales, she said, "Your turn's coming up."

He leaned forward in the seat. The lights from the dashboard controls lit up the determination in his expression. A few moments later the car slowed. On the left a single-lane road veered off into a stand of trees. "You sure this is it?"

I tried to see down the dark throat, but the darkness was as impenetrable as a black hole.

Gardner nodded. "This will take us around the outer perimeter of the vineyard. We'll be able to approach from the back of the building this way."

"Everyone go ahead and engage their bio-monitors now,"

Mez said. I turned and saw the headlights of the stopped van a few feet behind our vehicle. "I'll go camp out toward the entrance of the winery and monitor you all from there."

Turning back, I reached down and flipped the button on the monitor at my waist. About two inches round, the contraption sent a signal to Mez's computers with my heart rate, temperature, and whatever other biorhythms he thought it necessary to watch. Using the pin that attached my badge to my wallet, I pricked my finger and milked a few drops from the skin. The instant I touched the amulet with my blood, it warmed and started glowing in my hand. The magic inside allowed the wiz to track us without the need for satellites. The blood also engaged the magical force field of sorts that helped dampen potion attacks. When I put the amulet back around my neck, it felt heavy, and my skin crawled like someone had walked over my grave. I hated the sizzle of magic on the skin, but I reminded myself that if I hadn't agreed to this compromise, Gardner never would have let us move forward with the raid.

Pen's voice nagged at me, ticking off yet another principle pushed aside in favor of duty. I pushed it aside ruthlessly. Refusing magical protection when I was about to face down a psychotic wizard was damned near suicidal.

"Everyone good?" Morales looked back. I nodded despite the nausea roiling in my gut. When we all confirmed we'd engaged our defensive items, he told Mez we were a go.

"I see everyone on the monitor," Mez said through the speaker. "Happy hunting, guys. See you all in a few."

With that, the van pulled out and continued down the highway. I watched the taillights recede like two red eyes in the distance.

"All right, everyone," Gardner said. "Radio silence starting now."

Morales cut the lights and turned into the dark. The lack of light and sound created a dark vacuum in the car. The visceral pressure built in my chest and head until I wanted to claw my skin off and run through the woods like a night thing.

I wasn't sure if the journey took five minutes or fifty, but eventually a sliver of light up ahead signaled our exit from the tree tunnel. Morales pulled the SUV to a stop at the border between dark and dim light. Without speaking, we all exited the vehicle, bringing with us the tools of our trade: salt flares, S&P spray, hawthorn wood wands, potion bombs, and lots and lots of guns.

A wide field was the borderland between the woods and the first rows of vineyard. Grapevines snaked up wooden spikes in row after row after row. Far to our right, dim lights identified the winery's main house. And straight ahead, over the tops of the vines, the moon danced off the serpentine waters of the Steel River.

Crouching low, I jogged toward the fruit-heavy vines. My heart trotted in time with my steps, and a fine sheen of sweat coated my skin despite the smoky autumn chill. Out here in the countryside, the air smelled of yawning earth preparing for a winter's hibernation. The silence was broken only by the repetitive crack of my defensive wand against my cuffs and the creak of leather. Toads sang night songs along the riverbed, and the occasional hoot of an owl punctuated the night with a question mark.

Gardner and Shadi ran into one row of vines, which would dump them out toward the right of the winery house. Morales motioned toward me to follow him down a left-facing row. This course would bring us almost directly to the back door of the building. As I entered the track, I pulled my Glock and prayed Mez's detection amulets would warn us before we stumbled into a trap.

The uneven ground forced me to feel my way slowly across the terrain. Up ahead, Morales's shoulders filled my vision, and their width was a reassuring sort of shadow, blocking my view of what was coming. But just like he trusted me to go forward with the raid, I trusted him to warn me of danger.

We were almost at the end of the row when his left fist came up. I halted immediately and listened. At first, my ears were buzzing too full of adrenaline to hear it. But soon the noise in my head was drowned out by the sound of a shouted argument from somewhere in the compound.

I glanced at Morales. He shrugged, but tightened his grip on his gun like he suspected a trap.

Just beyond the vines, a low fence separated us from the gravel yard surrounding the house. A large barn-like structure that I assumed was the place where the wine barrels were stored stood probably fifty yards from the old Victorian, and an open stable-turned-garage held a rusty old truck. I couldn't tell which building the argument originated in, but I was pretty sure if we found the source, we'd find Dionysus.

I punched a button on my vest. "Chief, I smell trouble."

"Roger that," she replied in my ear. "Mez, you listening?"

"What's up?" came the reply.

"We got indications of an altercation on the premises. Call BPD and have them send backup stat. If Eldritch denies the request, call in the tactical wizes from the sheriff's office."

"Got it." With that the wizard clicked off to call in the cavalry.

"All right," Gardner said to the rest of us. "Hang back until we have confirmation of backup. But keep an eye out for imminent threats."

I wanted to argue with her that we needed to move now, but I knew better. Rushing in without confirmation of imminent danger to a civilian was a recipe for a shit show.

Morales pulled his binoculars from his vest and aimed them at the house. "All the windows are shaded."

"Might be coming from the barn," Shadi said through our ears.

Our earpieces crackled with Mez's voice again. "No go, sir. Eldritch is shitting himself because a group of costumed demonstrators have started a riot outside city hall."

"What about the tac wizes?"

"Bomb threat at the county jail."

Doubts crept like vines over the instincts that convinced me Dionysus was at the vineyard. "Shit," I said. "Maybe I was wrong."

Morales opened his mouth to say something. But before he could, the unmistakable sound of a shotgun blast exploded.

"Holy shit," Mez said. "Tell me you guys heard that."

Gardner replied, "Get us backup now! I don't care what you have to do. The rest of you, approach with extreme caution."

"But, sir—" Shadi began.

"I don't know if Dionysus is in there, but we can't afford to ignore shots fired. Shadi and I will take the barn. Morales, Prospero, clear the house. Everyone watch your asses."

Morales glanced at me and nodded.

I nodded back because I didn't trust myself to speak. Once I heard that shot, my adrenaline spiked and my muscles twitched with the need to run toward trouble.

In the next instant Morales burst forward like a sprinter from a block. His large body moved with surprising agility, hurdling the wire fence with ease. I followed behind him, my own legs shorter and less graceful. But I managed to leap the fence without too much trouble. Landing on the other side, we crouched, ready for ambush. To my left I saw Gardner and Shadi clear the fence as well, and run, blending in with the shadows closer to the barn.

Morales waved me on, and together we ran toward the house. Lights illuminated rosemary bushes with their sharp green scent all around the perimeter of the house, but all of the lower-level windows were dark, like closed lids on sleepy eyes.

When we got to the back door, Morales walked up the two steps and carefully touched the knobs. My eyes scanned the grounds for movement. Except for the leaves waving on the large tree in the center of the courtyard, the place was still, almost as if holding its breath.

The door cracked open easily. I turned to Morales and pointed my gun forward to cover him as he rolled into the room. Darker here. The air hot and heavy, like someone had punched the thermostat too high. The coppery scent of blood like a slap.

The *chunk-thunk* of a racking shotgun. Instant adrenaline.

Me rolling left. Morales lunged right. Blinding flash. Booming assault to the eardrums. Wood and glass splintered over my head. Stinging skin, cold welling of blood. Deafening silence. Then—

Chunk-thunk-BOOM!

I don't know where the second shot hit, but I knew it was only a matter of time before a bullet found my vulnerable fleshy parts. Scrambling on my belly, I crawled behind a chair. My heart pistoned in my chest. Thoughts scattered like buckshot.

Where's Morales? Where's the shooter? Can I get a clear shot? Can the shooter? Shit, this chair won't protect me. Need to move. But where? Gun's cocked. *Don't get shot, Kate, Don't get shot, Kate, Don't get shot, Kate.*

I peeked around the edge of the armchair. A shadow moved near another doorway. Shooter reloading.

"MEA," Morales shouted from the other side of the room. "Put down the gun."

"You got a warrant, secret agent man?"

I frowned. The voice was female. Definitely not Dionysus. I remembered what Shadi said about the property belonging to the Daniels couple.

"Mrs. Daniels," I called, "put down the gun before you get hurt."

Chunk-thunk. "Maybe you should be taking your own advice, Detective Prospero."

My stomach contracted. How the fuck did this chick know who I was? I scooted over to look around the chair to locate Morales. His eyes flashed like dark marbles where he crouched across the room. His brows rose as if to ask if I knew this woman. I shook my head to tell him no, shit was just a lot more serious than we expected. Because if this chick knew my name, chances were pretty good Dionysus did, too.

"Here's what's going to happen," Mrs. Daniels continued, "you're gonna lay down your weapons—all of them, and then we're gonna go to a party."

"What kind of party?" Morales asked. To me he made a motion with his hands. I nodded.

She made a dismissive sound with her lips. "A moon par—"

I burst up from my hiding space, yelling like a banshee. Time slowed. Mrs. Daniels's face opened into shock. She spun toward me, raising that double-eyed monster high. My fingers tightened on my trigger. But before she or I could make good on our promises, a third weapon exploded from across the room.

The bullet hit her in the center of her neck. The impact

forced her body into a death roll. The shotgun swept around. Her hand spasmed.

Boom!

The shotgun's blast hit about three feet from Morales's head.

Daniels's body slumped to the floor. Blood gushed from her neck like a fountain. I jumped toward her, kicking the shotgun to the side. I bent down to check her pulse, but there wasn't much left of her neck. Her cornflower-blue eyes were wide enough to see the Pearly Gates.

Two boots appeared in my peripheral. "You all right?" I asked without looking up. I couldn't stop staring at those eyes. Those deep watery pools were glazing over, like a pond choked with algae—stagnant. Dead.

"I'm good," Morales said above me. "How much you wanna bet Mr. Daniels is nearby?"

Something tickled the back of my mind. Some sensory memory. "Wait," I said, "the blood."

Morales made a pitying noise with his mouth. "Yeah that happens when you hit their carotid."

I shook my head and stood, my eyes finally scanning the room as a whole instead of flashes of input from when we were being shot at. A ratty sofa under a pair of windows looking out on the courtyard. The chintz armchair I'd used for cover. In the corner, a small, warped wood table with an old gas lamp. A river-rock hearth and mantel with weathered pictures of proper ladies and dapper gentlemen in old-timey costumes. But no blood, except the rapidly spreading pool at our feet.

"Prospero? What's going on in that head?"

I pulled my gaze from the photos and looked at him. "When we came in—before the first shot—I smelled blood."

The skin between his brows puckered, and his eyes scanned

the room. "You're right. I forgot about it once the shotgun shouted hello."

The sound of running footsteps outside had both of us reaching for our weapons again. But instead of Mr. Daniels or Dionysus, the rest of our team came through the door. "We heard more shots." Gardner froze, her eyes on the corpse on the ground.

"Mrs. Daniels, I presume," Shadi said.

"Did you find anyone in the barn?" I asked.

Gardner shook her head. "Wine barrels and potion ampoules, though."

A timid sort of relief bloomed in my chest. If we'd been wrong about the connection between Dionysus and the winery, we would have had a lot of explaining to do about the rapidly cooling body at our feet and why we'd gone to the vineyard in the first place.

Our earpieces buzzed. Mez's voice boomed in our ears. "What the fuck is going on in there?"

"We're all good," Gardner said. "Morales and Prospero took down a civilian with a shotgun. We'll need the ME. Where's my backup?"

"The bomb threat was a hoax, so Sheriff's sending the tac wizes."

"Shit," I said. "If they were at the county jail, it'll take them twenty minutes minimum."

"Thanks, Mez." Gardner looked around at all of our curious expressions. She sighed like she needed the oxygen to steel her resolve. "All right," she continued, sounding older suddenly, "let's clear this house. The husband's around here somewhere."

"Or his body is, anyway," I said. "We smelled blood when we walked in."

They nodded solemnly and split off toward the kitchen. To get there, they had to step over Mrs. Daniels's body. Funny how now she seemed just another set piece, another prop in this drama.

Shadi went through the kitchen first. "Goddamn."

We pushed through the doorway. The stink of dirty copper was stronger there.

The floor and walls were covered with Rorschach inkblots of blood. A gory butterfly. A sinister jack-o'-lantern with fangs. A melting clown's face.

A fucking mess.

"Where's the body?" Morales asked suddenly.

The room's layout offered up two possibilities. To our right a set of stairs led to the second floor. There was blood on the stairs, but from where I stood it appeared to be more spatter instead of the smears that might indicate a dragged body.

To our left, a closed door probably led down to the basement. Blood on the door, more on the knob.

"Shadi and I go up," Gardner said. "You two go down."

We watched those two climb the steps before approaching the door.

Morales grabbed a dish towel from the sink and used it to turn the knob. He stayed out of the way in case there was a nasty surprise waiting for us on the other side. Only silence and inky darkness greeted us. A single, bare bulb hung above the risers, but I didn't flip the switch because it would make us a target to anyone below. We'd have to rely on the glow from the kitchen that illuminated the first few steps down.

I stepped forward. "Cover me."

He opened his mouth to argue, but a raised brow on my part convinced him to keep his argument to himself. I took up less space. Easier for me to plaster myself against the wall on the right side of the steps and make it past the meager pool of light to see what was waiting on the dark side.

I pulled air in through my nostrils, willing it to shoo away the wasps swarming in my stomach. One step, two.

My heart was a distant drum in my ears and competed with the rushing of air in, out and in, out and in, out. Three, four, five.

The shadows played tricks on my eyes. Was that really movement beyond the light or an illusion?

Step six brought me to the edge of the wall. Beyond that point, two thin rails sat on either side of the staircase. I knelt down, my knees popping in protest, and squinted into the cave-like area beyond.

It took a few moments for my eyes to adjust. Those few seconds were all my mind needed to offer up a highlight reel of horrors. Knowledge from deep in my marrow whispered in my ear: *He's down here.*

The cold fist in my gut also told me there was a gun aimed at me. Inside that gun was a casing with my name engraved. And inside that casing was a bullet that wanted to make itself a home in my chest.

I squinted toward the center of the large basement. It took a moment before I saw the movement. Something swaying in the shadows. I raised my gun and pointed it at the...thing or person. "Put your hands up."

No response, except for a slight creak and a constant drip, drip, dripping.

With a trembling right hand, I grabbed the pin light from the utility belt at my waist. I turned it on and pointed it in the same direction my gun was focused. It took a few seconds to realize what I was seeing. A pale, hairy arm, a naked torso, another hairy arm. Back and forth it swung like a pendulum.

I lowered the light's aim, and the source of the dripping became clear: a large puddle of blood. I stuck the light between my teeth and groped for a switch with my right hand. Finally, my fingers found my goal and flipped the lever up. Another bare bulb in the center of the basement exploded into sudden brightness.

Pain behind my eyes. Confusion. Then...horror.

I grabbed the light from between my lips. "Morales."

His footsteps pounded down the steps behind me. I kept my gun aimed for the body just in case Dionysus or someone else came barreling out of a hiding space.

"That sick fuck," Morales said.

The body of a man who I assumed was Mr. Daniels hung from the rafters by a length of chain wrapped around his neck. The center of his chest was a gaping hole. That certainly explained the mess in the kitchen. But the gory wound wasn't what had bile crawling up the back of my throat and Morales cussing.

The man's penis and testicles hung from a length of rope around his neck. I'm no forensics expert, but judging from the copious blood and the visible clots where the penis used to be attached, the wound probably occurred before Daniels was shot.

"You think this was Dionysus or the wife?" I asked, recalling Mrs. Daniels's shotgun.

Before Morales could answer, my eyes caught movement in the shadows. I swiveled my gun that direction, blowing out air to dispel the surge of adrenaline. A silhouette emerged from the dark corner and into the pool of light.

"Freeze!" Morales and I shouted in stereo.

His head was down at first and his hands were clasped sub-missively behind his neck. He wore a white tank top spattered

red with blood, old-fashioned suspenders attached to frayed jeans. Cuffs rolled up at the ankles to expose combat boots smeared in more of Daniels's blood. Two full sleeves of tattoos covering sinewy muscles.

He raised his head and hit me with the force of two fevered green eyes. The violence in that stare took my breath away even as it made cold sweat crawl over my skin.

The magic detector amulet on my vest went apeshit.

"Prospero? Morales?" Mez's panicked voice came through the earpiece. His breath came out in loud bursts, like he was running. "What the fuck's going on?"

I lifted my free hand to my vest to respond. A blast of magical energy shook the house. The sickening stench of ozone rolled through the air. I ducked, looking up at the dust flying down from the rafters.

"What the fuck was that?" Morales shouted.

"Your team found my little booby traps."

My stomach did a death roll in my gut. I hit the button. "Mez?"

Silence.

"Shadi? Gardner? You guys, okay?"

Static was the only response.

"Fuck!" Morales gritted out.

I squeezed the gun so hard, my knuckles went white. "What did you do?"

"Relax, Kate," he said. Hearing my name on his lips made me feel dizzy. "They're alive. They're just . . . sleeping."

Morales took an aggressive step forward. "Do. Not. Move."

Something around the eyes changed. A tightening.

"Now!" I projected, deepening my voice.

His whole body undulated, and his eyes fluttered. I realized he didn't loathe being bossed around. He got off on it. I didn't have time to be unsettled, so I used it to my advantage. This time I lowered my voice to give the order extra punch. "Do not disobey me, Scott."

He sucked a deep breath, making his nostrils flare. His tongue darted out from his mouth. The shocking red of it contrasted against his beard in a way that reminded me of sex.

"I feel it, too," he whispered.

Something in my stomach pitched. My hand tightened on the gun. "ON. YOUR. KNEES."

This time he obeyed. His hands were still behind his head, but a smile hovered on his lips. With my right hand, I removed a set of lead cuffs from my back pocket. The weight was cold and heavy in my palms. The lead wouldn't offer me much protection if he had a magical trick up his sleeve, but they'd hold his hands through almost anything.

"She's going to cuff you now," Morales said behind me. "You so much as breathe on her and I'll make you bleed. Got it?"

The corner of McQueen's mouth twisted up in anticipation. His eyes stayed on me, daring me to be nervous. He shouldn't have looked so cocksure. I wasn't nervous, I was pissed off.

I reached out to grab his hand. But before I saw it coming, he struck like a snake. With one hand he grabbed my wrist, pivoted, and with his other hand slammed a weapon against my jugular.

At first I thought it was a Mundane gun. That bullet with my name engraved. Time slowed and my life flared behind my eyes like a stop-motion montage.

Click. Baby Danny gumming my pinkie.

Click. Volos whispering that he loved me right before he took my virginity.

Click. Mom's dead body laid out in a coffin.

Click. The day I earned my badge.

Click. The day I joined the task force.

Click. Morales screaming my name.

Boom!

I'd expected bigger pain. Total annihilation. Instead the pain was a sharp stab above my jugular.

My vision wavered.

Another loud snap. Morales grunted.

My knees buckled.

The world was a blur of red and sounds. I fell in slow motion. From the corner of my eye, I saw the dart gun in Dionysus's hand. I tried to open my mouth, but no sound emerged. Pain exploded on my right side. My face smacked into the concrete. I gasped in a lungful of air but it wasn't enough. My ribs felt too small, constricting my lungs. I opened my eyes and saw the puddle of blood from Daniels's body a few inches from my face.

If the attack had happened on a random day my protection amulet would have absorbed the excess magical energy. But the moon's erratic energy must have put the thing on the fritz. Besides, a potion delivered in the vein was twice as potent as one splashed on the skin.

My body twitched, helpless, on the floor. A shadow loomed over me. The warped sound of mad laughter. My limbs twitched and my left eyelid convulsed. I tried to work my lips to say... something, but it was no use. Whatever he'd hit me with left me totally short-circuited.

Dionysus knelt down. I saw his hand on my skin but couldn't feel it. "Shh now," he whispered. Up close his eyes were otherworldly and menacing. "Surrender, Kate."

Somewhere in my panicked mind, I realized I couldn't see Morales. A whimper reached my ears, and I recognized that it had come from my throat.

Dionysus grabbed my chin and jerked my head toward the base of the stairs. Morales's body lay in an unmoving heap. Before I could register that my partner might be dead, a hand rose above me and came down hard.

I couldn't even flinch in a vain attempt to avoid the hit. I didn't feel the pain, but a split second later the watery image of Dionysus's face wavered and dimmed. And then, there was nothing but black.

Chapter Twenty-Eight

October 31
Blue Moon

I woke on a gasp. The world rolled beneath me. The green haze of nausea clogged my throat and made my stomach protest consciousness. Blinking against the darkness, I tried to find my bearings. Unfortunately, the darkness didn't give me a clue about the time, so I had no idea if I'd slept a few hours or a few days.

I swallowed hard and tried to focus my senses on finding clues.

The rhythmic sound of water captured my attention first. Then the overpowering scent of algae and the chemical odor of a portable toilet made my nausea regain steam. A boat then, I decided. I'd spent a week on harbor patrol duty back during my time as a rookie, and I'd never forget the odor of that fucking chemical toilet.

I moved my fingers and realized my wrists were bound in

front of me. My head ached like I'd hit it, and my face felt like someone had tried to tenderize it with their fist. So basically, I was a mess physically. Mentally I wasn't faring much better.

My thoughts were caged animals in my head, pacing, pacing, pacing. Where was I? What could I use for a weapon? Were Gardner, Mez, and Shadi alive? Where was Morales?

A low groan next to me. I angled my head and saw a large body in a heap to my right.

Hope exploded in my chest. "Morales?"

A familiar grunt reached my ears. "Fuck."

"Thank Christ," I whispered. "Are you okay?"

"You mean besides the cracking headache, being bound in a strange boat by a madman, and having no weapons?" came the caustic reply. "Yeah, Kate, I'm peachy fucking keen."

I pressed my lips together to suppress a smile. If he'd been seriously injured he wouldn't have had the energy for sarcasm. "Injuries?"

A couple of beats of silence indicated he was taking a mental inventory. "Hit my head when I fell. Possible concussion." His tone was less acidic this time. "And I've lost some blood."

I craned my neck for a better look. He lay maybe five feet away. He was facing me so I got an eyeful of the small pool of blood under his face. I tamped down my instinctive fear and tried to remind myself that head wounds always bled a lot. Made them seem worse than they were sometimes.

"That bad?" His lips screwed up into a forced grin.

I realized then that the skin between my brows was pinched to the point of pain. Forcing my expression to relax, I tried to look into his eyes. But I was too far away to see his pupils. I couldn't be positive without a closer examination, but it was safest to just assume he had a concussion.

"You'll live," I said, more to reassure myself than him.

"What's your status?"

I took a quick inventory of my pains. "Nothing worth worrying about." Not like his head, anyway. Between the blood loss and the concussion he was definitely impaired, which meant I'd need to take the lead on escape plans.

"Whatever you do," I whispered, "do not fall asleep."

Before he could respond to that, a loud creak overhead signaled that our captor was about to pay us a visit. Morales perked up, his body going alert. "That's not going to be a problem."

Heavy footsteps echoed overhead. I sat up straighter, scanning the area for possible weapons. Now that my eyes had adjusted to the darkness, I could see a small galley kitchen on the other end of the berth, but with my hands tied and dizziness circling my head, I doubted I could make it there before the person coming down the steps arrived.

An instant later the door opened and Dionysus emerged. He'd changed into a long white toga and a wreath of ivy. In his left hand he carried a wooden staff topped by a cluster of pinecones.

"Oh good, you're awake," he said in a conversational tone. As if we were guests instead of prisoners.

"You need to let us go," I said. "Our team will be here soon."

He shot me a sweet smile that was totally creepy given the circumstances. "Kate, Kate, Kate. It's been almost twenty-four hours. If they haven't found us yet, they won't." His grin made him look like the god of chaos he pretended to be. "At least, not until it's too late."

I looked down at my chest. Mez's protection amulet was gone. I glanced at Morales and saw that his was, too. Dionysus must have taken them once he'd potioned us. I'd bet my left hand, the backup that arrived way too late would find nothing in the house to lead them to this boat.

I closed my eyes and cursed.

"It's invigorating, isn't it?" Dionysus asked.

I opened my lids and glared at him. "What?" I snapped.

"Living life without a safety net. That sweet ache of vulnerability."

"The only thing aching is my ass."

"Did you know sarcasm is defense mechanism?" he asked in a light tone. "People who rely on it too heavily tend to be hiding something." He shot me a pointed look. "It's a mask."

"Wow, you really got so much out of the Psych 101 class in college. Did you take it before or after you killed your parents, Scott?"

His left eye twitched. "They killed themselves. I was simply their suicide weapon."

He sauntered over the galley and pulled a bottle of wine down from the shelf. He didn't speak again until he was in the process of pouring the red into a glass.

"After I slit both their throats," he continued casually, "I skinned their faces off their skulls." He took an experimental sip of the wine. Sloshed it around on his tongue before swallowing. He smiled and nodded at the glass, as if approving of its flavor. "I think that's what doomed me in the eyes of the jury. I tried to explain that their skin was hiding their true selves, but no one believed me."

If I worked that nerve, maybe he'd make a mistake. "I find it ironic that you're ranting about your parents wearing masks when you're the one parading around as a Greek god."

He ignored me and took another sip. "The only one who ever listened was the one who told me Babylon was the perfect setting for my plans."

"Who?" Morales demanded.

"Dr. Flamel."

I frowned. Then I remembered what Shadi had said about one of Scott's doctors believing his story at the psychiatric hospital. "Your psychiatrist?"

He nodded dismissively and set down the glass. "Anyway, time to move this little party to a more appropriate location." With languorous movement, he produced a gun from a hidden pocket in his toga. "If either of you tries to fight, I will shoot the other one in the head. Am I clear?"

I nodded stiffly, but my eyes were busy scanning the room for likely weapons or tools. From the corner of my eye, I saw Morales execute a curt nod. But I had a feeling that, like me, he didn't plan on giving the asshole a chance to get a shot off when he struck.

"Rise," the psycho demanded. The gun's unblinking eye moved back and forth between us. "Slowly."

I rose unsteadily. This part was not faked. Between the seasickness and the aftereffects of the knockout potion, I felt watery. Morales reached over as if to help me.

"Ah ah ah," Dionysus said. "Hands to yourself."

Morales glared at him and rose to his full height. Dionysus didn't look impressed by the display, but then he was the one with the gun and the complete lack of moral compass.

Dionysus flicked the gun toward the room's only exit—the stairs leading up to the deck. Morales moved first. I guessed this was some noble move on his part to be the one who faced whatever was waiting up there first. I didn't argue. As it happened it worked well for my plans.

I took a couple of uneasy steps in my partner's wake. But just as I started to pass the galley, I feigned a stumble. I sprawled sideways into the low, laminate counter.

A flurry of activity erupted behind me. Morales shouting my name. Dionysus telling him to stand back. Rough hands on my shoulders, forcing me upright.

"Watch yourself, bitch," Dionysus snapped.

"Sorry," I said breathlessly. "I got dizzy."

He grabbed my arm and pushed me roughly forward. I stumbled a couple of steps, hunched over as if defeated. But really this just gave me a chance to shove the corkscrew I'd nabbed when I fell into my pocket. I wasn't quite sure how I was going to get the rope off my wrists without Dionysus seeing, but having something pointy made me feel light-years better.

We made it up the steps without further incident. But the instant Morales stepped out, he cursed. Not a good sign.

I stepped out behind him and let out a curse that made his seem like saying grace.

It had been a while since I'd seen her without her makeup, but I recognized the priestess the instant I laid my eyes on her.

"What the fuck, Shayla?" I snapped.

She stood at the back of the boat, just beyond the awning covering the wheelhouse. She used both hands to hang on to a Glock .22, as if she expected it to jump out of her grasp at any moment. The tight jeans, stilettos, and bright red boob top seemed a tad much for boating, but who was I to judge a whore's fashion sense?

"Surprise," she said with a serpentine grin. When Dionysus stepped up to join her, Shayla's posture transformed into the practiced movements of a professional seductress. She slowly swiveled her aim toward me. "Let's kill them and go have some fun," she said, her tone kittenish now.

"Two people are definitely dying tonight, sweetheart," Morales said, "but Kate isn't one of them."

Dionysus kissed her forehead. "We'll get to that, but first we need to have our pre-party."

Her face fell into a pouty moue. "All right."

"You framed Aphrodite," I said, as my mind played catch-up. We'd originally thought Dionysus worked alone, but if Shayla helped—

"She made it easy. She was dumb enough to keep a file on the mayor with pictures in case she needed to blackmail him. I stole them and showed up at the mayor's apartment one night with a bottle of my master's wine. The rest was easy."

"So you started working for Dionysus after the robbery?" Morales asked.

"Ha!" the priestess mocked. "Who do you think left open the window in Aphrodite's lab?"

The pieces clicked together. Dionysus had gotten to Shayla before he attacked the temple—just as he'd gotten to Little Man and Mary. I clearly hadn't given her enough credit if she'd managed to fool Aphrodite and the MEA about involvement in the robbery.

"You should have followed your mom into the business," Shayla said. "You can't possibly suck in the sack more than you do at police work."

I pressed my lips together in a bitch-please expression. "I wouldn't imagine trying when you got the market on sucking dick cornered."

"No, that was your mama."

Another door opened by accident. Mom on her knees. Pulling back in surprise. A line of drool from the tip of a white penis to her too-red lips.

My hands tightened into a fist. "Watch your mouth."

"You should ask your uncle."

"Ask him what?"

"How good your mama sucked dick."

A red haze propelled me forward. All thoughts of cool heads and strategy dissipated under the heat of my anger. But before

I could launch myself at the bitch, a male fist plowed into my gut.

The air whooshed from my lungs. Pain radiated from my navel in concentric circles of agony. I fell to the deck in a heap. Preoccupied with the fire in my belly, I curled into a ball.

Rough hands grabbed my chin and suddenly I was forced to look into Dionysus's fevered eyes. Something glowed in their depths—excitement? "Do you want your partner to die?" he asked in a reasonable tone.

I swallowed the curdled pride in my throat and managed a stiff head shake.

He patted my cheek. "If you do anything like that again, I will put a bullet in his skull and then fuck that hole while the bomb destroys your precious city. Am I clear?"

The mental image he painted made me want to scrub my brain with bleach. "Yes," I said in a gravelly tone.

He jerked me off the ground. "Chair," he snapped at Shayla. "Put the other one there."

I was still too foggy from pain to track their movements, but before I knew it, I was forced to sit in a deck chair. Directly across from me, Morales received the same treatment.

Dionysus placed his hands on my shoulders. His fingers massaged the tense muscles, which only served to make them contract until it felt like he was kneading rocks under the skin. "Now," he said, close to my ear, "we're going to play a game."

Across the way, a grinning Shayla produced a syringe with a long, gleaming needle. Inside the syringe's barrel was iridescent green liquid. Movement behind me indicated that Dionysus was mirroring her. I jerked my neck away from him, but it was too late.

The sting of metal through the skin, the burn of magic

seeping into tissue. My heart skipped and then took off galloping like a spooked horse.

On some level I was aware of Morales fighting a similar battle not six feet from me, but I was too busy gulping in air and willing my heart not to burst to pay it much mind. Magic sizzled through my neck and down into my chest. Sweat bloomed on my forehead, and my vision went all hazy.

"Now," our captor said in an underwater voice, "if you tell the truth, you'll feel pleasure." He leaned down and licked up my neck over the puncture wound. "But if you lie, you will suffer." His teeth sank into the tender skin below my ear.

My limbs were weighed down and useless. My head lolled to the side, and I was panting from fear and pain. Inside, the potion ricocheted around my insides like lightning.

Across from me, sweat coated Morales's face and his cheeks were flushed. His biceps strained as he fought magic's claws. His wide eyes met mine. The lack of hope I saw in those dark irises worried me. Normally he was the one to crack a joke to ease the tension. But now he looked like a man who'd run out of options.

I swallowed hard against the bile surging in my throat. Until I took my last breath, I'd never believe there were no more options.

"Now." Dionysus stepped back and tapped a finger on his full lips. "Who wants to share first?"

Morales and I looked at each other across the space. I could feel my secrets crowding on the back of my tongue like tiny daggers. Morales looked as worried as I felt, so I assumed he was experiencing the same urges. That being the case, neither of us said a word, worried we'd spill our secrets without any further prompting.

"No one wants to volunteer?" Dionysus said. "Well, I guess we'll have to just do this the old-fashioned way."

From inside his toga, he held up my anniversary token necklace. A shock passed through me. I hadn't noticed it was missing. "Arcane Anonymous, huh? Bet that means you have lots of juicy secrets, Detective Prospero."

I didn't rise to the bait. Instead I zeroed in on the necklace, which, in addition to the token still bore the tiny vial Baba had given me.

"Ohh, you look mad," he said in a taunting tone. "Do you want it back?"

Until that moment, I hadn't appreciated how precious both items were. And now they were in the hands of a man who'd likely kill me in the immediate future. But I wouldn't give him the satisfaction of having something to hold over me. "I couldn't care less."

He raised a single brow in challenge. Then, without a word, he tossed the necklace over the back of the boat.

I clenched my teeth and promised myself that no matter what this asshole threw at me, I would fight him with every last ounce of strength in my body. Unfortunately, with the truth potion surging through me like a high-speed train, my strength was quickly waning.

"Where was I?" Dionysus said, tapping his lips. "Oh yes, a coin flip. Shayla, my dear, would you do the honors?"

The priestess pulled a coin from the pocket of her skintight jeans. "Heads or tails?" she asked Morales.

"Fuck you."

"Tails it is, then," she said on a giggle. She tossed the coin into the air with a graceful flick of her wrist.

In what seemed like slow motion, it flipped end-over-end. In my head, I willed the coin to land on tails. It's not that I wanted Morales to suffer, but he was the last guy I wanted to admit my secrets in front of. If we survived this, I was worried he'd go straight to Gardner and it would be game over for my career.

Shayla snatched the quarter from the air and slapped it on the back of her right hand. She waited just long enough for the suspense to become agonizing. Her narrowed eyes ping-ponged back and forth between Morales and me. A bead of sweat rolled down Morales's temple. His jaw was rock-hard and his eyes were focused on that fist like it was a time bomb.

Finally, Dionysus went to join her. She lifted her hand to allow him to peek.

"Oh my," he whispered. Stealing glances at both of us, he chuckled. "We have a winner, kids."

He moved toward me with deliberate slowness. When he stood directly in front of me, he leaned down into my face.

"Tell me, Kate, what's your secret?" he whispered. He ran a finger down my cheek. "Won't it be such a relief not to carry the burden alone?"

He was the snake in the garden and I suddenly felt as naked as Eve. "I can't." My eyes shot toward Morales. His expression was grave, and I saw sadness and pity in his eyes. Like he knew before this was all over he'd know things about me neither of us was ready for him to know. Like he knew this would change everything—if we survived.

Words gathered at the back of my tongue, like eager lemmings ready to dive off the cliff. I ground my teeth together to keep the truth inside.

"I can see you fighting it," he said. "Means the secrets are extra juicy."

The longer I resisted, the more excruciating the effort. My heart struggled to keep up with the rising blood pressure. My temples pounded, my stomach churned, my tongue swelled. I squeezed my eyes and focused on trying to ride out the pain.

"Oh yes, I can see this will be a good one. What is it, Kate? Did you fuck someone you shouldn't have? Or no—you're a cop. Cops have the best secrets. Some kind of crime you covered up, maybe? A secret addiction?"

I tried to keep my eyes shut, I really did. But the instant he mentioned a cover-up and addiction, my eyes popped open.

"Ah ha!" he said, laughing. "Hit a nerve there, did I, love?" He caressed my cheek. His palm was hot and sweaty and made revulsion creep across my skin.

"I'm not hiding anything," I gritted from between clenched teeth. Pain was a boot heel to my gut. Doubling over, I struggled not to vomit.

His face pressed close to mine, those blazing eyes like twin flames in my pain-dimmed vision. "Your secrets will kill you," he whispered. "Literally."

I looked up quickly, hoping he was the one lying now. He pulled back a little, but smiled. "Didn't I mention that part?" He shrugged. "The more you resist telling the truth, the more the potion will attack your vital organs. Tell one too many lies and—" He slashed a hand across his throat.

I glanced at Morales. His normally olive complexion was now bone-white except for the blood streaking down his cheek.

"All right," I said, panting. "I'll tell you a secret."

Dionysus's eyes widened like a kid given free rein at an ice cream shop. He leaned forward so he wouldn't miss one sweet drop.

I licked my dry lips and swallowed before speaking. My breaths were coming in short bursts as I fought the pain and adrenaline. "I haven't had sex in eighteen months."

"Ha!" Shayla laughed. "That's a shocker."

Almost immediately the pain in my stomach eased. I let out a relieved breath. But before I could get too used to the less shitty sensation, Dionysus's palm cracked across my cheek. My head snapped back.

"Don't fucking patronize me, bitch!"

"I tore the label off my mattress," Morales called. "And when I was a kid I stole a piece of gum from a gas station."

Dionysus rounded on my partner but not before I caught a glimpse at the pure rage on the psycho's face. He marched over to Morales and placed the gun's muzzle between his eyes.

Fear crawled up my throat on spidery legs.

Morales's face morphed into an expression of bored contempt. A look that proved this wasn't the first time someone had pointed a gun at my partner. A look that dared the asshole to back down just like all the others had done.

"Don't tell him, Kate." He kept his eyes on Dionysus.

Instead of responding, the man with the gun lowered the barrel. The gun exploded. Shayla screamed. Morales groaned in pain. I reared up and was hit upside the head with vertigo. Through blurry vision I tried to assess the damage to Morales.

His body was slumped over, but he was moving. "Drew!" I shouted, blinking rapidly.

"I'm okay," he growled.

Dionysus moved toward Morales. A split second later my partner hissed. My vision cleared enough to see Dionysus pressing a thumb into a bullet wound on Morales's left leg. "Next time I will shoot him someplace vital." He turned wild eyes toward me. "Tell me, Detective." He pressed harder, and Morales clenched his teeth to trap a scream.

"Don't, Kate," he panted. "Don't."

But blood was spreading over the left side of Morales's body. And the pain in my midsection was creeping like poison vines. And telling the truth wasn't just a compulsion but a requirement, like breathing.

"I lied!" I shouted.

Dionysus went still. A devilish smile emerged from the beard. "About what?" he asked in a seductive tone.

I swallowed to wet my dry throat. "About the Bane case."

Morales stilled, and his eyes rose to look at me with an expression filled with fear. For some reason I knew this fear wasn't for him or us, but for me and what this admission would mean.

"I cooked magic for John Volos." I barreled ahead now because with each word the agony in my middle lessened. "I read the Gray Wolf potion, I used what I discovered to complete the antipotion, and then I promised Volos I would keep the identity of Bane's accomplice a secret so John could go after the guilty party himself."

Dionysus made a smacking noise with his lips, like he was savoring the admission. "My, my, that *is* juicy." He turned toward me. With his free hand, he jerked my face up by the chin. His fingers dug into the skin and his gaze bore into me. "But you only told part of the truth." He leaned in. "Who was behind the potion, Kate?"

Behind the madman, Morales was shaking his head, willing me to resist. But I was so tired. Tired of the pain, yes, and the fear. But more than that, I was fucking exhausted from carrying the weight of this secret around on my shoulders. Tired from pretending I was the kind of cop who could collude with criminals because the ends would justify the means. Tired of not getting credit for saving my brother's life. Tired of being in debt to John Volos and at the same time wishing he'd make good on his threats against Uncle Abe. Of knowing I needed him to exact the vengeance I couldn't legally pull off.

"Who was it, Kate?" Dionysus yelled.

I opened my lips to complete my confession. But before I

could form the words, Morales shouted his own confession. "When I was undercover, the coven I'd infiltrated killed a dirty cop. I helped them hide the evidence."

All sound evaporated. Air became an endangered resource. A chill passed through me like a ghost.

Morales's eyes were hot and focused on me. Waiting to see my reaction. But the muscles in my face weren't cooperating and all I could do was stare, slack-jawed.

There are moments set apart from reality. Like stepping off a treadmill and tripping into stillness. This was one of those times. I felt removed from my body, staring down at smug Dionysus, nervous Shayla, defiant Morales, and a pale, shell-shocked woman.

Dionysus spoke from far away. "Now we're really having fun!"

Time suddenly caught up with me and my conscience fell back into my body with the impact of a meteor.

"It's quite a shock, isn't it?" Dionysus said. "To find out that people you admire are nothing more than carefully constructed shells."

I couldn't take my eyes off Morales. "Is it true?"

"Of course it is," Dionysus said impatiently. Both he and Shayla were watching me, because that's where the drama was. "If he were lying he'd be dead."

Morales nodded slowly. I noticed his hands were busy plucking at his bindings. Then his eyebrows rose and his gaze darted toward our captor. Toward the gun in Dionysus's hand.

I knew instantly what he was planning. "Goddamn it, Morales! How could you cover up something like that?" I leaned over, as if trying to find comfort. The move allowed me access to the corkscrew and its dull knife.

"Don't you fucking judge me," he shouted. The outburst

captured the rapt attention of both Dionysus and Shayla. I furiously sawed at my bindings. "I did what had to be done, Prospero." His voice had a convincing defensiveness to it. So convincing I worried I'd misread his intention. "But who are you to judge? I'm not the only one here who's rationalized shitty decisions."

"I cooked to save Danny's life. You covered up a murder to save your job!"

"And you haven't kept your secret to save your job?" he challenged.

Dionysus crossed his arms and watched me closely, like he was anticipating a complete meltdown.

Part of me wasn't sure if we were acting anymore. The anger his comeback caused certainly didn't feel fake. I palmed the corkscrew and sat up, careful to hold my wrists together. Looking into my partner's eyes, I played out the charade. "Fuck you, Morales," I said in a low, mean voice.

"No, fuck"—in a burst of motion, Morales launched himself up from the bench—"you!" He slammed into Dionysus like a wrecking ball. The weight of both men slammed into the boat's bow.

Shayla screamed and started dancing around, as if she were confronted with a mouse instead of two grown men pummeling each other as they grappled for a gun. Launching myself out of my seat, I tackled her. We slid across the slick floor until her head slammed into the gunwale.

But instead of subduing her, the impact turned her into a rabid polecat. For a few adrenaline-soaked moments the world was a sea of scratching nails, vicious hair pulling, and the palpable heat of rage. Somewhere in the tussle I lost my grip on the corkscrew. By the time I realized this, Shayla had managed to get a grip on her gun and raise it.

I froze instantly.

She let out a calming breath and smiled. "Stand up."

With my hands raised, I stood as slowly as possible. She moved to put a little distance between us. Behind me, the men had gone silent, but I didn't have time to worry about who'd won when my own skirmish was far from over.

"Do not fucking move"—Shayla's voice rose with panic—"or I'll shoot you."

"No, you won't," I said. "You may be a whore, but you're no killer."

"You don't know me."

"I've known a lot of killers, Shayla." I jerked my chin toward her partner. "That asshole is one. Uncle Abe, too. And Aphrodite for damned sure. But you?" I shot her a pitying frown. "You don't have the hardness in your eyes or the steel in your gut."

I braced myself. My hands clasping into fists. Trying to focus through the pain and the disorienting surge of magic's energy through my cells.

"Actually, I lied," I went on, bending my knees slightly. "According to my mom, you weren't so hot at whoring, either. It's sad, really."

Time slowed to a crawl. The warped echo of a screech. That red fingernail pulling on the trigger. A flash of fire from the muzzle. My leg muscles screaming. Commotion behind me. Each frame of motion flashing like a slideshow. Shayla's body flying backward. The gun flying loose. Hands, feet scrambling. Fingers yearning for and finding hot metal.

Fast forward. My bleeding fists slammed the bitch's body against the wall. A smile bloomed on my lips even as the gun pointed at her face made her smile dissolve.

Her lower lip and jaw trembled, like she was too cold. My

forearm dug into her sternum, allowing me to feel the rapid pulse of her breath.

Over my shoulder I called, "How we doing, Morales?"

"Peachy keen."

I didn't look to confirm. He'd tell me if there was something to worry about. I suppose I shouldn't have been surprised at the confirmation he'd managed to subdue Dionysus, but part of me was pretty impressed.

"Maybe I should save you for Aphrodite to deal with," I said to Shayla. Her lipstick had smeared like a wound across her face and her hair stood on end, as if the violence had shocked her system.

Her chin rose despite the fear glinting in her eyes. "I outsmarted the Hierophant once. I could do it again."

"Tough talk from a dirty mouth."

"I'm surprised you didn't admit your other secret," Shayla taunted, clearly changing tactics. "Why didn't you reveal how you cooked the potion that killed your mama?"

My left eye twitched.

"Kate," Morales said.

Shayla's laugh was low in her chest. Her chin didn't tremble anymore. Now it was my hands that shook.

"I bet you still cry about it," she taunted. "But the saddest part is, it's not even true."

"What the fuck does that mean?"

"You'll have to ask your uncle about that." She pursed her lips. "Knowing Abe, though, I bet he'd let you go on believing it was your fault."

The dark place in my mind where the demons lived lit up like a volcano about to erupt. Their seductive voices urged me to remove that lying mouth from her face with a bullet. Hell, to even consider what she was saying as truth made me feel capable of leveling the city myself.

"Step away, Prospero." Morales used his cop voice now. Somehow I'd gone from partner to perp. "She's not worth you ending up in a cell next to your uncle."

I didn't know how Morales knew exactly what to say. But those words managed to break the spell of rage. Panting, I pulled back, lowering the gun.

I started to turn toward Morales. A blur from the corner of my eye. The flash of red nails. A scream of rage. Her weight landed on my back and I started to fall. Swiveling midair, I turned to face her. Hands grappling for the gun.

I don't know whose hand pulled the trigger. I don't know if she believed she could actually get the gun from me. But I did know her body went lax and that the breath on my face was her last.

The sound of two hands clapping cleared the foggy haze of shock. Turning my head, I saw Dionysus lounging on the low bench set into the bow, clapping as if he'd just watched dinner theater. Morales, stoic expression firmly in place, stood with a gun pointed at the asshole.

"It—it was an accident," I said.

"Sometimes accidents are merely manifestations of wishes long denied," the fake god concluded.

"Shut the fuck up." Morales grabbed the false god by his arm and jerked him to a standing position. To me, my partner said, "What now?"

In death, the priestess was a lot heavier than she had been alive. It took a couple of shoves to roll her body off me, and when it hit the deck, it did so with a hollow thump. I pushed myself to standing as gracefully as possible, which wasn't very.

Jaye Wells

Once I was upright, I had to steady myself against the wall of the boat. My hand left a red smear on the gleaming white hull.

As I stood, I realized the pain from the potion had dissipated a great deal. I was smarting from all the wounds I'd earned in my catfight with Shayla, but the sickening tingle of magic in my veins was almost gone. Volos's truth potion had been strong, but it hadn't been long lasting. Guess I'd have to mention that little defect to John if we survived the night. Right after I punched him for making the fucking thing in the first place.

The promise of being able to have that conversation gave me enough perverse pleasure to ignore the exhaustion rolling in my gut like an ocean tide.

"Now," I said, "we deal with the goddamned bomb."

Dionysus snorted. "You'll never figure out how to disarm it before the moon reaches its apex."

I punched him in the throat. He doubled over, wheezing and choking. Morales smiled at me like I was a genius. "Then I guess we'll just have to torture you until you share your own secrets."

Chapter Twenty-Nine

Dionysus's secret bomb location turned out to be a wooden platform that was anchored to a mooring buoy about half a mile away from the boat. To reach it, we had to row over in a rubber raft that had been tied to the cabin cruiser where we'd been held.

From the buoy, I could see the silhouette of the old Babylon lighthouse about a mile away. The full moon overhead illuminated the steel cage around the darkened light. The lighthouse had fallen into disuse years ago after the GPS technology that most of the freighters and fishing boats were now equipped with made it obsolete.

The water patrol cop I'd shadowed as a rookie was named Lieutenant Fred Harris, but he'd insisted I call him Cap'n. Anyway, the old coot had spent most of our time patrolling the Steel River telling me about the history of many of the fourteen hundred shipwrecks littering the bottom of Lake Erie.

I guess I needed to send Cap'n a thank-you note because

some of what he'd told me stuck. That's how I knew the buoy we tied the raft to had been installed by an organization that tracked Lake Erie's shipwreck sites. They'd installed the moored buoys so that dive groups didn't have to drop anchor and risk harming the wreck sites far below. From our position, I guessed that the site we were above was the *Cuyahoga*, a barge that went down during a storm in the 1920s.

The wooden platform on the water's surface was dominated by two large metal brackets, a mechanical catapult, and a big glass sphere containing two chambers, one filled with iridescent red liquid and the other with shimmering blue. Beyond the bomb, the bastard moon mocked us from its perch high above the Babylon skyline. Judging from its position in the sky by the time we reached the bomb, I knew we were reaching that deadly hour when the orb achieved its apex and became an officially full Blue Moon.

Once we'd all disembarked from the raft, Morales handed the gun over without a word. The GSW on his leg was bleeding freely. His complexion was pale, and he'd had trouble climbing out of the raft without my help. Considering the concussion, the hangover from the potion, and the bullet wound, I was amazed the guy was even upright.

"How much time until it goes off?" I asked Dionysus.

He glanced at the moon. "The bomb is set to deploy once the moon hits its apex."

"What time will that be?"

"Four twenty-seven a.m."

Morales glanced at his watch. "It's four ten right now." We exchanged a heavy look.

The thing was, the bomb didn't look all that complicated. It wasn't like the movies where there were different-colored wires sticking out of the damned thing. Near as I could tell, once the timer counted down, a charge would activate the catapult. Then it would fling the orb toward the city.

"It's too far," I said. "The catapult can't project the bomb that distance."

"Even if it doesn't reach all the way when it explodes, it will be high enough for the wind to carry the potion cloud over the city."

Eyeing the water, I cursed its lack of salt. If I'd been on an ocean, I could have tossed the entire damned thing into the water and interrupted the magic's ability to activate. But Lake Erie was infuriatingly free of salt, which meant we were fucked. In addition, the catapult was bolted to the platform, which meant throwing it overboard to sink to the bottom of the lake was also impossible.

"What happens once it's deployed?" I asked the asshole.

"Once the catapult flings the orb, the potions will mix, creating a chain reaction that will end in an explosion." He smiled a cocky smirk. "A trick and a treat just in time for Halloween." He raised his arms and looked up at the moon. "Between the fucking and the fighting, the entire city should be on fire before sundown."

My pulse had had so many shocks that night that it jumped for a couple of beats before settling back into its normal rhythm. "I'm going to give you one chance to tell us how to disarm it. If you fail, I will make you bleed. Do you understand me?"

"Why would I build the perfect weapon with the option of disarming it?"

I tilted my head. "You're lying." What I wouldn't have given for an extra dose of Volos's truth serum right then.

His eyes danced with manic glee. "Once it's set in motion, there is no stopping chaos."

My gun crashed into his jaw with a satisfying crunch. Blood

splattered from his mouth. A few cool drops hit my own skin, but I didn't care.

"Tell me how to stop this," I yelled.

His head swiveled slowly back toward me. His pink tongue jutted from his lips to lick away the blood. "You can't stop it." That smile again. Those red teeth, like a demon. "Surrender, Kate."

The moon mocked me over the wizard's shoulder. My right hand clenched into a fist. My teeth clenched.

"Surrender isn't an option."

"It's the only option," he countered.

In an instant the rage boiling in my chest parted to reveal a calm spot in the middle. And in the eye of that storm, a deadly calm cut through me like ceremonial athame.

I didn't hear the laugh escape Dionysus as he realized my intent. I didn't hear the gun discharge. But I saw his left hand explode and felt grim satisfaction.

His laughter turned into a scream.

Blood everywhere. Dionysus collapsed on the platform and rolled to protect his destroyed hand.

Morales's face was a mask of shock—mouth hanging open, face pale. "What the fuck, Kate?"

I licked my lips and tasted that bastard's blood. "Trust me."

"You shot an unarmed man."

Anger flared in my gut, the fire fueled by desperation and fear. "Don't judge me. You fucking covered up a cop's murder!"

His face hardened. "And you protected your uncle."

My stomach dropped to the bottom of the lake. "I never said—"

"You think I'm an idiot? Who else could it have been?"

I shoved the gun in the rear waistband of my jeans. "All

right, look," I snapped. "We're both assholes, okay? But we're also the only two assholes who can save the city."

"You...won't...succeed," panted Dionysus.

"Shut the fuck up," Morales snapped.

I grabbed the whimpering madman by the toga and dragged him toward the bomb. Reaching back for my cuffs, I remembered too late I didn't have them anymore. I looked around, my eyes zeroing in on Morales's waist. I snapped my fingers. "Bring me your belt."

He frowned. "What, you're going to beat him, too?"

"No, wise guy, I'm gonna strap him to his own bomb."

Morales's frown cracked into a crooked smile. "I like it." He limped across the platform to bring me the strip of leather. Judging from the grimace on his face that deepened with each step, that leg of his was giving him a world of hurt.

I grabbed Dionysus's right hand and strapped it tightly to one of the metal struts supporting the bomb. Then I stepped back and assessed the situation.

"Now what?" Morales asked.

I looked up at the moon, which winked mockingly from the ink-stained sky. It loomed so large and bright that I suddenly felt very small and full of shadows. The idea of me being able to stop this runaway locomotive of a clusterfuck was suddenly so inconceivable that I wanted to just jump in the water and let the currents pull me down to the wreckage below.

"Kate."

"What?"

"What are you thinking?"

I laughed bitterly. "I was thinking I wished Uncle Abe was here to summon the Lake Erie Lizard to eat this fucking thing." I kicked a metal brace.

"Actually," Morales said slowly, "that's not a horrible idea."

My eyebrows slammed down, worried. "You've lost a lot of blood, Morales. Maybe you should sit down."

He shook his head and stepped toward me. "Sometimes you have to fight magic with magic, right? Abe told you how he did it, didn't he?"

I shook my head and stared at him like he'd sprouted horns. "That's ridiculous. He was lying to a little kid, Morales. The monster doesn't exist."

He crossed his arms. "How can you be so sure? Every day we see all sorts of inconceivable things."

Morales's words came back to me from that day we'd gone to see Abe.

"This lake's gotta be what—a hundred feet deep?"

"Two hundred in some places."

"Right. Just saying, maybe there's things down there we don't want to believe in."

I shook my head again, as if doing so might shake some sense into him. "You're insane. I don't do magic, remember?"

He raised an ironic brow. "You did it to save Danny? Why wouldn't you do it to save the entire city?"

"Uncle Abe told me he summoned it using a potion he cooked using blood and water gathered under a full moon."

"Shh—don't spoil it," Dionysus said in a pained voice. "She's about to give up."

I rounded on him. The impossibility of the situation mixed with taunting by that sick fuck lit a fire under me. "No, I'm not—" I backhanded Dionysus. The blow forced the side of his head into the metal bar. He slumped over to the side.

I turned back to Morales, who wisely kept his opinions about my abuse of the psycho to himself. "I don't have any Gideon's Dew, remember? Dickhead over there threw it over the side."

"You said he used dew gathered under a full moon, right?"

I nodded sharply, ready to argue with anything he said.

"We're in the middle of a freshwater lake under a Blue Moon, Kate." He spread his arms wide. "Look, if you don't try what will happen?" I remained stonily silent until he answered his own question. "They'll die," he said, pointing toward the skyline. "But first they'll suffer. And it's up to us to make sure that doesn't happen."

All of my excuses dried up and a crystalline silence took their place. My head filled with a pressure that felt like I was swimming through water. The bell on the nearby buoy clanged every few seconds, but otherwise my ears were filled with the bass-drum kick of my heart.

Suddenly Pen's concerns about the sacrifices I made for this job twisted until I saw them in a new light. Yes, being on the task force had led to me using magic again. But it also had allowed me to use magic for the good of someone besides myself for the first time in my life. While my cooking methods might have been learned the dirty way, I was finally able to use them in a clean way, as far as my conscience was concerned.

"Time's running out, Cupcake," Morales said in a quiet tone.

I swallowed hard and looked into his brown eyes. "Shit."

He smiled and nodded approvingly. "You can do this."

I chewed on my bottom lip, ignoring the roiling fear in my gut. My brain scrolled through everything I'd need to make this impossible Hail Mary pass. I had plenty of blood and water. I had a Blue Moon offering its powerful energy to the air. What I didn't have was a heat source.

"I don't suppose you have a lighter," I said.

He patted down his pockets and shook his head. " 'Fraid not."

I went to the passed-out Dionysus but only discovered that the false god preferred to go commando under his toga.

Wiping my hands on my jeans, I looked around for something, anything I could use as a heat source.

The inflatable boat we'd came over on from the skiff bobbed off the edge of the platform. From our ride over, I remembered seeing a small metal box strapped near the back. I leaped into it and started feeling around the edges. When my hand hit the hard-sided case, I whooped in victory. I cracked it open and found two waterproof emergency flares.

I stashed the flares back in the metal box and climbed back on the wooden platform. The whole structure tilted dangerously, but I stilled long enough for it to stabilize before I proceeded.

"Tell me what you need," Morales said.

"The flare's potassium nitrate will add some punch to the potion, along with the heat I need to cook the ingredients," I explained. I handed him the second flare. "Hold on to this in case we survive."

He frowned.

"To call in the cavalry to come get us," I explained.

He smiled. "Good thinking, but why not shoot it now?"

"They won't get here before the bomb goes off, and I don't want anyone else to get hurt if this monster shows up and I can't control it."

His face paled at the thought of me summoning an uncontrollable beast. Ignoring his reaction, I placed the metal box under Dionysus's bloody hand. When I had a good puddle in the bottom, I stepped away. I didn't want to risk him gaining consciousness and interrupting me while I cooked.

I handed Morales the box. "Get some water. Equal parts to the blood."

While he went to do that, I took the flare from my mouth and ripped the plastic top off with my teeth. When he returned,

I tapped the flare onto the edge of the box to get a little of the potassium nitrate power mixed in with the blood-and-water mixture. Then I scratched the lid against the tip of the flare to ignite the flame. A loud hiss sounded and the light blazed, illuminating the area in an eerie red glow.

"Ten minutes, Kate."

Ignoring the pang of nerves in my center, I placed the flame under the box. The metal heated quickly, singeing my fingertips. I ignored the pain and tried to focus all my attention on the potion. I wasn't sure how long I had before the flare petered out, but I knew I had only minutes before I was totally out of options.

While I worked, I was vaguely aware that Morales had stepped back to watch me. I didn't have the luxury of feeling self-conscious about it, but it felt as intimate as him knowing my darkest secrets.

Lifting the box high, I willed the moon to speed the process. I closed my eyes and imagined a stream of neon magic zapping from the moon to the little box. A tingle of energy sizzled up from my chest, through my arms, and into my burning fingertips. Electricity shocked my fingers and pain burst behind my eyes.

A shock attacked my hands and the box leaped from my grasp. My eyes flew open in time to see it splash into the water. The potion sizzled, and a bright blue pool of light flashed before going dark.

"Shit." Rubbing my stinging hands together, I glanced at Morales with a heart sinking as fast as our last chance.

His face fell and he glanced at the moon like it was his biggest enemy. I suppose at the moment it ranked pretty high on the list.

I dropped to my knees on the platform. In the distance a few lights were still illuminated in Babylon's office towers despite the late hour. All across the city, hundreds of thousands of people slept peacefully in their beds. Children dreamed of jack-o'-lanterns and bags full of candy. Night-shift workers yawned and hurried to complete their work so they could clock out and head home. Junkies huddled in doorways, their eyes rolling back in their heads from the high of a potion-fix mixed with the Blue Moon's rising power.

Kneeling on that platform with Morales and a passed-out madman, I'd never felt so alone.

"I told you it wouldn't work," I said in a low, savage tone. I couldn't look at him.

"Kate, I—"

The entire platform swayed, as if lifted by a large wave. The unexpected movement threw off my equilibrium. I fell toward the bomb, grabbing the bracket out of instinct.

"What the fuck?" Morales yelled. His arms were outspread, and he crouched to keep from tumbling over.

"Morales—it's her!" Hope bloomed in my chest. Rogue waves didn't just appear in the middle of a lake—unless something under the water caused them.

At that moment a large, black hump crested out of the water, followed by a loud splash not fifty feet from our suddenly very small platform.

Cold fear and hot hope swept under my skin. Lake Erie wasn't home to whales or dolphins. I'd heard some large catfish lived in the deep waters, but the spiked tail I'd seen didn't belong to a fish. It belonged to a monster.

Another wave—smaller this time—rocked the platform. The monster was circling, trying to decide on the best approach.

A loud gasp sounded behind me. I turned to see Dionysus's

head jerk up and his unfocused eyes go wide. "Wh—what's happening?"

Now that I'd managed to summon the monster I'd invited to the party, I realized with a start that I had no idea how to control the beast.

"Cut the raft off the buoy!" I yelled at my partner. He jumped to do what I asked without question.

The monster roared and leaped into the air a good way from the raft. The hulking shape made my mouth fall open.

"Four minutes," Morales yelled, coming to stand beside me.

Underneath the instinctive fear, the kernels of a plan began to form. The kind of plan born of desperation, gut-wrenching terror, and lack of options.

The beast emerged from the depths again. This time a large head broke the surface. I had a quick impression of large yellow eyes and a gaping mouth filled with a few rows of sharp teeth. From the triple nostrils large plumes of water shot up into the night air. And above this terrifying image, the Blue Moon watched in judgment from the sky. It seemed to say: "Be careful what you wish for."

Another crest of water exploded beside the buoy. The wake threw my body through the air. "Kate!" Morales screamed.

I landed in the cold drink with a splash. My head went under; water shot up my nose, choking me. I couldn't tell which way was up or down. But if I didn't act fast I'd drown. Kicking my legs with every bit of strength I had left, I burst above the surface for a brief, victorious moment. I gasped in a lungful of air.

"Moral—"

My scream was swallowed by the water. Something tugged on my leg, pulling me farther underwater. I looked up, yearning for the surface.

Despite my body's instinctive struggle for air, in my brain a small voice urged me to just surrender. Maybe Dionysus had it right all along. Life shouldn't be a constant struggle, but lately it seemed to be nothing but one conflict after another. Ever since I'd joined the MEA—my dream job, I'd thought—I'd been forced to choose between my principles and the Arcane demands of the job.

I could just let go. Sink down. Let the abyss swallow me.

I closed my eyes.

Pain in my lungs, desperate for air. For life.

An air bubble escaped my mouth. Another tug. Stronger this time.

My eyes snapped open. The bright orb of the Blue Moon shimmered through the water, lighting my path toward the surface. Morales's words came back to me: *If you don't try what will happen?*

The thing I'd managed to successfully ignore this entire time suddenly loomed larger than the monster. Danny and Pen were in that city. Baba, Rufus, and everyone else I cared about. If I gave up now, they'd all suffer. My surrender would doom them all.

I kicked hard with both feet. Yearned for the surface with my grasping hands. My foot made contact with something solid, again. Again. And then, miraculously, I was loose, swimming like a wild mermaid toward the surface.

I burst out of the water, and panic fueled my arms to scramble for the edge of the platform. My eyes were blurry with dirty water. I struggled to reach the edge of the platform. Exhaustion threatened to pull me under again.

A warm hand grabbed mine and hauled me from the water like the catch of the day. The wood dug into my solar plexus, knocking what little air I had from my lungs. But I didn't care as long as I wasn't in the water with the monster anymore.

Morales grabbed me in a fast, hard hug.

"Jesus that was close," he gasped. His face was pale from blood loss, and his eyes searched the water for the beast.

I grabbed his wrist. According to his watch, we only had a minute and fifteen seconds left.

I leapt across the platform toward Dionysus. I slapped his face. His chin jerked to the side. "Wake up, Scott!" Cold water from my hair splashed over his eyes as they winked open.

"What—" he said in a groggy tone.

"You have a visitor." I jerked his chin toward the water.

The beast's huge head rose from the surface a hundred feet from the platform.

Scott's eyes widened. "What the fuck!"

I leaned forward and whispered, "You wanted chaos?" I pointed toward the beast. "Well, she's coming for you."

The monster's two large yellow eyes zeroed in on us. A loud roar filled the night. She was coming in hot.

"Untie me!" His voice cracked with fear. "Please!"

"Kate?" Morales said in an urgent tone. "It's go time!"

"No, you can't leave me!" The Raven struggled against the belt, but with his ruined hand he didn't have a hope of untying himself. "I'm begging you!"

Morales looked at me, unsure. Part of me wanted to leave the asshole tied to his own bomb—a little poetic justice. But in the end, I couldn't justify leaving him tied up. I certainly didn't intend to save him, but I also couldn't damn him to being unable to try and save himself.

"Untie him. Quickly!"

Morales dove across the raft and quickly unbuckled the belt. Dionysus froze, as if shocked by the tiny mercy we'd shown him. "W-why?"

Morales came back to join me at the edge of the raft before

he answered. "Because every man deserves to be able to go down fighting."

A roar echoed over the water. All three of us turned toward the spine-chilling noise.

The monster's mouth emerged from the water and opened wide enough to swallow a Volkswagen. A guttural sound escaped the maw. Morales and I edged to the opposite side of the platform from the bomb. Scott, clearly dizzy and weak from lack of blood, slipped and groped against the metal frame to regain his feet.

"Take me with you!" Scott yelled.

"Kate?" Morales was pushing against me.

"Patience," I said. A sudden calm descended over me as time slowed. I glanced at the clock. Thirty seconds.

"It won't work," Dionysus yelled. "You'll die, too, you stupid fucking whore."

I taunted the monster. "Come on, you big, beautiful bitch!"

"Oh shit," Morales said. "This is crazy!"

The beast's mouth grew closer until it filled our vision like a portal to another dimension. Bending my knees, I wrapped my arms around Morales. His came around me, too.

I cast one final glance at Dionysus. He was crawling toward the other edge of the raft, his knees slipping in his blood. "So long, asshole."

The monster loomed closer, closer. The man who claimed to love chaos screamed with a terror that would haunt my dreams.

"Now!" I shouted.

The first few boards of the platform crunched under the monster's enormous, sharp teeth. Lunging with all our strength, Morales and I flew off the port side of the platform. Slamming into the water felt like belly flopping onto concrete. The air whooshed from my lungs and cold, dirty water surged into my sinuses.

Morales kicked his good leg and I scissored both of mine until we were clear. Once my head emerged from under the water, the shrieking registered first. Then a loud crunch. The sound of sharp teeth on bone and wood. The monster's victorious roar filled the night. And then, silence.

We swam like mad things toward the raft he'd set adrift. I helped him in first, and then he pulled me up to join him.

An instant later a magical concussion spread through the water like an aftershock. Ripples spread in choppy concentric circles through the water, making our raft bob wildly in its wake.

I held my breath, watching the surface for signs of the beast's fate. When I'd formed the plan, I hadn't thought about what would happen when the bomb detonated inside the monster's body. If she exploded, would the lake be contaminated?

But then, breaking the silence, a loud splash sounded. The monster's body leaped out of the water fifty feet from our raft. The formerly black surface of her slick skin sparkled iridescent purple in the Blue Moon's glow. As soon as she appeared, the Lake Erie Lizard descended back into the depths, taking every trace of Dionysus and his ill-fated bomb with her.

I finally released the breath I'd been holding. "Holy shit."

Morales's eyelids were drooping. "Jesus, Prospero, if I'd known you were going to play chicken with that beast I never would have suggested you summon him."

"Her," I corrected. "That was definitely a lady monster."

He popped an eyebrow. "How can you tell?"

"I just know."

He laughed. "Well, guess what, Cupcake? Since you're so smart, I'll let you row." He tossed the oars to me. Despite the sarcasm, I could tell the suggestion was really a necessity.

He'd lost a lot more blood than me. Besides, he had the

flare, which he shot into the air as I rowed us toward the lighthouse.

By the time the rescue boat reached us twenty minutes later, we'd both fallen into shocked silence. What other choice did we have? It's not like we were going to talk about the secrets we were forced to know about each other. The ones we were both praying the other would never repeat.

I was shocked to see Gardner, Shadi, and Mez standing on the ship's railing, loaded down with every Mundane and magical weapon in existence. They rushed off the boat and secured the area before coming to make sure we were okay.

Then we were being bundled in blankets, having our wounds triaged, and being urged onto soft benches to rest. Morales's bullet wound was the most serious, so Mez focused his efforts there.

I went to sit while Shadi and Gardner peppered me with questions. I answered in a monotone, but my eyes were on Morales. His jaw was tight as Mez doctored his wounds with saline and iodine. His eyes met mine, and his face was a mask of solemn shock.

I'm not sure what Morales thought about during those moments, but I was thinking about the time I'd spent under the water. The moment when the moon that had caused a lot of my problems became a beacon of hope.

Eventually, Gardner explained that they'd been found by the sheriff's tac-wiz team not long after Dionysus managed to get us out of the farmhouse. Best they could tell, he'd had a boat waiting in the Steel River, which ran along one side of the winery's land. Of course they hadn't known that then and wasted a lot of time trying to find us on the road. They'd spent the last twenty-four hours tearing the city apart. They'd been loading onto the boat to sweep the coastline when Morales's flare exploded into the sky.

"Jesus, Prospero," Shadi said. "We're lucky it was you on that platform. The only other person who could have stopped that bomb was probably Mez."

Or Uncle Abe, I silently amended. Guess he hadn't been lying all those years ago, after all.

I pushed that thought aside and forced a smile. Inside, I was relieved that the team had taken news of me using magic so well. But the other part of me was terrified of what they'd say if Morales told them about the last time I'd cooked.

After that, Gardner and Shadi melted away to go speak to Morales in quiet tones. I stood wrapped in a blanket on the bow, watching the moon hanging over Babylon. The city looked so peaceful and quiet from this distance. Because I'd used magic, those dreaming children would get their Hallow-een. Because Morales and I had exposed our skeletons to the moonlight, the entire city was spared the horror of having *their* deepest secrets revealed. And because I'd refused to surrender, I emerged from that water with a new appreciation for the Adept genes in my body that had felt like a burden for so many years.

I guess when it came down to it, the entire night had been a baptism of sorts. And it never would have happened if that damned Blue Moon hadn't come around to fuck everything up.

Chapter Thirty

November 1
Waning Gibbous

On my way home from the hospital, I made Baba take me by an apothecary.

"I just need to get a couple of things the nurses suggested for the wound care," I said. "Just be a minute."

She simply nodded and turned up the Tom Jones cassette tape. Before I exited, I made sure no one I knew was suddenly going to spring out of nowhere and see me exiting the hoopty car. Or at least that's what I told myself. Actually, I was more worried about anyone seeing what I'd really come to buy.

The bell over the door dinged cheerfully. Unlike the apothecary under LM and Mary's place, this was a more upscale suburban outfit. It catered mostly to Mundane clientele who had extra scratch to spend on expensive wrinkle potions and youth serums.

As I walked through the aisles, looking for my prize, I threw some arnica cream in my basket to help with the bruises all over my body. According to Baba, I looked like I'd been beaten like a redheaded stepchild, which wasn't too far from the truth.

Passing a display of ice packs, I threw in a couple of those, too. As well as some Epsom salts scented with lavender. On impulse, I also grabbed a myrrh-and-sweet-almond-oil mix to rub into my scrapes and cuts to promote healing and prevent scars.

Satisfied I had enough purchases to use for cover, I went to the back corner of the store, where a small toy section was set up to entice kids. It took me a couple of minutes to find what I wanted, but when I did, I stared at the box for a full minute, debating with myself.

I hadn't seen Morales in the hospital. According to the call I'd received from Gardner that morning, he was to be released the next day. Mez was scheduled to pick him up and get him home. It would have been an easy thing to sweep by his room on my way out, but I didn't. In the hours that passed after our rescue, and with the distance between us in the hospital, I worried about how things would play out moving forward. Would he use my secrets against me? I didn't want to believe he would, but promises made under stress in the dark don't always come to fruition in the harsh light of day.

Shaking off the sense of dread, I decided not to worry about what would come. I couldn't control what Morales did with all the dirt he had on me. I looked at the box again. But I could make things right with Danny. I grabbed the box and marched toward the counter.

◆ ◆ ◆

Since Baba's arthritis had been acting up, she didn't offer to walk me to the door. "Sorry, doll. Until I can afford more Maslin's, I'm not feeling too spry."

335

"I thought you already bought more?" I frowned.

She looked away. "I shared it with Pen."

I sucked in a breath that didn't do much to alleviate the sudden heaviness in my chest. Looking down at my hands, I asked, "How is she?"

Baba made a wishy-washy movement with her head. "She's going back to work tomorrow. Her wounds are healing, but she's . . . subdued."

Instead of commenting, I made myself busy finding my wallet. "How much for the Maslin's?"

She made an argumentative sound. "I can't ask you for that."

"You're not asking. I'm offering. You do so much for us, let me help you for a change."

The old woman sucked her teeth for a moment. "A small bottle is eighty."

My eyes popped wide. "For a small bottle?"

She shrugged apologetically. "It's clean magic."

I pressed my lips together and pulled out my checkbook instead. I scribbled a quick check out to her for an even hundred. I figured the MEA owed me some hazard pay, so why not?

Baba took the check and quickly shoved it into her housecoat. "Thanks, Kate." She wouldn't quite meet my gaze.

"You'll tell me if you need anything else, right?"

"Oh sure," she said, nodding unconvincingly. "Wouldn't need this, but my Social Security check isn't due for another week."

I patted her hand. "It's no problem. Thanks for the ride."

Before I shut the car door, she called out. I leaned back inside. Baba's face was grave. "She won't make the first move."

I tipped my chin abruptly and slammed the car door shut before she could elaborate. I'd call Pen eventually and set things right, but for now I needed to put one foot in front of the other.

By the time I limped inside with my apothecary bags, I was exhausted. Danny was sitting at the kitchen table. A book was open in front of him, and he had a pencil jutting from his mouth like a cigarette. He looked up when I stepped in the door with a bag in my left hand, but his eyes immediately returned to his work.

"Hey, kid," I said. Baba and I had agreed he shouldn't come to the hospital, but she promised she'd filled him in on the bare basics so he wouldn't worry.

He made a noncommittal noise. His eyes narrowed on my bandages and bruises. "You okay?"

Judging from his tone, he was worried but didn't like it. We still hadn't had a real conversation since our argument.

"Yep. Just little sore." I placed the bags on the table. "I'll be good as new in a couple of days."

He nodded and looked down at his homework again. His movements were tense, as if he was bracing himself for another argument.

"What ya working on?"

"Math." He didn't look up.

I placed my hands on the back of the chair in front of me and leaned into it. "Let me ask you something."

He sighed and looked up. "What?"

"Now that you're in DUDE are you totally antimagic?"

He rolled his eyes. "Don't be ridiculous, Kate," he snapped. "DUDE is about spreading awareness of dirty magic. Clean magic is fine."

"Relax, I'm not trying to start an argument here. I'm just curious." I pulled the seat out and joined him at the table. I took my time getting settled, allowing my thoughts to solidify.

"You know, I never learned how to cook clean magic." I fidgeted with a pencil. "Uncle Abe always said clean magic was too expensive and time consuming to learn." I looked up. "He didn't explain that it's also generally safer and more stable. That sometimes it can help people."

Danny's posture opened a little, and I knew I had him. "That's sad, Katie."

"I agree," I said. "But when you asked me to teach you magic, I thought you wanted to learn the kind of magic I knew. The dirty kind."

His voice rose. "I tried to tell you that's not—"

I held up a hand. "I know, Danny. I get that now. But the thing is, I couldn't have taught you clean magic."

He nodded impatiently. "I know, I know. You hate magic in all its forms." He mimicked my voice in a not-so-flattering tone.

"That's not what I meant." I tilted my head and looked him in the eye. "Because I don't know how to cook clean."

His eyes lit up like he finally got it. "Oh. I never thought—"

I patted his arm. "Don't worry about." I reached down to the bag on my lap and placed it on the table in front of him.

"What's this?" He looked at it with a wary smile.

"Open it." Suddenly nervous, I chewed on my bottom lip.

The brown paper crinkled open. He gazed down into the bag with a frown. He reached in slowly, almost as if he expected it to be a trick. But then he lifted the box and stared down at it for a long time.

The picture on the cover depicted a kid in a wizard outfit, complete with pointy hat and magic wand. The Little Wizard Cooking Kit was most Adepts' introduction to basic magic.

"I'm sorry it's for kids, but it's all they—"

He looked up, blinking rapidly. "Are you serious?"

I licked my lips and nodded. "I know I promised I'd teach you, but I figured maybe we'd learn together instead."

He simply stared at me like he'd never met me before.

"When I was a kid," I said to fill the silence, "I watched the commercials for that kit with envy roiling in my gut like a green snake. Every year I asked Mom for it for Christmas, and every year I got a stupid doll in a pink dress."

A sad smile spread across my brother's not-quite-a-man face. "Why didn't you buy it when you were older?"

I shook my head, my eyes glued to the image of the happy Adept children dancing across the box. "By the time I was old enough to buy one for myself, I was so jaded about magic. I thought dirty potions were superior because they required a craftier mind." I laughed bitterly. "Anyway...what do you think?"

"I think it's pretty cool." He smiled at me with a smile I'd used on him more times than I could count. It wasn't patronizing exactly, but maybe...sympathetic and encouraging. Either way, I'd take it.

"Obviously we'll zoom through the stuff in here pretty quick. That's why I was thinking about talking to Mez about giving us some lessons."

"Seriously?" His mouth dropped open. "Mez?"

"Do you think you'd like that?"

"Are you kidding? He's a total magical badass."

I smiled. "Yeah, he is."

He quieted for a moment and then looked me in the eyes. "You're pretty badass, too, Kate."

I smiled. "Ditto, kid."

I toyed with the box on the table for a moment. I was screwing up my courage, but Danny didn't seem to notice because he was too busy looking at his present. Clearing my throat, I said, "There's something else."

He looked up. The smile on his face froze. "Uh-oh."

I sighed and leaned forward. "You know how I was at the old brewery the night Volos came up with the antipotion and Bane tried to kill both of us?"

A shadow passed behind his eyes. I didn't want to reopen these old wounds, but sometimes you had to rebreak an injury for it to heal correctly. "The truth is, Danny, I helped John cook the antipotion."

He fell back in his seat. "What?"

I chewed on my bottom lip. "John did most of the work. When I went to meet him it was almost there, but he was missing an important ingredient. I helped him by reading Gray Wolf to understand the hidden ingredients in the potion. What I saw revealed the missing ingredient."

Danny's mouth fell open, but I wasn't done.

"The thing is, before John could finish it, Bane busted in and shot Volos full of Gray Wolf. He was...incapacitated," I said in the understatement of the year. The real truth was that the potion had turned John into a slavering beast that tried to kill me. "So I had to complete the antipotion on my own to save him—and you."

"Wait," Danny said, his eyes wide, "you cooked?"

I nodded.

"But, I don't understand. Why did you lie about it?" His voice rose. "Why did you let me believe it was John who saved me?"

"It's complicated," I began. He made a disgusted sound, as if he expected me to brush him off. "Let me finish."

He relaxed a fraction, nodding.

"I'd spent weeks telling you I didn't want you to cook. And I've spent years preaching the dangers of magic. I was worried that if I admitted I'd worked with magic, you'd think I was a hypocrite."

"You're an idiot."

I pulled back. "What?"

"Jeez, Katie. You're a freakin' hero!"

I bit my lip, ready to deny it. But he wasn't done.

"I was angry because I thought you'd done nothing to try to save me thanks to your high and mighty principles. I thought—I thought you cared more about proving you could resist your desire to do magic than you cared about saving me."

"Now you're the idiot," I said. "You're the most important person in my life, kid. Can't you see that? I love you and stuff."

The corner of his mouth lifted. "Ah, man. Don't get all mushy on me."

I laughed. "Smart-ass."

My little brother looked at me with bright eyes. "I love you, too, Katie."

We both sat there for a long moment with goofy grins on our face. Finally, I said, "All right. What do ya say we bust out some ice cream and learn about clean magic?"

"Shit yeah!"

I was so happy I didn't even make him pay back the curse jar.

Chapter Thirty-One

November 4
Waning Gibbous

For some reason I expected the basement to look different. I'd been going to Arcane Anonymous meetings there for a decade, but in the nine weeks since my last visit I'd changed so much I guess I just assumed everything else had too.

But the air still smelled like old linoleum and stale coffee. The blue plastic chairs still sat in the same irregular circle. The windows set high in the walls were still barred shut. And at the front of the room, Jesus still wore his crown of thorns and watched us from his cross.

I was late on purpose, arriving at the tail end of the meeting. Rufus was already well into his closing statements. As I walked in, heads turned, whispers were shared, and eyes took in my bandages and bruises and downcast eyes.

"Well, well, well," Rufus said in an amused tone. "The prodigal daughter returns."

I glanced up and was surprised to see him smiling. "Hey, everyone." I waved my left hand. The bandage made it look like a white flag.

My gaze slipped toward the woman huddled on the far side of the circle. I hadn't seen Pen in a couple of weeks. Not since that night she'd used the pain potion and we'd had that wicked fight. I knew from Baba that she was back at work, but beyond that my best friend had become a stranger.

High off my reconciliation with Danny, I'd tried calling her every day since I got out of the hospital. After having four voice mails ignored, I'd decided the best way to end the ice age was to go to her. And I knew that Pen would never miss an AA meeting, especially after she'd had a recent relapse.

"I know it's out of order, but can I talk for a minute?" I knew if I sat down and waited for the talking period, I'd lose my nerve.

Rufus crossed his arms and narrowed his eyes. "You come here to preach or confess, sister?" His comment told me he'd been talking to Pen.

I swallowed hard. "Confess," I whispered.

He nodded. "Proceed."

I sucked in a deep breath and released it before speaking. "I haven't been to group in a couple months. I told you the reason was because I was too busy, but I was lying." I licked my lips. "I've been lying about a lot of things lately."

Pen's gaze jerked up.

"When Danny was in his coma, I willfully used magic and then covered it up. I lied to my family, my co-workers, and my friends." The backs of my eyes started stinging, but I was beyond fighting it. If there was one lesson I'd learned from Dionysus, it was that sometimes surrender is good for the soul. "I lied to all of you, and I'm sorry."

The room remained silent. I crossed my arms and continued. "I never should have accepted the anniversary amulet. I don't really have an excuse for taking it except I was ashamed." I cleared my throat. "I'd return it tonight, but it's at the bottom of Lake Erie at the moment."

Rufus's expression gave as much away as a sphinx. "Kate—"

"That all you got to confess?" Pen's voice cut through the room like a blade.

I turned to look at her. Her expression was diamond-hard. My stomach dropped. "I also used protective amulets in the line of duty, got hexed by a sex magic potion—against my will, but still—and used dirty magic to summon a monster." I took a step toward her. "But you know what? I'd do it all again."

Pen crossed her arms and stayed silent.

"I know you don't like hearing this," I said to Pen. "But I also need you to understand that being a cop helps me keep my demons at bay. If using magic can make me more successful as a cop, then all the better. I'm sick and tired of feeling afraid and ashamed of being an Adept." I blew out a shaky breath on the tail of that admission. "So, while I'm sorry for lying to you, I cannot and will not regret using magic to save lives."

I still wasn't quite sure how to balance all that with the demands of the job, especially since every case I'd had on the task force thus far had almost gotten me killed. But I also knew I wasn't willing to walk away from the work. I just had to figure out how to have both the job and the people I loved in my life.

"You know I don't go in much for religion," Jacob said in a soft tone that contrasted with his imposing appearance. He raised a tattooed arm to point at Jesus on his cross. "But when

I was in prison, all I had was a Bible to keep me company." He served five years in Crowley for stalking a woman after he'd taken a dirty love potion. "But there's some good stuff in there. Like in John, when J. C. says, 'Let he who is without sin cast the first stone'?" He shook his head. "That's some deep shit, man."

"What's your point?" Pen snapped.

I frowned at her uncharacteristic outburst. That's when I realized Pen hadn't admitted her own sins to the group. They loomed like shadows in her eyes.

"Point is," Jacob said, "way I see it we're all sinners here. We've all lied and cheated and stole and worse. But we keep coming back here every week."

Rufus leaned forward. "Why do you think that is, Jacob?"

The large man shrugged. "Because every day is a new chance at redemption."

Those words washed over me like a balm. Back when I was seventeen, I'd started over. Got myself on a new road. It's just, I'd taken a detour for a little while. Allowed myself to be lured into believing magic was to blame for my problems when it was my poor choices that caused the pain in my life. Choices like trusting John Volos and giving Uncle Abe power over my self-worth. Choices like lying to the people I loved. Like lying to myself.

But this main road—the one I'd set out on ten years earlier—was populated by a lot of other imperfect-but-trying souls. Like Rufus and Jacob, Baba and Morales—and Pen.

"I'm so sorry, Pen. I was so wrapped up in fighting my demons, I couldn't help you with yours."

"God, stop it," she snapped. "Just stop." She heaved in a breath, as if preparing to yell, but when she let it out her shoulders lowered. "Like you're some martyr. Jesus, Katie, you know damned well you did all that lying to protect your job on the task force."

I lifted my hands in a gesture of surrender. "You're right. I have compromised myself for this job."

Her expression bordered on smug, but I wasn't done.

"However, I've also done a lot of good." I took a breath. "I've learned that there's a positive side to magic that I never got to see before. One where I can use the skills I was born with to make a difference in this world."

Pen's mouth fell open. "That's some weak-ass bargaining, Kate."

"Is it?" I glanced at Rufus, whose expression gave away nothing. "I'm not so sure. Seems like I'd be more of a coward to run away from a major part of who I am."

She blinked. "That's...actually pretty insightful."

I frowned at her. "Really?"

She nodded. "If you want to be on the task force, I can't stop you. But you've seemed so conflicted about what you were doing, and I couldn't stand watching you self-destruct."

I raised an ironic brow. "Ditto, sister."

Her face paled. Without another word, she reached up and removed her own anniversary necklace. She turned to face the group with her chin trembling. "I have a confession, too."

She glanced at me. I bit my lip and nodded. She heaved in a shaky breath. "I used magic, too." She paused, as if gathering her courage. "It was the pain after the accident. I— It was too hard. So I stole an old woman's pain potion and started using again."

No gasps echoed through the group. No one called her out. I crossed my arms to keep from going to her protectively. She had to do this herself.

"It was just that one time, but I guess that doesn't really matter. I threw away years of sobriety for an easy way out of my pain." She walked to Rufus on wooden legs. She held out the necklace, which he took reverently and without comment.

She turned back to the group. "My name is Penelope Griffin and I'm a potion addict."

"Hi, Pen," the group answered as one.

Unable to hold myself back anymore, I went to my best friend. We collapsed into each other and held on for dear life. On some level, I knew that, unlike the *Cuyahoga* at the bottom of Lake Erie, our friendship was strong enough to weather a storm. But I also knew in my gut that this wouldn't be the last time magic came between us.

Rufus came forward and pulled Pen away. "Every day is a chance for salvation," he said, repeating Jacob's words. He slipped a small yellow disc into her palm. I recognized it instantly as the token AA gave newly sober members. In essence, it was a signal that Pen was starting over with a clean slate.

He turned to me next. I raised my chin and looked him in the eye. "You realize of course this means you can't attend AA anymore, right?"

My heart dropped lower in my chest. I hadn't thought about that part. "If that's how it has to be, then I'll respect it."

"I wish it were otherwise, but I think it's for the best all things considered. But I do want to give you this." He reached in his pocket and removed a small yellow disc. He walked to me and handed me the same token he'd given Pen. About the size of a quarter, the yellow plastic had words written on it in black: ONE DAY AT A TIME.

I swallowed the emotion that reared up in my throat like a certain lake monster. "Thank you."

"All right, all right," Rufus said in a gruff tone. He sniffed a little, but if I'd called him on it he'd say he was allergic to touchy-feely crap. "It's time to get this meeting wrapped up. Round up for the recovery pledge. Pen? Why don't you lead us?"

My best friend grabbed ahold of my hand. "Magic is a tool," she began. "If I am unable to use it responsibly, I will not use magic at all." She squeezed my palm meaningfully. "I am responsible for my own actions, and I pledge to act with compassion for myself and others, always."

◆ ◆ ◆

Half an hour later I emerged from the basement with Pen. We'd decided to go grab a drink at a nearby pub to catch up. So much had happened since our fight, and she had a lot of questions about what exactly went down with Dionysus.

The night was chilly, and I pulled my jacket tighter. The sky was clear, which offered a stunning view of the three-quarter moon.

Beside me, Pen's steps faltered. "Kate."

I pulled my eyes from the moon to see what was up. Her eyes moved toward something down the street, and I followed their movement. A long, black limo idled at the curb. The brake lights added a sinister glow to the plumes of smoke billowing from the tailpipe. The license plate read SHEMALE.

"Shit," I breathed. "Wait here."

Pen grabbed my jacket sleeve. "Wait—"

I shook my head to let her know she didn't need to worry. "It's okay. Just need to finish a little business. Then we'll go grab our drink."

She didn't look convinced by my reassurances, but nodded. "Be careful."

I walked toward the back of the car slowly. My piece was at my side, under my jacket, but it was too soon to tell if I needed it.

A low whirring sound reached my ears. I paused, but quickly realized the noise had just been the window rolling down in the back of the car. A masculine hand emerged and flicked through the air to summon me.

Placing one arm on the roof and keeping the other at my side for easy reach of my gun, I bent so my head was level with the open window.

The hermaphrodite's male visage was in shadow, except for a slice of light across the unsmiling mouth. "Katherine." The voice was deep. Looked like Aphrodite had decided this solemn occasion called for a little testosterone.

"When did they spring you?"

"Yesterday." His eye cut toward me. "In no small part thanks to your assistance."

I shrugged. "The evidence spoke for itself."

"That's the curious part." A single brow rose. "Considering my treacherous priestess's involvement, it would not have been difficult for you to manipulate the evidence to implicate me as an accomplice."

I frowned at him. "I hadn't thought of it that way."

He smiled, turning toward me fully. Now I could see the smoky eye and subdued nude lip on the female half of the Hierophant's face. Having both sides visible gave me the uncomfortable sensation of being regarded by two separate people. Almost like conjoined twins, only more attractive than the other set of twins I knew.

"Interesting." Now the voice had changed. *She* was in charge again.

"What's interesting?" I asked. "The fact I didn't screw you over."

She nodded. "Can't say I would have blamed you if you had. All's fair in the war on magic, right?"

"Don't misunderstand," I said, "I think you're guilty as hell for a dozen other crimes. But if and when I take you down, there won't be any doubt about the facts of the case."

She laughed, a deep, rich sound that probably had seduced more people than I'd arrested in my career. "This is going to be fun."

"What is?"

She tilted her head. "Didn't they tell you?"

"Who?"

"Your bosses?" She waved an elegant hand, as if dismissing an insignificant thing. "Even after I was cleared of the murder of our beloved mayor"—she said it like he was a stranger and not a customer who no doubt paid her very well—"your Special Agent Gardner still saw fit to charge me for obstruction for breaking into Dionysus's apartment."

"Which you deserved."

A slight tip of the chin was the only acknowledgment of that comment. "However, I managed to convince handsome US Attorney Stone that a person in my position might prove useful in future cases."

"And they believed you?"

The feline smile was back. "I can be quite persuasive."

"I'm sure. So what? They offered a reduced sentence in exchange for future snitching services?"

That half-painted mouth pursed in distaste. "Kate, please, I am no bitch's snitch. Let's just say I'll be a consultant, and leave it at that."

I barely managed not to roll my eyes. "You're a real piece of work, you know that?"

"Oh, honey, you have no idea." She chuckled. "Anyway, I just wanted to thank you personally for taking care of my little problem."

"Don't mention it."

"I mean it, Prospero. A person doesn't have as many enemies as I've collected without also fostering allies."

I opened my mouth to tell her we weren't allies, but she held up a hand.

"Relax, I understand where things stand. I'm just saying I like to pay my debts. And I owe you three. One for clearing me for the mayor's murder, and two more for punishing that fucking Raven and my treacherous priestess." She spat the words out. "Day's gonna come when I can be of service to you and yours." That shrewd gaze met mine. "Consider these my markers."

She held out her hand and dropped three tokens into my palm. I held one up to the streetlight. Most sex magic temples got around having their girls deal with cash by selling tokens to customers. Each temple had its own custom design, and some people even collected them, like other people collected stamps. Aphrodite's tokens bore her pentagram and spiral logo on one side and the words DULCE POMUM QUUM ABEST CUSTOS on the reverse.

"What's this mean?" I asked.

She smiled. "Forbidden fruit is the sweetest."

I clasped the coins in my fist until the metal bit into my skin. Seeing the tokens reminded me of my mother and Shayla's taunting words on the boat. "What happened to her?" I asked, looking up. "My mother."

The Hierophant's smile faded and she sat back, totally in shadow. "Are you sure you want to know?"

I held up one of the tokens. "I'm calling in my first favor. Tell me what happened."

"Telling you would do you no favors." She pushed the token away. "You want to know what really happened, you need to ask your uncle. But I'll give you some advice free of charge."

I raised my eyebrows and waited.

She leaned forward so I could see her full face again. "Some ghosts need to remain buried for the living to have peace. Don't go digging for secrets you aren't prepared to learn."

My stomach dipped. It wasn't an admission that Shayla was right, but it was damned close. I slipped the tokens into my pocket. "I'll take that under advisement."

She smiled, sadly this time. "No you won't, but don't say I didn't warn you. Good night, Detective." She flicked a hand to signal the driver.

I stepped back and watched the limo drive off into the night. Pen ran over to join me.

"What was that about?"

I released a deep breath. "It seems I have a new friend."

She flicked a suspicious glance at the retreating limo. "With friends like that, who needs enemies?"

Chapter Thirty-Two

November 6
Waning Gibbous

There are twenty-seven steps from street level to the door of city hall. With each one I climbed, my uniform felt tighter and tighter. By the time I reached for the handle of the huge wood-and-brass doors, the damned thing felt like a straitjacket.

I let out a breath and paused before allowing myself to enter the lion's den.

I hadn't seen Morales since the night we'd been fished out of Lake Erie. I knew he'd been released from the hospital. I knew that, like me, he'd had to report to the gym to make an official statement because Gardner mentioned when I was finished that he would be in that afternoon.

Debriefings were always framed as closure, but sometimes they felt like ritualized reopening of wounds. Having to stand in front of someone with the power to steal your badge and defend the choices you made in the line of fire felt like its own sort of hell. Not the watery hell of that lake with the monster and the madman, but a hell lorded over by the demons Would Have, Could Have, and Should Have.

Anyway, I also knew Morales hadn't tried to contact me. But then, I hadn't tried to call him, either.

The summons to report to city hall came from Gardner on Thursday night. "Just a press conference," she'd said. She tried to keep her tone casual, but there was an undercurrent of tension. "Be there at nine in your blues."

Considering all that had happened under that Blue Moon, part of me was worried the press conference was some sort of ambush where I'd be exposed for the liar I was. It wasn't my most rational thought ever, but then my life hadn't been unfolding in any sort of rational pattern lately, anyway.

I closed my eyes and pulled open the doors to surrender myself to the inevitable.

Flashes of light behind my lids. I opened my eyes. Hard to see through the blinding lights and the shouted questions and the spastic clicking of camera shutters.

I blinked a few times before trying to locate a familiar face among all the parasites. The first one I recognized belonged to John Volos. He stood near the front of the room next to fellow mayoral candidate Anton Rebis. Both men smiled broadly, more for the benefit of the cameras than me.

As if in slow motion, I looked down and saw the seal of the city of Babylon inlaid in the marble floor. On it, a proud lion protected the gates to the city. And in my head, I was telling myself to paste a smile on my face.

Morales's voice echoed inside: *Don't let them see your fear.*

"There's Detective Prospero now." Eldritch's voice boomed

through the room via a microphone. I blinked and tried to force my feet to not run the other direction.

But then, Gardner was coming forward with her hand extended and a smile on her face.

And all I could think was, *He didn't tell them. Of course he didn't*, my conscience argued in a dry tone. Morales wasn't a rat.

The next few moments were a blur of handshakes and smiles and pats on the back. Gardner led me to the front of the room, where a podium had been set up. Two large photographs stood on easels—one with my unsmiling picture and the other with Morales looking uncharacteristically serious.

"This is bullshit," I whispered to Gardner.

"Play nice," she warned under her breath.

My eyes scanned the room for Morales, but I didn't see him yet. Part of me wouldn't put it past him to skip the dog-and-pony show on principle.

John drew my gaze again. I wasn't sure whether his gesture was congratulatory or an I-told-you-so nod. Regardless, I pressed my lips together and looked away quickly.

The doors to the hall opened again, prompting another round of excitement. The broad-shouldered shape of Drew Morales was backlit by the bright morning sunlight outside. He paused at the threshold like I had, but recovered from his surprise more quickly.

He wore a charcoal-gray suit with the collar of his white dress shirt open at the neck to reveal his muscled neck. Shock hit me upside the head. He looked so at ease in the business attire, but no less lethal despite the buttoned-up formality.

It wasn't until he limped forward a few steps that I noticed the black cane. On some men, the aid would have signaled weakness. But in Morales's hand it looked like a weapon.

His eyes snapped toward me. Despite his poker face, I saw a glimmer of relief in his gaze.

At that instant, I knew part of him had expected me to rat on him, too.

I tipped my chin. His expression went from guarded to solemn. A lot passed between us in that look. Relief. Confusion. Respect. Promises. Maybe even a little intimacy, but I didn't have a lot of experience with that concept.

Soon enough, he was standing next to me. But we didn't have a chance to talk because suddenly lots of people were jockeying for the mike to take credit for our accomplishments.

First, Interim Mayor Hernandez spoke at length about the courage Morales and I displayed under fire, and how we offered our city hope despite the recent loss of our beloved Mayor Owens.

Soon, but not soon enough for my taste, he surrendered the mike to Eldritch. "The BPD is extremely proud of Detective Prospero, and we offer our sincere thanks to Special Agent Gardner's MEA task force for their assistance in bringing Scott McQueen to justice."

Gardner cleared her throat.

Eldritch ignored her censure and continued. "I would also like to offer a sincere apology to Aphrodite Johnson, who was framed by McQueen. She has been cleared of all charges." He said it in a tone that implied she'd threatened to sue if the public apology wasn't broadcast all over Babylon's airwaves.

"And now, I'd like to invite Special Agent Miranda Gardner to the podium."

Gardner pasted on a polite smile as she joined him. She stepped forward to say something, but Eldritch swooped in to say something else. "She'll be formally presenting Agent Morales and Detective Prospero with their medals."

Gardner paused briefly, as if she was considering saying a few words despite the snub. But then she thought better of it and accepted from Eldritch the boxes containing our medals.

"For their dedicated service to the city of Babylon and bravery in the line of fire," Eldritch said, "we formally present Agent Andrew Javier Morales and Detective Katherine Athena Prospero with the bronze medal of courage."

Gardner pinned Morales's medal first, since he held rank. When she leaned in she whispered something to him that made him chuckle. He responded in a low, rumbling tone that had her cracking a big smile. They shook hands and then she moved to me.

Standing before me, Gardner removed the second medal from the box. When she looked up, the smile was gone and a solemn frown took its place. She pinned the medal over my left breast. "You're a good egg, Prospero," she whispered. "Keep up the good work."

"I will, sir," I replied.

"This is a historic day in Babylon," Eldritch said. "Detective Prospero is the first Adept to ever receive the medal of courage."

I froze. It wasn't until that moment that the weight of receiving the medal hit me. Something resembling pride shivered through me. But then, past Gardner, movement on the front row caught my eye. It was John Volos rising to give me a standing ovation.

I met the twinkle in his gaze with suspicion. That's when I knew the awards ceremony had been orchestrated by the man who happened to be the city's first Adept candidate for mayor.

But before I could take that thought too far, the entire room burst into applause. And then there were more flashbulbs and shouted questions from the media. I tried to smile and answer the questions, but the entire thing passed in a blur and I have no idea if my answers made any sense.

Once the furor died down about half an hour later, Volos found me standing alone near a large potted plant, where I'd gone to escape everyone for a moment of privacy.

"Looks like you're the hero of the hour," he said.

I looked up and frowned at him. "Nice play."

He smirked. "That transparent, am I?"

"To me, anyway."

He raised his hands in a conciliatory gesture. "Why do you insist on thinking the worst of me?"

"Because you keep giving me so many reasons."

He let a beat of silence pass before changing the subject. "I'm glad you're all right."

I crossed my arms. The move made the muscles in my back scream. Even though Morales had gotten the worst of the injuries, I hadn't escaped totally unscathed. "I'm just glad we stopped him."

He nodded. "Have you given any thought to how to deal with Abe?"

I frowned. "What do you mean?"

He scooted closer and looked around to make sure we wouldn't be overheard. "He'll be in touch. To gloat, if nothing else."

I shrugged. "I'll leap off that bridge when I come to it."

"He'll want to stir some shit."

"I'm more than used to dealing with men who want to cause trouble in my life, John."

The corner of his mouth lifted. He started to reach for me, but just as I pulled away a throat cleared behind him.

We both turned to see Morales standing proudly with his cane and his medal glistening in the light coming through the rotunda skylights. "Am I interrupting?"

"Yes," Volos said.

"No," I said at the same time. "Mr. Volos was just leaving." I shot John a level stare that dared him to argue with me.

He tipped his chin with dignity. "Congratulations again." He turned to Morales. "To you both."

He held out a hand to Morales, who accepted the gesture. I might have been imagining things, but I could have sworn I saw both of their arms tense in a way that indicated they were both gripping harder than necessary.

"Yeah," Morales said. "And good luck with the campaign."

Volos pulled his hand away. "Luck doesn't win elections, Agent Morales. It's all up to the people."

Morales laughed. "By 'people' you mean Ben Franklin, William McKinley, and Grover Cleveland, right?" he shot back, referring to the faces that appeared on high-denomination bills.

Volos didn't take the bait; he simply shot us a parting politician's smile and walked away with his shoulders back.

"I can't believe you dated that asshole," my partner said.

"No shit." A laugh escaped with my exhaled breath. "How you doing, Macho?"

"Can't complain. Chicks dig the limp." He tapped the cane on the marble floor. "So...Athena?"

I punched him in the arm. "Fuck off. My mom loved Greek mythology."

"The warrior goddess of wisdom," he said. "Kinda suits you, Cupcake."

The warmth in his tone made me look up again. There was something bordering on...tenderness in those brown eyes that made my flight-or-fight instinct flare up. Stupid, maybe, since this brave guy standing in front of me, the one looking so handsome in his suit, the one who knew my darkest secrets, should have been the last person on earth to scare me.

"You want to go grab a drink?" he asked suddenly.

I blinked. "It's ten in the morning."

"So we'll get Bloody Marys and call it brunch."

His tone was casual, but there was an undercurrent of tension that told me he had plans for us after those Bloody Marys. And damned if I wasn't suddenly intrigued by the twist of events.

But hot on the heels of my discussion with Volos, a plan had formed in my mind—and as it happened Morales would be the perfect wingman.

"Actually, how about we skip the Bloody Marys and go check out this other place."

He stepped closer. The spicy scent of his cologne mixed with his natural Morales-ness made him Dangerous—with a capital *D*.

"Which other place?" he asked, his voice pitched low.

"You're going to love it. It has several bars."

His eyes widened. "All right. Am I dressed okay? I can lose the suit."

I enjoyed the view too much to encourage that plan. "I have a feeling the other guests won't care much what you're wearing."

Chapter Thirty-Three

After a sunny morning, a storm was rolling in over the water. Lake Erie was choppy and the color of the dull side of aluminum foil. I pulled my Jeep into a parking lot next to the dock. "Kate?" Morales said. "I'm pretty sure they don't serve brunch at Crowley."

I pushed Sybil into Park and turned toward him. "I need a favor."

He cocked a brow and crossed his arms.

"Abe hasn't called. I figure he's letting me stew. But I'm sick of waiting, so I want you to go with me to talk to him."

He blew a long breath through his nose. "Worst date ever."

I froze. "So you really were asking me out on a date?"

He just stared me down until I shifted uncomfortably.

"If you do this for me, I'll let you take me out to a really expensive dinner."

He snorted.

"And I'll let you get to first base."

He stilled. "Only first?"

I tilted my head at him. "Fine. Second, but I expect dessert."

He pursed his lips, as if thinking it over. I glanced toward the dock, where the ferry's captain was busying the craft for departure. Finally, Morales spoke. "All right, I'll go with you to see Abe. But you can forget about the date."

My shoulder drooped. "But—"

He leaned forward. I froze, believing for a heart-galloping moment he was about to kiss me. But at the final second, his mouth changed trajectory and veered toward my ear. "I don't do pity dates, Cupcake. When you're ready, you can ask me out."

With that, my partner exited the vehicle. I made a frustrated screech as I gathered my things. I supposed the worst part was I deserved that dose of my own medicine for bullshitting him into coming with me in the first place. "Insufferable ass," I groused, not because I believed it, but because it made me feel better.

When I joined him at the dock, he shot me a cocky grin. I narrowed my eyes at him. "Just remember, let me do the talking."

He rocked back on his heels with a self-satisfied grin. I wanted to be mad at him, but I also knew there was no one else I'd rather have with me for what was waiting on the other side of the lake.

♦ ♦ ♦

Abe leaned back in his chair with a reptilian grin. After we'd disembarked from the ferry and signed in, he'd kept us waiting a good hour for his grand entrance.

"Why'd you bring backup, Katie Girl? Don't trust yourself to handle me?"

"Nah," Morales said, deadpan, before I could respond. "I'm here to protect you, old man."

Uncle Abe laughed. "The day I need a crippled Mundane cop to protect me is the day they put me in the grave."

I didn't bother to correct Abe's presumption about Morales. He didn't deserve to know my partner had been born an Adept but had chosen to live life as a Mundane. Time to put Operation Turn the Tables into motion. "Do you know someone named Dr. Flamel?"

His eyes flared. "Who?"

"According to Dionysus, that was the name of his doctor in the psychiatric prison. He hinted this Flamel was something of a mentor."

Abe leaned back and wiped his mouth with the back of his hand. "I wouldn't know."

Lies. I made a mental note to follow up with Shadi on her research into Flamel when I got back to the office. But for the time being, we had more important ground to cover.

"I've been thinking. See, Dionysus lived in a shitty apartment in Babylon, but when the big showdown occurred he had a large boat, expensive materials, and lots of help with logistics. He also mentioned this Flamel suggested Babylon as a target. Maybe the good doctor was orchestrating from the shadows."

"I'm sure I wouldn't know," Abe said.

"Really?" Morales said. "From what Kate tells me you know a lot about orchestrating plots. I wonder if Ramses Bane would concur with that assessment."

Abe's gaze flicked toward me. I smiled.

"That's a serious accusation, Special Agent," Abe said in a hard tone, "especially without proof."

Morales pursed his lips and shrugged. "Not an accusation, just an observation."

"Why did you warn me about Dionysus coming to town?" I asked.

He licked his lips and wove his fingers together on the table-top. Anticipation lit his eyes from the inside. This was the moment he'd be waiting for. The moment when he'd finally reveal his plan. He leaned forward and looked me directly in the eyes. "This city needed to be reminded who runs the Cauldron."

Morales snorted. "If you run the Cauldron, why did you need the MEA's help to stop Dionysus?"

The corner of his mouth quirked. "I didn't need you to stop him. I needed you to understand you couldn't have stopped him without my help."

"The same day I met with you that asshole sent a letter to Owens," I said. "Without your vague intel we still would have figured out who he was."

"You're grasping, old man," Morales said.

Abe ignored him and zeroed in on me. "And you're forgetting where you come from, girl." He moved his arm to expose the image of a snake eating its own tail that circled his left wrist. Then he shot a pointed look at my own exposed left wrist, which bore an exact copy of the Ouroboros symbol that marked me as a made member of the Votary Coven. I self-consciously covered it with my right hand.

Abe smiled, but it didn't reach his eyes. "Maybe you've con-vinced the brass you're a hero, but I know that in your heart you will always be a wizard." He glanced again at my left hand. "You can try to deny it all you want, but I know better. Just like I know you've been doing magic." He leaned forward and sniffed. "You stink of ozone and guilt."

I didn't rise to the bait. No doubt he'd read the newspapers' breathless accounts of how I'd used magic to defeat Dionysus. Besides, he was wrong. I was done with guilt.

"But as it stands," he continued, "I can't blame you for questioning my intentions. After all, we've covered that I was indeed the catalyst for Ramses Bane's crimes against this city." He glanced at Morales, as if he expected my partner to leap up and charge him with the crime. Instead, my partner stifled a yawn.

Abe didn't let the lack of shock faze him. "But despite every horrible thing you believe about me, you know I vowed to you that I would never harm your brother."

I snorted. "Why would I believe that when promises drip like venom from your forked tongue?"

"Because while your betrayals are well documented, Danny remains innocent. There is still hope for him and his magic."

I leaned forward and forced him to look into my eyes as I made a vow of my own. "I will kill you with my bare hands before I let you get within ten feet of that boy."

An eyebrow quirked. "Are you going to let her threaten me like that, Agent Morales?"

Morales crossed his arms, flexing his muscles. "If she doesn't manage it, I'll finish you myself."

"That is a battle I look forward to with relish," Abe said. "But the fact remains that Bane acted without my permission or knowledge when he hexed the boy." He looked at me. "Whatever else lies between us, I need you to understand that is the truth."

I crossed my arms. "Why do you care what I think?"

"I don't. I care about balancing the accounts. Bane acted without permission and he used my own family in his machinations. This shall not stand."

My phone buzzed at my hip. I ignored it, but noticed out of the corner of my eye that Morales shifted as if his had buzzed, as well.

"Tell me, how is it that John Volos managed to create the antipotion for Gray Wolf on his own?" Abe continued.

My jaw clenched. His tone and self-satisfied expression told me he already knew the answer. "He didn't. But you already know that."

He smiled. "I could see the magic in you the moment you walked in here two weeks ago. How did it feel to use your powers again, Katie Girl?"

I didn't respond.

"I find it curious that you and your partner have both accused me of involvement, yet I have yet to be charged. Why is that?"

I looked him in the eye. "Because I don't trust the justice system to deliver the punishment you deserve."

"And who do you trust? Surely not John Volos?"

I raised my brows. "I don't need John Volos to fight my battles for me."

He threw back his head and guffawed. "I taught you well, Kate, but surely you don't think I taught you everything I know."

The phones buzzed again.

"You might want to answer that." The snake smile was back. My pulse picked up.

Morales did the honors. "Sir, we're kind of in the middle—"

He cut off as if she'd interrupted him. As he listened, his brows slammed down and his gaze jerked toward me. "Goddamn it! How?"

My heart leaped to my throat and then slid slowly back to my chest, leaving an icy trail behind. Across the table, Uncle Abe held my gaze.

When Morales finally hung up, Uncle Abe cocked his head in a facsimile of concern. "Bad news?"

Morales forced a casual shrug. "Some might think so."

I looked at him and waited for the bad news to drop.

"Ramses Bane," was all he said. He didn't say the word *dead* but it was there, hanging in the air like black smoke.

"How?" I snapped.

"Hung himself."

"Bullshit." I rounded on Uncle Abe. "You did this."

He raised his hands in an innocent gesture. "Why, Katherine, I have no idea what you mean. After all, I am locked up in this prison on a remote island. How on earth could I have killed Ramses Bane?"

I gritted my teeth and tried to keep a lid on my urge to throttle the old bastard. If I had to guess, he planned to murder Bane before he ever called the mayor to orchestrate our first meeting.

"A pity poor Ramses couldn't handle the pressure of his impending trial." Abe tipped his chin in a facsimile of sympathy. "Yet there is an upside."

"What?" The word bit into the air like a blade.

"His death settles accounts, yes? At least where Danny's concerned." He said this all magnanimous, like he'd done me a favor.

"You're welcome to think so," I gritted out. I stood up and loomed over the table. "But in all your planning, you failed to consider one thing."

He smiled and crossed his arms, so cocksure and untouchable. "I'm breathless with anticipation."

"Bane didn't just try to kill Danny. He also went after John Volos." Abe's smile wavered a fraction. "And I'm pretty sure Volos won't consider that Bane's death erases the debt he owes you."

"John Volos is a child."

"Who is about to become the mayor of Babylon."

He didn't look surprised by the revelation. Further proof he was keeping up with things on the outside. "As recent events have revealed, Babylon's mayors are hardly immune to violence, Detective."

"Hmm, time will tell," I conceded. In a breezy tone, I continued. "There's something else I've been meaning to ask."

"What is it?" he snapped.

"What really happened to my mother?"

All emotion and color drained from Abe's face.

Loud banging sounded from the door. The guard telling us time was up. I held up a finger. "You better hope they keep you in this prison for a good, long time, old man." Leaned across the table to get in Uncle Abe's face. Sweat beaded on his brow. "Because John Volos is the least of your worries."

Abe's eyes skittered toward the guard and Morales—anyone who'd listen. "She just threatened me. Did you hear that?"

The guard yawned from the doorway. "Didn't hear nothing."

Morales crossed his massive arms. "Me either."

I drew myself up and turned slowly to face the man who'd once been my mentor, but was now the closest thing I had to a mortal enemy. "Come on, Morales."

Morales's chair screeched against the concrete floor. I took two steps toward the door before Abe got in his parting shot.

"Ask your boyfriend Volos about Flamel."

I froze and turned. "Why?"

Abe rose from his chair and stood straight and proud. "That's always been your problem, Kate, you think you're smarter than you are. But there's gears at work you can't begin to understand."

"Kate, let's go," Morales said.

I held up a hand and turned toward Abe. Behind me, I felt Morales brace himself. I should have been angry, but I wasn't.

For the first time in my life, I looked at Abraxas Prospero and felt nothing except resignation. "You and I are going to have a reckoning one day." I paused to let him digest that. "I won't lie. I'm really looking forward to it."

He smiled like he was, too.

"But today? You're just a sad old man in an orange jumpsuit whose kingdom only extends as far as those bars."

The transformation happened so fast I didn't see it coming. One second Abe stood with perfect posture and a taunting smile. The next he lunged, his face contorted into a rage mask—all flashing teeth and pulled-back lips and wild, hot eyes.

Time slowed. The guard screamed. Morales cursed. My left hand jerked into motion. I don't remember grabbing the Taser, but suddenly it was in my hand. Bright blue electricity arced between the metal prongs. An instant later Abe was on me. The force of the collision knocked me back. I slammed the stun gun into his neck and pressed the button so hard my finger cracked.

He was suspended for a moment and then fell into a heap on the ground. Foamy spittle bloomed from between his gray lips, and his eyes fluttered as convulsions rocked his thin frame.

"Holy shit." The guard skidded to a stop next to me. He looked at the weapon in my hand. "How many volts did you give him?"

I shrugged. "A lot."

Morales turned me toward him. "You okay?"

I looked down at the man I'd once believed to be larger than life—the god of my small world. Now he resembled one of the potion freaks he'd profited from for so many years. "Yeah," I said. I raised my chin and turned my back on the man I'd made into my own personal monster. Seeing him on the floor like that reminded me of something I'd forgotten under the strain of all the memories I carried. Abraxas Prospero, for all his magic and manipulations, was simply a man.

A man who'd taught me that magic was supposed to be dirty. That it was a weapon and a gold mine. But I'd learned a few things since I'd escaped his influence, and I would use those hard-won lessons to bring his ass down when the day came.

"Kate?" Morales prodded.

I looked up at him and smiled the first real smile since I'd walked into that room. "I'm all good now."

Acknowledgments

As always, thank you to Devi Pillai and Rebecca Strauss for making up my own personal Team Awesome. Thanks for the guidance as well as the kicks in the pants.

Team Orbit also deserves a shout-out for the amazing covers, marketing, and production work. A special nod to Lauren Panepinto for getting why I'm so anal about the symbolism on the covers and for ensuring Kate actually looks like Kate.

Thanks to Krista McNamara, Annie Slasher, and Suzanne McLeod for the stalwart beta reading and continuity editing. Huge hugs to all the Up N Comers: Elizabeth Essex, Julie Glover, Christina Delay, Lori Freeland, Chris Keniston, Sylvia McDaniel, and Kat Bladwin. Thanks, especially, to Margie Lawson, who has done so much for my writing, I dedicated this book to her.

To Nicole, Mark, Leah, Heather, Molly, Judy, and the League of Reluctant Adults: Thank you for reminding me not to take myself or this crazy business too seriously.

Zach, thank you for your tireless support and for helping me build this dream. ILYNTB.

AJW, watching you write the story of you is the absolute joy of my life. I love you, buddy.

extras

orbit

meet the author

On Location Portraiture

Raised by booksellers, *USA Today* bestseller JAYE loved reading from a very young age. That gateway drug eventually led to a full-blown writing addiction. When she's not chasing the word dragon, she loves to travel, drink good bourbon, and do things that scare her so she can put them in her books. Jaye lives in Texas with her husband and son. Find out more about Jaye Wells at www.jayewells.com.

introducing

If you enjoyed
CURSED MOON
look out for

CHARMING

Pax Arcana: Book 1

by Elliott James

John Charming isn't your average Prince…

He comes from a line of Charmings—an illustrious family of dragon slayers, witch finders, and killers dating back to before the fall of Rome. Trained by a modern-day version of the Knights Templar, monster hunters who have updated their methods from chain mail and crossbows to Kevlar and shotguns, John Charming was one of the best—until a curse made him one of the abominations the Knights were sworn to hunt.

That was a lifetime ago. Now John tends bar under an assumed name in rural Virginia and leads a peaceful, quiet life. That is, until a vampire and a blonde walked into his bar…

Prelude
Hocus Focus

There's a reason that we refer to being in love as being enchanted. Think back to the worst relationship you've ever been in: the one where your family and friends tried to warn you that the person you were with was cheating on you, or partying a little too much, or a control freak, or secretly gay, or whatever. Remember how you were convinced that no one but you could see the real person beneath that endearingly flawed surface? And then later, after the relationship reached that scorched-earth-policy stage where letters were being burned and photos were being cropped, did you find yourself looking back and being amazed at how obvious the truth had been all along? Did it feel as if you were waking up from some kind of a spell?

Well, there's something going on right in front of your face that you can't see right now, and you're not going to believe me when I point it out to you. Relax, I'm not going to provide a number where you can leave your credit card information, and you don't have to join anything. The only reason I'm telling you at all is that at some point in the future, you might have a falling-out with the worldview you're currently enamored of, and if that happens, what I'm about to tell you will help you make sense of things later.

extras

The supernatural is real. Vampires? Real. Werewolves? Real. Zombies, Ankou, djinn, Boo Hags, banshees, ghouls, spriggans, windigos, vodyanoi, tulpas, and so on and so on, all real. Well, except for Orcs and Hobbits. Tolkien just made those up.

I know it sounds ridiculous. How could magic really exist in a world with an Internet and forensic science and smartphones and satellites and such and still go undiscovered?

The answer is simple: it's magic.

The truth is that the world is under a spell called the Pax Arcana, a compulsion that makes people unable to see, believe, or even seriously consider any evidence of the supernatural that is not an immediate threat to their survival.

I know this because I come from a long line of dragon slayers, witch finders, and self-righteous asshats. I used to be one of the modern-day knights who patrol the borders between the world of man and the supernatural abyss that is its shadow. I wore non-reflective Kevlar instead of shining armor and carried a sawed-off shotgun as well as a sword; I didn't light a candle against the dark, I wielded a flamethrower...right up until the day I discovered that I had been cursed by one of the monsters I used to hunt. My name is Charming, by the way. John Charming.

And I am not living happily ever after.

1
A Blonde and a Vampire
Walk into a Bar...

Once upon a time, she smelled wrong. Well, no, that's not exactly true. She smelled clean, like fresh snow and air after a lightning storm and something hard to identify, something like sex and butter pecan ice cream. Honestly, I think she was the best thing I'd ever smelled. I was inferring "wrongness" from the fact that she wasn't entirely human.

I later found out that her name was Sig.

Sig stood there in the doorway of the bar with the wind behind her, and there was something both earthy and unearthly about her. Standing at least six feet tall in running shoes, she had shoulders as broad as a professional swimmer's, sinewy arms, and well-rounded hips that were curvy and compact. All in all, she was as buxom, blonde, blue-eyed, and clear-skinned as any woman who had ever posed for a Swedish tourism ad.

And I wanted her out of the bar, fast.

You have to understand, Rigby's is not the kind of place where goddesses were meant to walk among mortals. It is a small, modest establishment eking out a fragile existence at the tail end of Clayburg's main street. The owner, David Suggs,

380

had wanted a quaint pub, but instead of decorating the place with dartboards or Scottish coats of arms or ceramic mugs, he had decided to celebrate southwest Virginia culture and covered the walls with rusty old railroad equipment and farming tools.

When I asked why a bar—excuse me, I mean *pub*—with a Celtic name didn't have a Celtic atmosphere, Dave said that he had named Rigby's after a Beatles song about lonely people needing a place to belong.

"Names have power," Dave had gone on to inform me, and I had listened gravely as if this were a revelation.

Speaking of names, "John Charming" is not what it reads on my current driver's license. In fact, about the only thing accurate on my current license is the part where it says that I'm black-haired and blue-eyed. I'm six foot one instead of six foot two and about seventy-five pounds lighter than the 250 pounds indicated on my identification. But I do kind of look the way the man pictured on my license might look if Trevor A. Barnes had lost that much weight and cut his hair short and shaved off his beard. Oh, and if he were still alive.

And no, I didn't kill the man whose identity I had assumed, in case you're wondering. Well, not the first time anyway.

Anyhow, I had recently been forced to leave Alaska and start a new life of my own, and in David Suggs I had found an employer who wasn't going to be too thorough with his background checks. My current goal was to work for Dave for at least one fiscal year and not draw any attention to myself.

Which was why I was not happy to see the blonde.

For her part, the blonde didn't seem too happy to see me either. Sig focused on me immediately. People always gave me a quick flickering glance when they walked into the bar—excuse me, the pub—but the first thing they really checked out was the clientele. Their eyes were sometimes predatory, sometimes cautious, sometimes hopeful, often tired, but they only returned to me after being disappointed. Sig's gaze, however, centered on me like the oncoming lights of a train—assuming train lights have slight bags underneath them and make you want to flex surreptitiously. Those same startlingly blue eyes widened, and her body went still for a moment.

Whatever had triggered her alarms, Sig hesitated, visibly debating whether to approach and talk to me. She didn't hesitate for long, though—I got the impression that she rarely hesitated for long—and chose to go find herself a table.

Now, it was a Thursday night in April, and Rigby's was not empty. Clayburg is host to a small private college named Stillwaters University, one of those places where parents pay more money than they should to get an education for children with mediocre high school records, and underachievers with upper-middle-class parents tend to do a lot of heavy drinking. This is why Rigby's manages to stay in business. Small bars with farming implements on the walls don't really draw huge college crowds, but the more popular bars tend to stay packed, and Rigby's does attract an odd combination of local rednecks and students with a sense of irony. So when a striking six-foot blonde who wasn't an obvious transvestite sat down in the middle of the bar, there were people around to notice.

Even Sandra, a nineteen-year-old waitress who considers customers an unwelcome distraction from covert texting, noticed the newcomer. She walked up to Sig promptly instead of making Renee, an older waitress and Rigby's de facto manager, chide her into action.

For the next hour I pretended to ignore the new arrival while focusing on her intently. I listened in—my hearing is as well developed as my sense of smell—while several patrons tried to introduce themselves. Sig seemed to have a knack for knowing how to discourage each would-be player as fast as possible.

She told suitors that she wanted to be up-front about her sex change operation because she was tired of having it cause problems when her lovers found out later, or she told them that she liked only black men, or young men, or older men who made more than seventy thousand dollars a year. She told them that what really turned her on was men who were willing to have sex with other men while she watched. She mentioned one man's wife by name, and when the weedy-looking grad student doing a John Lennon impersonation tried the sensitive-poet approach, she challenged him to an arm-wrestling contest. He stared at her, sitting there exuding athleticism, confidence, and health—three things he was noticeably lacking—and chose to be offended rather than take her up on it.

There was at least one woman who seemed interested in Sig as well, a cute sandy-haired college student who was tall and willowy, but when it comes to picking up strangers, women are generally less likely to go on a kamikaze mission than men. The young woman kept looking over at Sig's table, hoping to establish some kind of meaningful eye contact, but Sig wasn't making any.

Sig wasn't looking at me either, but she held herself at an angle that kept me in her peripheral vision at all times.

For my part, I spent the time between drink orders trying to figure out exactly what Sig was. She definitely wasn't undead. She wasn't a half-blood Fae either, though her scent wasn't entirely dissimilar. Elf smell isn't something you forget, sweet and decadent, with a hint of honey blossom and distant ocean. There aren't any full-blooded Fae left, of course—they packed their bags and went back to Fairyland a long time ago—but don't mention that to any of the mixed human descendants that the elves left behind. Elvish half-breeds tend to be somewhat sensitive on that particular subject. They can be real bastards about being bastards.

I would have been tempted to think that Sig was an angel, except that I've never heard of anyone I'd trust ever actually seeing a real angel. God is as much an article of faith in my world as he, she, we, they, or it is in yours.

Stumped, I tried to approach the problem by figuring out what Sig was doing there. She didn't seem to enjoy the ginger ale she had ordered—didn't seem to notice it at all, just sipped from it perfunctorily. There was something wary and expectant about her body language, and she had positioned herself so that she was in full view of the front door. She could have just been meeting someone, but I had a feeling that she was looking for someone or something specific by using herself as bait... but as to what and why and to what end, I had no idea. Sex, food, or revenge seemed the most likely choices.

I was still mulling that over when the vampire walked in.

introducing

**If you enjoyed
CURSED MOON
look out for**

FORTUNE'S PAWN

Paradox Series: Book 1

by Rachel Bach

Devi Morris isn't your average mercenary. She has plans. Big ones. And a ton of ambition. It's a combination that's going to get her killed one day—but not just yet.

That is, until she just gets a job on a tiny trade ship with a nasty reputation for surprises. The Glorious Fool *isn't misnamed: It likes to get into trouble, so much so that one year of security work under its captain is equal to five years everywhere else. With odds like that, Devi knows she's found the perfect way to get the jump on the next part of her Plan. But the* Fool *doesn't give up its secrets without a fight, and one year on this ship might be more than even Devi can handle.*

Chapter
1

Y ou're quitting the Blackbirds?" The shock in Anthony's
voice was at odds with the finger he was languidly sliding
over my naked back. "*Why?* You just made squad leader last
year."

"That's why," I said, swatting his finger away as I pulled on
my shirt. "Nowhere left to go. Squad leader's the last promotion before they stick you in a desk job."

I stood up, grabbing my pants from the chair. Still naked,
Anthony rolled over to watch me dress with growing displea-
sure. "I don't get you, Devi," he grumbled. "The Blackbirds
are the top private armored company on Paradox. It takes most
mercs ten years in a lesser outfit before they can even apply.
The fact they let you in straight out of the army should be the
miracle of your career. Why the hell are you leaving?"

"Some of us have ambition, Anthony," I said, sitting back
down to put on my shoes. "I had five good years with the
Blackbirds, made a lot of money, got my name out there. But
you don't get noticed if you sit around on your laurels, do you?"

"If you got any more noticed, I think they'd have you
arrested," Anthony said. "They were talking about that stunt

386

you pulled on Tizas in the office just yesterday. The duke of Maraday's apparently thinking of offering you a fat contract with his Home Guard."

I rolled my eyes and combed my fingers through my hair, wrestling the dark brown mess into a ponytail as best I could. My hair never could take mornings. "I am *not* joining the Home Guard. I don't care how good the money is. Can you imagine me sitting around on some noble's pleasure yacht playing bouncer for his cocktail parties? No thanks."

"Home Guard *is* dull," Anthony agreed, his boyish face suddenly serious. "But it's safe." He reached out, catching my hand as it dropped from my hair. "I worry about you, Devi. You've done eight full fire tours in five years. I know you want to make a name for yourself, but that kind of work will kill you, and I'm not talking about taking a bullet. If you got a job with the Home Guard, you could take it easier. Hell, if the Maraday thing actually came through, the duke never leaves the capital. You could live here, with me. I'd even let you redecorate, and we could be together every night."

I didn't like the way this conversation was going, but I knew better than to let that show on my face. Instead, I smiled and gently pried his fingers off mine. "It's a sweet offer, Anthony, but I'm not looking to settle down. Here or anywhere else."

Anthony heaved a huge sigh and collapsed on the bed. He lay there facedown for a moment, then rolled onto the floor and started pulling on his boxers. "Can't blame me for trying."

When he was dressed, we took the plush elevator down to the building café. I didn't regret turning down his offer, but I had to admit Anthony had a nice setup. His apartment was in one of the new sky towers that dominated Kingston's shoreline. Through the enormous windows, the royal capital lay spread out as far as I could see. Enormous skyscrapers rose like silver and glass trees from the dense underbrush of the older, smaller buildings. The sky was hazy with the usual smog and the clouds of commuter aircraft darting between the official sky lanes. The café was on one of the sky tower's middle floors, but we were still high enough to see the starport and the towering shadow of the Castle behind it from our booth.

I might just be sentimental, but seeing the Castle's shielded battlements and the shadows of the building-sized batteries of plasma guns behind it always filled me with pride. It wasn't the tallest building in the city anymore, but the Castle was still the largest, dwarfing even the deep-space trawlers that were waiting their turn to dock in the starport below. It was a good, strong fortress, feared by all on planet and off, and a worthy guard for the Sainted Kings of Paradox.

As always, I bowed my head before my king's sacred fortress. Anthony followed suit a second later. He'd never been as much of a believer in the power of the king as I was, but then, he hadn't taken as many bullets as I had.

Once we'd paid our respects, Anthony called the waiter over. He ordered large and well, and the spread of food that arrived at our table was a mini-heaven all in itself. Thanking my king again, I fell to with a mercenary's efficiency. Anthony watched me eat with amusement, drinking something red out of a tall, frosted glass that looked like a cocktail. I really hoped it wasn't. Even I didn't drink this early in the morning.

"So," he said, spinning his now nearly empty glass between his fingers. "Why are you really here, Devi?"

"Last night wasn't enough?" I said, popping a tiny coffee cake into my mouth.

"Last night was marvelous," Anthony admitted. "But since we've established you aren't exactly pining for my company, I thought we might as well get to the point before you crush my ego again."

He was still smarting from the rejection, so I let the comment slide. I'd known Anthony a long time; we'd been in the army together before he got his captaincy and his cushy desk job with the Home Guard. We had good chemistry, and he was always the first person I called when I came home. We'd been friends with benefits for nearly seven years now, and I'd thought we had a good understanding. Obviously, things had changed. Still, this was Anthony. An apology would only make him feel worse, so I honored his request and got to the point. "I need you to tell me the qualifiers to become a Devastator."

I had his full attention now.

"Are you out of your goddamn mind?" he cried. "*That's* why you quit your job?" He flopped back against the booth's deep cushions. "Devi, you can't be serious. The Devastators are the king's own armored unit. They're *above* the best."

"Why do you think I want to be one?" I said. "I'm sick of wasting my time on the edge of civilized space crashing pirate camps for corporate money. Devastators serve the Sacred King directly. They get the best armor, the best guns, they go on the most dangerous and important missions. They have power you can't buy; even the nobility listens to them. I was the best in the Blackbirds—"

"This isn't like the Blackbirds," Anthony snapped. "I can't even tell you the qualifiers, because there are none. You can't apply to become a Devastator. They ask *you*, not the other way around, and they don't ask anyone who hasn't spent a minimum of twenty years in active field service."

"Twenty *years*?" I cried. "That's ridiculous!"

"They want experience—" Anthony started.

"What do you think I spent the last nine years getting?" My

shouting was attracting weird looks from the other diners, but I didn't care. "I got twelve commendations in four years when I was in the army. You know, you were there. *And* I've gotten five promotions in five years in the Blackbirds. I'm not exactly fresh meat."

"Devi, you're not even thirty." Anthony's voice was calm and reasonable, the sort of voice you'd use with a child who was throwing a tantrum. It made me want to punch him. "You've already proven that you're exactly the sort of suicidally brave, workaholic lifetime soldier the Devastators look for. They'll come calling, I'd bet money on it, but not yet. Not until you've got at least ten more years on your record."

"In ten more years, I'll be dead." I said it plainly because it was a goddamn fact. The average life span of an armored mercenary was just shy of twenty-five. I was two years past that. After thirty, survival rates fell to almost nothing. Shooting for cash was a game for the young. You either got a desk job, applied to the Home Guard, or went back to your parents in a body bag. A desk wouldn't impress the Devastators any more than it impressed me, but I couldn't do crash jobs and pirate clearing forever.

"I'm good enough to serve the king right now," I said, lowering my voice. "I've seen Devastators in their thirties, so I know they make exceptions to the experience requirement. I want to know what and how, and I'm not letting you out of here until you tell me." And just in case he didn't believe me, I kicked out my leg and slammed my boot onto the booth beside him, blocking him in.

Anthony glanced at my foot with a deep sigh. "You're impossible. You know that, right?"

I didn't answer, just leaned back, crossed my arms, and waited for him to cave.